JOHN
J. NANCE
TURBULENCE

PAN BOOKS

First published 2002 by G. P. Putnam's Sons, New York

First published in Great Britain 2002 by Pan Books
an imprint of Pan Macmillan Ltd
Pan Macmillan, 20 New Wharf Road, London N1 9RR
Basingstoke and Oxford
Associated companies throughout the world
www.panmacmillan.com

ISBN 0 330 49225 X

9 8 7 6 5 4 3 2 1

A CIP catalogue record for this book is available from
the British Library.

Typeset by Set Systems Ltd, Saffron Walden, Essex
Printed and bound in Australia by
McPherson's Printing Group

To the Memory of my Father
Joseph Turner Nance
1917–1977
Senior International Lawyer
Army Air Corps and United States Air Force Officer-Pilot-Veteran
And the best Dad – and inspiration – a boy could want

ACKNOWLEDGMENTS

Every novel I write leads me on a wild and unpredictable journey of research, and *Turbulence* was no exception. Problem is, there are always too many good folks to thank for help along the way, and some of those must remain nameless because of perceived worries about discussing their job with a writer, however much an integral part of professional aviation he might be. Therefore, I want to express "in the blind" my great appreciation to those guys and gals in both the hard-working ranks of the air traffic control world, and the operational side of the airline industry, who helped so much with a very difficult and squeamish subject: the precipitous deterioration of airline service and the correspondingly dangerous increase in passenger air rage.

But this page is about thanks.

As always, the evolution of this story began with editorial and developmental assistance from my wife, Bunny Nance.

In New York, special appreciation to friends at Putnam and Berkley, David Highfill, Leslie Gelbman, and Phyllis Grann, for being wonderful and steadfast partners.

My eternal thanks, as well, to my longtime agent and friend Olga Wieser of the Wieser and Wieser Literary Agency in New York.

Here in the Pacific Northwest, the woman who shouldered the demanding task of line-editing, polishing, and shaping this work deserves special mention and thanks. Patricia Davenport, who wields a master's in English with the rectitude and authority of the best of senior grammarians, also happens to be my business partner, president of my professional speaking division, and my world-class *in-house* editor.

My great appreciation as well to our world-class staff, Operations Administrator Gloria Liu, Executive Assistant Lori Carr, and Administrative Assistant Sherrie Torgerson, all of whom keep us on track in the face of continuous challenges.

And thanks to Theo Onuoru in Little Rock, Arkansas, and Tom Nomakoh in Oakbrook, Illinois, for assistance with Gen. Onitsa's background.

And most of all, my thanks to you, my reader, for your humbling loyalty and enthusiasm, even when I keep you up all night.

As the song says, I do it for you!

JOHN J. NANCE
University Place,
Washington
(www.johnjnance.com)

TURBULENCE

PROLOGUE

Dr. Brian Logan careened his Lexus past a frightened patient and shot out of the parking garage of the hospital that had just fired him. An impossible mix of embarrassment and anger spurred him on, and he jammed the accelerator repeatedly to the floor, driving like a madman, shooting across the Charles River into Cambridge and daring any cop to stop him. He ran every red light he found and skidded around the corners through the quiet neighborhood streets until he screeched to a halt at last in front of his own address—the empty Georgian two story that he and his wife had loved so much.

Logan put the car in park, but his hands wouldn't complete the job of turning off the engine or opening the door. He glanced down, realizing he was still wearing the green surgical garb he'd donned for the bypass procedure they had canceled without warning. The memory of storming through the corridors to confront the medical director was little more than a hazy procession of images now, fading against the kaleidoscope of thoughts whirling through his mind and obliterating the beauty of a late spring day.

He couldn't recall when he hadn't had surgical privileges at Mercy Hospital. He could easily find another place to practice, but to be thrown out was a horrible, disgraceful shock.

There was an endless blue sky overhead framed by an explosion of green leaves from the row of sturdy elms, but all he could see was the disapproving face of Dr. Jonas Kinkaid, his former mentor's words still burning their way through his brain after his latest outburst: "You're out of control, Doctor, and you've thrown your last tantrum in this hospital."

Deep inside Logan realized Kinkaid was right, but to admit that was unthinkable, even now. Surgeons weren't allowed to be human, to lose control. But in the year since Daphne's death there had been no recovery and no form of deliverance, only numbness and disorientation punctuated by bursts of frustration and fury too often aimed at the nurses. The hurt had oozed into his personality like primordial mud, encasing and calcifying the chasm within, taking the form of the compassion that had once lived there.

Brian Logan forced himself out of the car and into his house. He closed the door and stood for a moment in the hallway listening to the hollow ticking of the grandfather clock, his mind replaying the music of Daphne's voice and the way she used to sing out a greeting and run to his arms—sometimes with nothing on but a smile. The memory left him drained, and he trudged to the living room to sink into her favorite easy chair as he tried to conjure the feeling of her arms around him once more. She had been the only true love of his life, her beauty and sexuality beyond his wildest dreams, made all the more exciting and wonderful by her sparkling intelligence and the way she embraced life—not to mention the sharp contrasts with his first wife, Rebecca.

Brian's eyes fell on the wing-back chair by the piano where he'd been sitting the day the call came. "We're so sorry to tell you, Doctor," an airline representative had said, "but your wife suffered a medical emergency in flight." Daphne Logan, the center of his universe, had hemorrhaged to death at thirty-five thousand feet, taking their unborn son with her when the jetliner's captain had refused to make an emergency landing. For an hour and twenty minutes she'd begged the crew to land, but if she was well enough to ask, the captain concluded, her condition wasn't serious enough to justify the cost of an unscheduled landing. The hundred-million-dollar negligence suit Brian had filed would come up for trial next year, but there was no satisfaction in his attorney's assurances of success. A million, a billion, so what? The money could never replace his wife and unborn son.

He could have saved Daphne. Of that he was sure. Even with crude instruments. Even airborne. And he could have gone with her on that trip to see her parents, but he'd stayed behind in Boston to work. He had been stupid and selfish, and now he was alone, and fired, and coming apart.

Brian jumped to his feet and began pacing, an array of thoughts cascading through his mind, including a useless urge to call Rebecca, his first wife, now remarried and living in Newport, Connecticut. She would be underwhelmed by such a call, though not unreceptive. She expected him to fail. He'd been a long-term disappointment to her, a project she couldn't complete. Rebecca Cunningham, the beautiful, educated debutante from a proper monied New England family had been raised a dour pragmatist, and the young M.D. she'd brought home for her parents' inspection so many years ago held promise only if she could mold him into the dutiful image of her father, a tenured professor of medicine at Harvard. Brian should plan to practice for ten years, she decreed, before entering academic medicine as a professor. He should publish. He should speak. He should smoke a pipe and be interested in long evenings of polite conversation. He should learn to regard the word *fun* as slightly subversive, as she'd been taught.

But Rebecca hadn't counted on her new husband having a fun-loving nature. Such things were irresponsible and clearly unacceptable, and in the end, she decreed the project a failure by divorcing him.

Daphne had blown into his life five years after the divorce like a Caribbean zephyr, inspiring a renaissance and waking a sleeping heart. She was a starry-eyed romantic with a Ph.D., a true bohemian in designer dresses to whom all things were possible and beautiful, and she liked him just as he was. He had fallen for her absolutely—utterly, shudderingly in love with the very idea of her.

Brian glanced over quickly at the portrait of her he'd centered over the formal couch. Daphne stood there among the flowers of her garden, the petite vixen who loved being in love, and to whom sex was language and light. Brian the unchangeable had become a bumbling puppy falling all over himself to please her, and he was amazed that all she wanted was him in his original state. In the three years of their marriage, life had blossomed from a duty to a wild joy, and whereas Rebecca had held pregnancy at bay pending Brian's probation during what he used to sneer was the "Federal Reconstruction of Brian Project," Daphne wanted children as soon as possible.

Brian forced himself from the chair and wandered absently into the kitchen, spotting a forgotten airline ticket on the table. He'd agreed months ago to do a surgical lecture series in Cape Town, South Africa, and he was supposed to leave from Boston's airport in two days. These were the tickets, and there was no point in canceling with a fat fee involved, especially since he'd be needing it while he looked for another hospital to take him in.

The need to *do* something propelled him back to the

coffee grinder to start a fresh pot, a ritual as comforting and familiar as scrubbing before surgery. His hands went through the motions automatically, the aroma barely registering as the coffee pot filled. He poured a cup and sat heavily at the table, flipping absently through the airline ticket, reading everything on it with the desperation of an early riser studying the fine print on a cereal box.

He was on Virgin Atlantic from Boston to London. But on the London–to–Cape Town leg, his office manager had booked him on Meridian Airlines.

Oh, God. No! Brian thought, jumping to his feet as he held the offending ticket at arm's length. He could feel his heart racing. Meridian was the airline that had killed his wife and son twelve months before. There was no way.

A handwritten note had been stuffed in the envelope, and he found it now and opened it.

> *Dr. Logan, Virgin Atlantic doesn't fly to Cape Town. I'm really, really sorry, but there were no other seats available on anything but Meridian, and I snagged the last one. So it's Virgin to London. Stay overnight. Then Meridian to Cape Town.*

He wadded up the note and threw it at the wall, watching the crumpled paper fall short, just as his life was falling short of the acceptable. He would have to endure it, but it meant surviving for ten hours in the belly of a beast he wanted badly to gut.

Brian had prayed for Meridian's bankruptcy, and even—much to his own horror—found himself turning on the network morning shows each day hoping for pictures of smoking wreckage with the Meridian logo clearly in view. The thought sickened the part of him that remained calm and reasoned, but incited a riot among the other facets of his personality. The need to hurt them, to retaliate, to extract the rawest form of revenge was almost consuming.

And now . . .

Dr. Brian Logan felt a sudden stillness descend over him like a dark veil of impenetrable rage, and for the first time since Daphne's death, his mind became quiet and cold and calculating. And within that whirlpool of inchoate pain, the horror of the impending encounter with the enemy began to metastasize into something else.

ONE

"This is nuts!"

Shift Supervisor Jake Kostowitz shook his head in pure exasperation as he muttered vague epithets to himself. The day was going to hell already.

Again he felt the deep craving for a cigarette, the fallout of quitting after twenty years. The FAA's no-smoking policy inside control towers was unshakable, and he still felt a pang of resentment every time the urge became too strong to bat down without a surrogate stick of gum.

He hated gum. But he dug into his right pants pocket anyway now to find some.

All around him—spread out for three hundred sixty degrees and some two hundred feet below the new, glassed-in, air-conditioned O'Hare FAA control tower— the gridlock of overheated, delayed airliners inched

9

forward along crowded taxiways past jammed intersections, baked by the relentless glare of the summer sun.

What was that figure he'd heard? Jake mused. Was it fifty, or sixty flights that were scheduled to depart O'Hare at precisely the same time every day? Whatever the figure, at least the system was fully recovered from the nationwide passenger panic following the loss of the World Trade Center. Jake shook his head slightly, a gesture no one else noticed. Never did he ever want to see his airport looking like a ghost town again, but the endless flow of airliners was now back to ridiculous, and the airlines refused to change it.

The aroma of hot cinnamon reached his nose, and Jake turned toward the stairwell to see one of his off-duty controllers munching on a huge roll and grinning. Jake shook his head in mock disapproval. The controller was at least eighty pounds overweight and a walking heart attack. He climbed the last few steps licking his fingers and stood beside Jake, surveying the intense action in the tower cab.

"Well, you think they'll do it, boss?"

Jake turned to glance at him, trying to read his meaning. "Sorry?"

"That's a good word for them. *Sorry*. I'm talking about America's most dysfunctional airline. Dear old Meridian Air, or as a pilot friend of mine who works there calls 'em: '*Comedian* Air, where service is a joke.'"

Jake shook his head. "I sure hope they don't walk.

They've got twenty-six percent of this market now. That's a lot of delayed passengers."

"How would they know the difference?" The overweight controller laughed. "Besides, that would also mean twenty-six percent fewer flights for us to sort out."

Jake chuckled and shook his head. "Yeah, right. As if United and American wouldn't pick up the slack. We'd be just as stressed." Jake pointed to the half-eaten sweet roll. "Any more of those in the break room?"

"Yeah. I bought a box. Have at 'em," the man said, watching Jake slip past him down the stairway.

A TV was droning away in the corner of the break room as Jake swung through the door and headed for the box of Cinnabons, the mention of air traffic control catching his attention.

The set had been tuned to C-Span, and a congressional hearing was in progress. Jake recalled reading something about it the day before. Some congressman had seized on the latest air rage incidents to justify a hearing.

Another useless exercise in political grandstanding, Jake thought, his curiosity piqued by the sight of an Air Force officer sitting alone at the witness table in a hearing about the civilian airline industry. The officer wore the silver eagle emblem of a colonel.

"Mr. Chairman," the senior officer was saying, "every day we have hundreds, if not thousands, of enraged passengers flying this airline system and just barely

11

containing their fury. While excess liquor consumption often makes things worse, the underlying causes are a combination of massive overcrowding and poor passenger treatment, not enhanced security procedures."

A gallery of still photographers was sitting on the floor in front of the witness table, and the click-whirr of their constant shooting formed a strange audible backdrop to the televised image.

"So how do we fix it, Colonel?" the chairman was asking. "Is your task force ready with recommendations?"

Jake absently picked out an outrageously caloric Cinnabon and began munching it as he watched. There was a small sign on the witness table, and it identified the officer as U.S. Air Force Colonel David Byrd of the FAA.

Ah! An Air Force liaison officer, Jake thought. He had fond memories of working with a Navy liaison captain assigned to air traffic control several years back.

"No, sir," Colonel Byrd was saying. "We're not ready to issue the final report as yet, but I can tell you this from my own research: Tougher criminal laws won't do it, because people don't plan to get angry and out of control. In other words, we can't adequately change human nature by criminalizing it, and these incidents reflect the predictable responses of humans under great stress. You pack overheated people into overcrowded airports and airplanes and treat them like dirt, lie to them, manipulate them, and price-gouge them, and the numbers of rage incidents are, by definition, going to increase. Mr. Chairman, this is a ticking bomb."

The committee chairman raised his gavel to call for a recess and the next witness and Jake headed toward the stairway to climb back to the tower cab, the muffled roar from a departing 727 catching his attention as he stepped back on the top step. He tracked the departing jetliner for a few seconds, wondering how long that particular crew had had to wait at the end of the runway.

It was, indeed, a ticking bomb, Jake thought, because the delays and the crowding were worsening all the time, and it was already a typical day: there would be no on-time takeoffs the rest of the afternoon, yet the airlines would keep on shoving their jam-packed airplanes back from the gates to join the hour-long taxi delays while recording each push-back as an "on-time" departure. Only when the air traffic control system ordered them to stay at the gate would they do so, and even then, too often the airplanes were shoved out of the gate to make room for an inbound flight. The "penalty box"—as the ramp designated for waiting airliners was called—was usually full these days, and the airlines usually knew precisely which flights would be late. The passengers, of course, weren't supposed to know.

What a scam! And we get blamed. It's always the FAA's fault.

The same thing happened every day with depressing predictability, and today the rapid approach of a line of heavy thunderstorms now beating up Springfield, Illinois, to the west was poised to make the daily air traffic snarl even worse. When the storm finally moved over O'Hare, everything would come to a halt and stay that way until it passed.

Jake looked to the west, catching the glint of lightning a hundred miles out. Hanging in the western sky between the black thunderstorms and O'Hare was a seemingly endless procession of expensive aluminum moving steadily toward the airport with landing lights sparkling against the dark clouds beyond. Their pilots, Jake knew, were struggling to comply with the precise airspeeds ordered by the harried men and women of Chicago Approach Control, located several floors below the quiet tower cab in a windowless room. Airliners as big as office buildings traveling at two hundred miles per hour were reduced to electronic blips on radar screens monitored by air traffic controllers who snapped off continual speed changes as they tried to keep the minimum legal distance between them.

"American Seventy-five, slow to one forty. You're overrunning the Eagle flight ahead. United Three Twenty-six, I said maintain one eighty, sir."

Pilots who flew too fast, or slowed too late, ended up in pilot hell: vectored around for a half hour by unforgiving controllers who would eventually have to squeeze them back into the traffic flow for another try at landing—while the passengers checked their watches and fumed. On the ground, heat undulated in great waves from the blazing-hot metallic skin of the queues of idling Boeing and Airbus products interlaced with smaller regional jets and turboprops to form billion-dollar waiting lines stretching toward the horizon of O'Hare's real estate.

Jake caught the eye of one of his controllers across the room and rolled his eyes in shared agony. The man smiled and nodded.

The background din of strained pilot voices always grated on Jake's nerves, especially when aircrews became testy in response to the staccato instructions of his ground controllers, who usually talked about as fast as human speech allowed.

"All right, United Two Thirteen, O'Hare Ground, I SEE you, and I told you to hold your position. Meridian One One Eight, stop it right there, give way to the Eagle ATR Seventy-two on your right. Lufthansa Twelve, speed it up, sir, I need you out of that alley NOW. Delta Two Seventeen, are you on the frequency?"

"Ah . . . Delta Two Seventeen is with you."

"Roger, Delta, follow the Meridian Triple-Seven on your left. Air France Twelve, change to tower frequency and wait for him to call YOU."

Diane Jensen, Jake's favorite controller for mostly sexist reasons, appeared at his side from the break room below, adjusting her headset as she prepared to pick up the rhythm and take over for one of the male controllers.

She ruffled her short-cropped, honey blond hair and smiled at him. "And now is the season of their discontent," she intoned with mock severity.

"Ours, too," he replied. "Herndon's slowing the inbounds already," he said, his eyes on the distant traffic as he invoked the name of the FAA's Air Traffic Control System Command Center near D.C., "and we're running out of ramp space."

"And I've got a short-tempered brother in that mess down there trying to get to Dallas. I just dropped him off. You'd think he was preparing for battle."

"He was," Jake remarked.

"I suggested Amtrak," she said, moving forward to plug in next to the man she was preparing to relieve. "But he wouldn't listen."

The tie-line from Approach Control was ringing again, and as Jake reached for the receiver, his eyes caught a bright glint of sunlight from a distant car in the clogged traffic outside. He was glad he didn't have to be down there among all those flaring tempers.

Very glad.

RAYBURN HOUSE OFFICE BUILDING
WASHINGTON, D.C.

Colonel David Byrd picked up the papers he'd spread out on the witness table and shoved them in his briefcase before turning to take the outstretched hand of Julian Best, chief of the Aviation Subcommittee staff.

"Nicely done, Colonel," Best said, a grin creasing his craggy features.

"Thanks," David Byrd replied as the insistent chirping of a cell phone began somewhere in the room.

Colonel Byrd tapped the surface of his briefcase. "By the way, Julian, I'm not exaggerating," he said, a dead-serious expression on his angular face. "While we've pretty much solved the terrorist threats, the air rage threat is becoming critical. The summer's just beginning, and this isn't FAA posturing."

Best was smiling. "I know you're not blowing smoke, Colonel. I know your record. Anyone who commanded a special ops squadron, has a row of ribbons that impressive, and handled the things you've handled is too tough to send to Capitol Hill on a B.S. mission."

The chirp of a cell phone interrupted them and Byrd shrugged as he gestured to the phone.

"Sorry."

"No problem, Colonel. I'll be in touch," Julian said as he turned to go.

Byrd opened the phone and turned toward the nearest wall to concentrate on the call, momentarily puzzled by angry words on the other end.

"This is Lieutenant General Overmeyer, Colonel. What in holy hell do you think you're doing testifying to Congress without my approval or a Pentagon handler?

I just saw your ugly mug on television *in uniform!* Who gave you authority to go on C-Span in uniform and make policy statements?"

Colonel Byrd pulled up a mental image of General Overmeyer, the Air Force deputy chief of staff, a man known to most of his subordinates as "General Overreactor." The general was powerful and dangerous to the career of any officer who crossed him. Even a full colonel.

"General," the colonel began, "you put me directly under the command of the FAA administrator, and I was testifying at her direction."

"Byrd, you're not there to be a civilian lapdog to be trotted out at the administrator's discretion to chase pet issues up a tree anytime it pleases her."

"General, I take offense at that. I'm hardly a lapdog, I . . ."

"I want you in my office in thirty minutes, Byrd. Is that understood?"

"Yes, sir. If you insist."

"Apparently I just did. That's a goddamned order. Oh. In case you've forgotten your roots, Colonel, do you need any help *finding* it? The Pentagon, I mean? It's a big structure near Reagan National."

"General, sarcasm isn't necessary."

"GET YOUR ASS IN HERE!"

The general hung up, leaving David Byrd off-balance, as he calculated the fastest way across the Potomac.

TWO

The windy city awakened to the usual traffic mess of a weekday June morning with temperatures hitting the mid-seventies by eight. By noon, the thermometers were pushing ninety and rising at roughly the same rate as the tempers of many of those converging on O'Hare by bus, van, taxi, and car through the medium of hopelessly jammed freeways.

The airport itself was in a state of meltdown. O'Hare was overcrowded, overheated, and overused, with no relief in sight from the constant pressure to add more flights and more passengers, and keeping the intricate airport machine balanced, oiled, and running was a daily battle. There was little margin for error, and any outside disruption could cause a cascade of delayed and canceled flights, the effects of which would ripple back through the airline system to create gate holds, delays, and more cancellations across the United States.

And disrupting the Meridian system was precisely what the infuriated flight attendants of Meridian Airlines were determined to do on this hot summer morning.

As passengers alighted at the Meridian check-in area at O'Hare, they were immediately sucked into a tornado of angry flight attendants brandishing picket signs. "We're not on strike yet!" the signs proclaimed. "But Meridian's being UNFAIR!" A handful of passengers gave them thumbs up, but most brushed past the pickets, pretending they weren't there.

Among the melee, hundreds of pounds of bags clunked, plunked, and thudded their way onto the sidewalk as a tide of passengers lined up for the skycaps running curbside check-in. Other passengers struggled through the sweltering heat and crowded confusion of the sidewalk to get to the ticket counters inside, which were grossly undermanned and defined by unending lines. Movable stanchions marshaled the supplicant passengers into a back-and-forth line that provided only the vaguest of promises that one would actually reach an agent before departure time. It was a depressing game understood by most. Agents cost money, and Meridian wanted as few of them as possible.

A Meridian Airlines customer-service agent in a wrinkled blazer and badly stained tie turned from his latest close encounter with a furious customer and checked his watch, disappointed to see it was only fifteen minutes past twelve. He could see a frazzled-looking couple approaching from the right, their eyes locked on his red coat, but he raised his eyes instead to the driveway outside, his attention snagged by a stretch limo. Who, he wondered, would emerge from the long, black Cadillac? It could be Madonna, who was in town, or some political superstar. But most likely it was just some unknown fool with too much money. In any event, it gave him an excuse to ignore the obviously unhappy couple a few seconds longer.

He hated the customers. He hated Meridian. And he hated his job. More than anything else, he hated the fact that he'd worked for Meridian too long to quit, and had too much invested not to care about being fired— something he and most of the contract employees were threatened with weekly.

The driver of the limo came around and opened the rear door, and the supervisor watched a young Asian couple unfold themselves from the rear seat. The man and woman stood on the curb, trying to come to grips with the confusion.

It's nobody, the supervisor said to himself. *Just a couple of overgrown children with too much money*. He turned to other oncoming customers instead.

At the curb, Jason Lao pulled his briefcase from the interior of the ostentatious limo and nodded uncomfortably to the driver. He'd signed the invoice and paid a reasonable tip before getting out, and now all he wanted was distance from the car before someone recognized him.

Linda Lao was several paces ahead. She turned and

smiled at him, the warm, sensuous smile that had captivated his heart since their Silicon Valley days. She waited for him to pull the handle up on his bag and catch up.

"Now, babe, wasn't that better?" she said.

"No. That was mortifying."

"Jason . . ."

"I order a town car and they send me a rolling bordello."

"It was a bit much, I'll admit, but it was comfy and cool, and you're filthy rich now, remember? We can *afford* it!"

A skycap had turned and spotted them as likely candidates as they each pulled their large rolling bags across the inner drive.

"Folks, can I help you?" he asked.

Jason nodded and let him take charge of the bags.

"Where are you going today?" the skycap added.

"London," Linda said with a toss of her head, not caring who knew how excited she was.

He nodded and began loading the bags on a handcart as Linda took Jason's arm and guided him through the automatic doors, then spun him around.

"What?"

"Okay, repeat after me, Mr. Chairman. I'm going to enjoy this."

"What?"

"Come on. Repeat it."

"That's silly."

"Maybe, but say it anyway. I . . . am . . . going . . . to . . . have . . . fun!"

"Yeah, okay, I'm gonna have fun."

She put her hands on his shoulders, mock seriousness painting her features. "You want me?"

"Of course I want you. I *always* want you."

"Okay. No smile, no fun, no sex. Got it?"

He sighed and tried to smile. "Okay. I am going to have fun."

"And you're going to relax, right?"

"One thing at a time," Jason replied, smiling a bit at last.

Linda Lao knew she was dealing with a lit fuse whenever Jason had to go to the airport. He was tightly wound, demanding much of himself and others, the engine of success for one of the few surviving dot-com superstar companies. He was successful because he lived and breathed customer service—a term that, in his words, had become an oxymoron in commercial aviation.

Every foray to the airport was an agony for Linda, who hated watching her husband angered and stressed by typically hideous service. Even the snowstorm of post-flight complaint letters he usually wrote wasn't as annoying as just watching the tension eat at him—which was why she had all but begged him to charter a jet for the trip to London.

The reaction had been predictable. Jason was a frugal man from a frugal family who had survived and prospered in Hong Kong by *being* frugal. A price tag approaching thirty thousand dollars for a chartered jet compared with coach fares under two thousand had horrified him.

"At least get us first class, then," she'd begged.

"Our employees don't fly first class, and neither do we," he'd said. "I have stockholders to think about."

"But your company isn't paying for this trip. We are."

"All the more reason. We're not so good we can't fly coach."

"Jason, honey, coach is all right for domestic flights, but it's *horrible* for international!"

The limo was the only exception he'd make, and she knew she'd be hearing about that for the next two weeks: the cost, the embarrassment, the wrong message it sent. It amused her sometimes that he was so careful of finances and of his image as a leader. They had struggled for years in California to make it, and now they had. "But precisely when," she asked him on a regular basis, "are we planning on spending some of the fortune we've earned?"

"Over my dead body will we pay thirty thousand for transportation, and that's that," he'd said, and her years as the dutiful child of Chinese parents had kicked in, forcing concession to her husband's feelings. Coach it was to London.

And now she regretted giving in.

The trip through the conga line of sweating passengers to the indignities of the ticket counter had taken thirty minutes. Characteristically, Jason had brought them to the terminal two hours early, so time wasn't a problem, but keeping him under control was.

Linda glanced up at the passenger security portals, relaxing somewhat at the sight of the uniformed federal officers now running the process. Jason had been delighted by the change and even cooperative, but the memory of their last foray through the old system some years before still sent shivers down her back.

They'd been headed to Los Angeles when the officious attitude of a snaggle-toothed security guard all but pulled the pin from Jason's temper.

"There is no rational reason to check my computer beyond what you've already done," Jason had snapped as the man tried to wrest the briefcase from his grasp, and a tug-of-war ensued.

"Sir, take the computer out or you'll have to leave the secured area."

Two Chicago cops had immediately turned and approached. The morning had been boring. They were itching to arrest someone, and Jason was emerging as a likely candidate.

"Jason," Linda whispered in his ear, "this isn't the place. These people are certified idiots. You can't reason with them."

Jason had turned to her, his teeth clenched, his anger almost out of control as she whispered again in his ear.

"I want to get to L.A., baby, not bail you out of jail. Don't say another word. Just nod to the stupid person and show him your computer."

She'd seen his jaw muscles twitching frantically as he fought to control himself while the security guard fumbled around trying to find a switch to turn on the computer.

"Here!" Jason had said in exasperation, his finger jabbing the on button. "And what the hell is that going to prove? The screen lights up. Big damn deal!"

A large woman had moved in from the other side, her uniform straining against her apparent love of food. She was nodding to the cops, who were getting closer.

"You giving us attitude, mister? We don't need no attitude. You give us attitude, we'll get the police here to 'splain it to you. You don't be cussing at us here."

Linda had tightened her grip on Jason and dug a fingernail into his wrist to the point of drawing blood, as his temper had reached the boiling point and teetered for a few seconds while the forces arrayed against him waited for the one additional snarl they needed in order to make an arrest.

Linda remembered their disappointment when Jason had suddenly exhaled and replaced his computer in his briefcase, saying no more as he avoided the eyes of the security guards and turned to take Linda's arm.

"Thanks," he'd said under his breath.

"Gotta stay cool, babe," she'd whispered, well aware

of the glares of the Chicago cops who had been cheated of their prize. "They live for guys like you."

"Which gate?"

Linda looked around, startled. "What?"

Jason was smiling. "Which gate?" he asked again as he pulled the carry-ons off the X-ray belt, snapping Linda back to the present. She realized they were already through the checkpoint, and it was disorienting to see her volatile husband still calm.

"Gate . . . B-Thirty-three," she replied, fumbling with the ticket. "Meridian Flight Six. I saw the screen. It's showing *on time*."

They changed course for the adjacent concourse, dodging the obnoxious beeping of a passenger-carrying electric cart rushing by at breakneck speed, driven by an agent wearing a half-maniacal expression.

THREE

Colonel David Byrd straightened his uniform and entered the outer office of the Air Force deputy chief of staff. A "get-your-ass-over-here" order from Overmeyer was a lower-level emergency than such a summons from the secretary of defense, but it was still chilling. The general had a reputation for getting angry very easily, though he usually got over it just as fast.

"Good morning, Colonel," a secretary said without a moment's hesitation. "The general is waiting." She led the way to a small conference room where Lieutenant General James Overmeyer was sitting on the opposite side of a conference table flanked by two men in business suits. David saluted formally, and the general returned it in a dismissive way before gesturing to his right.

"Colonel Byrd, meet Billy Monson from Defense Intelligence and Ryan Smith from Central Intelligence."

They exchanged handshakes and sat down, David warily eyeing the general, who had a canary-eating grin on his face. "So, David, you're probably wondering why I called this little meeting."

"Yes, sir. I recall some four-letter words about my testifying and an order to haul my posterior over here within thirty minutes."

The general laughed and checked his watch. "And you made it with two minutes to spare. Good man."

"May I defend myself, sir?" David asked.

General Overmeyer shook his head no and leaned forward. "No. The FAA administrator called me three minutes before you walked in to confirm that she asked you to testify, but I already knew that."

"Then . . . I guess I'm confused."

"Well, you really *should* have called me first, but that's okay. David, I've never explained why I agreed to loan you to the FAA last year."

"No, sir, you didn't."

"Well, I wanted one of us over there to keep an eye on this increasing problem with passenger rage because of a possible terrorist connection."

Byrd looked puzzled. "What?"

Overmeyer nodded. "Both DIA and CIA have been sweating bullets that some remaining terrorist group might arrange to manipulate a passenger rage situation on a civilian airliner and turn it into an attack."

David Byrd was glancing from face to face. "But how? Airborne anger incidents are spontaneous by nature."

"Are they?" General Overmeyer asked, his face serious. "Can we be absolutely sure of that? Or could the right group of passengers be goaded into an explosion of rage at a moment convenient for someone with other plans?"

"I don't know," David replied.

"Neither do we." The general sighed. "Mr. Monson and Mr. Smith here are going to brief you on the nightmarish possibilities as they see them. It's all Top Secret, or Top Secret Crypto, and as of now, you *do* have a need to know at my direction. We'll talk later." The general rose from the chair and headed to the door as he motioned to Monson.

"Billy, you've got the floor."

HEADQUARTERS, CENTRAL INTELLIGENCE AGENCY,
LANGLEY, VIRGINIA
I:00 P.M. EDT

Among the countless messages moving through the labyrinth of "the Company's" warrens at Langley, a small communiqué from one of the growing force of clandestine operatives working for the U.S. had made its way through initial screening to the electronic "in-basket" of the appropriate working group. By six-thirty in the morning, the two-man, one-woman group had read what the operative had presumably risked his life to provide, and had decided it was a missing piece to an emerging puzzle.

"What we don't have a clue about yet is what type of aircraft, or the type of weapon," one of the team said as she explained their conclusions to a deputy director.

"But," one of the men interrupted, "what we can conclude from this report is the following: Provided this is accurate, the origin of the aircraft carrying the weapon will be Africa, and I mean sub-Saharan Africa. That probably means an intercontinental flight."

"Something like a Boeing 777 or a 747 headed for Europe?"

"Right, or an Airbus 340, a DC-10, or an MD-11. Any of those. We give that a high confidence level."

"But we've no idea who the target might be?"

They shook their heads in unison. "Any city in Europe."

"Timing?"

"Within the next forty-eight hours. And our guess is the agent will be biological, such as weaponized anthrax, or something equally terrifying. All they have to do to spread it all over a civilian population is hide a bag of it in the wheelwell. The gear comes out, so does the agent."

The deputy director nodded and stood.

"Okay. We sound the alert and start watching everything that flies over Africa for the next two days."

FOUR

In the crowded boarding lounge Martin Ngume felt himself jerk awake before his eyelids fluttered open. A momentary panic gripped him as he searched for a clock, wondering if he had overslept and missed his flight.

There was a digital clock across the concourse, its readout showing a minute past noon. His flight would leave at 1:30 P.M.

Martin relaxed, but for no more than a second, his mind flashing back to the chilling news from South Africa that his mother's tiny house had a padlock swinging from the only door.

Why padlocked? Where was she?

There was no telephone in the house. The shanties in Soweto barely had bathrooms, and to use a phone, you had to walk a quarter mile to a dusty store—which is what she did once a month on Sunday to receive a call from her son.

But this time the phone had been answered by someone else, a stranger who didn't know his mother. It had taken several more calls to find a villager who would agree to make the trek to her house, and more calls to get him back on the phone for word on what he'd found.

"She is not there."

"You looked inside?"

"I could not look inside; there is a padlock on the door."

"A . . . what?"

"A little padlock. A combination padlock, you know. It's on the door."

"Did you ask anyone if she's been seen?"

"Yes, but no one knows where she is."

Martin rubbed his eyes. He'd been without sleep for two days, trying to find out what had happened to her—trying to find out why a sick old woman who'd used every penny she could save to send her son to school in America was nowhere to be found.

He was panicked, and he couldn't help it. He'd ditched his classes for two days to stay on the phone and by the phone, but in the end, there was nothing to do but find a way to fly home. There was simply no one else in South Africa who seemed to care enough to search for her.

"Excuse me," a feminine voice said from his left. "You okay?"

He swept his eyes past the empty seat to the row behind and met the eyes of an attractive woman who'd been watching him.

"Yes, thank you."

"You looked so startled when you woke up. I thought you were going to break your neck the way you were sleeping," she said, smiling.

There was a bank of public phones to the right, just down the concourse, and his mind had been heading there, but he focused now on her words.

"I'm sorry . . . . I don't understand."

"You were falling asleep, and your head would slowly drop down, like this . . ." She let her head loll forward, then jerked it back up to look at him. "And then you'd pop back up, and do it again."

"I'm sorry," he said again, feeling somehow guilty.

"Nothing to be sorry about. But my neck hurt just watching you."

He nodded, returning her smile. Normally, he would be pleased that a pretty American woman was concerned about him, but all he could think about now was that bank of telephones, and whether his phone card would still work. He thrust his right hand in his pants pocket, fingering the small amount of cash there. Eighty dollars and a Visa credit card were all he had to get him through the next few days. The plane ticket was another matter. The kindness of his landlord had brought tears when she told him not to worry, that she would get him a round-trip ticket.

"It will take time to repay you," he told her.

"It costs me nothing," she said, explaining that his three roommates had relayed his plight to her. "I've got all these frequent-flyer miles, Martin, and no time to use them. It's no big deal."

She'd only been able to get him a standby listing on the first leg to London, and he approached the podium again now, standing quietly to one side until the agent had finished setting up her computer keyboard before checking in the flight.

"Excuse me, I . . ."

"I'm not ready yet, sir. I'll make an announcement. Please have a seat."

"I'm on standby, you see, and I'm worried . . ."

"SIR! I said, please sit down and I will make an announcement when I'm ready. Okay?"

"Okay." Martin turned and headed for an idle pay phone. His call went through to the little store his mother frequented, but no one answered.

He closed his eyes again, trying to convince himself that she had simply gone on some small adventure. Maybe she'd decided to take the train to Cape Town, he thought, knowing better. She was afraid of traveling, and her eyesight was so poor now that she sometimes had trouble walking through her own house without stumbling.

And the padlock.

He knew there had been trouble with the landlord. The man had threatened to evict her a year ago, and

Martin had taken an extra campus job to send money to remove the threat. Could the landlord have padlocked the house and thrown her out? Surely not.

But when he'd thought about everything else, it still came down to one fact: A woman who hadn't left her village in thirty years was suddenly missing, and her house was padlocked.

His brow furrowed in anxiety, Martin returned to his seat, hardly noticing the woman who had spoken to him before.

But she was still watching him, and he met her eyes once again and managed a smile, a difficult feat with his heart so low. She appeared to be in her mid thirties and was exceptionally tall and carefully groomed with just a hint of makeup. Her sandy hair was worn shoulder length. Not beautiful, he thought, but a striking Caucasian female.

"You're going to London?" she asked.

"No, Cape Town," Martin said, and in spite of himself, began to tell her why, stopping a few minutes later when he realized he'd become lost in his own anxiety.

"You think she's still in the house, don't you?" the woman asked. "You're afraid something's happened to her, and I don't blame you, but I'm sure she's all right."

He looked into her eyes and saw a warmth there that began to penetrate his defenses, unleashing some of the wrenching fear and loneliness he'd bottled up, causing tears to well up no matter how hard he tried to be the strong, impervious, twenty-one-year-old straight-A scholarship Northwestern University senior his mother was so proud of. Fleeting thoughts of the classes he was missing passed through his mind. But he had to get home, and fast. That was the only thing he could think about now. He could make up the classes later.

Twenty feet away, Jimmy Roberts checked the front of his ticket envelope and shifted a bag to his other shoulder as he looked up at the gate number. The aroma of food from a nearby overpriced fast food snack bar was annoying him. He was hungry, but so far nothing they were hawking in the terminal was appealing, especially at the prices they were charging.

"Is this it, Jimmy?" His wife asked as she lowered her tote bag toward the filthy concourse floor, then thought better of it and pulled it back to her shoulder again.

"Yeah, darlin', I think so. B-Thirty-three."

The grossly overboosted voice of a gate agent down the concourse was growling an indecipherable announcement over the PA system, wiping out for the moment the elevator music playing in the background.

"That's a long line," Brenda said, looking toward the gate's check-in counter.

"Well," Jimmy began, "why don't you go find us a couple of seats while I wait."

She looked around, confirming her initial impression. "Aren't any seats here, hon. I'll just stand here with you, and keep the women away. "

Jimmy turned to look at his wife. He wasn't the catch. *She* was. He couldn't help but smile, she was so beautiful—blond hair, five feet six, perfectly sculpted in her jeans. Jimmy was acutely aware that her passage was constantly watched by most of the men in the vicinity, like an array of radar antennae tracking a target as it flowed past. As long as they kept their distance, Jimmy figured, their interest in his lady was somewhere between amusing and flattering.

God Almighty, I'm a lucky guy! he thought to himself for the thousandth time. Lucky to have her as his wife and lover, and unbelievably lucky that she liked to enter raffles and sweepstakes, although he'd always teased her about it—until the registered letter arrived with news that they'd won a free international trip on Meridian Airlines anywhere they wanted to go.

"Why South Africa?" Jimmy had asked when the shock wore off and she'd decided on a destination.

"'Cause I've never been there, and because I had an uncle who lived there a long time ago and I've always wanted to see it, and because . . ."

"Okay, okay, okay!" he'd said, chuckling. "We'll go to South Africa. Hell, darlin', the only place I've ever really visited is Dallas, and that was just one time. South Africa will really be somethin' to write home about."

The flight to Chicago through DFW had been exciting. They'd been on an airplane before, flying Southwest to El Paso once for a funeral, which almost broke their meager bank account. Meridian was different, Brenda thought. They served food instead of peanuts, but the flight attendants all seemed kind of distant and angry. Nothing like Southwest, where they were all friendly good old boys and girls just having fun, as Jimmy put it.

"I ought to call Roy and make sure everything's okay," Jimmy said. Brenda recognized the look. They were scratching out a living running a small auto-repair garage on the western edge of Midland, and Jimmy's brother had promised to look after things for two weeks. The whole idea of leaving the business in anyone else's hands had terrified Jimmy, but his brother had a business degree and should be able to take care of things, even if he didn't understand the mechanics Jimmy employed.

"Hon, you leave your brother alone. He can handle it."

"He'll probably fire everyone before nightfall as soon as he finds out how strange they are. We've got a weird bunch, Brenda." Jimmy pointed to an overhead sign. "You want to try that rest room?" The other one she'd entered down the concourse had been so filthy she'd come out immediately with her face all screwed up.

"I'll just hold it," Brenda said. "You wouldn't believe how bad that other one was. I've seen outhouses less disgusting."

"This whole place is filthy," he agreed, stepping back slightly as a skycap pushed a wheelchair-bound passenger past him.

There was a commotion a few feet away in the middle of the concourse, and Jimmy looked up to see two airport cops running past on foot with no apparent quarry in sight.

The line slowly oozed toward the counter until just two people stood ahead of them. A loud voice caught Jimmy's attention. He glanced up, surprised to hear one of the female agents raising her voice at a customer.

"Lady, you're not on this flight. Okay? *Okay?* What part of the phrase 'no reservation' don't you understand?"

The passenger, a petite woman in a conservative suit, was holding a computer case and almost straining to see over the counter. She couldn't be more than four foot eleven, Jimmy figured, maybe an even five feet at best.

"Look, it's got to be there," the woman was saying in a calm voice. Jimmy had to strain to hear her.

"Your name again?" the gate agent said, scowling as she glanced up at the long line of other passengers now being held up by the small woman before her.

"Douglas. Sharon Douglas."

The agent began pecking at the computer keyboard, then let out a loud sigh.

"As I told you, Ms. Douglas, you're not on this flight, and I've got no seats left. We're sold out. If you'll have a seat in the waiting area, when the flight's gone I'll see what I can do about getting you another reservation."

The woman had been rummaging through her purse, and she looked up suddenly and pushed a folded piece of paper across to the agent.

"What's this?"

"My confirmation number."

The agent took it gingerly, as if it were contaminated. She examined the print, then slid it back.

"This is for another date."

"Is this the sixteenth?" Sharon Douglas asked evenly.

"Yes, ma'am."

"Then you misread it. Look again, please."

Jimmy glanced at Brenda, who was listening to the same interchange, a dumbfounded expression on her face. She looked up at him, eyebrows raised in an "I don't believe this!" expression.

With another sharp sigh and a disgusted shake of her head, the agent once again took the paper, this time letting an arched eyebrow register her surprise.

"Well . . . I wish you'd shown me this before."

"I gave you the confirmation number. That's all a passenger should have to do with an electronic ticket. That shows I'm confirmed on this flight to London, seat fourteen C. I expect a boarding pass for that seat."

"Well, Ms. Douglas, you can expect anything you want. That seat's already taken."

The woman shook her head slightly, as if trying to

expunge the growing feeling that she'd entered some alien world. "Okay. You know what? I really don't think you're listening to me, so I want you to call your supervisor."

The agent shook her head. "He doesn't have time to come over here."

"I'm not asking you; I'm instructing you. Call your supervisor. I know your company's rules, and you have no choice when that request is made."

"Call him yourself," the agent sneered. "They don't pay me enough money to listen to rude people."

"*I'm* being rude?" Sharon Douglas stood with her jaw open for a few seconds, trying to fathom the chutzpah of someone who could so blatantly accuse a customer of her own behavior. "Listen to me," she told the agent. "Listen carefully. Your job is on the line here. You do not have the right to refuse. Call . . . your . . . supervisor!"

The agent leaned toward Sharon Douglas with a smirk and widened her eyes in a mocking gesture. "But I AM refusing! How's that? I'm not calling my supervisor—and, lady, if you try to order me around once more, you're out of this line. Oh, and when you write your little complaint letter, be sure to spell my name correctly." She fingered her ID badge and held it out contemptuously as the next customer in line—a tall man in a business suit—moved forward suddenly and tapped the counter for emphasis.

The female agent met his eyes angrily. "What do you want?"

"What do you suppose would happen," the man said,

keeping his voice low, "if your airline's president, not to mention your supervisor, found out you'd treated a VIP the way you just treated this lady?"

"Mind your own business, sir!" the agent snapped.

He ignored the retort. "And what do you think would happen to your job if the very important person you sassed like that turned out to be, oh, let's say, the chairman of the United States Senate Aviation Subcommittee, one of the senators who bailed your industry out a few years ago with a few billion public dollars?"

Sharon Douglas placed a hand on the man's arm in a gesture of restraint. "That's okay. I'm all right."

"So who are you, sir?" the agent sneered. "A close personal friend of our chairman, like everyone else claims to be? Or maybe *you're* a U.S. senator."

"No, ma'am," he said, gesturing toward Sharon Douglas. "I'm not a senator. But *she* is. The lady you just insulted happens to be the senior United States senator from Illinois."

The agent's expression slowly melted from arrogant to confused to cautious to alarmed as the man continued. "And after you fall all over yourself trying to apologize, I'd suggest you get your supervisor over here sometime yesterday, just as the senator ordered."

"Are . . . you really a senator?" the agent asked Sharon Douglas, who nodded.

"Yes, but that shouldn't make any difference. You shouldn't be treating *anyone* the way you just treated me. Now, I'd like my boarding pass."

The male passenger had turned sideways and was gesturing at the others in line, and nodding at Jimmy as he spoke in a raised voice. "Senator, this is how this airline treats us all the time, every day. They begged us to come back and buy their tickets a few years ago, and we did, and now they're back to treating us like pond scum."

"Pretty impressive demonstration, I'd say," Senator Douglas added, watching the wide-eyed agent fumbling with her phone.

Within seconds, walkie-talkies were coming alive all across the terminal as several red-coated figures turned immediately and beat a path for B-33.

FIVE

LONDON, ENGLAND
6:10 P.M. LOCAL

Captain Phil Knight slid open the patio door of his friend's air-conditioned London home and stepped outside, letting the suffocating heat of a late-summer afternoon enfold him. The scent of flowers perfumed the air, but he had no knowledge of horticulture. He merely noted the pleasant aroma in passing as he sipped a frozen daiquiri and studied the cumulus cloud formations lazily floating by overhead. It was understandable how someone could enjoy such surroundings, Phil thought as he looked around the lush little garden in the well-manicured and very private backyard encircled by an eight-foot high cinder-block wall. Someone else, that is. Ever since he'd arrived he'd been trying to suppress the urge to make apologies, beg off dinner, and crawl back to his hotel near Heathrow.

Phil glanced around, relieved to see Glenn Thomasson still on a phone call in the distance, the man's posture ramrod straight as he stood in his kitchen holding the receiver.

Captain Thomasson was a gracious host who'd done nothing to make his far younger American guest feel unwelcome or uncomfortable, but Phil couldn't shake the feeling of being an interloper. What made it worse was not having a clue *why* he felt that way.

He smiled in spite of himself. Captain Thomasson was full of the usual tales pilots tell each other with hands held high in the air in a "there-I-was" formation, and it was entertaining to listen to his animated and strongly embroidered stories. The British captain had logged thirty-eight years in the cockpit and over twenty-eight thousand hours of flight time, first as a copilot and captain for British Overseas Airways Corporation and then as a senior 747 skipper for BOAC's successor, British Air. He was sixty-six now, hale and hearty, and a divorcé who was all too quick to claim a Professor Henry Higgins independence of women—a protest Phil refused to believe.

Phil Knight had dined with the retired British Airways captain once before, a delightful memory of a leather-trimmed men's club in the central London area. It had been an evening of swapped stories of airplanes and fishing, capped with brandy and cigars before Thomasson dropped him back at the hotel.

But this was different. Perhaps it was all the plaques

TURBULENCE

and photos on the walls testifying to Thomasson's apparently happy years as a commercial pilot that made Phil strangely uncomfortable. Or maybe what was so unsettling was the clear impression that there had never been a time in the past thirty-eight years when Captain Glenn Thomasson had ever doubted his abilities.

That was the trait in Thomasson he most admired.

The sound of powerful turbofan engines rumbled over the house, and Phil looked to the south in time to catch a glimpse of a departing Airbus A-340. The four-engine jumbo was climbing slowly, its structure heavy with fuel and passengers, obviously heading for some foreign destination. In the cockpit of the Airbus there would be a pair of pilots for whom the complexities of international flight were second nature, a team with no worries about understanding thick accents, deciphering international rules, or knowing the so-called "secret handshakes" about how to stay safe above the African continent by providing your own air-traffic services. Phil felt a flash of envy, laced with a twinge of regret. It must feel good to be so prepared—so competent. If Meridian had even hinted at how much extra knowledge was required to fly overseas, maybe he would have made a different decision.

A chill rippled down his back, and he could feel his stomach tighten as its acid content pegged the meter once more. Constant indigestion was part of the price he paid for bidding Meridian's international routes as a 747

47

captain. He was working his way to an enormous ulcer, but that couldn't be discussed with any other human being, let alone another pilot.

Phil glanced at his watch. *Six-thirty P.M. here, and just past noon in Chicago. That leaves me about eleven hours, he told himself. I've got eleven hours before the flight leaves and the agony starts again.*

The flight he was assigned to command from London to Cape Town, South Africa, was scheduled to arrive from Chicago at two-thirty in the morning. That meant a 3 A.M. wake-up call and no time to eat before reporting to operations by 4. By then, Meridian's Heathrow ground handlers would be readying his Boeing 747-400 to take over the Flight Six call sign, while the Boeing 777 that had used that flight number from Chicago prepared to return to the States as Flight Five. Departure for Cape Town would be just after 5 A.M.

Another shiver, this one sustained.

Phil turned once again to check on his host, but Thomasson was still on the phone, gesturing in animated conversation in his kitchen. Phil moved back inside to the living room and slid the glass door closed behind him. The air-conditioning felt good, and he lowered himself into a wing-back chair, his eyes still on the distant sky as he unconsciously tensed, thinking about the inbound flight. Like Marley's ghost dragging stratospheric chains, it was coming to haunt him for letting greed enmesh him in a dangerous charade.

Phil looked at his watch. Flight Six should be getting ready to leave Chicago right now. Phil could visualize the pilots arriving from their Chicago-area homes and flight planning in Meridian Operations, just as he'd done two days before. Their night over water to London would be easy, with nothing more confusing than a Canadian or British accent to deal with among the fraternity of controllers who carefully watched over the North Atlantic air routes. That would bear no resemblance to the challenge *he* would face, the part of the job that roiled his stomach and made his head hurt. African airspace was as much a jungle as some of the equatorial landscapes below. Each country insisted on providing its own version of air traffic control in order to collect user fees from the airlines, but the equipment, the training, and the procedures were wildly different and dangerous, and nothing like in the United States. Even when Phil could understand the thick-accented versions of English, even when the controllers bothered to answer radio calls, the "system" was completely untrustworthy and the experienced pilots who flew over Africa had developed their own backdoor air traffic control system by calling out their positions constantly and talking to one another on common frequencies in what was sometimes a near-desperate effort to keep from colliding with someone else.

And, Phil knew, there were informal "rules" for the "IFBP," the in-flight broadcast procedure, as it was called. Garth Abbott, his copilot, knew the rules and the procedures and the frequencies by heart. Meridian, however, had taught Phil almost nothing.

Phil felt his hand shaking slightly and willed it to stop. The last thing he wanted was for Glenn Thomasson to find him looking anywhere near as upset as he was.

SIX

Chuck Levy squeezed his wife's hand tighter and tried to focus on the gauntlet ahead, but the phone call kept replaying in his mind. The voice of the emergency room physician calling from Zurich to tell him his daughter had been in a horrible car wreck and was near death.

"Who are you again?" he had managed.

"Doctor Alfred Knof. You must come quickly to Zurich. We are doing everything for Janna. However, I fear there is little time."

Janna's rental car had been overrun by a loaded truck, and the results were gruesome.

Anna, his wife, had sat bolt upright beside him in bed.

Chuck shook his head to suppress the memory. There was less than a mile to go to the terminal, and the cabby was asking which airline in a voice so heavily influenced

51

by his native tongue, Chuck had to concentrate hard to make out the question.

"Oh. Meridian Airlines," he said.

"Madidiam?" was the reply.

"Mer-ID-ian. Meridian. Understand?"

"Yes, yes. Madidiam."

Chuck nodded. There was too much to plan, and the crushing fatigue of the terrible news coupled with the struggle to snap into motion to fly a world away with less than four hours' sleep felt like the description asthmatic friends had used to explain an asthma attack: like having an elephant on your chest.

He glanced at Anna. She was squeezing the blood out of his hand as she sat with her eyes shut tight. He could feel her shaking with fear for the fate of their only child. The same elephant, sitting on both of them.

Think! Chuck commanded himself. Two interminable hours spent on the phone with untrained, uncaring airline reservationists after holding for fifty minutes had drained him as well. No special fares, crowded airplanes, bad schedules, no seats, and no willingness to do anything but peck at a keyboard on the other end. All of it had made the experience a special torture, especially since it tied up their only phone line. He should have paid for call waiting, Chuck scolded himself. He'd called Zurich three times between the airline calls, trying to make sure he hadn't missed a call from Dr. Knof.

But nothing had changed. Janna was barely clinging to life, and the prognosis was grim.

He had to organize his thoughts.

Okay, we've got two bags. We'll have to wait in line, get the ticket, check the bags, then go to the gate. Must make sure the bags go all the way to Zurich, but is it Meridian or Swissair we're booked on out of London? There had been so many false starts and possible flight combinations with over-booked flights, he couldn't remember what they'd finally confirmed.

Passports? Yes. We've got both of them. Thank God I had them renewed last year. Money? No. Need a cash machine. Would that be before security or after? If I screw it up and it's outside, I'll have to go back through security again and it'll take too long. Do it in London.

It was going to be very, very tight. Getting everything done in the right sequence was critical. They were already behind for the 1:30 London flight.

It was so depressing, Chuck thought, how many "hoops" the airlines, Meridian in particular, made you jump through to buy their product, even after the federal bailout, even after their near-death experience with frightened passengers staying away in droves following the attacks on New York and Washington. He'd been a salesman all his life, and a good one, but if he'd used the same attitudes with his customers, he would have starved to death by age twenty-five.

And the expense! Nearly five thousand dollars for two last-minute round trips. There was no way they could afford it, but there was no time to call around for a better deal. He'd have to figure out how to pay American

Express later. The airline had acted like a bandit . . . a criminal. You want to see your daughter before she dies? Just fork over your bank account while we hold your hearts hostage.

"My daughter's near death. Is there no discount for this type of disaster?" he'd asked in shock. "I . . . heard there was a special fare for families with a medical crisis."

"Oh, yeah," the female reservationist had replied. "You're thinking about the old bereavement fares. But those are only when someone dies, and we cut them out a long time ago anyway for international flights. After all, sir, we're in business to make money."

The O'Hare terminal was looming up in front of them now, and the cabby was slowing. Chuck turned to Anna and gently pressed her hand. "We're almost at the airport, honey," he said.

She squeezed harder in response, her eyes still welded shut, but not tightly enough to stem the constant flow of tears.

Outside Gate B-33 in the cockpit of Meridian's Flight Six to London, the captain pulled off his headset and ripped a piece of paper from a notepad, handing it to the first officer in the right seat of the Boeing 777.

"What's this?" the copilot asked as he glanced up at the boarding area, visible through the glass wall ahead of B-33.

"The usual. From Ops. We're due out at one-thirty, but they say we'll be on gate hold for at least an hour. And we've got that line of storms coming in."

"You need a crew duty time analysis, right?"

"Right. When do our efforts become futile? How late can we be at the end of the runway and still make it to London before violating the maximum time requirements?"

"You want to hold their feet to the fire? Right to the minute?"

The captain shrugged. "If we don't enforce the rules, Meridian won't."

The copilot snorted. "No shit, Sherlock. They'd handcuff us to the yoke if the FAA let them."

"Would you mind telling the passengers?" the captain asked.

The copilot looked at him with an incredulous expression. "You bet, I mind. I hate doing PAs."

"Well . . . so do I. But they're going to get upset if someone doesn't talk to them, and since your captain refuses and there's no flight engineer, I figured . . ."

"Captain," the first officer said, "I think you've got me confused with someone who gives a damn."

"Okay," the captain said with a sigh. "Then I'll talk to them in-flight. I don't want to upset them."

"Too late. They were born upset, and then we give them such wonderful ticket agents to burnish their fine mood. Wait till they sample the food."

The captain gave the copilot a quizzical look. "A little sour today, are we, Jeff?"

"You noticed! How nice. Yesterday I was just disillusioned. Today I'm full-scale disgruntled."

SEVEN

ABOARD VIRGIN AIRLINES FLIGHT TWELVE,
BOSTON TO LONDON
OVER THE ATLANTIC

A degree of calm had finally settled over the first-class galley as the Virgin Airbus A-340 cruised past the halfway point at thirty-seven thousand feet on the way from Boston to London. After serving a sumptuous dinner, dessert, coffee, snacks, and uncounted drinks, the cabin service staff assigned to keep Virgin's most important passengers happy had finished stowing and cleaning their equipment, and were daring to relax for a while.

There was little time. The breakfast service would begin in two hours.

The welcome tranquillity of a jetliner at altitude was affecting them all, the white noise of the muted background roar an audible, sleep-promoting sedative in stark contrast to the sudden commotion of a man bursting into the galley interior in obvious distress.

"Miss! Miss!"

The three startled flight attendants turned immediately toward the wild-eyed passenger as he stopped and pointed over his shoulder toward first class.

One of the women came forward immediately. "What's the matter, sir?"

"Your first-aid kit. Where is it? My . . . my . . ."

He looked around in confusion and pulled away from her, rushing back out with the flight attendant on his heels.

"What's the matter?" she asked as another flight attendant appeared.

Dr. Brian Logan was moving rapidly up the aisle, stopping at each seat, his eyes darting in all directions as he searched the floor. "She's . . . Where *is* she?" WHERE IS SHE?"

The lead flight attendant grabbed him by his shoulders from behind and tried to spin him around.

"Sir! SIR? Calm down, now. Please! Tell me what's wrong."

Logan straightened up and turned on his own, blinking rapidly as he tried to focus on the uniformed woman before him. She could see recognition flare, and feel his body slump as he lowered his head. "Oh, God."

She tried again in a gentler voice. "Sir? Can you tell me what's wrong?"

A third flight attendant came up from behind with a printout of the passenger list and whispered in the ear of her senior, "His name is Brian Logan. He's a doctor."

The senior flight attendant nodded, keeping her eyes on the distraught physician, who was crying softly.

"Doctor Logan? Can you sit down and tell me, please, what's wrong?"

He nodded and let her guide him back to his seat, and she knelt in the aisle beside him, still holding his arm.

"I'm sorry. It was . . . a very real nightmare, I guess."

"That happens," she said.

"I thought my wife was aboard and . . . in medical trouble . . . and . . ."

"I understand."

"Where am I? I mean, I know we're on the way to London, but . . ."

"Three hours from Heathrow, Doctor. Is someone meeting you there?"

He gave her a long, uncomprehending stare. "Sorry?"

"Is anyone meeting you at Heathrow?"

He shook his head slowly, a faraway look in his eyes.

EIGHT

THE PENTAGON, WASHINGTON, D.C.
1:45 P.M. EDT

Colonel David Byrd quickened his step to keep pace with General James Overmeyer as they swept down a stairway and headed for the Pentagon's north entrance. The combined intelligence brief had taken nearly an hour, but there had been no time to discuss it. The general reappeared just long enough to issue a string of instructions to his secretary and turn to David with a directive.

"Follow me," he'd said. "We're going to Andrews. I talked the Eighty-ninth into readying a Gulfstream to get me down to Hurlburt."

"We're going to Hurlburt Air Force Base?" David asked as they climbed into a staff car.

"No. *I'm* going to Hurlburt on a Special Operations matter. You're just riding along to Andrews so we can talk. After that, the driver can take you wherever you'd like . . . within reason, of course. You know. Take you to your apartment, your mistress, your church, whatever turns you on."

"I don't have a mistress, sir."

The general grinned over his shoulder as he reached the curb and nodded to the driver who was holding open the right rear door. "Neither do I. For some reason, the idea irritates my wife and probably violates a few regulations."

The driver accelerated smoothly into traffic as Overmeyer turned to David. "So, what do you think about that briefing?"

"General, I think both Mr. Monson and Mr. Smith have been spending far too much time in dark rooms. I mean, I know we've been overworking these fellows since the attacks . . ."

"So, are we all nuts?" Overmeyer asked.

David shook his head, trying not to be distracted by the sight of a drop-dead beautiful blonde wearing a skimpy halter top in a silver Mercedes convertible keeping pace to the right. He forced himself to look at the general.

"There's no question we should be concerned, maybe even paranoid, about the possibility that some one of the remaining groups we're trying to ferret out could slip past our other intelligence nets and try to sneak a bomb or biological agent into the U.S., or anywhere else, masquerading as a legitimate flight. You know, no hijacking involved, just piggybacking on the cargo or maybe even the airframe itself. But, if you ask me, Monson and Smith are connecting dots that don't connect."

"I did ask you. Explain."

"Okay. How on earth is anyone going to mount a reliable terrorist operation in the middle of the world-wide war we're waging against them and somehow get the chance to sneak a weapon on board by creating a diversion based on manipulating angry passengers? Their song and dance makes no sense. We've been studying angry passengers at FAA under my direction for a year now, so this is more than just my opinion."

"Okay."

"This concept is far too random. No one can know that a particular load of passengers on any given day is going to be upset enough to be manipulated. And what on earth are they supposed to be talked into doing, anyway?"

The general nodded.

"You want me to go on?" David asked.

"You hate dead air, don't you, David?"

"Sir?"

"Dead air. I was a part-time radio DJ in high school in the early sixties, and that's an old radio term. When the station goes silent because you run out of things to say, it's dead air . . . and it's scary. Program directors get really upset."

"I was never a DJ."

"No, but you hate dead air. Most people do. Yes,

David, I want you to go on. You think they're full of it."

"Yes, I do. We can concoct all sorts of far-out possibilities, but the *probability* of some remaining terrorist cells still having enough ability and money . . . after all we've been doing to eradicate them . . . to goad an otherwise unstable individual or group of passengers into creating an airborne incident that could be used for an attack just doesn't rise to the level of reality. They're looking for a Trojan Horse, General, and that's not the way you'd construct one."

"I agree."

"You do? But, you said you put me in that assignment specifically to . . ."

"No," the general interrupted. "I put you in that assignment because I owed our FAA administrator a favor, and because I know what happens when our Defense Intelligence Agency in particular approaches FAA on major air security questions."

"Terrorist intelligence matters, in other words?"

"Yes. After all, after the World Trade Center attacks, FAA's folks have developed a propensity for getting far too excited far too fast and losing their analytical edge. Can't blame them, really. By the way, you do recall, don't you, that I headed up DIA for three years?"

"I'd forgotten that, General."

"Well, I did, and I dealt with FAA, and got burned a few times. That's why I sent you. I couldn't see the connection either, and I knew you'd be able to give me a more intelligent answer. David, write me a talking paper on what you just heard. Classify it appropriately, but refute their worries with what you know. I may need it."

"Why? I mean, why might you need it?"

"Because I'm afraid Langley and DIA are going to go off half-cocked on this issue. They're essentially on a twenty-four-hour alert right now looking for a Trojan Horse somewhere in the world. That's too much of a hair trigger."

"You want that paper yesterday, I take it?" David smiled.

"Of course. And you stay the hell out of the public eye on this issue of angry, misbehaving passengers. Understand?"

"Yes, sir."

"I want you to make brigadier general, and I may have already hurt your chances by diverting you to this assignment when you ought to be commanding a deployed fighter wing in Saudi, so we have to be careful with you from here on out."

"Meaning that anything I do publicly . . ."

Overmeyer sighed. "The promotion boards are suspicious of colonels who enjoy being on camera or talking to Congress. Understood?"

"Understood."

"Now, one other matter." The general opened his briefcase and began fumbling with the various papers. He pulled a plain envelope out at last and handed it to David, then pointed to it. "This has the name and contact numbers of a guy I want you to work with. After you drop me at Andrews, call him."

"About the Trojan Horse threat?"

"Yes. John Blaylock is his name. Somehow we made him a full bull colonel some years ago. He's a reservist, and he's an utter disgrace to normal officer grooming requirements. He's sneered at them all his career."

"Has he been activated?"

"No. But he . . . works for us a lot."

"Why do I want to meet this man, sir?"

"Let me finish. He's an airline captain, now retired. Flew all over the world for several carriers looking and acting like the boorish ugly American, considering his omnipresent cigars."

"As I said . . . ," David began, recoiling from the verbal image.

The general held up his hand and smiled. "I know, and he's a classic case of the so-called raggedy-ass reservist, but that doesn't explain it either." The general fell silent, and David started to speak, then stopped and smiled, waiting patiently until Overmeyer began laughing. "Okay, okay, I hate dead air, too," the general said.

"Why, sir, I repeat, would any self-respecting senior officer want to meet the likes of Colonel Blaylock?"

"Because for thirty years he's been one of the sharpest intelligence operatives we had in the Air Force. While everyone rolled their eyes at him, he was out in the field finding out precisely what was going on when no one else could. Peru, Brazil, Colombia, Paraguay, most of Africa, Asia . . . the ugly airline captain would always come sauntering back with exactly what we needed when all our air attachés, and all the CIA's moles and covert ops types hadn't a clue."

"Interesting."

"He's a kick, David. And he knows the airline business. Just don't expect spit and polish. You can learn a lot from him."

"So . . . he's retired from the reserves?"

"John? Hell, no! He just looks like it. John Blaylock is a slightly bohemian national asset with a very strange sense of humor."

"Sounds like a real character, but I've been warned."

"Just don't introduce him to your wife."

"I don't have a wife. Why?"

"Women are his main weakness. After cigars, that is. I have no idea how someone like John attracts females, but he always has, and you wouldn't believe the messes we've had to repair."

NINE

Four hours of sitting on a delayed, overheated aircraft were taking their toll on Karen Davidson. She was already exhausted, and the sight of her son being escorted back down the aisle of the Boeing 777 by an angry-looking flight attendant wasn't helping matters. Four-year-old Billy Davidson was stir-crazy and cranky, and she'd already chased him down once. But this time when he'd thrown off his seat belt and run, she was engaged in breast-feeding his infant sister. Chasing him hadn't been an option.

She had seen the lone male flight attendant on the crew grab Billy none too gently and march him back.

"Ow!" Billy protested. The man turned the child around and forced him back into his seat before pointing a finger in Billy's face. "You put that seat belt on right now, young man, or we'll open the door and throw you out on the concrete."

"Hey! Don't threaten my son," Karen said, as startled as she was embarrassed.

The man turned. "Control your kid, ma'am, and there won't be a need for any threats."

"You know," she began, fatigue canceling caution, "I don't particularly appreciate your attitude. We're all tired and hot and disgusted, including my little boy. I don't know why your air-conditioning isn't working, but this is miserable, and you're being rude. My son wasn't racing up and down the aisle. He just got away."

The flight attendant snorted and knelt down beside her, his voice still loud enough to be overheard in the adjacent rows. "Lady, you're bordering on interference with a crew member when you challenge me. Know that? I could have you arrested for not complying with my orders. This is a public place. It isn't a day-care center."

He stood and walked off, leaving Karen Davidson and a host of nearby passengers aghast.

In the rear of the main coach cabin, one of the eleven flight attendants turned when she felt her sleeve being tugged and found herself smiling at a silver-haired man in a business suit.

"Sorry to bother you," he said, "But . . . someone made an announcement about cellular phones and the door?"

"Yes, sir," she said. "You can only use them while

we're on the ground with the front door open, because otherwise they interfere with the airplane's navigation system."

"If the door is closed, they interfere, but not when it's open?"

"Yes, sir. That's the law."

"The *law*? And why would the law say that?"

Her hands migrated to her hips. "Because cell phones are dangerous and can interfere with the navigation equipment of the aircraft on the ground."

"And . . . the captain needs that equipment to find the end of the runway?"

There were several snickers from adjacent passengers as the flight attendant realized she was being interrogated.

"Yeah, probably," she said. "Look, I've got to go."

"Do they teach you this drivel in some class?"

"I'm sorry?"

"This utter nonsense you've just been spouting through complete ignorance. Do they really *teach* you to say these inane things?"

"I don't know what you mean, sir, but I told you what the law is."

"Young woman, I'm a lawyer with forty years experience in communications, and an electronics engineer. Not a single thing you said is true. That's merely an airline rule. It's not a regulation, and it's not a law. There is virtually no chance of cell phone interference on the ground with this modern aircraft's navigation gear or any other circuitry. And the only reason for prohibiting the use of cell phones in the air is the fact that the FAA hasn't done enough studies to prove they can be used safely, not because they can't. It has nothing to do with the door being open or closed. And ... on top of everything else, if the phones presented a hazard of fuel explosion, using them on the ground at the gate would be the most dangerous time of all."

She turned without a word and walked away as quickly as possible as a dozen surrounding passengers broke into applause.

In the first-class galley, Janie Bretsen, the lead flight attendant, picked up the interphone and rang the cockpit to brief the pilots on the growing unrest.

"Captain, we've got a guy in business class who's demanding to get off. He wants you to go back to the gate."

"We can't do that."

"He's not feeling well."

"Well, neither am I."

"What do you want me to tell him?"

"Tell the man we've got over three hundred paying passengers who want to get off the ground, and if we break out of this line and go back to the gate, it'll mean at least another two-hour delay. Does he feel *that* bad?"

"I'll ask him."

Within two minutes she was back on the interphone.

"He just says he's feeling bad and he demands to be let off."

"So, he's not really sick?"

"No. I mean, I guess not. But maybe we should listen to him."

"He's just whining, and I'm not impressed. Tell him there's no way the company would understand our going back, unless I have him hauled away by ambulance. Otherwise, he can deal with it in London."

There was a click of finality as the captain hung up.

In the rear galley of Flight Six, Lara Richardson had been deep into a copy of the latest *People* magazine when a passenger call chime caught her attention. She slapped the magazine closed and rolled her eyes at another flight attendant as she got to her feet. "*Now* what?"

Lara began walking toward the front, looking for an illuminated call button, which she found at row 28.

"Okay, who's the troublemaker?" she asked with a forced smile as she scanned the four passengers in the row. "Who rang the call chime?"

A middle-aged man with an ashen face raised his hand. "We did. We're . . . concerned about getting to London," Chuck Levy began.

"Yes, sir, we're all concerned about getting to London," Lara said, rolling her eyes.

There was a long pause as the man studied her face,

then continued. "I . . . just need to know if you have any idea when we're actually leaving?"

"No one knows, sir. We're all stuck out on this taxiway because of that rainstorm, and because the FAA can't get their act together. It's up to them."

Chuck glanced at Anna, his wife, who was looking equally grim and gray.

A real fun couple, Lara thought to herself.

"Look, miss . . . ," he said, his voice conveying a crushing fatigue.

"Sir," she broke in, "you'll know when we know. Okay?"

"I just need to know whether there might be another flight, maybe on another airline, that could get us there faster. The cost doesn't matter."

She snickered. "So what am I, a ticket counter? I don't know."

"Miss," he tried again. "You don't understand . . ."

"No, *you* don't understand! You can't get off this airplane unless we go back to the gate. If we do go back to the gate, you can get off and go call reservations. In the meantime, I can't help you, and I'm busy. Okay?"

"Hey. Excuse me," a male voice called from the opposite side of the aisle. Lara Richardson turned to find herself in the crosshairs of an angry glare from a young man in a Navy uniform.

She smiled broadly and cocked her head. "Hi, sailor. New in town?"

His expression didn't change as he motioned her closer, speaking in a low voice. "Ma'am, you want to treat those folks with a little more respect."

Lara reached out and patted him on the head as she walked off to the rear. "You sail your little boats, fella, and I'll fly my airplanes."

The report of a seat belt being snapped open was followed by a rush of white as the Navy ensign scrambled to his feet in pursuit of the flight attendant. He caught up with her in the rear galley.

"Ma'am, just a minute."

She turned, hands on hips, fixing him with an icy stare. "Yes?"

"There's a young girl in a hospital near Zurich, Switzerland, at this moment with two shattered legs, serious internal injuries, and a head injury, and she's not expected to live more than another twenty-four hours at best. Her rental car was flattened early this morning by a truck. The girl is twenty-two, single, and was in the middle of a graduation trip her parents had saved to pay for. And those are her parents you just treated like dirt."

Lara's jaw dropped slightly. "Oh, Jeez, I didn't know."

"You never asked, did you? I was talking with them before we boarded. They're scared to death their daughter's going to die while we sit here on the ground at O'Hare. Don't you think they're entitled to some consideration?"

"I'm sorry," she said. "Yes. They are."

She pushed past him and headed quickly up the aisle.

A small commotion had begun in the rear of the business-class section, and Janie Bretsen pulled back a galley curtain to see a large man in a business suit with his tie askew walking toward the rear of the aircraft with his ear to his cell phone as one of the female flight attendants chased after him.

"Sir! Sir! You can't use that in here unless the doors are open."

"Then open the damn door," he muttered over his shoulder.

"You can't use that in here," she repeated.

He whirled on her. "Oh? Your flyboys turned off the aircraft's phone system and we're still on the ground. Who the hell says I can't?"

"The FAA regulations . . ."

"Screw the regulations! Everybody with a brain knows these phones couldn't blow up a barrel of nitro-glycerine in a paint mixer. The rule is a sham, and so is this airline."

He jammed the phone back to his ear.

Another flight attendant, a slim, classy-looking woman in her early thirties, moved up the aisle to reinforce her friend, as the male flight attendant stuck his head around the corner from first class.

"Sir!" the second flight attendant said.

The man lowered the phone momentarily and held out his hand in a stop gesture. "You leave me the hell alone! Either turn on the aircraft phones, get me back to the gate, or leave me alone!" He leaned over, responding to a voice on the other end, leaving only an adjacent passenger within earshot of his words.

"Yeah. My name is Jack Wilson, and I want to report a kidnapping."

TEN

In Meridian Airlines' operations control center near Denver, a harried crew of dispatchers and managers stared at a mission control layout of monitors as they worried about the deteriorating schedule.

"What's O'Hare's status?" one of the men asked.

"Twenty-six flights holding on the taxiways. Two have gone back for fuel and are back at the end of the line, but the airport's just opened again, so takeoffs should start momentarily."

"Everyone will make it out, then?"

"Ah . . . not sure about Flight Six to Heathrow, Bob," a woman named Janice said, holding up several printouts. "We're close on crew duty time and the captain's making noise about taxiing back."

"How much time?"

"Fourteen minutes more."

"Call the captain, Janice. Tell him we need a break. Ask him to stretch the crew duty limits a few minutes."

Janice looked at her colleague with the expression of someone who's just discovered a friend is hopelessly insane. "You came here from Alaska Airlines, didn't you?" she said.

"Yeah. Why?"

"At Alaska, I'm told, the pilots actually like their company."

"Yes. Mostly."

"This is *Meridian*, Bob. Everybody hates everybody, and the pilots especially hate the big, bad company."

In the cockpit of Flight Six, both the captain and copilot had verified the image of the flight attendant on the small video screen as she stood outside the door and requested entry, her hand placed in the new cipher-lock identification slot.

"Okay, she's alone," the captain muttered as he pushed the lock-release button to complete the security procedure.

Janie Bretsen pushed her way in, closing the door behind her to stand with her hands on her hips behind the center console.

"Hello," the captain began. "Jane, is it?"

She ignored the question. The name "Janie" was clearly visible on her name tag, and presumably he could read, she thought. She despised pilots who came aboard without introducing themselves.

"The passengers are revolting," she said simply.

"Is . . . that a qualitative analysis, or a warning of impending action?" the copilot asked, grinning at her.

A pained expression crossed her face. "What?"

"Never mind," he said.

She shook her head in confusion. "I'm trying to tell you we've got a planeful of angry people."

"Why's that?" the captain asked.

"Well, let's see," she said as sarcastically as she could manage, "for starters, you told me not to serve any meals, so we haven't, and they're mad about that. We've got a passenger in first class I called you about who says he's sick and wants to get off, and I had to tell him you refused. His wife is furious, and there's a U.S. senator down there listening to their complaints."

"Wait . . ." the captain interrupted. "A *senator*?"

She ignored the question. "We're short by thirty coach meals, and way short in business class on meals and pillows. When this aircraft came in from its previous leg, the crew wrote up two of the rear rest rooms as broken, filthy, and locked. Well, they're still broken, filthy, and taped shut. And, it's still hotter than hell back there." She looked at the first officer and pointed to the overhead panel. "Is that thing on full?"

"What 'thing' would that be, dear?"

"Don't get cute. The air-conditioning."

"I'm running an air-conditioning pack," the copilot said. "You want more?" He reached up to the overhead panel in anticipation of her response.

"Are you joking? It's gotta be ninety degrees back there. *YES*, I want more. If you're not pumping as much cool air as this plane will pump, you're creating problems. I mean, these people are near revolt, and if you'd come through that overcrowded terminal, you'd be, too."

"Hey, calm down, Jane," the captain said.

"*Janie*, for God's sake. It's on my bloody name tag."

"Oh. Sorry," he said.

The captain turned to the first officer. "Turn all the packs to full cold."

Janie swept a stray tendril of hair from her forehead. "Okay. I may need one of you square-jawed heroes to come back and intimidate some of the passengers. One guy's walking around with a cell phone he won't turn off."

"You're kidding?" the captain asked.

"No, I'm not kidding," she replied in disgust. "You know, it really doesn't help things when you guys refuse to talk to them. They get to the point where they don't trust a thing we say, and the anger just builds and builds."

The *whoosh* of a departing jet heralded the first takeoff after the thunderstorm's passage.

"How tall are you, Janie?" the captain asked.

"*Excuse me?*" she replied, a look of confusion on her face.

"Well, we don't have many pretty, petite, female flight attendants."

Janie stood still for a few seconds meeting his gaze.

"You are kidding, right? You're just pulling my chain to get a feminist reaction or something?"

"Well, no . . ."

"Captain, I met the minimum five-foot height requirements just barely when I was hired. I'm still the same size. Thanks for calling me pretty, and yes, I'm female. Now, should I ask in return, have you always had that paunch?"

He shook his head slightly and looked wounded. "No."

"Good. Now that we've finished appraising each other's bodies, would you please tell me when we'll begin flying somewhere? Inquiring minds below want to know."

The captain sighed. "I think we've got a chance of getting out of here in a little while."

"Good. I love precise answers," she said, pulling a half dozen folded pieces of paper out of a pocket in her uniform.

"What're those?" the copilot asked.

"Love letters to you two," she snapped, opening one of them.

"'Captain,'" she read from the note, "'yours has got to be the worst display of arrogance I've ever experienced as a passenger.'"

"'Arrogance'?" The captain asked in a pained voice.

She looked up. "Yeah, 'cause you two won't talk to them." She selected another. "Quote, 'If there's not a federal law against keeping people trapped in a hot cabin, there should be. What's the matter with you people?'"

She selected a third. "Here's another. 'What the hell do you think we are back here? Cattle?' Shall I go on?"

"No," the captain replied. "I get the point. They don't like us."

"Hell," the copilot chimed in, "judging from our last union meeting, *WE* don't like us!" He twisted around and gestured to Janie Bretsen. "You flight attendants hate us pilots *and* the company. The mechanics hate the company and the pilots. And the Teamsters hate everyone. Take a number."

"We don't hate you," Janie said. "We just don't like being told we're a team, and then being ignored. By the way, we have only half a tank of water. We won't make it to London without running dry, which means no coffee or tea for breakfast."

The captain sighed. "Doesn't matter, probably. We're almost out of crew duty time anyway."

Janie looked crestfallen and let out a small moan. "Don't tell me there's a chance, after all this, that you two may have to be replaced?"

"Well . . ."

She sighed. "*That* one you'll have to explain yourselves, and may God have mercy on you. The passengers are already mad enough to kill." She started to leave but turned back. "By the way, do you two have names?"

The pilots exchanged glances, and the captain turned and nodded.

"I guess we should have said hello or something when we came in."

"'Or something,'" Janie replied. "Yeah, I guess you should have." She leaned down to make sure no one was waiting outside the door, her eyes scanning the video screen carefully.

"Cleared to leave?" she asked the captain.

"If you insist," he replied. She turned and slammed the door behind her before he could say anything more.

"Jeez," the captain said, watching the copilot shaking his head.

"Just another cute bitch on wheels, Bill. They're all being bitchy because of their contract."

"Oh, you mean those pickets out front?"

"Absolutely."

"I didn't know what that was all about."

"The usual. Madder than hell and not going to take it anymore. And they're trying to get us to honor their silly little picket lines if they strike."

"Fat chance," the captain snorted.

"Tell me about it. I should give up a month of pay and hurt my stock options because they don't have enough cash to clean out Neiman's on every layover. The company's gearing up to replace them with office staff anyway if they strike." He pointed out front. "We're moving at last."

"How much time left?"

The copilot shook his head as he looked at his watch. "One minute. No way we're gonna get off the ground in time."

The captain looked at him. "You want to hang it up and go back?"

"Hell, no," he said. "Janie the little dragon lady back there will tell the passengers we did it out of spite and start a revolt. I don't want to deal with angry passengers."

"And our fuel's okay for London?"

The copilot nodded. "Barely. We're legal. We're not fat."

"Then we're outta here." The captain released the brakes and began inching forward, following the 747 ahead as the copilot reached up to change to the control tower radio frequency. A voice from ground control beat him to it.

"Meridian Six, O'Hare ground."

He punched the transmit button as he glanced at the captain.

"This is Meridian Six."

"Okay, Six. When you get up to Taxiway Alpha, pull off to the left and make sure you're clear of the outer. Give your operations a call."

"What's up?"

"Ask them," the controller replied, continuing the string of instructions for the dozens of other aircraft jockeying for position around the field.

"Dammit! It's our crew duty time," the captain said with a sigh. "They're gonna force the issue."

The first officer dialed in the right frequency and made the call, which triggered an instant answer.

"We've been trying to reach you, Six. Hold your position. We're sending out portable air stairs."

The captain raised his right hand to stop the copilot and toggled his transmit switch, a plaintive tone in his voice. "We're almost number one for takeoff after hours of waiting. Are you guys crazy? We're going to lose our place in line *and* run out of crew duty time."

"Do you have a medical emergency aboard, Six?"

The captain and copilot exchanged incredulous glances.

"No. Absolutely not."

"Is there any hostile activity in progress in your cabin?"

"*What?* No!"

Another voice came over the company frequency. "Six, this is the station manager. We're pulling you aside because the Chicago police are ordering you to stop, and the FBI has ordered a ground stop. They're going to come aboard. Seems one of your passengers has called 911 to report three hundred twenty people being held against their will, and someone else just reported he was having a heart attack and said you wouldn't get him any help."

ELEVEN

LONDON, ENGLAND
11:30 P.M. LOCAL

Phil Knight waved to Glenn Thomasson as the British captain accelerated away from the hotel. He glanced at his watch, surprised it was only eleven-thirty. The evening had seemed interminable.

Phil entered the lobby and turned toward the elevators, but changed course for a bank of telephones to call Meridian Operations. The inbound flight was often late. Maybe he could pull an extra hour of sleep.

"It's running way late, Captain," a Meridian agent told him. "The usual Chicago nonsense. It's already three hours behind, and I doubt it'll get off for another hour and a half."

Phil thanked the agent and hung up, calculating the result. He wouldn't need to wake up until half past six at the earliest. Suddenly the night seemed young and wide open to anything he wanted to do.

So, what do I want to do? he thought, no ready answer coming to mind.

The aroma of cigarette smoke hung in the lobby, which was otherwise deserted, and he could hear voices coming from the hotel bar in the distance. He glanced at his watch again. The rule on drinking was twelve hours between bottle and throttle, and he had just enough margin for a drink—something he seldom did on layovers.

So what DO I want to do?

He repeated the thought. There were TVs in the rooms with movies available. Maybe he could go watch one. But that was a lackluster option. And it was too late to go into central London, even if he had a reason.

Phil entered the bar instead and sat at a small table, ordering a brandy from the barmaid as he took note of the discontent on her face. A faded mid-thirties, he decided, her body shapely but harshly laced into a skimpy costume some male had designed to resemble that of a sixteenth-century tavern wench: tight around the midriff, her not inconsiderable breasts artificially cupped and thrust out, forcing her to kneel rather than lean over a table to set down drinks.

The thought of engaging her in conversation crossed his mind. Maybe he could bridge the gap between them by sharing their respective agonies.

But the hard look on her face warned him off.

He thought of Doris, his wife of twenty-three years, and the fact that he'd never cheated on her. He should

be proud of that, but somehow it now seemed an indict-
ment of sorts, and that was confusing. Garth Abbott, as
far as he knew, wasn't running around on *his* wife. Nor
were the other copilots he'd flown with in the international division, who all tried to act so sophisticated and
worldly around the bumpkin stateside captain in their
midst. Yet, the feeling persisted, deep and strong, that he
was far too conventional and boring and ordinary to ever
keep up with this league, and now, he told himself, the
concept of marital fidelity, even if by default, somehow
just seemed to confirm what he perceived was their
image of him as a hopeless provincial.

He thought of his copilot, Garth Abbott, who tried
to hide his contempt behind a facade of forced courtesy.
But Phil could see through that. *That sanctimonious little
bastard!* Phil thought. He was out to prove that Garth
Abbott and not Phil Knight should be in command.

Phil closed his eyes and shook his head to expunge
the anger and confusion just as a gentle zephyr of
perfume wafted across his consciousness accompanied by
the sound of a chair being pulled out.

He opened his eyes, startled to find a gorgeous
redhead in the process of seating herself at his table, her
hair cascading over her shoulders. She was clad in a short
fur jacket that stopped just above her long, shapely legs,
a pearl necklace visible around her neck even before she
opened the coat to flash a plunging neckline and heart-
stopping cleavage.

"Hi," she purred.

Phil looked around in confusion, then back at her. "Ah, hello."

"You look lonely," she said.

He smiled, feeling flushed and cornered. "Well . . . I mean . . . yes, a little."

"I'm available," she said, glancing around herself before continuing. "I'm not cheap, but I'm available, if you're interested."

"I'm sorry?"

The woman sat back slightly and cocked her head. "You aren't getting this, are you, ducks?"

"I guess not."

She leaned forward, deftly presenting her chest to him as she placed her mouth next to his left ear.

"I'm a professional, honey. You pay me two hundred pounds and I come to your room and have sex with you for an hour. Five hundred pounds for all night. Clear enough?" She drew back with a knowing smile, watching conflicting emotions play across his face.

A cascade of jumbled thoughts crackled through his mind all at once: There was at least £300 in cash in his map case. But what if she had AIDS? And what if one of the copilots had set him up, and was watching, maybe with a camera? But, if not, could they get upstairs without being seen?

God, she's sexy! Yes, I'll do it. No! Yes, dammit! No!

What did he want to do? What did he WANT? The question screamed through his mind but he couldn't answer it, and as he tried to form the words to say yes, he realized with a start that any sexual desire she might have ignited was now completely deflated by panic.

"That's okay, sugar," she was saying as she got to her feet. "Your eyes are about to pop out. I think I scared you." She patted his shoulder and leaned over to give him a light kiss on his cheek. "Some other time, then."

Phil sat in embarrassed confusion for nearly ten minutes, chastising himself from all angles, convinced his inability to act had been observed by the enemy. He would be the laughingstock of the first-officer force. He would be the laughingstock of the airline!

But you didn't cheat, he kept thinking. *You didn't give in.* He tried to cling to the thought, bolster himself with it, perhaps even hide behind it, but it was no use. His own image came back to him: ineffective, indecisive, scared, and all but impotent. He hadn't wanted the woman; he'd just wanted to be able to *decide* without being scared.

And he'd failed.

A small anthology of self-loathing pummeled him like the impacts of collapsing flats on a poorly designed set.

Phil waited until the barmaid was occupied at the far end of the bar before leaving enough cash to cover the drink and a tip. He slipped out, half expecting to hear laughter behind him, and closed the door of his third-floor room a minute later, thankful for the solitude and anonymity, his face crimson.

He sat on the end of the bed and rubbed his eyes.

What would it have been like? That was the same question, he realized, that had led him to bid the international division to begin with.

But what *would* it be like to have sex with such a woman? For that matter, he thought, what would it be like to do *anything* bold without being consumed by uncertainty?

TWELVE

DOWNTOWN MARINA,
ANNAPOLIS, MARYLAND
6:45 P.M. EDT

The young deliveryman in the door of the marina office consulted his clipboard and nodded before looking back up at the manager standing behind a small counter.

"Yeah. The name I'm looking for is Blaylock. J. Blaylock. All he gave us was this address."

"He's in slip eighteen," the manager replied.

"So, he's on a boat?"

"Well, not exactly."

"But you said 'slip eighteen.'"

The manager closed the master list of his customers and came around the counter to stand beside the young man in the doorway and point to the jumble of boats and masts beyond.

"You see that tall mast, just to the right of the green boathouse?"

"Yeah."

"Well, look just to the left of it. See that metallic blue metal roof?"

"That thing with the dish antennae that looks like the top of a bus?" the young man said.

"That *is* the top of a bus," the manager replied. "Like the type rock groups use on the road."

"What's a bus doing in a marina, man?"

"Floating, mainly." The manager chuckled.

"A bus?"

"It's actually a motor home. Get Captain Blaylock to show it to you."

"A *floating* motor home? Like a houseboat, right?"

"Well, he decided he wanted a boat, but he already had everything done just the way he liked it in his custom bus, which he lives in, so he had a shipyard build him a custom barge for his custom bus. When he wants to go to sea, he drives his bus aboard and kind of . . . drives away. The rear wheels of the bus engage big rollers that connect to twin screws."

"This I gotta see."

The young man drove his minivan the short distance to the edge of the slip and loaded several boxes on a handcart before pulling them to the edge of a gangplank. On the side of the huge, forty-five-foot bus facing the dock was a beautiful blue-and-green painting, a watery mural of graceful whales swimming with the smaller, but equally elegant, figure of a well-endowed mermaid trailing at least ten feet of platinum blond hair. The coach looked brand-new as it sat in the drive bay that bisected the barge. The surface it rested on was three feet below the surrounding teak deck, making the wheels of the coach invisible and giving the upper body of the bus the look of a permanent superstructure. Brass railings surrounded the decking of the barge, which itself was on two levels, with the forward end forming a normal, pointed prow.

A small lecternlike stand had been installed at the edge of the gangplank with a phone and a speaker attached. The deliveryman reached for the phone, but jumped slightly when a deep male voice boomed from the speaker.

"Okay, Billy's Market. I see you out there, and it's about damn well time. Come aboard."

A large door opened in the side of the bus, and the owner emerged with a broad smile to guide him in.

"The marina owner told me you might show me around," the deliveryman said, as he unloaded the boxes.

"Yeah, well . . . drop by tomorrow. This isn't a good time."

"Okay."

Blaylock took the clipboard and signed the charge slip. "It's just that right now I've got a dinner to prepare." He looked more closely at the young man, judging him to be in his mid-twenties. "You married?"

"No, sir."

"Good. Then you'll understand. My guest is a lady. I intend to shamelessly seduce her with food, and she has no idea she's walking into a culinary trap. Be gone."

JOHN J. NANCE

"Hey, good luck, sir," the deliveryman said, smiling as he pocketed the ten-dollar bill Blaylock handed him.

John Blaylock pulled the door closed behind him and began rifling through the boxes, stowing some of the items and arranging the produce on a built-in chopping board. Most of the ingredients for the dinner he was preparing were already laid out in proper order. Two separate sauces simmered on the stainless-steel gas stove, filling the air with the complex aromas of their wine-enhanced, multilayered ingredients.

Blaylock glanced around the interior of his four-hundred-thousand dollar bus-boat, appreciating what he saw. The continuous battles with the conversion shops had been worth it. In the end he'd gotten exactly the interior he'd designed: a third of the coach contained the gourmet kitchen, dining, and living area; a third was devoted to an electronically sophisticated bedroom decorated in what he laughingly called "early cathouse," with heavy use of red velvet; and the remaining third was a combination wheelhouse and driver's station crammed with enough instrumentation to make Boeing proud, arrayed like a miniature of the *Starship Enterprise*'s command bridge. The woodwork was custom-crafted walnut and oak, the fixtures brass, and the wheel—for both driving and controlling the helm while afloat—a six-spoked ship's wheel.

And all of it was his, paid for by a career of banked salary and careful investing, fueled by the fees he still occasionally collected for various projects.

He checked his watch. Ninety minutes until the unsuspecting female was supposed to arrive and be so dazzled she'd fail to see the carnal plot. He chuckled, then grew serious as he struggled to recall her first name.

Damn! Janice? Jan? Where is that slip of paper? He fished through the pockets of his jeans and extracted a dog-eared business card.

Jill! Of course. He stuffed it back in his pocket, turning the name over in his mind as the phone rang.

He glanced at the displayed number. Jill had said she had a D.C. cell phone. This was the same prefix, and she was supposed to call for directions.

He toggled the speakerphone to the "on" position.

"Hello, beautiful! You on the way?"

There was the sound of someone fumbling with a phone, and then a confused male voice. "Ah . . . I'm sorry . . . I'm calling for Colonel John Blaylock."

"He's dead," John Blaylock said. "Hanged himself last week over a lost lover whose phone call was blocked by someone he didn't care to talk to."

He disconnected and turned back to the counter to start chopping onions.

The phone rang again after a minute, and he hit the answer button without saying anything.

"Ah . . . Colonel, please don't hang up. I'm betting that's you, dead or alive. This is Colonel David Byrd."

"Unless you're a mighty cute biological female with an exceptionally low voice, I do NOT want to talk to you right now. Call me in October."

Once again he reached for the switch to cut off the call, but the voice on the other end shot back a single name.

"Overmeyer . . . General . . . one each. Jim Overmeyer told me to call you."

John Blaylock hesitated, then yanked up the receiver. "You think you said the magic word, don't you?"

"Well, I'm trying."

"Tell that three-star windbag . . . Wait a minute. I can't say that. I'm not really retired. Okay, what do you want?"

David Byrd fired back a quick synopsis and waited.

"So, a bird colonel hanging out with the FAA is trying to figure out why people get mad on airlines. They get mad because they're treated like dirt. I'll send you a bill."

"I need to meet with you. Is this evening possible?"

"Not without a federal court order. Tomorrow will work, though."

"Okay. Where and what time?"

"Zero-seven-hundred, here in Annapolis." He passed on the address and the slip number. "I'll give you no more than an hour, unless I'm alone."

"I . . . what?"

"Never mind, Colonel. Give me your cell number . . . Wait! I already have it here on the screen." The sound of a call-waiting beep pulsed into the handset. "Time's up. I'm on a prelaunch checklist. See you at six." He punched the appropriate button without waiting for a response, relieved to hear a woman's voice on the other end, the same cellular prefix displayed on the screen.

"Is that you, Jill?" he asked carefully.

"Yes," she said, her voice forming a tonal question mark.

He relaxed, a broad smile covering his face. "Then hello, beautiful! You on the way?"

THIRTEEN

The Boeing 777 had been airborne for less than eight minutes when Janie Bretsen began reaching for the buckle of her seat belt and hesitated, calculating whether there were any FAA inspectors on board who might write her up for getting up too soon. She'd been disciplined several times before for popping to her feet to start the cabin service before the pilots rang the cabin chime twice to indicate they were climbing above ten thousand feet, but that was back when she had the misguided idea that it mattered and her company cared. Now she knew better. No one cared, and the fact remained that there was simply too much to be done to sit any longer than absolutely necessary.

The sudden sound of the PA system caused her to jump.

Folks, this is the captain.

Thank God! Janie thought. The original cockpit crew had been replaced at the end of the runway where they'd sat for a half hour, and now it looked as if the replacement pilots were going to be communicating with the passengers. They'd even introduced themselves to her as they hurried aboard.

She hoped the original two were in trouble, but she doubted it. They would be sitting in some management office about now, she figured, whining and pointing fingers at the cabin crew, and it would all end with her being called into the office again and made a scapegoat. At Meridian, any contest between a pilot and a flight attendant ended badly for the flight attendant.

Something the new captain was saying caught her attention.

. . . be frank with you. We were about to pilot a trip to Paris when they asked us to come over and fly your flight, because our other pilots had run out of crew duty time. But they also warned us that you were an angry and unruly bunch, and that the last hour of delay was courtesy of someone who illegally called the cops and filed a false report. I know one passenger was taken off by ambulance, but we're told he was only mildly sick. Now look, folks. I'm the chief pilot for the triple-seven fleet here in Chicago, and while I want you to have a good flight and come back and all that, anyone who fails to obey the orders of my crew will be physically restrained and arrested at the other end, and that includes anyone using cell phones or turning on a laptop before we give you permission. We take security very, very

seriously. We appreciate your business, but this airline is simply not going to put up with disruptive passengers anymore, and for the majority of you who would never act that way, you should be as angry as I am at people who try to flout our authority.

Janie Bretsen hid her face in her hands and wondered if she could find an alcove somewhere to crawl into. The passengers were already furious at them. The last thing she needed was another insensitive throttle jockey fanning the flames with the PA. She stood and turned toward the galley.

"Excuse me." A cultured female voice stopped her, and Janie turned to find Senator Douglas at the edge of the galley.

"Yes. I'm sorry," Janie said, feeling off balance. She knew Sharon Douglas from television but had had no idea she was on board until one of the supervisors upgraded her to first class. The supervisor's explanation had been cryptic: "One of our gate agents messed up, and this seat is an apology."

"You're the chief flight attendant?" the senator asked.

She nodded and remembered to hold out her hand. "Yes. Janie Bretsen," she said, before quickly adding "Senator."

Sharon Douglas shook her hand briefly, then inclined her head toward the cockpit. "Are they all that hateful?"

"Excuse me?"

"The pilots. Are they all that militaristic and abusive to the passengers?"

Janie felt the blood draining from her face. This was a powerful woman in her galley. If she said the wrong thing, she could be fired.

Sharon Douglas recognized Janie's discomfort while the flight attendant searched for safe things to say.

"Look, Janie," Douglas said, holding up the palm of her right hand, "it's cool, okay? I know you're worried that anything you say to me might end up hurting your job, but that's not true. I'm just asking you personally so I can get a feel for what's wrong here. Everyone working for this airline seems furious."

"Well . . ."

"Would you accept my word of honor that absolutely nothing you say will ever be attributed to you?"

"Yes, Senator," Janie replied, hating the fact that her eyes were probably huge with fright.

"Okay. Now. Call me Sharon, not 'Senator,' and tell me, woman to woman, what in the hell is going on with this airline?"

Janie looked at her watch before answering. "I . . . hate to ask, but . . . could we wait until the dinner service is done?"

Sharon Douglas nodded immediately. "Of course. When you've got time, then. There's an empty seat next to me . . . but you know that."

"I'll come up as soon as we're through. I promise,"

Janie said. She could feel her heart still fluttering as the politician considered the most powerful woman in aviation slipped back to her first-class seat.

Janie moved alongside the galley by the privacy curtains and surveyed the coach cabin behind, wondering whether mollifying the passengers was even possible. Seldom had she dealt with such a high level of fury on the ground. Then again, she'd never before had to write up two of her crew members on one leg even before takeoff.

There was no choice with the male flight attendant, Jeff Kaiser, after the arrogant way he'd treated a young mother in coach, and especially after he'd responded to Janie's dressing him down by shoving her and warning her to "watch your backside, little girl!" Any unwanted touching at Meridian was a firing offense, and even if it wasn't, his attitude could not be tolerated.

And there was Susan, another veteran flight attendant, who had caused a major problem with a couple named Lao by calling Mrs. Lao bitchy when she didn't want to check a computer bag. The husband had exploded when he'd found out and Susan had jumped the chain of command and called back the replacement captain who threatened to arrest both of the Laos, all of which had inflamed half the coach cabin.

Undoubtedly the Laos would sue.

Janie closed her eyes for a second and rubbed her forehead. The confrontation with the current captain had been just as difficult, and now he, too, was angry, which would mean yet another pilot complaint about her.

Is there anyone working for this poor airline who actually likes the job? she wondered.

Janie sighed and let go of the curtain, turning to move back into first class to do a walk-through. She felt like plunking herself down in the nearest empty seat and just going unconscious. It was like watching Pan Am die over twenty years before, amid assurances that it could never happen. She'd been in college when they parked the fleet of familiar blue-and-white jetliners and went out of business. It had been a jet-set equivalent of a child of the fifties losing Buddy Holly, or a child of the sixties losing John Lennon. An end to innocence, especially for young girls who dreamed of the glamour of being a sexy, jet-setting stewardess for Pan Am, or Meridian.

Airlines had offered a strange, magical world of travel and fun and unlimited possibilities. Airline people were special, exciting folk living exciting lives in which depression and discouragement were altogether impossible.

How she wished that were true. But depression was a constant companion, especially in the previous five years as her once-proud airline lost its way, and then its passengers, the pampering of whom had been its reason for existence. They'd been in bad financial shape even before the horror of the attacks on the Pentagon and the World Trade Center forced the federal financial bailout.

She'd expected a rededication to passenger service after that, but it hadn't happened. They were back to abnormal.

"Meridian Airlines," she had once been told, "is the best there is. The epitome of customer service. The number-one-rated airline in the world."

And it had been, in decades past, which was why its slide from excellence to pedestrian mediocrity was so hard to take. It was akin to Kmart running Neiman Marcus, or Starbucks selling Folgers.

No, she thought, it was worse. At least those were solid brands. Meridian had sunk to the level of a poorly run bus line.

Janie maneuvered quietly around the first-class seats. Sharon Douglas was asleep at last, using an eyeshade and earplugs, and Janie found herself trying to review what she'd told the senator. They had talked—or rather, *she* had talked and the senator had listened—for two hours after the dinner service was done. But what had she *said*? The memory was jumbled, but if Senator Douglas was not a woman of her word, Janie's career would come to a screeching halt as soon as Meridian's leaders discovered she'd blabbed.

Not that she knew any smoking-gun secrets, but she did know how dysfunctional Meridian had become in the cabin. The senator wanted to know the routines and where the problems were, and Janie had told her. "There's so much wrong, it's hard to know where to start."

"Well," Sharon had said, "tell me what you're upset

about right now. Tell me what you'd tell your chairman *if* he was willing to listen to you."

Janie began with the hatefulness of the little notes left in her box in the flight attendant crew room—not only the ones from fellow flight attendants who thought she was sucking up to management but also the constant barrage from the company itself. Each official memo ended with the same sentence: "Compliance is mandatory! Failure to comply will be met with severe disciplinary action, up to and including termination."

"What a great a way to begin each trip," Janie said. "Getting endearing little love notes in the box with things like: 'Bretsen, J., you were seen with a run in your panty hose last week. That must not happen again' or 'Bretsen, J., you reported two minutes late last month. This is the second tardy check-in within the past six months. Five tardy check-ins require disciplinary action.' On and on. I mean, I was very briefly a temporary flight attendant base manager, and I never would have given such mean, catty notes to my people. It's my airline, too, but I'm not allowed to help. I'm not allowed to give even a little. I'm supposed to thrust the union contract in the face of our crew schedulers with glee and say, 'See? You can't make me fly. You've got to dump three hundred paying passengers over to Delta when *we* desperately need the money because Janie will get beat up by her union if I help out.'"

"When you do give a little, does the company at least appreciate it?"

Janie laughed, without humor. "No way."

"Never anything positive?" the senator had asked.

"The pilots have a phrase: Ten thousand 'Attaboys' are instantly extinguished by a single 'Aw, shit!' Same with us. But the union's got a big point, too. The company's trying to get rid of our union. They want a strike. They want to replace us, and the union's just trying to hold them to their contract. I understand that, but . . ."

"It's still your company?"

"Yeah. Exactly. I even own some stock, and it gets terribly confusing. When I do what the union says, it's like I'm shooting my own foot, you know? Boom, company. Take that. Ow!"

It was amazing, Janie thought, that a powerful United States senator would have the patience to listen to a two-hour rant. "I'm trying to figure out what's gone wrong with this system, Janie," she'd explained. "Meridian may be by far the worst in customer service, but almost all of them are awash in unhappy people, substandard service attitudes, and furious passengers these days. In the terminals, in the cabin, in the cockpit, on the ramp . . . everywhere I look, people are fed up and furious with this form of transportation, and employees like you are fed up with their treatment and fed up with the passengers. The thing is, it's getting dangerous."

"You mean, air rage? Furious passengers doing things?"

The senator nodded. "Any experiences yourself?"

"No," Janie told her, deciding not to tell about the drunk in a first-class aisle seat a month before who'd assaulted her when she leaned past him to reach a window seat tray. The shock of realizing the man was actually biting her left breast through her bra was impossible to describe. Somehow she'd expected a sky marshal to jump up and collar the man, but none had appeared. She'd been too startled to even slap him, and when the company quietly warned her not to sue, that had been the end of it. It was better to think of it as a nightmare anyway.

"I don't see much of anything resembling customer service anymore," Senator Douglas had continued. "I'm convinced your leaders would take out the seats and put in overhead leather straps if the FAA would let them get away with it, just to get a greater return on investment."

"It's the rat principle," Janie said.

"I'm sorry?" Sharon Douglas had leaned a bit closer.

"Rats in a maze. It's an old, classic experiment I remember from my psych classes in college. When rats were put in overcrowded conditions, their behavior became increasingly bizarre in direct proportion to the crowding. The greater the crowding, the worse the antisocial, even psychotic, behavior. Fighting, cannibalism, catatonic rats . . . they couldn't take it, and neither can we."

" 'We' meaning airline personnel?"

"And passengers."

Janie shook her head to end the mental replay of their

conversation. She paused just behind the forward galley with a blanket in her hand, looking for any of her passengers who might need it. The cabin felt comfortable, and all but one of her first-class people were sleeping. Pitch darkness filled the windows with a timeless void as they soared over the Atlantic, rushing toward the belt of twilight currently approaching middle Europe and marking the division between night and day. Astronauts in orbit saw it eighteen times per day, she'd been told. An eastbound transatlantic flight saw it twice, once with sundown after takeoff, and again after a short night over cold waters.

She took a deep breath and felt the tight muscles around her shoulders relax. She couldn't remember the last time anyone had really listened.

Janie had no illusions left about her airline career. She needed to be thinking hard about finding another job.

FOURTEEN

First officer Garth Abbott stood at the window of the small hotel room buttoning his gold-braided uniform coat with his left hand while he pressed the GSM cell phone tightly to his face with his right, as if the force of his grip could squeeze a few more words out of the now-silent device.

What had she meant, "Perhaps?"

His mind was suddenly far away, chasing his wife back through the thousands of miles of digital connections to their Wisconsin home and playing the same old gut-wrenching game of trying to decide whether there was something to worry about.

"I'll see you Thursday," he'd said.

"Perhaps," was her only response.

He checked his watch, relieved to find he still had the twenty-five minutes he'd allocated for getting to the restaurant and wolfing down some breakfast before "Captain Sunshine" lumbered through the lobby and wilted the morning.

It was 8 A.M. in London, and 2 A.M. in Wausau. Her call had startled him. She knew he always kept his phone on, but she seldom rang it.

Is she worried I won't return on time? I've always come home when I said I would.

Garth zipped his roll-on bag and put on his hat, making one last check of himself in the mirror before sweeping out the door. He'd been grateful to find the inbound flight was so delayed. It had meant hours of extra sleep, but suddenly he felt just as tired as he would have been with a 2 A.M. wake-up call on the original schedule.

Maybe she's worried about my flying with Phil Knight. Maybe I shouldn't have shared that frustration.

The third-floor elevator lobby was devoid of other crew members, and he was secretly relieved. His mind was grinding through the possibilities, and he wanted no distractions. Like a computer condemned to use all its capacity to calculate the ultimate value of pi, he had to fight the desire to find a chair and fold in on himself as he fought for an answer—partially in puzzlement, partly in fear.

Dear God, is there a chance she's planning to leave me?

The possibility had hovered at the edge of his consciousness for months like a persistent rumor, though she professed to be content. There had been little incongruities, and he realized he'd refused to think about the possibility she was seeing someone else. Yet, sometimes the faraway look in her eyes defied that reassurance, and he worried that she was ready to run and didn't even know it herself.

But there was only so much they could say to each other on the subject of contentment, and he'd concluded that bridging the gender gap with words was impossible. If he was from Mars, she had to be from somewhere beyond Alpha Centauri.

He left the elevator at flank speed and hurried across the lobby past a stationary formation of potted ferns and into the restaurant through a large double door, spotting Knight at a table near the entrance a moment too late to escape.

"Oh. There you are, Phil," Garth said weakly, his heart sinking as he realized Knight had already seen him. Garth feigned a smile, expecting none in return.

The captain had been hunched protectively over his cereal bowl, but he looked up and nodded now to his copilot as he motioned toward the adjacent chair, his left arm still partially encircling his meal.

"Morning," Phil Knight managed. Garth pulled out the chair and sat down. There was an international copy of *USA Today* on the table in front of Knight, but it was folded and untouched.

"So," Garth began as cheerfully as possible, "did you get into the city this time?" He already knew the answer.

"London, you mean?" Knight replied.

No, you twit. Bangkok! Garth thought, carefully

sequestering the mental retort a safe distance from his mouth. "Yes," he said. "Central London."

"No," he said with a sharpness that startled Garth. "I, ah . . . had dinner with a pilot friend near here."

Yeah, sure you did, Garth thought. *Probably spent the evening with a book of foreign phrases. I've never seen a captain so uptight about dealing with foreign controllers.*

A waiter bustled past with a heavily laden tray of food for an adjacent table, bumping Garth's chair as he passed. Another waiter appeared at the table with a pot of coffee and a bored demeanor.

"You are having the buffet?" he asked.

The former allure of breakfast had paled with Carol's strange response over the phone and evaporated completely in Knight's company. Garth shook his head. "Just coffee, thanks."

The waiter poured a cup and disappeared, leaving another of the deep and embarrassing silences that Garth had come to expect in Phil Knight's presence. He stirred some sugar into the coffee and began reading an article in the folded newspaper. He wanted to reach out and unfold it—the story concerned a stock he owned—but Knight was strange about such things. If it was *his* newspaper, magazine, or anything else, he didn't want anyone fooling with it. Even moving such an item seemed to trigger a high-voltage wave of anger, never stated but clearly felt, as if the act of touching something Phil Knight had placed somewhere was a condemnation of his decision to put it there.

Garth averted his eyes and made a mental note to get his own newspaper before leaving the hotel.

Knight was concentrating on his cereal again, carefully shoveling in the contents a spoonful at a time, his shoulders hunched in a way reminiscent of Richard Nixon.

Two more weeks and two more international trips were still left before the month of flying trips with Knight would be over. Garth had already bid away from him by carefully examining the captain's selection of requested trip pairings before making certain he bid differently. Carefully bidding the trips one wanted to fly was a monthly ritual for airline pilots, but occasionally, like now, it became a matter of emotional survival.

"Is he dangerous?" Carol had asked.

"No, not dangerous, and not incompetent, exactly," Garth had replied. "Just . . . very unsure of himself. And I really think he hates me, not to sound paranoid. For that matter, I think he hates all copilots."

A chair scraping backward with a sudden burst of noise startled Garth. He looked up to see Knight push away from the table, grab his flight bag, and turn toward the door without a word.

"See you at the bus," Garth said to the captain's back.

There was no response.

ABOARD MERIDIAN FLIGHT SIX, LONDON
HEATHROW
8:45 A.M. LOCAL

Janie Bretsen had already unstrapped herself by the time
the seat-belt chime sounded seconds after the 777 lurched
to a halt in its Heathrow gate. She deactivated the
emergency slide at door 1-L now before moving to the
first-class cabin to collect the Levys and get them ready
to exit first. She shot a cautioning glance at Lara Richardson, who would now be her third crew member with a
disciplinary write-up. The pilots had begun the initial
descent into London before Lara got around to telling
her about the couple's daughter and the agony they were
going through. Janie had immediately reseated them in
first class, but in the meantime they'd been subjected to
a night of agony with all the other passengers crammed
together in coach.

The coach seats alone caused people to become angry,
she thought. Supposedly they could empty the airplane
in an emergency in ninety seconds on the ground, but all
the flight attendants knew that was a sick little joke. The
passengers were jammed so close together with so little
leg room it would take at least five to six minutes to get
them all out. Leaving a bereaved couple in that environ-
ment all night long had been nothing short of cruelty.

She'd gone to the cockpit to use the company satellite
phone to call the London operations chief for Swissair,

the Levys' connecting airline, who promised to meet them at the gate with a special customs clearance. Then she'd called the hospital in Zurich, holding her breath until she heard that Janna Levy was still hanging on to life—a hopeful fact that she immediately relayed to the couple.

Janie hugged Anna Levy at the door, fighting back tears herself. "My prayers go with you both."

"Thank you," Chuck Levy said, taking her hand.

"And again, I sincerely apologize for the boorish conduct of my crew."

"That's all right. We appreciate your help," he said, turning to put his arm around his wife as a delegation from Swissair moved forward to greet them.

"We have a car to take you directly to our Zurich flight," the Swissair station manager was saying. "We're locating your bags, and we want to assure you that our people will meet you at planeside and take you directly to the hospital on arrival in Zurich."

They enfolded the Levys in a blanket of compassion and eased them down the jet-way stairs. Janie watched them go with a lump in her throat.

Why can't we treat our passengers like that? she wondered.

"Excuse me, who's the lead flight attendant?" a young woman in a Meridian uniform asked.

"I am," Janie replied. "Can I help you?"

"I have an urgent message for Bretsen, J."

★

Several miles away from Heathrow, Garth Abbott collapsed the handle on his rolling overnight bag and hefted it into a shuttle bus waiting on the hotel's front drive. He stepped inside and glanced down the aisleway, verifying that Phil Knight was already aboard. As usual, the captain had gone to the last seat in the bus and was sitting and staring impassively at the seat back before him.

The copilot spotted an empty window seat halfway back, a safe distance from the zone of required small talk around Knight. He put his pilot case in the overhead, swung past the knees of the passenger in the aisle seat, and sat down before glancing at his seatmate. The man had almost the same vacant look Knight usually adopted, and for a brief moment, Garth entertained the hilarious idea that the man was doing a Phil Knight impression. He suppressed a laugh and looked at the passenger a bit more closely.

The man was in his late thirties or early forties, his black hair neatly trimmed, his clothes expensive. The man's tie was loosened, the collar of his white shirt unbuttoned, but he was clean shaven.

Garth looked away, then glanced back, specifically looking at the man's hands. He was wearing a wedding band, and on the third finger of his right hand, a class ring of some sort. He leaned over the aisle, pretending to look forward, and the fleeting moment gave him a closer look at the embedded gold emblem on the ring's red stone. It was a caduceus, the internationally recognized symbol of the medical profession, a staff encircled by a snake.

A physician.

The man's eyes flickered in the direction of the copilot and Garth hurriedly looked away, slightly embarrassed to be caught staring.

Brian Logan had spent much of the night in central London in a park he and Daphne had loved, until the London Metropolitan Police eased him into a taxi and sent him back to his hotel near Heathrow. Brian remembered paying the driver and refusing his offer to walk him to the lobby. He had thought of collapsing on one of the lobby couches, but his bag was in his room, and one way or another he'd have to visit it and shower and shave before leaving in the morning. He couldn't arrive in Cape Town looking like a bum, no matter how he felt. It was a hopeful sign, he concluded, that he even cared.

He had wobbled to the room and shed his clothes, curling up in a fetal position beneath the covers as he finally drifted to sleep thinking about Daphne, their nights in London, and how amazing it had felt just to hold her.

The sun streaming in the window had awakened him, and with a loud buzzing in his head, he'd called Meridian's reservation line. He was sure he'd missed the flight, and almost relieved at the prospect.

"No, sir, Flight Six for Cape Town is quite delayed this morning," the agent reported. "The flight is posted now for a nine-forty-five departure." Brian replaced the receiver with strange memories of the night before swirling through his head.

When he entered the lobby twenty minutes later, the aroma of breakfast wafting from the restaurant nauseated him. Food was the farthest thing from a mind wholly occupied by the impending agony of dealing with hours aboard an airplane bearing Meridian's logo. Even their emblem on the ticket folder had roiled his stomach, and he thought again about canceling the trip. But it would be too late for his host to find a replacement cardiologist. He had to go.

The ride from the hotel on the north side of the huge airport to Terminal 4 was a numbing series of tunnels and traffic. Brian followed the others out of the bus at the other end, wondering how something as simple as the name of the airline on the terminal entrance could create such instant stress.

Inside the Meridian logo was everywhere. It pressed in on him, mocking him, fanning an incendiary reaction he knew had passed the illogical. It took a Herculean effort to stand in their line and present their ticket to their personnel without coming apart. Three times he had to return to the TV monitor to read the number of his departure gate, a necessary bit of information his mind refused to retain. After the third try he wrote it down, but the piece of paper with the gate number instantly became as offensive as the fact that Meridian was still in business. He forced himself to memorize the gate number and crushed the scrap of paper to the size of a spitball, tossing it as far away as he could manage.

The gesture was seen by a police officer usually intolerant of litter in his airport, but something about the demeanor of the offender warned the officer away. There was deep anger there, and besides, the scrap of paper the man had thrown had immediately rolled under an ATM machine and disappeared.

No evidence, no offense, he concluded.

As the local passengers departing on Flight Six converged on Heathrow's ticket counter, Meridian Station Chief James Haverston walked quickly to the head of a utilitarian stairway off the main concourse and stopped to consult his clipboard. Ancient technology the clipboard, he thought, but it got the job done. The computer rosters had come off the printer many hours before in operations, but now the job of corralling the through passengers who had just arrived from Chicago and getting them to the gate and eventually back on the aircraft would keep him unnecessarily busy. He'd begged Meridian's brass in Denver to keep the through passengers aboard, but Heathrow authorities wouldn't hear of it. There were merchants in the terminal waiting to separate the inbound masses from their money.

His two-way radio squawked to life with a question from one of his agents, and he raised the walkie-talkie without looking.

"Say again, please?"

"I need the through count on Flight Six, James," a woman said, the voice low and the accent precise.

"One hundred and six through passengers to Cape Town," he answered.

By now, he knew, far too many of those continuing passengers would be roaming Terminal 4 at will, doing progressive damage to their credit cards and the potential gross weight of the airplane by stocking up on overpriced so-called "duty-free" items they scarcely needed. Some, of course, were merely sitting like stunned cattle near the gate waiting to reboard the flight, while a lucky few from first class were being catered to in Meridian's so-called "Regents' Lounge." Through the dirty windows of the lounge, the inbound Boeing 777 could be seen as a tug pulled it away to be replaced by the outbound 747, but hardly anyone noticed.

James turned to descend the stairs just as a flight attendant rounded the landing below, her well-proportioned, petite figure triggering an initial flash of pleasurable recognition as she looked up at him.

"Janie! How are you, old girl?"

Janie Bretsen trudged the last few steps to the top and hugged him briefly, giving him a tired smile when she pulled away.

"Exhausted, James," she said with a sigh. "But it's good to see you."

"And, the call from crew sked?" he asked, already suspecting the answer. He'd relayed the message by radio to his agent as the jet pulled into the gate to have her call crew scheduling in Denver immediately.

"They . . . didn't talk you into continuing on to Cape Town, did they?" James asked.

She shook her head and forced a short laugh. "As if you didn't already know, Judas."

"Janie," he protested, trying to sound hurt. "I didn't put them up to it. I just reported the other girl's illness."

"Yeah, well, it was the usual," Janie said, adopting a whining voice. '*Please*, Janie! *PLEASE!* If you don't go, we won't be legal and we'll have to cancel the flight, shoot the station manager, fire all the crew members, and withdraw from serving London.'"

"Dear me." He laughed.

"Oh, they're good, James!" she said. "At least Golden Globe–level performances for the asking." She dropped her voice back into a feigned accent. "Janie, I promise, all you have to do is get back on board and lend your body to the cause. You'll have a first-class seat. You can sleep! We'll be legal, and you get more money."

"Who's senior on the outbound leg?" James asked.

He heard her sigh again, this time with greater fatigue as she ran her hand through her chestnut-colored hair, fluffing it slightly.

"Our favorite Machiavellian firebrand. Judy Jackson."

"Good heavens! After all the troubles you've had with her personally?"

"Well, that's ancient history, but she's still never forgiven me for suspending her."

"When you were the Denver manager of flight attendants?"

"*Temporary* manager of flight attendants. After that, I had to go rob little old ladies and abuse children to regain my self esteem."

"I'm always surprised when she shows up here. I keep thinking the company's going to can her. I've never met a meaner woman."

Janie's hands migrated to her hips as she cocked her head. "Why would they can her, James? You guys in management won't tell Denver what she's really like out here, so she goes on reducing flight attendants to quivering wreckage, alienating passengers, and pissing off pilots at a furious rate."

"She is good at it," he said.

"Sorry. I shouldn't say 'pissing off.' Isn't ladylike."

"But, you're bang-on right about Jackson."

"Well, anyway . . . thanks, old friend," Janie said, patting his arm. "If I survive two legs with Mistress Jackson and her chamber of tortures, I'll see you day after." Janie moved past him heading back to the gate as James watched her go in mild alarm. When they'd first met, Janie was filled with the energy of an eighteen-year-old with the face and body to match. She'd been a devastatingly attractive twenty-six at the time, her petite, perfectly proportioned figure making her seem at a distance like a well-dressed child until one drew closer and discovered the very capable woman within. Janie had always had an elegance about her that made her sexy and desirable—an allure that had propelled them into a brief affair many years ago, a six-month-long delight marred by his neurotic concern that his six-foot frame would eventually injure her somehow. She seemed fragile, though she was anything but.

Yet, those same years, he thought, were taking an inordinate toll on her. He could see the struggles beginning to show in her face, around the corners of her widely set eyes, and in the slight slump of her little shoulders as she trudged off to do a major favor for crew schedulers who, he was sure, had already completely forgotten her concession.

No one but a close friend would notice her fatigue, he thought. Janie still turned male heads in waves, like a stiff breeze through a wheat field. But he could see the damage.

FIFTEEN

The temperature had climbed to the lower seventies by eight o'clock, portending another scorching summer day for the U.K. in the age of global warming.

Three Meridian gate agents—all of them British citizens increasingly alarmed at the decline of their American employer—took up positions at the podium in the gate area and began shuffling the stacks of paper and endless strings of computer entries needed to fuel a 365-passenger airplane with the human cargo that produced airline revenue. The continuation of Meridian Flight Six to Cape Town, South Africa, was a thrice-weekly affair, but seldom were they as full as this morning. Two hundred eighteen people would be joining the original one hundred and six from Chicago in the maw of the uncomfortably warm boarding lounge, many of them eyeing the door to the jetway as if boarding normally began with the crack of a starting pistol.

Several hundred feet down the concourse, Martin Ngume replaced a pay-phone receiver and sat in silence for a few moments trying to part the curtains of fatigue that were clouding his mind. Once more he had asked the owner of the little store in Soweto to take a crowbar, walk the quarter mile down the road, and pry the padlock off his mother's door. "Please, Joe, please be sure she is not inside and injured or something." At last Joe had promised to do so. But there would be no chance to call again until Cape Town. There were satellite phones on the plane, but they were far too expensive.

Martin got to his feet and picked up the small valise he'd carried aboard in Chicago, wishing London hadn't been the destination of the American woman, Claire, who had been so sympathetic. She'd checked on him in-flight several times on the way to London and knelt by his seat to talk. He felt good around her, even while drowning in worry.

"What am I to do if ... if my mother is dead?" Martin had asked her somewhere in the night over the Atlantic.

"Survive," Claire had replied. "You'll survive, as we all have to learn to do when our parents die." She had patted his arm and he appreciated her sympathy, but he could never explain to her or to anyone how every single day living in the United States had been lived for his mother as well as himself. He had written her daily in a large, cursive handwriting, since her eyes were so bad, and mailed the journals weekly. She had written back

JOHN J. NANCE

several months ago that for the first time in her life she felt her spirit soaring free of her mean circumstances in Soweto. "I am living this wonderful experience of yours through your words, son. I am seeing and feeling and learning these things as if I, too, were a university student." The letter had moved him to tears, and he longed for the day, not too far in the future, when he could bring her to America and show her his new world in person. He had said the same thing to a newspaper reporter who had come to the campus to research a Sunday feature on foreign students, and the resulting article had been accompanied by the picture of his mother he always carried.

Martin smiled at the memory. He'd sent her several copies but didn't know if she'd seen them yet.

He returned to the lounge and found a seat across from a young mother and her two children, winning a weak smile from the woman as he sat down.

Karen Davidson was beyond exhausted, and with more than ten hours of flight time to go, she couldn't let herself think about it. Her infant daughter was finally asleep again, as was Billy, who alternated between being reasonably good and marginally controllable.

Karen watched the handsome young black man as he sat across from her, and wondered again about the haunted look in his eyes. There were human stories of all kinds among the exhausted travelers and those joining them from London, but there was a special air of sadness and mystery about him.

Two of the agents bustled past, but one came back and knelt beside her.

"Are you and the kids quite all right?" she asked. The thought of asking which airline she worked for crossed her mind, but Karen suppressed it. The agent was obviously being kind, and obviously British, and obviously nothing like the hateful, uncaring Meridian personnel she'd encountered thus far.

"Thanks for asking. We're okay."

"Very well, then. We'll be boarding soon." She smiled and returned to the podium.

"Would passenger Martin Ngume kindly come to the podium?" one of the agents said over the gate area PA. "Mr. Ngume, if you are currently in the waiting area, won't you please respond?"

Martin jumped to his feet as if scalded, his heart rate leaping into overdrive as he moved toward the ticket agent, wondering if she had information about his mother.

"I am Martin Ngume," he said as quietly as possible.

"Oh! Smashing. We have an upgrade for you, Mr. Ngume."

"I'm sorry . . . a what?"

"An upgrade to first class all the way to Cape Town."

Martin tried to give her an appreciative smile through his confusion. "Thank you, but that's not necessary, you know."

"Well," the agent said, reading a note fresh off the printer. "Do you know someone named Claire Langston?"

His smile was immediate and apparently infectious, since the agent smiled broadly in return as she waited for him to answer.

"Ah, yes. Claire. She was very kind to me coming from Chicago."

"Well, Mr. Ngume," the agent said, still smiling as she took his right hand and gently laid the new, gold-colored ticket envelope in his hand, "she has also been very kind to you going to Cape Town. Ms. Langston purchased the upgrade for you a little while ago at our front counter."

With the cabin cleaners finishing up their interior preparation of the Boeing 747's cabin and the flight attendants setting up their galleys, all that remained was a call from the lead flight attendant. It was a small, but somewhat traditional, rule with Meridian. Only the lead attendant could trigger the avalanche of boarding passengers, no matter how eager the gate agents were to empty the boarding lounge.

At the end of the jetway, lead flight attendant Judy Jackson stepped from the aircraft into the jetway to make the "ready for boarding" call, but stopped for a moment at the sight of her image. Someone had decreed that mirrors be placed in the jetways as apparent insurance against arriving passengers being confronted with an unkempt agent, thus giving the wrong image of British workers. Good idea, Judy decided. At times any woman could accidentally look like a nightmare, and even male agents could look scary with a case of jet-blasted hair and reddened eyes.

She studied her reflection for a few seconds, satisfied with what she saw: slightly fluffed, shoulder-length dark blond hair, and very few lines in her nicely tanned forty-year-old face. Her eyeliner was on just right, and she had no traces of lipstick on her teeth—the bane of her existence. She straightened her back, trying to stretch to the five-foot-seven height she always claimed.

And for what?

The thought intruded like an unexpected spark of static electricity. Her history with men was a void for the past few years, and some mornings—had there been no airline image to keep up—the nightmare look would have suited her just fine. Why try, after all? Guys didn't seem to target her any more, no matter how fit she kept her bikini-friendly figure.

Judy leaned over and looked through the small window of the jetway into the terminal. Her latest passenger load was milling around, impatient to be scrunched into their Boeing-built aluminum tube. She glanced at her watch.

They could wait a minute more, Judy decided, as she pressed her face against the small window again and tried to catch a glimpse of the man she'd noticed a half hour before.

He was old enough to be her father, and that was the problem: he looked disturbingly *like* her deceased father, and the resemblance had sent cold chills down her back. Not that she ever wanted to see her father's face again, but it—or effigies of it—kept popping up all over the world and destabilizing her whole day in ways she could never explain. As if he were watching her. As if he wasn't through torturing her.

There! she thought to herself. *The one on the left . . . No, that's not him.*

She made a mental note to walk the aisles after takeoff and search for the man. It was a strange obsession, she knew, and she'd exhausted three psychologist-counselors over time talking about it. She was weary of trying to answer their same question, asked in so many unimaginative ways: "Why do you obsess about such faces in the crowd?"

"If I knew that," she'd yelled at one of them—a rotund male with a Vandyke beard—"I wouldn't need a shrink! Right?"

There had been another instance years before that had added grease to the skids of her marriage. A face in the crowd at an airport on vacation had distracted her so profoundly she'd left her already dissatisfied husband at the gate for nearly an hour as the flight boarded. He had become increasingly frantic. She'd returned at the last second after chasing the look-alike all the way to a parking lot, but the damage had been done. Her soon-to-be ex refused to speak to her for days, and the vacation collapsed in a bonfire of accusations.

But whenever the face appeared again, it compelled

her attention. She had to find it and confront it and expiate it in person.

"You're simply trying to make sure he's still dead," one of the psychologists had concluded, somewhat grandly.

"And for that 'Well, DUH' observation I'm supposed to *pay* you?" she'd snapped.

Judy brought her mind back to the present as she watched an agent walk to the window of the Heathrow boarding lounge and press her nose against the glass, wondering what was going on out at the aircraft.

I guess I've toyed with them long enough, she mused, reaching for the phone. "Okay, this is the head mama. Open the cattle chutes."

Jimmy Roberts suppressed another huge yawn and smiled at his wife as Brenda hefted her shoulder bag and prepared to slide into the boarding line slowly snaking toward the jet-way entrance.

"What's our row again, darlin'?" she asked.

"Twenty," he replied, checking the boarding passes, aware they were standing beside one of the most vocal of the complaining passengers from Chicago. That whole aircraft had been filled with angry people, Jimmy knew, and it was upsetting to see so many of the same faces now as they got back on.

"You see that fellow with the computer off to the right?" Brenda asked in a whisper.

"Yeah."

"I heard him ask a man in front of him real nice to please not recline the seat, and the guy got furious, and shoved it back so hard the computer screen snapped shut on the fellow's hands. I thought they were going to get in a fistfight."

Jimmy shook his head. "I've never seen anything like it, not even when I was in high school and a bunch of us would go over to Pecos on Saturday night to raise a ruckus. Right now, I just want to get us to Cape Town before these people start rioting."

James Haverston stood at the podium watching the boarding process and his watch at the same time as he spoke quietly to the three agents at the podium.

"We've only fourteen minutes. Let's look lively, shall we?"

"We *are*, James," the closest one protested, only half smiling.

"I'm serious, ladies," he continued, returning what was more a smirk than a smile. "I'll not tolerate a late push-back due to boarding again today. Understood?"

One of them broke away and trotted to the jet-way entrance to speak to the boarding agent, who immediately picked up the PA microphone.

"Boarding all rows now for Cape Town. If you would please . . . move onto the aircraft as rapidly as possible, so we can get you off on time . . . for your convenience."

James had backed up to one side to monitor the progress, when he felt a tug on his sleeve and turned to find another one of his gate agents. She leaned over, cupping her hand over his ear with irritating familiarity and speaking too loudly. "Sir, we may have a problem. There's a distraught-looking man sitting over to the right who fits one of our profiles." She motioned with a small incline of her head toward a seat where a man in a business suit sat staring at nothing. "He's been sitting there in a near-catatonic state for a half hour, responding to nothing."

James Haverston had been a station manager and airline agent for decades. The security profiles of passengers who justified greater scrutiny were second nature, but so was his trust of his own sixth sense. James spotted the man and immediately raised his two-way to call quietly for a security officer. He walked over and sat in an empty seat next to the man his agent had indicated. Something *was* odd, he concluded, but there was nothing concrete he could put his finger on. Boarding was almost complete and the man had made no move to get to his feet and approach the gate, even though his boarding pass was clearly visible in his lap.

This fellow could be sleepy, drugged, grief stricken, or have some other logical reason for looking so distracted, James thought.

But there was always the possibility someone like him could be suicidal or even harboring some other evil intent.

"Good morning, sir," James began. "You *are* headed to Cape Town, are you not?"

Slowly the man looked over at him, his eyes partially dilated and unfocused. He tried to smile, but it was obviously an effort.

"Sorry?"

James held out his hand. "James Haverston. Meridian station manager here in Heathrow. Just wondering if you're okay."

James saw the man's face harden, his lips tightening in an effort to control himself. He made no attempt to shake hands.

"I'm fine, thanks. And I've got no choice but to fly with you people."

He stood up suddenly and lifted his carry-on and briefcase as James dropped his hand and stood, too, partially blocking his path.

"May I ask your name, sir?"

"Dr. Brian Logan."

"I see. Well, Dr. Logan, have we done something to offend you?"

The range of expressions crossing Brian's face prompted James to step back in slight apprehension. He glanced to the side, relieved to see one of the airport police officers he knew approaching. Dr. Logan was trying to speak and apparently searching for the words.

"You . . . want to know if you've done something to offend *me*?" Logan said in a staccato growl.

"Yes, sir, I certainly do. I'm concerned that you seem really upset with us. What on earth have we done? If you tell me, perhaps I can make it right."

Brian brushed past him and moved forward toward the agent at the jet-way entrance, effectively pulling James with him as the police officer circled around behind, watching carefully.

"You want to know what you've done," Brian repeated slowly as he handed his boarding pass to the woman at the door, who watched her boss for any signals. She was aware of the officer approaching from the right side.

James nodded to her in a signal to continue.

"Ah, welcome aboard, Dr. Logan. . . . We have you in first class, seat three-D."

Brian took the boarding pass without looking at it. His eyes were boring into James Haverston's. "Your airline killed my wife and son. Is that enough?" Logan turned away from Haverston and brushed past the agent to hurry down the jetway as the police officer moved forward.

James raised his hand to stop the officer just as he reached the jetway.

"No?" the officer asked.

"Wait a second." He leaned past his agent and typed a series of commands into the gate computer, waiting for the passenger case-file subdirectory to appear with the answer.

Logan, Brian, M.D.—Currently plaintiff in a one-hundred-million-dollar wrongful-death action against us for the loss of his wife and unborn son on one of our flights. Do not discuss his case, details of our procedures, or provide copies of any official-use materials under any circumstance. Handle with extreme care and respect. Unlikely ever to fly us again.

There was a brief recitation of Meridian's version of Daphne Logan's death. The moment of decision had arrived, James realized, and the agents he'd spurred to get the boarding done on time were now looking at him.

James stood for a moment, balancing his customer-service sensibilities and his security responsibilities against the revenue of a first-class passenger and the image of the man, his carry-on bag, and his title of doctor, then turned and nodded to the officer. "My mistake, Alf. Sorry to have bothered you."

"A false alarm, then?"

"Indeed."

Unseen at the end of the jetway, Dr. Brian Logan took a deep breath, and forced himself to walk through the entrance.

Janie realized Judy Jackson was consciously avoiding her the minute she stepped aboard the cavernous 747-400 and introduced herself to the two crew members working the door, Cindy Simons and Elle Chantrese. She could see Judy turn her back and slip out of the galley.

Nothing changes with you, does it, Judy? Janie thought in mild amusement.

"Where do you suppose I can be of the greatest assistance to you girls?" Janie asked Elle and Cindy, who simultaneously arched their thumbs toward the back of the aircraft.

"Synchronized gesturing. Very nice," Janie teased as both women laughed in response. Elle broke away to keep greeting passengers as Cindy leaned closer. "We're one short today, and Jackson's on the warpath as usual."

Janie inclined her head toward first class. "I'll put my things by my seat and head back there."

She moved a few feet up the aisle and turned, watching Cindy with the eye of a veteran as the compact brunette smoothly transitioned back to greeting duty with Elle, who was more than a foot taller.

Good attitudes, they both look elegant, and they're both friendly. Why couldn't I have had them from Chicago? she mused, the task of writing up most of her previous crew still ahead of her.

Janie checked her boarding pass again, verifying she was in seat 3-A. 3-B was vacant so far, and she hoped it would stay that way. It would be easier to relax if she didn't have to worry about a seatmate.

The six seats in row 3 of first class were placed in groupings of two seats each—two on the left, two on the right, and two in the middle, each of them comparatively huge and equipped with its own video screen and ample legroom.

Three-F was already occupied by a distinguished businessman in an expensive suit who was pulling a folder out of his briefcase.

There was movement at the rear entrance to first class, and Janie looked up to see a man enter holding a leather briefcase in one hand and his boarding pass in the other. He looked around in confusion, trying to locate his seat. Something about him pulled her attention away from the small task of putting her carry-on under the seat, and Janie realized with a momentary flash of self-consciousness that she was purposely fumbling with her purse to keep an eye on him as he settled into seat 3-D in the center group. Dark hair, late thirties . . . no, early forties . . . hard to tell, she concluded, but handsome and poised and well groomed. He was wearing a hard expression, almost angry, in fact, but somehow it didn't seem natural for him.

Janie watched the way he carefully placed the brief-case in his lap, then thought about it and put it under the seat in front of him, only to pull it back to his lap. He sensed her presence and looked around, and she smiled.

There was a flicker of a smile in return, but he was obviously preoccupied, and she forced herself to stow her bag and head for the rear of the aircraft, stopping briefly in the first-class galley at the rear of the first-class compartment to check the computer printout.

Three-A, me . . . Three-D, Dr. Brian Logan. Aha! A doctor. Interesting.

Janie moved aft through the still-crowded aisles, stopping to smile at the passengers one by one and help with the inevitable task of stowing bulky carry-ons in high places. But she lingered on the image of the doctor in first class wondering if there was a story there she should know.

In the cockpit overhead, First Officer Garth Abbott sat in the right seat of the ultramodern Boeing flight deck and watched the Heathrow terminal recede slowly in the windscreen. The unseen tug four stories below pushed the loaded 747 steadily backward, and then to one side to make room for another Meridian 777 that had arrived early. Garth could see the triple-seven in the distance, its crew waiting impatiently to nose into the same gate Flight Six had just vacated.

His mind kept returning to Carol, and the follow-up call he'd made to her while down on the ramp doing the ground inspection of the aircraft. He'd tried to compartmentalize his anxiety, but it wouldn't rest.

He'd awakened her and heard that delicious, recently loved rumble in her voice that always excited him.

"What did you mean, honey, earlier, when I said I'd see you when I got home and you replied, 'Perhaps'?"

"*Hm-m?* What?"

He repeated his words and heard the bedcovers rustling in the background. "We've talked about it before, Garth."

"About what?"

"Us. Look, just . . . come home safely, and we'll talk."

"That's always my intention, babe. But talk about what? Are you having some premonition? Some bad feeling about this trip?"

There was a long silence before she replied, and he heard her clear her throat first. "No. Not the trip."

"Then *what*?"

"I've been trying to tell you for years, Garth. I've *told* you for years, but you're too in love with airplanes to listen."

"Airplanes? What, this is about my being gone so much?"

Silence, though he could hear her shift the receiver.

"There's . . . something I have to tell you, Garth. But now isn't the time."

"About us?"

"Yes."

"You're not happy?"

"How would you know?"

There was a noise in the background, and Garth ignored it. "Baby, please! You're going to make me crazy. What's going on?"

"When you get home, we'll talk. Not now. I'm going to hang up now, Garth. I'll see you when you get home." The line went dead, and he'd sat for a few moments in shock before redialing. But this time the call went directly to voice mail, which meant she'd forwarded it.

Garth glanced over at Phil Knight, who was busy with the engine start sequence. He wanted to rip off his headset, tell Knight to get someone else as copilot, and find the first flight back home. But he couldn't leave now and keep his job.

His mind was whirling, his need to fix things immediately feeding a growing panic against the background of well-founded fears. He loved her deeply, he needed her, but he had always been unwilling to put the flying second. A sick feeling washed over him now, a realization that he'd been away for too long.

Maybe we can salvage it, Garth thought.

"Oil pressure, number four," Knight was saying, half under his breath. Garth could see him glancing in puzzlement at his first officer, wondering why there was no echo from the right seat. Engines one and two on the left wing and number three, the inboard on the right wing, were now idling, and Phil was raising the start lever to fire off number four, the outboard engine on the right.

"EGT rising," the captain was saying, watching the temperature climb. "But the rpm's stagnant."

"Okay," Garth said, just to fill the space with something verbal, then realizing what the instruments were saying. "I . . . think we've got a hung start, Phil." Garth glanced at the sweep-second hand on his watch, estimating how long it had been since Knight had raised the start lever. The exhaust gas temperature indication was rising steadily toward the red-line maximum.

"Shutting it down," Phil announced, taking the engine start switch back to the off position. "I'll let it wind down to zero, and we'll try again."

The second attempt was a mirror image of the first. The engine's internal fires had lit, but for some reason the engine itself could not accelerate to normal idle speed.

Once again, he shut it down. Garth relayed the problem to Operations over the radio before turning to Phil Knight.

"Phil, number four's also been giving false fire warnings for the past few months. I found a long history in the log book . . . but I didn't see anything about it having hung-start problems. There was, however, a bleed valve write-up a week ago."

The captain didn't respond, and before he could say anything more, the Operations frequency came alive.

"Maintenance is on the way, chaps," the Operations chief assured them as Heathrow ground directed them to wait on a side ramp just north of Terminal 4.

"Just find a place to park."

"Should, I, uh, tell the folks what's going on?" Garth asked when they'd set the parking brake.

"No," Knight replied immediately.

"No?"

"No. *We* don't even know what's going on."

"Yeah, I understand, but . . ."

"Have the flight attendants do it." Knight shot a glance to the right. "I don't want announcements made from up here and then have some idiot back there misinterpret what we mean and find a way to sue us or something."

"*Sue* us? I'm sorry, I don't—"

"Look, dammit! When you get to the left seat, you can chatter away on the PA all you like, but this is my ship, and I don't want any PAs made from my cockpit. Understood? You seem to question every damn thing I do, and I happen to be the captain."

"Phil, you're the one always giving me hell for not following the operations manual, and the manual clearly says . . ."

"It says the passengers will be kept informed!" he snapped. "It doesn't require the pilots to do it."

Garth suppressed a flash of pure anger. He was authorized—even required—to challenge a captain on safety-of-flight matters. But PA announcements on the ground weren't necessarily safety-of-flight items.

What a jerk! Garth thought, as he picked up the interphone and gave one of the flight attendants a briefing about the balky engine, then toggled his PA monitor to listen through his headset.

The flight attendant's voice came on within a half minute:

Ladies and gentlemen, this is your lead flight attendant. The captain has asked me to inform you that we're going to have a brief delay here by the runway before we can take off.

In the alcove of the forward entry, Judy Jackson lowered the PA handset for a moment in thought, then smiled as she raised it back to her mouth.

They've asked us not to tell you, but I'm going to anyway. The Queen's aircraft is inbound, and just as they do for Air Force One and the American President, when Queen Elizabeth arrives or departs here in London, all air traffic is held up. Please bear with us. From experience, I'd say we'll be here about a half hour.

Judy replaced the handset as Cindy, one of her bright-eyed young crew, came out of the coach cabin.

"Really?" Cindy asked. "The Queen?"

"Of course." Judy smiled.

"Wow! Oh, by the way, we're getting complaints that it's too hot back there. Should I call the cockpit?"

Judy shook her head no. "I'll do it. No one on this crew talks to the cockpit or goes up there but me. Understood?"

"Okay, Judy," she replied, a confused look crossing her face like a fleeting cloud.

"Oh, Cindy, is that refugee from Chicago back there? Bretsen?"

"You mean Janie? Yeah, she's helping in the rear galley."

144

"Tell her to get her tail up here. They gave her a seat in first class, and I want her in it."

"But, we're short—"

"Don't question me, little girl!" Judy snapped. "Do it! We've got ten hours. You can handle it one girl short."

The young flight attendant nodded and turned to head back down the aisle, missing the smug smile that spread across Judy Jackson's face.

In the right seat of the cockpit, Garth Abbott quietly tapped the PA button and turned to the captain with Judy Jackson's explanation still ringing in his mind.

"Did you . . . tell anyone back there on the interphone, or when you came aboard, that the Queen was coming in and causing our delay?"

Phil Knight turned and shot him an irritated glance. "What? I haven't talked to them."

I'm sure that's the truth, the copilot thought. Phil Knight never talked to the flight attendants, other than to grunt or mumble a hello if he was forced to. It was up to the copilots to introduce themselves and try to brief the cabin crew. Sometimes getting dinner to the cockpit depended on it, since none of the cabin crew liked Capt. Phil Knight, or wanted to come into his lair.

"Why'd you ask that?" Phil asked.

"Because our lead gal back there just told the passengers that we were being delayed by the Queen's arrival."

JOHN J. NANCE

"So?"

"So, that's not true, Phil, as far as I know. I was under the impression that we were sitting here because one engine won't start and the company and the FAA get irritated if we take off with one shut down."

"Look, I don't much care what she tells them as long as she keeps them quiet."

"My point, Phil," Garth said, "is that once she tells them a big yarn like that and they subsequently find out it's false, our credibility goes to hell."

"It's their cabin. Let them deal with it."

"What, and we're just unseen gnomes driving the engine on the train?"

"Something like that."

"Jeez, Phil, you should be flying boxes for UPS or something. Those people back there pay our salaries. Don't we owe them a little consideration?"

"DAMMIT!" Phil exploded, his eyes bulging as he looked at Garth. "What is it about the word *captain* you don't understand?"

"What?"

"I'm the captain, whether you like it or not! Quit trying to run this show."

Garth raised both hands in a gesture of complete puzzlement. "Phil, what on earth are you talking about? I *know* you're in command, but a good first officer . . ."

"A good first officer knows how to shut up and say 'yes, sir.'"

Garth stared at Phil Knight for a few seconds before shaking his head sadly. "Phil, this isn't a contest. It's supposed to be teamwork."

"Yeah, right. I make decisions and you undercut them. Some team."

"What? If I give you my professional opinion, that's *undercutting* you?"

Phil forced himself to turn to the copilot and look him squarely in the eye. "You think I'm not sharp enough to know your little game, Abbott?"

"What little game?" Garth asked, a look of astonishment covering his face.

Phil Knight leveled an index finger at him, his face contorted in anger.

"All month you've just been looking for opportunities to challenge every decision I make. You're just hell-bent on proving that you're the great authority on all things international. You're supposed to support me, not play 'Gotcha.'"

Garth was shaking his head. "Jeez, man, I *am* supporting you. I'm not out there calling the company every time I disagree with you. I'm telling *you* about it. You still make the final decision."

"You got that right," Phil said as he diverted his eyes to the instrument panel and began fussing with the altimeter. A deep silence settled over the cockpit for an agonizing number of seconds.

Garth Abbot broke the impasse.

147

"Well . . . what *do* you want me to do, Captain? You want me to sit over here like a deer in the headlights and nod yes on cue?"

"That would be an improvement," Phil snapped.

"How about the small fact that Meridian Airlines says copilots are required to speak up and be assertive when they think there's something the captain almighty needs to hear?"

"Just get that 'Gotcha!' tone out of your voice when you have something to say."

Garth Abbott fell silent again for a few seconds, his mind whirling between the desire to scream at the man and the reality that they had to fly together for several more weeks. He let out a loud sigh and shook his head.

"Phil, you know what? Somehow I guess I'm sending you the wrong signals. I'm not trying to criticize you, I'm just trying to do my job."

"So shut up and do it."

Garth felt slightly dizzy from the effort of stifling the explosion of epithets he wanted so badly to launch at Phil Knight, but he kept his jaw clamped shut and simply nodded.

This, he thought, *is going to be an agony.*

SIXTEEN

Senator Sharon Douglas stood at the desk in her hotel suite with her unpacked bags on the bed and dialed her administrative assistant in Washington, D.C. Bill Perkins came on the line immediately.

"Bill, I'm sorry to wake you up at this ungodly hour over there, but I need you to get an early transcript of what they're doing in the House hearing on airborne rage incidents and e-mail it to me as soon as you get to the office. We're going to call our own hearing."

There was an anticipated period of grunts and coughs as Perkins woke up. "Sharon, we agreed that was a red herring . . ."

"I was wrong, okay? Our buddies on the other side of the Capitol Building happen to be right. You wouldn't believe what I just went through getting here."

"What, you mean the flight was bad?"

"No service, no civility, no accountability, poor training, incredible overcrowding, and what a new friend of mine calls the 'rat syndrome.' Bill, we may have the terrorist threat at bay, but if we don't get some cold water on this system really soon, something terrible's going to happen internally."

HEATHROW AIRPORT, LONDON
9:40 A.M. LOCAL

Martin Ngume had entered the first-class cabin of Meridian Six with the wide-eyed reverence of a commoner in a cathedral. After more than twelve hours shoehorned into the diminutive agony of a coach seat, the first-class seats looked like thrones trimmed in leather, all of them equipped with the electronic gadgets he'd grown to love in American life.

Elle Chantrese, a tall and startlingly blonde flight attendant, noticed his hesitation as she greeted him at the door and pointed to the left, toward the nose.

"Welcome aboard, Mr. Ngume. You're in Two-A, sir, to your left."

"I'm sorry?"

"A left turn here, and up that way through the curtains. You're in our first-class cabin."

Martin brightened and smiled broadly. "Oh, yes. I am. Thank you."

He moved cautiously until he found 2-A, hardly

believing the American lady could have been so kind. To make the rest of the trip in such luxury excited him, and he settled into the seat with great appreciation, breathing deeply of the rich leather aroma, running his hands lightly along the soft armrests, and carefully unfolding the small liquid crystal screen as he read the instruction card.

"Would you like something to drink before departure, sir?" another of the flight attendants asked him as she appeared suddenly by his seat. He looked around for the usual metal cart carrying the drinks, but it wasn't there, and he wondered where she'd left it.

"I . . . would like some orange juice, please."

"You bet," she said, disappearing toward the galley to get it.

Like a restaurant, then, he thought to himself. *Mother would love to see this*, he thought, the reality of why he was making the trip in the first place having momentarily slipped from his mind.

The crushing weight of his worries about her returned, before he remembered her constant admonition: "One who ruins the enjoyment of a wonderful experience with worry about things beyond his control is wasting a gift."

He was in a wonderful place, thanks to a generous gift. He would enjoy it as best he could. There was nothing else he could do for his mother until reaching Cape Town anyway, except pray.

ABOARD FLIGHT SIX, HEATHROW
11:38 A.M. LOCAL

On the opposite side of first class, Robert MacNaughton had been drumming his fingers on the edge of the leather seat for some time, the rhythm and intensity of his unheard tattoo increasing substantially after the last PA announcement. A window was at his right elbow, and through it he could clearly see the maintenance stand that had been moved up to the number-four engine just before the cowling had been opened. Several maintenance workers in white coveralls bearing the Meridian logo were now buzzing around the engine, and it was quite clear that their labors had virtually nothing to do with any alleged travel plans for the Queen of England.

There had been a growing feeling of disgust in the first-class compartment since push-back, and Mac-Naughton had felt it. A male passenger named Logan in a seat to his left had been the most vocal critic, complaining about the temperature, the delay, and the attitude of the airline's personnel. Mr. Logan, MacNaughton concluded, had apparently come aboard upset, and in the absence of a decent crew, it had been all downhill from there.

Logan was once again on his feet trying to talk to the lead flight attendant, this time pointing to his watch and gesturing in disgust toward the maintenance crew outside the aircraft, his voice almost loud enough to hear across the cabin. The exchange over, he sat back down as he glanced over and rolled his eyes in shared exasperation.

Robert MacNaughton's own breaking point had been reached several minutes before with the latest installment of what had become a long series of increasingly obvious lies over the PA. He could put up with certain indignities, such as an aircraft with no seat phones, but being lied to was quite unacceptable.

MacNaughton flung off his seat belt, got to his feet, pivoted his compact five-foot-eight frame, and aimed for the first-class galley. He threw open the curtain just as the same flight attendant triggered the PA.

She turned, startled, and replaced the handset.

"Yes? Can I help you?"

"You are obviously the lady making those announcements for the past two hours, correct?" he said quietly.

"Yes," she replied, her eyes registering the fact that this was a first-class passenger and an impeccably groomed man with a full head of silver hair wearing a suit worth at least a thousand dollars.

"Would you be so kind as to tell me your position on this crew?" the gentleman asked, his voice friendly and thoroughly controlled, his words devoid of any trace of upset or anger. Judy visibly relaxed as she smiled.

"Of course, sir. I'm the lead flight attendant."

"Very well," he said, smiling slightly, his accent cultured British. "And there is, I presume, a captain up top?" He flared his eyebrows and smiled, causing Judy to chuckle.

"Yes, of course. It's hard to fly without one, you understand."

"Perfectly. And one other thing before I share a little something I've been thinking about. Are the words you've been speaking yours, or his?"

"I'm sorry?"

"Your words, as spoken into that instrument." He motioned to the interphone receiver still in her hand, which also served as the PA microphone. "Am I to understand that everything you say is dictated by the captain? You have no choice in the matter?"

Judy tossed her head in a defiant gesture. "Good grief. Of course not! I mean, yes, it is my choice. I'm in charge of the cabin. I find out what's going on, and I tell my passengers."

"Of course. Now, I need just one clarification if you would be so kind."

"Certainly," she said warmly. "What would that be?"

"I'm having a few difficulties with your factual recitation, you see."

"Oh?" she said, still smiling.

"Indeed. First, you informed us that we were being delayed by the Queen, yet I happen to know personally that the Queen is in India this week and not due back from that state visit until Friday. Air traffic control delays occupied center stage of your apologies for the next thirty minutes, whilst your own airline's aviation band channel on the entertainment system, tuned to the control tower, rendered no evidence of any delays whatsoever."

Judy Jackson's smile had begun to fade. "Well, that's what we were told," she managed.

"Really? Extraordinary, because you then provided the excuse of ramp congestion on an uncongested ramp, followed by an arriving medical emergency in the total absence of ambulance activity, and finally, your pièce de résistance, apparently, was a magically materializing line of invisible thunderstorms in a clear blue sky, despite the fact that as of eight a.m this morning the nearest convective weather activity was eighty miles north of Denmark."

"There was weather in the area, and . . ."

"And that transparent weather undoubtedly caused some sort of sympathetic malfunction in the right outboard engine of this jumbo, eh?"

Judy was totally off balance. She adopted an angry expression, her hands migrating to her hips. "If you knew much about airplanes, *sir*, you would understand that when there are delays, our mechanics must make certain ground checks."

"I'm certain you're right. I've only been a licensed jet pilot for a short thirty-two years, and my corporation has only owned a Boeing Business Jet for the past two years, which, I might add, I am now rated to fly. For the uninitiated, that's merely a Boeing 737."

He's shouting at me! she thought, realizing that somehow his words had accelerated in force, but not a bit in volume. The recognition left her momentarily speechless.

"So, young lady, my question to you would be this:

Are you a bloody frustrated fiction writer, or do you simply enjoy lying like hell to your passengers?"

"Just who do you think you are, talking to me like that?" Judy snarled.

"Oh, no one of consequence, really," he said in the same quiet tones. "Other than being one of your paying passengers."

"Then I suggest, *sir*, that you get back to your seat."

"As you wish," he said with a small hint of a bow. "However, I should like to request that in future announcements, you confine yourself to the rather quaint and obviously archaic practice of telling the truth. Contrary to your obvious belief in assuming psychological commonality with your passengers, we are, in fact, not idiots."

MacNaughton returned to the fourth row in the first-class cabin, sliding past the empty aisle seat to maneuver into his by the window and brushing past his briefcase in the process. A small, leather identity tag with the logo of English Petroleum caught the fold of his pant cuff and turned over, revealing his name embossed in gold: ROBERT MACNAUGHTON, CHAIRMAN OF THE BOARD.

The sound of the PA coming alive focused his attention on the overhead speakers. The woman's voice was back, but now there was a case-hardened edge to it.

Just a follow-up note, folks. Because of all the other problems that have delayed our departure, our maintenance department elected to do a routine inspection of the right outboard

engine, which is what you may have noticed out the right.
Nothing wrong, in other words. Just routine. I appreciate
your patience, but now that the line of weather is clearing
the area, we should be ready to go shortly.

Once more Robert MacNaughton's fingers began a
small drum coda on the seat arm as he shook his head
slowly in astonishment, almost missing the sudden motion
to his left as a man plopped down next to him with his
hand outstretched.

Robert stopped drumming and looked at the man.

"I'm sorry to bother you," the man said. "I'm Dr.
Brian Logan. I'm a physician from the U.S."

MacNaughton took the doctor's hand and shook it
without enthusiasm. "Delighted to meet you, Doctor.
Robert MacNaughton, here."

"I got the impression, Mr. MacNaughton, that you
were upset by those announcements, too."

"Indeed." MacNaughton quickly studied the physician's eyes, trying to decide whether to say more and
weighing the emotional need for alliance in the face of
such stupidity against a small voice of caution—which he
decided to ignore. "She's been spouting a pack of lies,
you see, and I'm bloody tired of it!"

Logan nodded, his eyes narrowing. "That's the way
they run this lousy airline. All that garbage about the
Queen and weather and traffic, and I think they've had a
problem with the right outboard engine since we left the
gate."

"I'm beginning to agree with you, Doctor," Mac-Naughton said. "I spoke to her about it, but as you can hear, it was of no consequence."

Brian nodded again and raised himself up in the seat, looking around as if checking for eavesdroppers. The gesture sent a small jolt of alarm through MacNaughton. Brian turned to him again, lowering his voice. "May I count on you to testify?"

Robert MacNaughton paused as he watched the physician's face. "I'm sorry? Did you say, 'testify'?"

"Yes. About their lies! I think we've caught them red-handed."

Rising caution slowed MacNaughton's response, and he chose his words carefully. "Ah, Doctor, I entirely agree their conduct is outrageous, but . . . even though I'm not a solicitor . . . I seriously doubt what's happened constitutes grounds for legal action, if that's what you're contemplating."

Brian stared back for a few seconds, then blinked and shook his head. "Sorry, I'm . . . I didn't phrase that correctly. If I file a complaint with aviation authorities, may I count on you to back me up?"

"Oh, I see." Robert MacNaughton pulled a business card from an inside coat pocket and handed it to him. "Indeed you may. Simply contact my office. The fact is, I've been sitting here contemplating the same action myself."

"Finally!" the doctor said, startling Robert Mac-Naughton until he realized the doctor was pointing to the window. MacNaughton followed his gesture and looked to the right, relieved to see the maintenance team pulling the stands away and resecuring the engine. He watched as one of them spoke unheard words into a handheld radio, and within seconds, the power fluctuated in the 747's cabin as the rising whine of the engine could be heard.

The creak of leather caught his attention, and he looked toward the aisle seat again in time to see the doctor getting to his feet and moving rearward through the dividing curtain.

Odd, his behavior, MacNaughton thought to himself, as he pulled his briefcase to his lap to retrieve one of the voluminous reports he needed to study. He had to prepare for a meeting in Cape Town that had come up suddenly, and with the company's jet fleet already busy, Meridian's flight had seemed the best choice. He was beginning to regret that choice.

The sound of the PA system clicking on again caught his attention, and he paused with the briefcase open, wondering if the pilots were finally going to speak.

The voice, instead, belonged to Dr. Logan.

Folks, this is Brian Logan, one of your fellow passengers. There's something you need to know.

The lead flight attendant had been fluffing pillows and doing what appeared to be busywork at the front end of the first-class cabin, all the while carefully avoiding MacNaughton's eyes. She turned suddenly at the sound of Dr. Logan's voice on the PA, her eyes darting in all directions as she broke into a run toward the coach cabin.

In first-class window seat 3-A on the opposite side of the cabin, Janie Bretsen came bolt upright.

The crew has been lying to us for hours. The nonsense about the Queen was a lie, there's been no bad weather anywhere close . . .

Judy Jackson came flying past Robert MacNaughton's seat and shot through the curtains. He could hear her footsteps receding into the next cabin and hear her shouting as Dr. Logan continued on the PA.

. . . the airport isn't traffic-jammed, and all along they've been trying to hide the fact that . . .

The sound of something striking the PA handset was followed by the unmistakable noise of its falling to the floor as heated shouts filtered through in the background. Janie was off duty, but now she came to her feet and moved aft. Over the speakers she heard a sudden grunt and an audible scuffle, as Logan tried to wrest the handset from whoever had taken it.

. . . you . . . WHAT YOU NEED TO KNOW . . . . .is . . . LET GO! . . . .they had a problem with the . . . engine . . . AND THEY DIDN'T WANT TO TELL US! ARE YOU GOING TO PUT UP WITH THIS?

Once more the handset was yanked from Brian's control and Judy Jackson's voice came over the speakers, out of breath but determined.

Ladies and gentlemen, we apologize for that outburst. One of our passengers seems to be having emotional problems.

The outboard engine on the right side was running now, and two more cabin chimes rang out as the 747 began taxiing, the gentle motion swaying the plane to the right.

MacNaughton looked over his shoulder and strained to see something through the privacy curtain, but decided not to interfere. He'd been somewhat unsure of the physician's stability. Perhaps this wasn't the time to get involved.

Angry voices and the sounds of a mild struggle were working their way forward until Brian Logan burst backward through the curtains, herded by a phalanx of flight attendants led by a furious Judy Jackson.

"SIR! If you don't get your butt in that seat and strap in, I'll have the captain return to the gate and have you removed in handcuffs!"

"Go ahead, damn you," he was saying, his voice low and threatening. "I'm already suing this lousy company for murdering my wife and unborn son. I'll just add another twenty or thirty million to the claim." He turned around to take his seat.

"Do what you like when you're off my aircraft, but if you don't . . ."

Brian Logan whirled back around, an index finger pointed in Judy Jackson's face. "Don't you *dare* presume to order me around," Logan growled.

"SIR! SIT ... DOWN ... OR WE'RE GOING BACK!" Jackson turned to one of the other flight attendants and pointed toward the cockpit. "Get up there, grab the interphone, and stand by to inform the cockpit about this. Watch for my signal."

The younger woman moved aft immediately, using the parallel aisleway to avoid coming within Brian's reach.

The doctor stood for a second, surveying the forces arrayed against him. Five of the crew had appeared to back up their leader, including, apparently, the off-duty flight attendant, and all of them were staring at Logan.

Brian glanced at Robert MacNaughton, who shook his head ever so slightly and motioned palm down for Logan to sit. Slowly the physician gave in and eased himself all the way into the chair.

Judy Jackson's eyes flamed with anger, but caution sparked by the volatility of the man held her back.

"I don't want to see you out of that seat again, sir," she said.

"It's *Doctor* Logan, and I'll damn well do as I please."

"I don't care what your title is. If you touch any crew equipment, or crew member, or interfere or ignore our orders again, you're going to be arrested and removed, charged, tried, convicted, and imprisoned. Keep in mind we carry armed sky marshals, and if they decide to jump on you, you'll spend the next ten years in jail if you survive . . . probably in the U.K., where they have no tolerance for infantile misbehavior. Understand?"

"Are you through?" he asked.

"Yes."

He leveled his index finger at her again, his voice low and threatening. "Woman, you lie to us again about anything else, and you're going to have me backed by three hundred angry passengers."

"Don't *you* threaten *me*, either," she said, swallowing hard enough to betray her nervousness and moving quickly aft through the curtains, well aware there were no armed officers flying on Meridian's international flights.

Janie Bretsen had been standing near her first-class seat watching the exchange. When Judy Jackson turned to leave, Janie followed hot on her heels, cornering her in the business-class galley.

"What on earth was that all about, Judy?" she asked, gesturing back over her shoulder.

"What do you mean?" Judy said without turning.

"Well, I mean is it a full moon or something? We had a load of furious people on the Chicago-to-London leg, too. What set the doctor off?"

Judy turned suddenly, looking Janie up and down and frowning at her appearance. "We look a little less than stellar this afternoon, don't we, *Miss* Bretsen, ma'am? You sure you're in compliance with what the manager of in-flight services would approve?"

"What are you talking about?" Janie responded.

Judy snorted and gestured to her. "Never mind. I guess former management is entitled to look haggish."

"Hag . . .*what?*"

"What do you want, Janie? I'm busy."

"I can see. I . . . saw that whole exchange and wondered if you'd like me to help in any way?"

"What, we can't handle it without the services of a supervising flight attendant?"

"Judy, cut it out! That suspension is ancient history, and you deserved what you got. You're being childish."

Judy moved a step closer, poking a finger at Janie's chest. "Bretsen, let's get this straight. *I'm* in charge of this cabin and this crew. *You* are no longer in a position of authority in this company, even though we all know you're a company stooge. They threw you on here to pretend to be legal and to spy."

"What? You know better than that. But now that you mention it, if you don't have a legal crew, why are we going?"

"With your carcass aboard we're technically legal, as you know. But you are *not* one of my girls and I do *not* need your help, and I wouldn't take it if I did need it. Go hibernate and stay out of my way."

"Never change, do you Judy? Same old snitty, combative attitude, and the same utter lack of customer skills."

"Sit down, Bretsen! Or do I have to have you arrested, too?"

Janie sighed and pointed upward as the two-chime pre-takeoff warning sounded in the cabin. "Are you going to inform the captain about what happened, or should I?"

"No one talks to my cockpit but me. *Capiche?*"

"They need to know, Judy."

"Get the hell out of here!" Judy snapped, pointing forward. Janie retreated through the curtains, reaching her seat just as the engines came up to full power and the heavily loaded 747 began its takeoff roll.

SEVENTEEN

Phil Knight engaged the Boeing 747's autopilot as they climbed through eight thousand feet and London Center turned them to the south. He watched now as the sophisticated auto-flight system gently leveled the big jet at thirty-seven-thousand feet and the auto-throttle system adjusted the engine thrust to cruise power with an equally gentle touch.

The captain glanced to the right, verifying that the copilot still had the laminated checklist in his lap. In the hours since their sharp exchange at Heathrow, the only communication had been required call-outs. Phil Knight knew he'd overreacted. That had been the wrong place and time to confront the copilot's snobbery, but he hadn't figured out how to repair the damage. The copilot might have been asking for it, but Phil was supposed to be the leader, and he knew he should have been more careful. His explosion had just made things worse.

"Cruise check," Phil said.

Garth Abbott looked up and nodded. "Roger. Altimeter?"

"Two-nine-nine-two."

"Pressurization?"

"Set. Cabin's at seven thousand."

They ran through the remainder of the challenge-and-response checklist without additional comment.

"Cruise check complete."

"Thanks."

"You bet," Garth replied, hesitating a moment and wondering what that meant. Knight never thanked a copilot for anything. *Must've been a slip*, he thought.

Brenda Roberts had been fairly bouncing up and down in the window seat on takeoff. Now she turned to her husband with wide-eyed excitement and grabbed his collar to pull him closer.

"Jimmy! You've *got* to see this! Wow!"

"What, darlin'?"

"The Parliament building, and . . . and Big Ben . . . and that's got to be the Thames River. Remember I showed you that picture?"

"Yeah."

"Well, baby, there it is in *person*!"

Jimmy released his seat belt and leaned on her knees

to peer out the window, wondering if one of the crew was going to come swooping down on him for not having his seat belt fastened.

It didn't matter, he decided, if they embarrassed him. He loved seeing Brenda so excited.

"Boy, howdy, darlin', that is the real thing, isn't it?"

She nodded, her head bobbing up and down too fast for her cascade of hair to follow, leaving her with a wild and windblown look that always made him lustful.

But there was nowhere to take her to carry out such a mission just now, so he suppressed his body's suggestion, his eyes following her finger as she pointed to something new.

"Is that Stonehenge, Jimmy?" She turned to him all bright eyed and smiles, and he beamed back, trying to see what she'd spotted.

"Can't tell. It's somewhere in south England, I think."

Her nose was back at the glass. "It *looks* like the pictures, but it's awfully small."

"Someday, we'll just have to take a trip over here and stay for a while."

She turned again, positively aglow, and threw her arms around his neck, almost hugging the breath out of him.

"I love you so much, Jimmy Ray!" she said, pulling away just as suddenly to look him in the eye. "Thank you for making my dreams come true!"

"Now, *you* won the contest, darlin'."

"But *you*, you big Texas lug, were the good ole boy what said, 'Hell, yes, let's go!'" She kissed him deeply, leaving him slightly flustered and embarrassed, even after all their years together. Then she turned to the window again and squealed.

"*DOVER!* Jimmy, that's got to be *Dover!*"

Garth Abbott watched England fall away from the 747 and let his mind drift home. Flying with Phil Knight was difficult enough, but it paled in comparison now with the anxiety Garth was feeling about his wife. He'd hoped the routine of takeoff and climb and cruise would help shove the burning doubts to some smaller, containable section of his mind. But it hadn't worked, and now he just wanted to be alone somewhere, anywhere, for a few minutes.

"I'm . . . thinking about going back to get some coffee and stretch, Phil. Do you mind?"

Phil Knight glanced to the right, expressionless. "No. Go ahead."

"When I come back, you want anything to drink?"

He shook his head no as he looked down to inspect the security screen, verifying no one was in the small hallway behind the cockpit. He punched through the various cameras showing each cabin of the multi-level airliner before returning to the first scene.

"Everything seems calm down there, and the hall is clear. You can leave."

Garth released his seat belt and got up, grabbing his hat before disappearing out the heavily reinforced cockpit door and carefully re-securing it just as Paris Control ordered a frequency change.

"Roger, Paris," Knight said. "One-twenty-four-point-five."

"No, Meridian, that was one-two-four-point-*zero*-five. Readback?"

"Okay, one-two-four-point-zero-five."

"Oui. Bonjour."

"Good day," Phil replied, dialing in the new frequency. He made the check-in call to the controller and sat back, feeling his stomach knot up again as he thought about the terrible accents he'd have to decipher ahead. It just wasn't fair. English was supposed to be the international language of aviation, and he'd depended on that fact when he decided to bid for the international division. He'd never taken a foreign language in school. He had no ear for them. But why hadn't he been warned that the version of English half the controllers in Europe and Africa spoke was essentially gobbledygook? Why didn't Meridian teach their pilots that fact?

The copilot, of course, had no trouble at all, which was galling. Phil could feel himself flushing slightly at the memory of having to admit on the first trip that he couldn't make out what they were saying. Abbott had pretended to be gracious, helping with the translations and taking over the calls himself, but Phil was sure that the copilot was counting the hours until he could spread the news of Phil's incompetence around Meridian's international division.

Phil glanced around toward the cockpit door, glad to see it still closed. He wished he could order the copilot to go take a seat in first class and not come back for hours, but the rules were clear: a pilot on a two-person crew could only be out of the cockpit for physiological reasons, and now there were a host of additional rules and procedures to make sure no one but the flight crew ever gained access to the cockpit, rules which made entering and leaving a necessary pain. He'd have to put up with the copilot's presence, though the trip would be a lot more enjoyable without Abbott and his withering disdain now made worse since they'd openly clashed.

"You don't deserve to be a captain" that smug look of Abbott's always seemed to be saying. "You don't know what you're doing out here."

Phil looked down at his flight bag and pulled out the wallet he always carried, flipping it open now to the pictures of his family. His wife, Doris, and their three sons stood smiling on the beach in the Bahamas where he'd taken them on vacation. A celebration, really. He'd just received the captain's bid to the 747 and the international division, and that had been grounds for celebration. Fifty thousand dollars more a year, although Uncle took thirty percent of it. But at last he was at the top of his profession. All his career he'd wanted to break out of domestic flying and see some of the world and call himself a senior 747 international captain. But until then, twenty-five years as a Meridian pilot had mainly consisted of driving Boeing 727s and later 737s around the Midwest to all the familiar airports. He'd made captain ten years back with moderate effort. He was already intimately familiar with domestic flying, the controllers all spoke English, he never flew into an airport he didn't know backward and forward, and his copilots were always respectful.

So why in the world did I leave? he asked himself.

Phil looked out the left window at a collection of towering cumulus in the distance to the east, wondering whether he could see the Swiss Alps. He reached down and fumbled for a map of Europe and extracted it from the case, unfolding it on his lap. He knew very little about European geography, but he had tried to memorize where the different countries were.

No, we're too far north for that to be Switzerland. It's Germany, I guess.

He imagined he could already see the spine of the Swiss Alps in the distance, but he'd have to cross-check the instruments to know for sure.

Another small wave of envy rippled across his mind, and he tried to suppress it. Abbott would know every feature out there, and loved to point them out. The copilots on the international runs were walking travelogues. They looked down their noses at anyone who had less experience, and they hated veteran domestic captains who suddenly bid the international runs to make more money. Phil felt that smoldering disdain on a daily basis.

His mind snapped back to the exchange at Heathrow, and he winced at losing control. Of course, Abbott deserved it, and maybe it had been the right time to clear the air, let the younger man know that the captain was fed up with his attitude.

No, I should have kept quiet, he thought, his mind nevertheless ringing with a litany of Abbott's advice over the previous weeks:

"Excuse me, Phil, but down here they *normally* have you turn right."

"Phil, sorry to interrupt, but in my experience . . ."

"Hey, Phil, I think it's this airport over here."

Teamwork, indeed. Every flight felt like a final exam that he'd flunked just by showing up.

The seat next to Brian Logan was empty, and Janie had reached the end of her endurance of solitude. The two-chime warning that they'd climbed above ten thousand feet was minutes behind them but the seat-belt light was still illuminated, yet Janie could stand it no longer. She had always met frustration and anger with motion. Pacing, walking, running, traveling—anything but sitting and stewing over Judy's insulting behavior exacerbated by her fatigue. She quietly maneuvered herself out of the seat and into the aisle, straightening her skirt and tucking in her blouse before sliding into 3-C next to the physician, who looked over, somewhat startled.

"Hi," she said, smiling at him and meeting his gaze. She could see his features soften a bit as she held her right hand out somewhat awkwardly over the armrest.

"I'm Janie Bretsen."

His right hand enfolded hers, tentatively at first, then with slightly greater pressure and she could feel a smoothness, neither soft nor callused—a powerful hand, nonetheless capable of great precision.

"Brian Logan. Nice to meet you ... Janie." He looked around as if a mother superior might burst through the privacy curtains at any moment and catch him molesting one of her brood.

"I ... thought you were a flight attendant," he said, releasing her hand.

"I am," she said, raising an eyebrow and adopting a conspiratorial tone. "But I'm playing hookey."

"Really?"

Janie slid her shoes off and retracted her legs beneath her, shifting around sideways in the wide seat to face him. "Actually, I worked this flight in from Chicago as lead, but they were one flight attendant short for Cape Town, and crew scheduling forcibly recruited me. So, technically, I'm on the crew, but in realistic terms I'm semi-deadheading."

She saw his hand withdraw to his lap and clench, as if he was suddenly embarrassed to have touched her or even be talking to her.

"I see," he said, his voice turning cold as he looked forward, pretending to search for something on the forward bulkhead.

Did I do something? Janie asked herself. The change had been instantaneous. *No, I didn't.*

"You know, I couldn't help . . . ," she began. "I mean, it's a small cabin up here and voices carry . . ."

He turned suddenly, a flint-hard look on his face. "You can go tell Ms. Jackson that this was a cheap trick and I'm not falling for it."

Janie looked stunned.

"I'm sorry?"

"Sending you up here to schmooze me, to . . . to try to win me over. It won't work."

Janie refused to take her eyes off the side of his face, even though he wouldn't look at her.

"You're very wrong, Doctor. I came over here to just chat with you. Judy Jackson had nothing to do with it."

"Nevertheless, it won't work," he repeated.

"What won't work, Dr. Logan?" she asked, her voice quiet and soft. "Should I call you Dr. Logan, or could we use each other's first names?"

"Doctor will do fine."

She nodded. "Okay. Doctor it is. But please tell me why what I'm *not* trying to do *won't* work."

The hint of a smile flickered across his mouth before he regained control and snorted. "That's a double negative."

"Is it?"

"I suspect you know that," he said, less stridently. "You're well-spoken. Better than most of the garrulous flotsam working for this so-called airline."

"Thank you . . . I think." She smiled. "Gee, Doctor, you're fun to chat with." Janie put her hand over her mouth and spoke through it in muffled fashion. "Sorry. That was a dangling preposition."

"What?" he replied, forced irritation in his tone.

She pulled her hand away from her mouth. "The old rule is, never end a sentence with *with*, and I just did, which is normally something up with which I would not put."

"Oh."

"This conversation is really catching fire, isn't it?"

"You've got an empty seat over there," he said sharply.

She let a few seconds pass. "Would you rather I left you alone?"

"If you're here to manipulate me, yes."

"I'm not. I promise. I'm not here to manipulate, convince, cajole, or shmooze you. I could not do that, would not do that, should not do that."

Another flicker of a smile.

"Thank you, Dr. Seuss," he said.

"Yeah." She chuckled. "Green eggs and ham."

He nodded, working hard to keep a grin off his face as she continued.

"I always liked Dr. Seuss as a girl. Oops. That sounds kinky, but you know what I mean."

He was nodding. *A good sign*, she thought. "My wife and I . . . ," he began, but the rest of it caught in his throat and he turned away, his teeth clenched, his hand to his chin.

"Doctor, look, I overheard you say to Jackson, that Meridian had . . . killed your wife and child . . ."

"Murdered!" he snapped.

"Yes, you said 'murdered.' You did say that."

They sat in silence for a few seconds before he turned and glanced self-consciously at her, then ahead, pursing his lips.

"I will go away if you want me to," she said, "but . . . I guess I'd like to know what happened."

He was surprised to find he didn't want her to go away.

"Was it a crash?"

He shook his head no and related the basics, working to keep himself under control. When he'd finished, they sat without talking for nearly a minute as Janie made her hands fuss with her skirt, then looked down, shaking her head.

"I had no idea," she said softly. "No wonder you hate everything Meridian. I would, too."

"You have any idea what it's like being on this airline?" he asked, pain replacing anger. "Being . . . being *inside* a Meridian airplane?"

"No, I don't," she replied, triggering a curious look. "No?"

"I can *try* to understand, Doctor, and I am trying, but

for me to say yes would trivialize the incredible pain you've endured."

"Brian," he replied.

"Sorry?"

He dipped his head and grimaced slightly as if apologizing for a painful faux pas. "Please call me Brian."

She nodded. "Thank you, Brian. And I'm Janie."

"I . . . ah, want to thank you for being understanding. I didn't expect that from . . ."

"You're welcome," she said, purposefully ending the need for further explanation.

"I'm . . . just sorry to see a lovely woman like you with such a hideous airline."

"So am I," Janie said, startling herself and wondering why the words hadn't passed her conscious scrutiny before they rolled out.

Brian Logan was looking puzzled, and she put a hand on his forearm.

"Brian, we have some terrible people at Meridian, including one woman on this airplane you've already encountered . . . and we have some who are burned out . . . and we have a lot who, like me, are simply sick to the depths of their being about what's happened to our company."

He nodded, unconvinced, and she related the conversation with Senator Douglas and the problems with the Chicago-to-London flight, losing herself in the narrative at times, but conscious of the fact that he was listening carefully. She knew she hadn't defused him, but it was a beginning.

It had taken Karen Davidson thirty minutes to figure out a way to safely suspend the child carrier from the magazine rack. She'd worked hard to get the handle to hook into the rack and make sure the attachment was secure but at last she'd fashioned a better solution than placing her baby on the cold floor.

Cathy Eileson, one of the flight attendants, had come slowly up the aisle at the same moment, and spotted Karen Davidson's handiwork with the child carrier. Cathy knelt down beside her. "Now *that* is clever!"

"Thanks," Karen replied. "Some airlines provide hooks for just this purpose, but I had to jury-rig this."

"That's a great idea, but . . . I hate to tell you, we aren't allowed to let a mother do this."

"Don't worry," Karen added. "I'll take it down before landing."

"I know you would, but . . . we've got a monstrous set of rules to follow, and they don't give us much flexibility. If we hit turbulence, this could fall off."

Karen nodded and sighed as she unhooked the child carrier and set it down at her feet. "I put it up there because the floor gets too cold," Karen said.

"I'll try to find more blankets," Cathy replied. "I'm really sorry."

Karen looked closely at her. "You work for this airline?" she asked.

Cathy Eileson moved back a few inches in surprise, unsure whether the question masked an attempt at humor. "Sorry?"

"I just wondered if you were really a Meridian flight attendant? Other than the lead flight attendant out of Chicago, Janie somebody, you're the only other one I've met so far who . . . well, seems to give a darn about any of us."

A look of confusion dissolved to a momentary flash of panic as the young woman pushed a cascade of soft, brown hair back from her eyes and shook her head. "I . . . I hate to hear . . . I mean . . ."

Karen held up her hand. "That was unkind of me. I'm sorry."

"No," Cathy replied, shaking her head. "I need to hear about it if we've mistreated you. I'm so sorry." Cathy got to her feet in silence and then leaned over, whispering, "Ask for me if there's anything you need the rest of the flight, okay? I'm normally working in the back galley."

Karen waited until she'd turned and disappeared before carefully leaning over to reattach the bassinet to the bulkhead.

On the upper deck of the Boeing 747-400, Garth Abbott emerged from the small toilet behind the cockpit and moved quietly to the nearby galley to pour himself some coffee and think. There was movement in his peripheral vision and he looked toward the rear of the cabin, catching Judy Jackson's eye.

It was, perhaps, the last thing he'd wanted to do at that particular moment.

Garth knew Judy all too well, having flown with her off and on for years. "She's mad at the world for no apparent reason," he'd told another new captain a month before when Judy had stormed into the cockpit after takeoff and chewed out the four-striper for some perceived slight.

"Who the heck's in command here?" the captain had asked Garth in genuine puzzlement after she'd left. "I mean, I know being an airline captain these days means we get no respect, but, *good grief*, Garth! She called me some choice names there."

"You should feel honored." Garth had chuckled. "She only insults pilots she likes. The rest of us die of starvation on her flights. No food, no drink, no quarter."

"Well, maybe it's time someone complained to the company about her."

"Be very careful," Garth had warned. "The last cappy who wrote her up ended up fighting for his career with an undeserved sexual harassment charge. At least, we're pretty sure it was undeserved."

"Really?"

"She owns the cabin, Captain. She's tough as nails, and we've all given up trying to wrest it away from her."

When Judy spotted the first officer in the galley, she gave him a small wave before moving in his direction.

Oh, wonderful, Garth thought to himself as he tried to decide if being in Phil Knight's company was any better. He thought of his wife again with that same sinking feeling, wishing he could just close his eyes and try to decipher their predeparture conversation without interruption. There was a tiny crew rest compartment behind the cockpit, and he'd thought of crawling inside for a while, but it opened into the cockpit, and Phil Knight was sure to notice.

"I could have brought that to you," Judy announced, tossing her hair and smiling as she pointed to his coffee cup.

"Oh, that's okay. I needed to stand up and get out of there anyway."

Judy shifted her weight slightly, the small motion broadcasting the shape of her hips beneath the well-tailored uniform skirt as she watched his eyes, wondering if they were going to travel down her body. She saw him look away instead, studying the galley, the rug, the ceiling . . . anything but her.

"You, young man, look worried about something," she said, her voice surprisingly gentle.

Garth looked at her, the unexpected words sparking a curiosity he expected would be answered by a smirk. But her eyes were wide and exceptionally blue, and he saw no mockery there.

"I, uh . . . just personal stuff," he managed, instantly irritated at the inept response.

"It's all personal stuff," she said. "Lord knows, I've gone through a lifetime of it. That . . ." She began maneuvering herself to the left a bit to stay in his shifted line of vision. "That's why I can always spot a worried man. I know I'm prying, but . . ." She glanced at his left hand, instantly recording the wedding band, which she hadn't paid attention to before. "Problems at home?"

Garth smiled involuntarily and squelched it as he shook his head. "What? No." He tried to chuckle, but it came out wrong and he coughed instead. "I, uh, just . . . wish I were somewhere else, you know? You ever feel that way?"

She laughed. "Only about every other hour. Welcome to the club."

His eyes found hers again for a very unsettling second. He'd always had trouble meeting a woman's gaze. The act was so personal, so . . .*intimate*. But Carol had taught him well the low opinion women had of men who wouldn't look them in the eye. "Either they're shifty and unreliable," Carol had said, "or they just can't tear their eyes away from your boobs. Either way, you don't trust them."

"Dollar for your thoughts," Judy was saying, her voice bringing him back to the present. Garth shook his head and looked at her again. "I'm sorry?"

"You were off in another dimension there for a second."

He nodded. "Yeah, well ... I'm going to be off looking for another job if I don't get back up there with Captain Sun ... ah, with Phil."

She smiled, confusing him even more. This was the firebrand he'd seen in action? This was the caustic woman he'd maligned a few minutes ago? How could she suddenly seem so nice, so ... *feminine*?

"See you later," he said, turning awkwardly to reach for the interphone and the cipher lock.

"Count on it," she said to his back.

EIGHTEEN

David Byrd stopped at the foot of Slip 18 and looked up at the squadron of gulls that had snagged his attention with their sudden coda of shrill cries. He stood for a moment, watching them bank and turn effortlessly in the early orange light, tracking the subtle movements of wing and tail with the wonder of an experienced pilot immersed in the never-ending thrill of probing the mysteries of flight.

The postdawn air wore a hint of midnight chill as it slowly warmed its way toward morning, but it was already redolent of a cocktail of aromas radiating like a biological perfume from the glassy green waters of the harbor. The slightest rumor of a sea breeze ruffled his hair as he closed his eyes and breathed in the mixture of salt air and day-old kelp brushed by a hint of fishiness—a pleasure almost spoiled by the sudden assault of diesel fumes from a nearby yacht idling in predeparture.

David checked his watch. It was two minutes to seven. General Overmeyer had warned that John Blaylock was an unpredictable sort, a strange mix of bohemian and disciplinarian who was well known for arriving at a high-level meeting precisely on time down to the second, clad in a rumpled uniform with shoes that hadn't been polished since they left the factory.

David stepped on the teak deck of the hybrid yacht and raised his hand to knock on the door of the motor coach, surprised when it was suddenly pushed open about twelve inches. A man's face appeared in the gap, his eyes suspiciously examining the visitor in silence.

"Hello?" David said.

The door was pulled shut without a word.

David raised his hand to knock again, but the door flew open once more, this time revealing a man wearing the lightning-bolt-encrusted uniform cap of an Air Force colonel—and clad only in a pair of Mickey Mouse boxer shorts.

"Colonel Blaylock?" David said.

The six-foot-three Blaylock saluted in exaggerated fashion before extending his hand.

"Welcome aboard, Colonel Byrd. I appreciate a man who's right on time." Blaylock turned and motioned David to follow him toward the galley. David stepped up to the planked, oaken main floor of the coach and pulled the door closed behind him as he watched Blaylock move easily behind the butcher-block counter in his galley. John Blaylock, David noticed, still had a full head of dark hair framing a tan face over an equally tan chest and a moderate gut. His face relaxed naturally into a pleasant smile, which he could instantly broaden to fifty-megawatt proportions.

"Coffee?" Blaylock asked, using the fifty megawatt mode.

"Please. Just cream, no sugar."

"Roger. Pull up a stool there."

David complied, watching Blaylock smoothly perform what had to be a morning ritual of retrieving and grinding a stash of beans from a Starbucks container before using the finely powdered results to prime an elaborate brass-trimmed commercial espresso machine far too big for a motor home.

John Blaylock took off the Air Force wheel hat and slid it down the counter with one hand as he scratched his hairy chest with the other. His espresso maker was clearly designed to dominate the galley, and almost on cue he inclined his head in its direction. "My prime addiction," he said. "Wait! I mean my prime addiction *after* consideration of the female of the species."

"Ours, I assume?" David shot back with a grin. "Species, that is."

John Blaylock's eyebrows climbed to an unnatural altitude. "Hey, I'm impressed! A Pentagon weenie with a genuine sense of humor!"

"For the record, I'm not a Pentagon weenie," David replied.

"For the record," Blaylock echoed, "I refrain from

involvement with females from species *other* than human."

"Good, since I think there's an Air Force Instruction about that."

"I'm not into Air Force Instructions," John Blaylock answered as he squinted at the dials of his espresso maker. "I'm a reservist. Reservists are, by nature, suspicious of regulations, inhabitants of the Pentagon, and colonels who show up dockside seeking information."

"I'm seeking information?" David asked.

Blaylock grinned at him. "Okay, coffee *and* information. Speaking of which, what is it, precisely, that the good General Halftrack thinks I can do for you?"

"Well, to begin with, this is an official visit."

"I gathered that," Blaylock replied, forcing himself to look serious as he pointed to the wheel hat. "That's why I wore my blues this morning."

"Yeah. But see, I'm pretty sure Mickey's boxer shorts are nonregulation."

"Nonsense! How many times in your career, Colonel Byrd, have you muttered to yourself that we're working for a Mickey Mouse organization?"

David chuckled. "Okay. I get the point."

"But you were going to tell me why you're here." Blaylock opened a valve and drew a cup of black coffee from the machine as David briefed him on the task force he'd led at FAA and the intelligence community's concerns about terrorist manipulation of disgruntled passengers. By the time he'd finished, his host had placed a gigantic cup of incredibly good coffee under his nose, pulled on a Hawaiian print shirt, and settled on a stool on the opposite side of the counter.

"That's it?" John Blaylock asked.

"Pretty much," David replied. "Is there a magic answer?"

Blaylock snorted. "I don't even have a magic *question*."

"Personally," David prompted, "I can't see how the airborne Trojan Horse threat even relates to air rage."

"It doesn't," Blaylock responded. "Which is why they're concerned."

"Sorry?" David replied.

John Blaylock put down his cup and gestured grandly to the ceiling. "It's the conservation-of-paranoia principle. I assume you've not heard of it."

"No."

"Probably because I just made it up. Seriously, when the intelligence community finds two problems like this that don't connect? All their basic conspiracy sensitivities are jammed into high gear, their analytical juices start boiling, and they begin looking for a way to affirmatively answer the question 'Is that what they *want* us to think?' Especially when we're fighting a war."

"The 'they' being an unnamed, and unidentified . . ."

"Right. Shadowy force of enemy conspirators staying one step ahead of us."

"You believe that?"

"Of course not. Most of my career has been devoted

to coming back from some far-flung place, waltzing into the Pentagon or Langley, and reporting that the dark, pivotal, revolution-planning summit of drug chiefs in Colombia they'd whipped into a top-secret hurricane of alerts and probabilities had, in fact, been nothing more than one of the cartel members throwing a garden party for an old buddy from Lima. You know, Langley is racing to the White House for strike authorization and these guys are just tossing down tequila by the pool."

"That's what you did?"

"Yeah, I drank some tequila, but I didn't swallow. No, what I did was just amble around on layovers acting like a dumb-fool American with too much time on his hands getting to know the natives in their quaint and colorful costumes. Amazing what you hear when you listen. Provided you buy the *cerveza* . . . the beer . . . smile, and belch on cue."

"So, using your 'conservation-of-paranoia principle,' you see a connection here?"

John Blaylock squinted at him. "You're wondering if there's a connection between this thoroughly laudatory tendency of outraged passengers to want to pound the excrement out of airlines that still give hideous service and our blood enemies, the terror mongers who want to create a plot of empty real estate stretching from La Jolla to Kennebunkport that glows in the dark without benefit of electricity."

"Sorry?"

"Disappear in a nuclear cloud. The U.S."

"Oh. Yeah, something like that."

"No. Not a planned connection."

"Which leaves open . . ."

Blaylock screwed his face into a squint and held his hand to his forehead. "Well, duh, let me see now. Could it be an *un*planned connection?"

"Okay, obvious answer." David raised the palm of his hand. "Look, what *do* you see as a possible connection between the dissimilar dots in this murky picture?"

"A smokescreen. Let's say you're the replacement head terrorist and you're determined that your selected deity, Beelzebub, wants two hundred and eighty million Americans killed. You've got a big problem, because any operation you start is probably going to leak to the Americans through a thousand different channels and your hired rats brigade will end up caught or killed. The Americans are driving you nuts, in fact, because they've become so irritated over you blowing big holes in the sides of their Navy ships and supporting groups that use airliners to destroy American buildings and citizens that now they've gone and declared war and seem to know precisely what you're planning and where. While they're watching you that closely and chasing your trained rats all over the globe, you can't really move. So what do you do?"

"I have no idea."

"You plan to go after a lightly defended target, and then you sit tight, do nothing, and wait for your bastard-ized substitute for Allah to give you a diversion big enough to take everyone's attention away just long enough to slip through their security net."

"I'm not following this."

"You wait for something to happen newsworthy enough to obscure your preparations for the attack. While they're hysterical about happenstance B, which you did nothing to create even though they think you did, you launch plan A."

"And . . . an incident of passenger anger aboard a commercial aircraft could be what you're calling happenstance B. But how? Most air rage incidents just shake up the crew and lead to an emergency landing and arrests."

"You're examining the molecular structure of the bark and forgetting the forest."

"So, what's the forest?"

"Would you like some breakfast? Eggs, fried pig, that sort of thing?"

"Ah, sure."

"Scrambled, fried, boiled?"

"Scrambled. And . . . do you have a rest room?"

"Two of them. Use the small one there to your right."

"Thanks."

"Your cell phone is buzzing," Blaylock said.

David looked at his belt and unclipped the phone, punching a button to stop the alert. "Just a voice mail." He placed it on the counter and slipped into the bathroom.

When David returned, John Blaylock had already begun to assemble the necessary ingredients in an effortless display, breaking eggs in a bowl and discarding the shells with one hand as he talked. "You, yourself, just testified yesterday that if the causes of passenger fury weren't addressed, someday something far worse was going to happen."

"How did you . . . ?"

"Little thing called C-Span."

"Oh. Of course. Lucky you happened to see it."

David saw a brief smile cross John Blaylock's face as he glanced up, then back at the food before continuing. "The more I think about this, the more I think what DIA and CIA are worried about isn't what I was saying a minute ago. I mean, they *are* worried about unplanned diversionary incidents, but I'll bet you they're really about half panicked with this airborne Trojan Horse possibility. After the WTC attacks, an off-course mosquito gets their attention, and we're still flying fighter cover over D.C. Naturally they're paranoid, but as the old phrase goes, just because you're paranoid doesn't mean the bad guys *aren't* out to get you."

"I hear that."

"They don't know how a Trojan Horse might be coming, but they're convinced it is. They've probably received one or more alerts from operatives in the field. So they're jumping on everything and trying to figure out anything and everything that could lead to such a nightmare. I can speculate on all this openly for the moment since I don't have any immediate classified information on it. Just instinct and experience."

"Okay."

"It's what they do."

"And that's your world?"

Blaylock looked up and smiled. "Not really. I just spent a lot of years helping to keep the paranoia under control. You know, stand up at the appropriate moment, clear my throat loudly, and point out that the king is apparently naked as a jaybird." He turned several sizzling strips of thick, smoked bacon, dropped bread into a toaster, and poured the eggs into a buttered skillet before continuing. "One thing you need to keep in mind is the Intelligence community's equivalent of the uncertainty principle as reduced by Murphy's Law."

"And, let me guess. You're going tell me about this in detail, right?" David asked, feigning worry.

"Of course. The principle is simple: No matter how wild a theory is, what actually happens will be even more off-the-wall, unpredictable, unlikely, or improbable."

John Blaylock finished cooking the eggs and smoothly parceled them onto each plate, adding the bacon and toast before placing the plate in front of him.

"Impressive. My compliments to the chef."

"The chef thanks you, and accepts cash or gold bullion. A little Chablis, perhaps? I keep a case in the wine cellar."

"You have a *cellar* in here?"

"No. But it sounds wonderfully pretentious, doesn't it? Like sniffing a plastic cork. Actually, my wine cellar is one of the lockers outside. I've even got some screw-top wines in there, vintage"—he looked at his wristwatch—"four-thirty."

"No, but thanks. This is great."

There was a soft noise of a door opening to his left, and David looked over in time to see a raven-haired young woman with nothing on but a sleepy expression appear in the opening, rubbing her eye with one hand and holding the door with the other.

"Good morning, beautiful!" John Blaylock said, as if this was a daily occurrence.

"Mornin', John," she purred.

"Meet a fellow colonel, babe. David, this is Jill. Jill this is David."

Jill stopped rubbing her eye and looked slowly down at herself, as if only then fully registering the fact that she was nude. She looked up at David with a slightly embarrassed smile and nibbled a fingernail.

"Oh," she said quietly, waving at him with her fingers before disappearing back into the bedroom and quietly pulling the door closed.

"So," John Blaylock continued without missing a beat, "what else can I help you with?"

David inclined his head toward the bedroom. "Unless she has a sister in there, a cold shower will do fine."

"No sister. But you're welcome to jump in the bay. It's cold enough."

"May I ask how old you are, Colonel?"

"I could say 'old enough.'"

"But that would be corny, and . . ."

"Yeah, I'd never use such a line. I'm sixty-four, going on twenty-nine, and before you ask, son, I'll tell you the secret is nothing more than how you treat a lady."

"Right."

"You look stunned."

"Ah . . . forgive me for asking, but shouldn't you be sitting on the top of a mountain somewhere in Tibet teaching this to the world?"

NINETEEN

Judy Jackson wiped a bead of perspiration from her forehead. The temperature in the 747's cabin was far too hot, and she'd already asked the copilot to cool it down. The passenger complaints didn't impress her, but they were increasing.

"See that little eyeball thingy over your head, sir?" she'd asked the latest malcontent. "Why do you suppose we put those in here? Gee, let me see," she said, rolling her eyes to the ceiling and planting her index finger in her cheek as if trying to think deeply. "Oh, *maybe* to cool off passengers." She rotated the vent to the on position and focused it in the man's face with a smile. "See? Problem solved."

Now, however, it was Judy Jackson herself who was uncomfortable, and she pulled the interphone from its cradle to order the copilot to cool it down.

197

That mission complete, Judy moved to the privacy curtain separating the business and first-class cabins from coach and carefully pulled open a small peephole. As many as thirty or forty passengers were standing and milling around, none of them wearing smiles. She could see two of her flight attendants, Cindy and Elle, moving among them with drinks and smiles, but it was obvious the level of discontent was still high from the delay at Heathrow and the interference of the doctor in first class.

She felt a shudder of revulsion at the thought of having to deal with a cabinful of whining passengers. They were getting the tickets for next to nothing these days yet they always wanted more, and she was sick of them.

And this bunch was going to require heavy-handed control.

Two men, both dressed casually, spotted her standing at the head of coach and moved in her direction. Judy started to retreat behind the curtain, but changed her mind. They looked angry, but they couldn't be any more angry than she was about the unruly behavior of this motley collection of passengers.

"Are you the chief flight attendant?" one of the men began.

"I'm the lead flight attendant, yes." She pointed to the ceiling. "Did you men happen to observe that little seat-belt sign, and the fact that it was on?"

"Yeah, whatever," the second one said. "Look, lady, we've complained at least three times to your crew that it was too hot in here, and my wife's getting sick back there."

"Already taken care of, sir. Now both of you get back to your seats."

The two men exchanged glances.

"Did you two hear me? The seat-belt sign is on. Get in your seats."

"You know," the larger of the two men said, "I've just about had it with your snotty attitude."

She moved to within an inch of his face. "And I've just about had it with passengers violating federal law by refusing to follow my orders. GET . . . IN . . . YOUR . . . SEAT . . . NOW!"

"Come on, Jim," the second man said, pulling his friend away from the confrontation by his sleeve.

"You've bought yourself a huge complaint, woman," the man said, his face crimson.

"Spell my name right, if you can, *man*!" Judy snapped, reaching simultaneously for the PA handset and punching it on.

Okay, people, this is your lead flight attendant. Listen up. For those of you who are pretending not to notice the seat-belt sign or understand what it means, let me make it simple for you. It means get yourself in a seat and buckle up this instant. I know some of you think it's your birthright to whine and complain about everything, but this group has gotten to the point of ridiculousness. We ARE cooling the cabin down, so I don't want to hear another word about that. We ARE taking you to destination, so the subject of delays in London is closed. We ARE going to serve you a meal in a little while, PROVIDED I don't hear any more whining from anyone. And, you know, I couldn't care less what complaints you want to write when you're off this airplane, but in the meantime, I see anyone else standing in the aisle without my specific permission and I'll have you arrested and charged and prosecuted for interfering with a crew member when we reach Cape Town, and you won't like their jails. Now, you boys in front here, SIT DOWN! NOW!

A small chorus of catcalls and angry retorts rang through the coach cabin and Judy started to ignore them, but most of the passengers were complying and she was on a roll. She pointed to a younger man on his feet booing several rows away.

All right, smart ass, you in seat . . . twenty-six-F . . . I've got your name on my seating chart and you can consider yourself under arrest. And you in the red shirt? You've got three seconds to sit down and shut up. I'm serious, people. I'm not going to tolerate a riot.

Judy lowered the handset as she watched the remaining passengers slowly sit down, as many as a dozen in the aisles melting away until she could see a man in the next cabin waiting to return to his seat. He looked up at her, and even across the seventy or eighty feet between them she could see that same face—her father's face.

Judy felt a buzz of adrenaline. She replaced the handset and walked rapidly down the aisle, ignoring the hostile stares and muttered comments. She hurried through the divider between the second and third coach compartments and began scanning the faces in the section where he'd disappeared. Her father had been dead for a decade, and there were no names on the manifest remotely similar to his, so the man she was looking for couldn't be some long-lost uncle.

She remembered seeing the face through the boarding lounge window back in London, and realized she'd forgotten to search him out. This was obviously the same man, but where?

Judy stopped midway through the section, her eyes landing on the owner of the face, which up close looked somehow different.

"Excuse me, sir, could I ask your name?" Judy said, leaning over two other passengers who were glaring at her, their jaws set in anger.

The man looked up. "I thought you knew who everyone was?"

"I . . . yes, but what's your name?"

"None of your damn business!" the man snapped. "And before you give your little 'I'm going to arrest you' speech, you should know I'm a retired state police officer from Maryland."

"Okay, but please, I need to know if we're related."

The man stared at her in disbelief. *"What?"*

The fact that dozens of passengers were staring openly now grabbed her attention, and a small wave of self-consciousness flowed over her.

"You look like . . . a relative of mine."

"God forbid," he said, his words acidic. "But what's your maiden name?"

"Jackson."

"No relation, thank God."

"Is your family from New Jersey?"

The man rose from his seat, his hand on the seat back ahead of him. "I've got a dozen witnesses to the fact that you're harassing me, young woman. Leave me alone or I'll have *you* charged!"

Judy searched for an answer but could think of nothing to say. They had to be related. That was her father's face, as much as she'd hated him.

She backed away and turned, trying not to show the confusion she felt as she retreated up the aisle with his seat number playing in her mind.

Thirty-eight-B . . . thirty-eight-B . . .

She would look up the name. It had to be Jackson.

In the cockpit, the coastline of North Africa had come into view minutes before, swimming out of the indeterminate blue-gray haze of the horizon ahead and coalescing into a sharp dividing line between the blue of the Mediterranean and the tan-colored coastline, with the great, trackless wastes of the Sahara beyond.

The copilot glanced to his left, wondering whether to point it out, but Phil Knight was head down in the operations manual and the last time he'd pointed out something below to the captain, Knight's response had been curt and frosty.

Garth sighed inwardly and nudged a bit closer to the forward panel, almost hanging his chin over the edge of the glare shield as he listened to the continuous whoosh of the slipstream flowing past them at 81 percent of the speed of sound.

"Meridian Six," the Spanish controller said in a heavily accented, bored tone, "change now to Algiers Control, one-two-six-point-five."

Garth triggered the small transmit rocker switch on the back of the control yoke. "Roger, one-two-six-point-five. *Buenos tardes.*"

The Spanish controller merely clicked his transmitter in response, and Garth made the frequency change on the forward panel before triggering the transmitter again.

"Algiers, Meridian Flight Six checking in. Level, flight level three-seven-zero."

"Roger, Meridian Six, flight level . . ."

The remainder of the air traffic controller's words were suddenly drowned out by a loud bell coursing through the cockpit, momentarily disorienting Garth. There was a red light somewhere to his left, but he was too close to the forward panel to realize it was coming from one of the four engine fire handles.

A flurry of confused sounds broke out to his left as Phil Knight fought to be free of the operations manual in his lap, finally shoving it off to one side and letting it clunk to the floor.

"What?" Knight asked, thoroughly startled.

"I don't . . . Wait!" Garth leaned back, focusing on the fire handle, which was mounted with three other identical handles on the forward glare shield, each one capable of instantly shutting down its respective engine when pulled.

"We've got an engine fire warning on number-four engine!" Garth yelled over the noise as he reached to press the button that silenced the cacophonous warning bell.

Phil was staring at the fire handle with wide eyes. "Number four?"

"Yes." Garth looked out the right window, remembering he could barely see the outboard engine from the cockpit but unable to restrain himself from the effort. A sudden blur of motion caught his attention to the left, and he glanced over in time to see the captain's right hand snake out and grab the number-four thrust lever and pull it to idle. The 747 yawed immediately to the right before the autopilot could compensate.

"Phil . . . ," Garth began, but the captain's right hand was in motion again, this time moving to grab the number-four engine fire handle.

"NO!" Garth heard himself yelp. "DON'T PULL IT!"

Phil Knight was glowering at his copilot. "What the hell do you mean, 'don't pull it'? It's on fire!" Phil replied, completely shocked at Garth's intervention, yet holding back.

"No it isn't. That's a false alarm."

Phil Knight's hand was still resting on the T-handle. "What are you talking about, Abbott?"

"There's a long history of false fire alarms with that engine, Phil. Really. What you're seeing isn't real."

Knight was hesitating, trying to decide what to do as he cranked in left-rudder trim to compensate for the loss of thrust on the right wing. "How do you know that?"

"Because I know it's been doing this periodically for the past three months—giving false fire indications. I briefed you in London when we couldn't get the engine started. Remember?"

"I don't recall you saying anything about that."

"I DID! I sat right here and told you that number four has been giving false fire alarms while airborne and maintenance can't seem to find out why, and we're all . . . well, kind of unofficially carrying the engine along."

"Doesn't matter. A fire warning is a fire warning." Garth could see Knight tighten his grip on the T-handle, preparing to pull.

"Phil, don't do it! The second you shut down that engine, we'll be forced to make an emergency landing for nothing. Ever heard of the concept of supporting indications?"

Phil Knight turned toward the copilot. "Don't you dare take a superior tone with me, Abbott."

"I'm not, Phil, I just . . ."

"I'm the captain. When I want your goddamned advice, I'll ask for it."

"Phil, the company says you've got to listen to my advice. Look at the damned panel." The copilot pointed to the center instrument readout. "See the exhaust gas temperature gauge? It's reading normal. Fuel flow is normal. Rpms are steady. Everything's normal but the fire light."

Knight was looking, too. A hopeful sign, Garth concluded as he pulled the interphone handset from its cradle. "Let me check with the cabin and see if they see anything burning out there."

Phil Knight nodded without comment, his jaw set and his eyes remaining on the engine gauges and darting every few moments to the fire light, which was still glowing red and pushing at him to do something.

Garth lowered the handset within a half minute. "Nothing's different out there, Phil. They can see no fire or smoke. Nothing. It's another false alarm."

Phil Knight looked at Garth in confusion and sat back suddenly. "I can't fly on like this. Declare an emergency, Abbott. Ask them for immediate clearance to"—he glanced at the flight computer—"Algiers International."

"ALGIERS? No! Good Lord, Phil, Algiers is bad. They've got a big airport but it's a dangerous place, and I can guarantee you the company would string us up. Remember, they already know about this glitch."

"I said, get me the damn clearance."

"Phil, please listen. If you divert in there and declare an engine fire or shut it down, we're stuck in Algiers and the flight's over. We have no maintenance there."

"We have to land at the nearest suitable airport with an engine fire indication even if we don't shut it down, or have you forgotten the rules?" Phil snapped.

"Out here, *Captain*, you've got to temper the goose-stepping rules with reality. We've got Spain behind us, and Gibraltar, and other airports *much* better suited to us than Algiers if you just have to land and imperil both our careers, especially when the damn engine isn't burning!"

The sound of an interphone call chime interrupted them, and Phil Knight yanked the receiver to his ear.

"Yes?"

"Captain, the aircraft just kind of shuddered and threw us to the left. What's happening?"

"We've got an engine fire, and we're going to make an emergency landing in Algiers."

"Really? Are you going to tell them?" Judy asked.

"No. You do it," he said, terminating the exchange and replacing the receiver as he turned to Garth. "Algiers is the nearest suitable. There's no room for quibbling."

"There's no friggin' fire, Phil, and no reason for an emergency landing. Can't you understand that? THERE'S NO FRIGGIN' FIRE!" Garth was shaking his head and trying desperately to hang on to his temper. "Phil, listen to me. I know you attended the same required crew resource management courses I did. Don't you remember anything they taught you?"

"I said SHUT UP, Abbott. I listened to you, and I'm rejecting your suggestion."

207

But Garth saw him pull his hand away from the T-handle.

"You haven't been listening, Phil. The company *requires* you to seriously take into account what your first officer recommends, and your first officer recommends in the strongest terms that we NOT divert to Algiers for a nonexistent problem."

For a moment Garth considered taking over the aircraft and ordering Knight to let go of the yoke. But there was no way the captain would relinquish command, and all he'd accomplish would be an airborne fight for control. No, better to go along with whatever he decided, no matter how ridiculous.

He glanced down at the satellite phone control head. "Phil, we should call the company before we do anything drastic."

"Why? I'm in command."

"Why? Well, maybe you hadn't noticed, Captain, *sir*, but we both work for Meridian Airlines, not Phil Knight's Airline. They're going to be light years beyond pissed off if we divert. This is the international division, Phil. It runs differently from domestic."

Phil Knight remained silent.

"Hoo—kay!" Garth said. "Let the record read that I tried to advise you."

Phil snapped his head to the right. "What the hell does that mean?"

Garth looked at him in puzzlement. "What?"

"What's that 'let the record read' stuff?"

The copilot motioned to the overhead cockpit voice recorder microphone, then dropped his hand. "Nothing. Forget it." Garth pulled the satellite phone from its cradle and punched in the appropriate numbers, aware that Phil Knight was glaring at him. A voice from the Denver Operations Center came on the line, and he quickly summarized the problem. He could hear Judy Jackson in the background on the PA system downstairs telling the passengers they were diverting to Algeria's capital city.

"Say again, Flight Six," the Denver dispatcher requested.

"I say we've got a fire indication again on number four," Garth repeated. "We've got no supporting indications, but the captain feels we ought to declare an emergency and divert into Algiers."

There was a flurry of noises on the other end, and Garth could hear the phone being passed urgently to someone else.

Someone new came on the line, his voice carrying a hard and urgent edge. "This is the DFC. Whatever you do, don't divert into Algiers."

"Just a second, sir. This is only the first officer. I'm going to put Captain Knight on the line." Garth thrust the phone toward the left seat. "The director of Flight Control wants to talk to you," he said.

Phil snatched the phone from his hand with undisguised disgust. "This is Captain Knight." He listened, nodding several times before replying to whatever the DFC was saying. "But I still have a fire indication light up here."

Garth watched Phil's face growing beet red. He could hear a raised voice on the other end without making out what was being said, but the captain's end of the conversation was telling enough.

"No, I told you it's a full-blown engine fire warning. I was going to shut it down and Algiers is the closest suitable. . . . Yes . . . yes, I understand that, but the rules are clear. Okay. But I'm not flying this thing to Cape Town with a malfunctioning engine. Then where do you suggest I take it? Back to London?"

A loud string of words flowed from the other end at a higher volume, and Garth could see Phil Knight working hard not to wince. "Okay. If it doesn't go out, then we'll return to London." He sighed and nodded as he rubbed his temple with his free hand, carefully avoiding eye contact with Garth as he ended the call and disconnected the satellite phone.

"You just couldn't wait to call them, could you?" Phil said after several long, quiet moments had passed.

"God, Phil, I told you they'd hate the idea."

"Don't touch it again."

"Excuse me?"

Phil Knight turned to glare at Garth, the veins in his neck almost purple. "Don't touch the damned satellite phone again! Only I make the calls. Understand?"

"You want a clearance to turn around?" Garth asked.

"Yes," the captain replied.

Judy Jackson stood in the entrance to the first-class galley and surveyed the wide-eyed reactions of the passengers arrayed behind her throughout the coach cabin. She could see two of her flight attendants coming forward equally alarmed at her PA that one of the engines was on fire and they were making an emergency landing. Judy punched up the cockpit again, surprised to get Garth Abbott on the line this time.

"You want them in a brace position?" she asked.

"No, Judy. There's no fire and we're not going to Algiers, but apparently the captain does intend to go back to London, even though it's probably a false alarm."

"I've already told them it was *Algiers*," she protested.

"Well, tell them you were wrong," Garth said. "Or I'll do it if you . . ."

"No!" Judy snapped. "I'll do it. London, now?"

"I'm afraid so."

"Shit." She toggled the handset off then punched in the PA code.

Ladies and gentlemen, this is your lead flight attendant again. The captain tells me he's now extinguished the fire, and instead of going into Algiers . . . which I'm sure you'd all like . . . we're now going to turn around and return to

London. We're sorry for the inconvenience, but we've got to do things safely, and that's just the way it goes. We should have enough fuel to safely return to London.

She punched off the PA, stifling a grin. That little flourish of creative tension about fuel would keep them scared and obedient, she decided.

The reaction in the cabin was an immediate eruption of voices and questions and ringing call chimes, and Judy pointed at Elle and gestured toward the back of the cabin. They could handle the bitching without her.

TWENTY

"Colonel David Byrd?"

"That's me ... Hold on a second ...," David said into the cellular phone headset as he reached over to turn down the volume on the radio while simultaneously trying to keep his car from hitting the metal barrier dividing traffic moving in opposite directions on both sides of Highway 301.

The female voice on the other end was insistent. "Colonel, this is Senator Sharon Douglas, chair of the Senate Aviation Subcommittee."

He'd been daydreaming down the highway on the drive from Annapolis, when the chirp of the cell phone rudely dissolved an interesting little fantasy starring the naked woman in John Blaylock's bedroom. For a split second his mind pasted the senator into the same role—a silly juxtaposition, but it triggered an involuntary smile. Sharon Douglas was also a good-looking woman.

213

"Are you still there, Colonel?" she asked.

"Yes, ma'am. What can I do for you, Senator?"

"I need you to come tell my subcommittee the same thing you told the House subcommittee yesterday. My staff saw it on C-Span and told me your task force has done a remarkable job of putting this problem in perspective."

"Ah, angry passengers in the commercial airline world, you mean?"

"Absolutely."

General Overmeyer's warnings coursed into his head from several directions, triggering mental caution lights as she continued. He was already dangerously over-exposed on the Hill.

"Let me tell you why this is suddenly a major issue for me, Colonel Byrd. I just flew over here to London from Chicago yesterday on Meridian Airlines. Meridian Flight Six, a call sign that will live in infamy in *my* memory, at least. By the time I arrived, *I* was ready to take a crash axe and attack the crew with feral ferocity." She described what she called the "trip from hell," beginning with the cavalier treatment she'd received at the gate through all the delays they'd endured, finally ending with the rude behavior and burned-out attitudes of the crew.

"And all that with a ranking U.S. senator aboard?" David asked.

"*Oh*, yeah! It's out of control . . . David. May I call you David?"

"Certainly, Senator."

"Well, then, you should call me Sharon."

"Okay," David replied reluctantly, trying out the concept in his mind of referring to such a powerful woman by her first name. He had just begun to get used to dealing with congressmen, but senators were somewhere above the Joint Chiefs and unknowable for a mere colonel.

There was a pleasant chuckle on the other end. "Please call me whatever makes you comfortable. Just tell me you'll come testify."

"Senator, I'll be delighted to work with you and your staff . . . ," he said, as he maneuvered the car around a slow tractor-trailer rig hogging the fast lane.

"That's not what I want to hear," she interrupted.

A beat-up red pickup slowed suddenly in front of him, causing him to hit the brakes. He sighed and steered the car to the shoulder, braked to a halt, and put the car in park.

"Well," David said, "I'll need to get someone else on my task force to do the actual testifying."

"I see. And that would be a direct result, would it not, of someone in the puzzle palace yanking your chain hard in the last twenty-four hours, right?"

"Ah, let's just say that certain Air Force members in my chain of command were singularly unimpressed by the fact that an active-duty Air Force colonel appeared before the subcommittee."

"Nicely put," she said. "Look, I'll be back in

Washington in a few days. Why don't you let me take you to lunch and talk about this? I won't bite, but I do need your help. As you warned, David, this mess with the airlines is going to explode. My staff will call you to arrange a time and place."

"Okay."

"By the way, it's probably best not to tell your general we're talking."

"Believe me, I won't."

He heard the phone disconnect, punched his own phone off, and removed the headset, his mind on the conflict inherent in trying to please two masters at the same time.

ABOARD MERIDIAN FLIGHT SIX

Judy Jackson had barely moved into the first-class compartment when she heard the forward galley interphone ringing. She returned to answer it and found Garth on the other end.

"The fire light's out, Judy. We're turning back around for Cape Town."

"You're joking!"

"No" was the singular reply. "The fire light went out. We're going on."

"You're sure this time?"

"Hey, I'm just the first officer. Phil's making the decisions."

216

She stowed the handset and moved to the divider curtain, aware of an uncharacteristic knot in her stomach from having to deal with the out-of-control doctor in first class. Or maybe it was the clash with MacNaughton. It wasn't every day she had someone aboard as rude and confrontational as he.

Stuffy Brit! she thought. He'd been quiet ever since, but the effect of his verbal attack back in London had been to intimidate her from making her normal PA announcements, and that was irritating. She loved to get creative on the PA. Lying, indeed! It wasn't lying; it was creativity. So what if the Queen was in India or some-where else? Who cared? Passengers just wanted to hear a plausible explanation. She'd never worried about the truth.

Judy picked up the handset again and began to punch in the PA code, but hesitated. There was that unsettling feeling again that she was losing control. She closed her eyes and shook her head to expunge it. *This is B.S.*, she told herself. *I'm the queen of passenger control.*

Judy pushed in the last digit for the PA system as she watched the sea of coach passengers. The sound of the PA coming alive triggered yet another wave of move-ment as they raised their heads to look at the speakers. It was a sight that usually excited her, a confirmation of her power to raise three hundred heads anytime she pleased.

Okay, people, this is your lead flight attendant once again. Remember I told you we were returning to London because our pilots told me to tell you that? Well, put your British pounds away once more because it turns out they've changed their minds again in the cockpit. Now we're back to Plan A. We're going on to Cape Town as planned.

She paused, trying to think of something else to say, and was startled that the words weren't coming.

Ah, our engine problem was apparently cured, and for those of you who felt it was too hot, I've asked the pilots to boost the air-conditioning to its coolest level, so if we get you too cold, let one of us know.

Good! Judy thought. *The old crowd-psychology lessons are kicking in. Tell them they're too cold in order to psychologically cool them down.*

She replaced the handset, feeling off balance. *That was the strangest PA I've ever given,* Judy thought, feeling a small flush of embarrassment coloring her cheeks. The sound of the passenger call buttons being pushed again was already chiming through her consciousness.

Judy turned to go back to the first-class galley as Elle and Cindy pushed through the curtains in search of her.

"Judy, help!" Elle said.

"What?"

Cindy arched a thumb in the direction of coach. "Several people are asking if this is the same engine that needed maintenance in London, and I think they're scared."

"*I'm* scared, too, if it is," Elle added.

Judy crossed her arms and looked at them for several uncomfortable seconds. Elle was a strikingly tall blonde with angular features, and Cindy was a pretty five-foot-four compact brunette, but both of them now looked frazzled.

"You need to fix your eyeliner," Judy said to Elle, receiving a startled reaction in response.

"Judy!" Cindy pressed. "We have to know the answer. Have the pilots said anything?"

Judy licked her lips and glanced toward the stairway leading to the upper deck and the cockpit before looking back at Cindy. "No. I'll have to call them. Wait." She turned and moved to the interphone handset again, punching in the two-digit cockpit number and relaying the question before hanging up and turning back to the women who were now standing with two more crew members.

"Yes, it is the same engine, but it's an unrelated problem." She relayed the remainder of Garth Abbott's explanation about a false fire warning.

"So, all of you okay with that?" Judy asked, letting a little sarcasm slip into her tone.

Elle looked around at the others, then back at her. "*We're* okay with that, Judy, but these people—they don't believe us anymore. They're pretty upset."

"Didn't they hear my PA?"

Cindy was nodding. "Yes. But, Judy, after that guy said what he said back in London, they . . . I mean . . ."

"They don't believe a word any of us are saying," Elle added.

Judy saw the movement in the corner of her eye and looked around as Janie Bretsen pushed through the curtain from first class. "Judy?"

"Oh, hell. What do *you* want, Bretsen?"

"We've got some problems in the cabin."

Anger instantly replaced uncertainty, and Judy felt a tiny flash of gratefulness for the interruption. "I certainly do have problems, Bretsen, and they're all *you*. Get back to your seat."

"No. That physician . . ."

"I'll take care of my own cabin, thank you," Judy added.

"Dammit, listen to me!" Janie insisted, startling Judy and the others. "I'm assigned to this crew whether you like it or not. Dr. Logan isn't far away from coming unglued, Judy. I've been talking to him, and the man is hair-trigger angry for a reason that . . ."

"Who gives a rat's patootie? He gets out of that seat once more, I'll handcuff him."

"Cute, Judy. Good answer. Problem is, every time you come on the PA he tenses, as do most of them." Janie looked around quickly at Cindy and Elle, then back at Judy. "By the way, are we all female on this crew?"

Judy snorted derisively. "What's the matter, babe? Little bitty Janie hungry for a big, well-endowed man?"

"Oh, grow up, Judy. You know darn well what I

mean. Are there any male flight attendants on this crew with hand-to-hand training? Someone physically intimidating?"

Judy was standing with her hands on her hips glaring at Janie Bretsen. "Not unless one of my girls had a sex change operation on layover."

"Well," Janie continued, "I doubt seriously that any female's going to be able to contain some of the male passengers if they get physical. There are at least a half dozen really angry men in the second and third coach sections, if you hadn't noticed, and two of them, physically, are really big boys."

"So?"

"So, unless there's a deadheading crew aboard of barrel-chested male pilots who can bench-press a small car, and you can talk them into violating the new rules and coming out of the cockpit, it's all up to us if someone really loses control. Neither of the working pilots can come back and spend much time getting involved, just in case you'd forgotten that."

A shadow of concern passed across Judy's face. "So what do you expect them to do?"

Janie shook her head, glancing back over her shoulder quickly to make sure they weren't being overheard. "I don't know, but I've got a very bad feeling. Did you also know we have the chairman of the board of English Petroleum up there in three-F?"

"No."

"Well, he is. Mr. MacNaughton."

"MacNaughton . . . ," Judy replied, her lower jaw betraying her surprise.

"That's right. *And*, I'd say you've already encountered problems with attitude in coach I haven't seen, right?" Janie addressed the question to Cindy and Elle, who both nodded affirmatively.

"Okay. So what I'm saying is, I'd get that captain up to speed and get this quelled before it becomes a revolt."

Judy's hands had migrated to her hips again, her tone hardening. "Thank you very much, Professor Bretsen."

Janie had her arms folded as she met Judy's hostile stare head on. "You know, Jackson, I don't care whether you like me or not, but if things get rough this evening, we'd better be a team. And right now I'd say you don't even know the meaning of the word."

TWENTY-ONE

CAMP DAVID, MARYLAND
II:IO A.M. EDT

The President of the United States fairly burst out of the door of the main lodge at Camp David with two casually dressed men close behind, their progress tracked, monitored, and coordinated by several Secret Service teams arrayed around the grounds of the Presidential retreat.

Don Nederman, a senior CIA analyst, took the President's right flank while Ryan Jacobs, a deputy director of the FBI, kept pace on his other side.

"It's really beautiful out here, isn't it?" the President said as he turned up the lane toward one of the pathways into the woods.

"Certainly is," Ryan Jacobs said.

"All right, fill me in, guys. And by the way"—the President dodged a water-filled pothole in the road—"I appreciate your both coming up here on short notice. The helicopter ride smooth enough?"

"Absolutely," Jacobs answered.

"Up this way," the President said, pointing to an intersecting lane as he glanced at the two men. He'd assembled them into a special advisory team on terrorism months before with the job of filtering the daily avalanche of intelligence warnings, searching out ones that really mattered to the leader of the free world.

They were walking as fast as possible up a small incline, the President pushing himself, and slightly out of breath. "Okay . . . I read the alert you sent this morning, and I'm alarmed, too."

"And the Pentagon is wholly in sync with your worries?"

"Yes, sir."

"After all, they're in charge of pressing the battles."

"We have everyone's authority to brief you, Mr. President," he replied, stifling a flash of growing irritation and the desire to remind the President that he knew his job, thank you very much.

"Okay," the President was saying. "I understand we're watching middle Africa for some sort of airborne chameleon . . . What'd you call it, a Trojan Horse?"

"Yes, sir."

"But what I got from your message is that the broader intelligence community you guys represent isn't taking it seriously because they think the target has to be North America. Right?"

The two men exchanged glances and nodded.

"I want to make sure I understand this. We've . . . made two major, seemingly unrelated arrests in the past week in two different places, and you two think the arrests are not only related, but that they may be a setup to mislead us. Right?" The President topped a small rise and picked up his pace.

"Yes, sir," Ryan Jacobs responded as he struggled to keep up.

The President stopped suddenly and turned around, hands on hips. "Go ahead."

Jacobs and Nederman both stopped.

"Yes, sir," Jacobs replied. "This threat comes, we think, from some of the remaining overseas cells of the one we pretty much destroyed in Iraq last spring. Of course they've vowed revenge. The usual saber rattling and silly statements of defiance. But we also know this subgroup has some capability left, and we can't find them. They're well funded, and we think they're trying to create a diversion. But we think they've inadvertently tipped their hand that the attack they're planning is *not* going to be on our shores, but in Europe. That's the opposite of what they want us to think."

The President looked at both men in turn, then inclined his head down the lane. "Let's continue walking. Keep going."

Ryan Jacobs summarized the arrest in Canada of two men who had quietly sailed a forty-foot yacht into Halifax harbor and tried to clear customs at dockside with two thousand pounds of plastique explosive hidden in the hull, along with nearly a hundred pounds of biological lab apparatus.

"I figured that was just great police work," the President said over his shoulder. "You know, a sharp officer with a sixth sense?"

"We thought so, too, at first," Jacobs said, trying not to pant, and wondering how he'd ever make it through the FBI Academy physical training again in such lousy shape. "I think . . . we were all *supposed* to think so. Whew! Could you slow down a bit, sir?"

The President looked around and chuckled. "Going too fast?"

"The pace is all right for the CIA, sir," Nederman said, grinning.

"All right. I'm just a bit out of shape." Jacobs smiled back. "It happens to all headquarters types. Sir, the small things that made the Halifax officer suspicious could have been planted in order to accomplish precisely that result."

"They *wanted* to get arrested?"

"Not the two men. They were probably dupes. Couriers. But whoever packed the boat almost certainly arranged the little flaws that caught her attention just to make sure they'd be caught. For instance, there was something off-kilter about a couple of odd, poorly built hatches leading to the bilge area."

"Okay."

"The officer spotted the incongruous hatches and couldn't get a good answer out of the two men because we think they themselves didn't know they'd been set up. If she hadn't caught it, there would have been some anonymous phone tip, we think. They were both naturalized Canadians from Pakistan and ripe for manipulation, and we're sure they were set up."

"And the other incident?" the President asked.

"This one's even more interesting, sir. This was an aircraft part, a hydraulic landing gear piston with components for a nuclear trigger carefully hidden within and shipped to an aircraft parts company in Atlanta with a great reputation for quality. Whoever sent the parts knew the contraband would be discovered by the Atlanta company, and they were right. The FBI arrested the two green-card Japanese who showed up to take delivery, but we think they were dupes, too."

The President held up a hand to stop them again and pointed to a distant tree line. "An eagle. Just over the trees there."

The three men squinted in the glare of the noonday sun for a few moments before the President put his hands on his hips and turned to face the two men. "So, we've got terrorists sending shipments into North America which could be used in weapons of mass destruction, and the masterminds intend that those shipments will be intercepted. Why? To divert us from Europe?"

Ryan nodded. "If we take the bait and decide these two intercepted shipments mean they're attacking North America, the surviving splinter group knows we'll get frantic and deploy all our investigatory talent to prevent a U.S. attack. While we're scurrying around in a frenzy on our shores, we're far less likely to see a European attack coming, even with all the forces we've got deployed in the Middle East."

"Mr. President," Don Nederman interjected, "there simply isn't enough evidence to get the British, French, or Germans interested in this theory. They still think the U.S. is the real target. All the evidence we have seems to point over here, and that leaves these cutthroats an open field, provided they don't make any mistakes on the Continent and call attention to themselves before they're ready."

"How would they move a weapon of mass destruction into Europe?"

"Could be by rail through a weak border," Ryan continued, "or by air through a type of threat Langley's labeled a flying Trojan Horse, or even through incremental shipments over time through normal commercial means."

"What, like using FedEx to send in their anthrax?"

"Almost that bizarre, but we're convinced the method of choice *will* be a commercial airliner either pretending to be on a regular flight or actually on a regular flight, and we think this morning's alert that the threat will come in the next forty-eight hours from middle Africa dovetails perfectly. We think, in other words, that this is it. Imagine delivering a weapon by using one of thousands of regularly scheduled airline flights. No hijacking. No assaults on the cockpit. No using the airplane itself as a bomb but as a delivery system. No one aboard knows there's something deadly in the cargo hold or the wheel well. If someone on the ground is waiting for the flight, that operative could use simple radio control to explode the aircraft on approach over Rome, or Paris, for instance, or just pop a bagful of dust and unleash a thousand pounds of anthrax or something else equally terrifying. A nuclear weapon is possible, but I vote for a biothreat. Our satellites do a very good job of spotting fissile material from space whenever it's being moved, and they know it. If the warning is right, then we've got a chance to intercept this because we know what to watch for."

"And that would be?"

"Any commercial or private jet big enough to carry such a weapon. We need your immediate authority to track virtually everything coming north into Europe for the next few days, examine flights on the ground before departure, keep tight communication with all affected airlines, and look for anything out of the ordinary, no matter how slight. We have the Seventh Fleet in the Mediterranean as a buffer, but we need a presidential finding."

The President looked at each man in turn and nodded. "You've got it."

TWENTY-TWO

Judy Jackson pushed through the curtains into the first-class cabin and walked quickly to the small closet at the pointed front end of the 747's main deck. She pretended to search for something there, then reclosed the door and started walking slowly back, catching the eyes of as many passengers as possible as she approached the passenger she'd tangled with before over the PA. She had noticed his briefcase was sometimes beneath the seat in front, but more often on his lap, and the image was making her suspicious.

Janie Bretsen was working away on something with a pen and paper in her window seat, a small set of reading glasses balanced on her nose, and she looked up as Judy approached.

Brian Logan had spotted her as well and the pupils of his eyes retracted to mere pinpoints when he saw who

230

was approaching him She could almost feel the animosity radiating from him. Janie had said he was on the verge of losing control, and his leather briefcase was on his lap again, his hands resting on it protectively.

"Would you like me to put that in the overhead for you?" she asked as nicely as she could force herself to sound.

"No," he replied, his eyes still boring into hers.

Judy leaned over slightly toward him. "Doctor, I'm sorry we got off on the wrong foot back there, but surely you can understand my reaction when you grabbed the PA microphone."

There was no response, and Judy felt a strange crawling sensation up her back.

"So, ah . . ." she continued, ". . . I just wanted to apologize for being rough with you. Of course, you were pretty rough with me, but . . ."

"Leave me alone!" Brian Logan snapped. "Go arrest the rest of the passengers."

Judy straightened up, resentment clashing with caution, and officiousness winning out.

"*Doctor* Logan. Since you won't respond to an apology, we have one more item to resolve."

"We've got a lot more than one item to resolve," he replied, his voice barely audible.

"I'm going to have to ask you to show me the contents of that briefcase."

He looked down at the briefcase, his face reflecting puzzlement, then looked up at her again. *"What?"*

"Your briefcase. I need to see what's inside."

"Why?"

"Because I have the right to ask, and I'm . . . concerned, because you keep holding on to it."

"Go to hell!"

"Sir! I am in charge of this cabin . . ."

"You touch this briefcase and I'll break your hand in some very effective places," Brian said through clenched teeth, snapping off his seat belt. He stood and glared at her as she backed up. Heads were turning all over first class, and she could see Robert MacNaughton looking alarmed in his window seat.

"GET OUT OF MY FACE!" Logan bellowed, causing her to wince involuntarily. At least six other first-class passengers were turning around in their seats to see what the commotion was this time.

Brian was holding the briefcase by its handle. He raised it up now as he snarled at her. "Over my dead body will you or any other employee of this godforsaken excuse of an airline touch this or anything else I own."

Judy retreated quickly back through the curtains to the galley at the back of the first-class section. She thought she saw Logan sit down again as she fled, but she half expected him to come bursting through the curtains after her. She felt a sudden need to be anywhere *but* close to first class.

I'll do a coach walk-through, she decided.

Judy tried to get her hands to stop shaking as she checked herself in the galley mirror. She turned and headed back into coach, still feeling the waves of fury radiating from first class and unprepared to find two of her flight attendants standing wide-eyed in the alcove with Janie Bretsen.

"What is this, a convention?" Judy Jackson snapped. Elle and Cindy moved back in response, looking guilty. Janie, however, stood her ground, speaking in a low voice.

"I saw that gratuitous confrontation," she began.

"So?" Judy replied, as if it made no difference. She could feel herself flushing all over again.

"Well, *if* I were really a management flight attendant, I'd fire you on the spot for the most obnoxious display of hostility I've ever witnessed in flight, starting with your incredibly stupid announcements and threats, and ending with that completely unnecessary confrontation."

"You go to hell," Judy replied, her teeth gritted, not expecting Janie to start nodding.

"That's roughly what he told you, yes. And if there *were* something lethal in that briefcase, you just invited him to use it before we can find a way to take it from him. Brilliant!"

Judy started to move past, but Janie stepped in her way, blocking the path to coach. Judy shoved her out of the way, her greater height and weight pushing Janie off balance. Janie exhaled sharply as she fell back against door 2-Left, but Judy didn't turn around.

There was an even more visceral mood of hostility in coach, and Judy could see it in the eyes of the passengers who watched her coldly as she passed. Not hatred, as when the doctor looked at her, but an underlying discontent wrapped in obvious distrust.

This is all his fault, Judy told herself with the image of a snarling Brian Logan still filling her mind and destabilizing her instincts.

All her girls were retreating from her advance. She could see Elle move through the middle galley and peek out from the other aisle as she walked slowly through, trying to use her practiced flight attendant smile on those who met her eyes, regardless of the upset and fury she saw on their faces.

It was the usual passenger load of widely varying ages and ethnicity, some well dressed, others not, women wearing dresses, women wearing jeans, one woman in a halter top that barely contained her substantial breasts and a pair of shorts that revealed legs marred by varicose veins. A damned bus station in the air. No, worse, she decided. One of the few who had smiled at her in London was avoiding looking at her now: a man in a rumpled business suit with the baldest head she'd ever seen. He was sitting next to a mousy woman in a white sari who was busily knitting at a furious pace. Two wide-eyed little girls were sitting next to them.

Judy spotted the young Asian couple she'd noticed earlier, the woman wide awake, the husband in a deep sleep. She'd noticed how the woman always watched her whenever she walked through the cabin.

She passed the mid-galley and moved into the second

section of coach again, feeling the hostility of the stares. It was like a wave of anger pushing her back, and she decided she'd gone far enough.

Something caught her eye to the left, and she turned to see a child carrier hooked on a magazine rack on the bulkhead in front of a young mother's seat. A small infant was asleep inside as the mother watched sleepily.

"What the heck is this contraption?" Judy asked no one in particular as she leaned down to find out how the child carrier was suspended.

There was movement from the mother, who leaned forward and pointed to the bulkhead. "I found a way to suspend it the way the other airlines do."

Judy looked at her. Late twenties, two kids, obviously tired, and obviously ignorant of the rules.

"You can't do this!" Judy pointed to the child carrier. "Take that down, right now."

Karen Davidson looked puzzled. "One of your flight attendants helped me with it, and I'm not going to use it on takeoff or landing."

"This is ridiculous," Judy said, more loudly than she'd planned. Several other passengers were looking in her direction now, wondering what the commotion was about. "Take it down! Otherwise, one bump of turbulence and your child will end up dumped on the floor."

Karen Davidson took a deep breath and sat up straight. "Excuse me, but have you noticed, perhaps, that we're in stable flight? There's no chance this is going to fall off. I've got it firmly attached."

A man in the adjacent aisle seat touched her arm, and Judy jumped.

"What?"

"What are you gonna do? Arrest the baby? Leave the poor woman alone, okay?"

"Are you with her?" Judy asked, gesturing to Karen.

"No, but . . ."

"Then mind your own business. This is a crew matter."

The man sat back in angry silence as more heads turned in coach. Judy was aware of the hardening glares and rising indignation. But this was her cabin, dammit, and she wasn't going to let these people boss her around any more than she would let Janie Bretsen try to tell her what to do.

She turned toward Karen and leaned forward.

"Take . . . the . . . carrier . . . off . . . the . . . wall! Understand?"

"No, I do *not* understand!"

"I'm the authority here!" Judy snapped. "Get that thing off the wall now! How would you like it if I came into your living room and screwed a new drink holder into your coffee table?"

"What?"

"You heard me. This is about as boorish a thing as I've seen a passenger do."

"What, trying to take care of my child? What the heck does that have to do with living rooms and coffee tables?" Karen said, shaking her head.

"Hey, sheriff," a male voice called out from several rows behind. "All of us are telling you to leave her alone!"

Judy ignored him as she leveled a finger at Karen. "Take it down, or I'll do it for you."

"Hey!" Another male voice rang out and Judy glanced across the aisle from Karen to face the glare of a middle-aged man in jeans and a sweater who was sitting next to the woman's older child.

"What are you, her husband?"

"What the heck difference does that make?" he asked. "That's a sexist question, but I'm telling you, if I *were* her husband, I'd probably be at your throat right now. Leave the woman alone. There's nothing wrong with that child carrier being there. What the hell's the matter with you?"

"Regulations are the matter with me," Judy said, turning back to Karen. "This is your last warning. Get it off of there," she ordered, balling her left fist and banging it hard against the bulkhead for emphasis as she barked, "NOW!"

At that same instant she felt the bulkhead vibrate violently. The child carrier was coming loose before her eyes, catapulting the baby inside off her tiny mattress. She saw the mother's eyes widen in the same instant as Karen Davidson lunged forward, her hands barely missing her falling child.

There was a simultaneous blur of motion from the right as the man across the aisle leaped in front of her, his arms outstretched, catching her baby in midair, his body impacting the edge of one of the seats with a dull thud as the empty child carrier clattered to the floor.

Judy felt herself instinctively dropping to one knee to help. She saw people standing all over the cabin and heard seat belts clicking open.

The man who'd caught Karen Davidson's baby daughter was on his side, the little girl held safely in the air for her mother to take as he turned with a painful grimace and held his chest. The young mother was on her knees as well, holding her daughter and trying to check on her rescuer at the same time. Judy became aware of voices and scuffling feet and movement and shouts and suddenly realized they were all aimed at her.

She knelt down and tried to help. There was motion all around, and Judy looked up to find a sea of angry faces closing in on her. She stood, but they weren't backing down.

"Get in your seats!" she ordered.

"Screw you!" someone snapped back.

The crowd pressed forward, causing her to retreat instinctively. Judy backed into the alcove between the coach sections and reached for the interphone handset, but there was at least one set of hands trying to grab her, and she kept retreating.

"GET BACK! DON'T YOU TOUCH ME!" she shouted.

"HEY! HOLD IT RIGHT THERE!" a large man in a business suit ordered. There were other shouts as they moved forward, pure rage showing on their faces, and Judy's instincts suddenly dictated retreat. She turned and broke into a run for the base of the stairway to the upper deck, incredulous that there was a host of running footsteps behind her accompanied by angry shouts to stop.

She shot past a galley, clipping one of her girls in the process, as an angry male voice reached her from behind.

"HEY, BITCH! COME BACK HERE AND FACE US!"

Judy rounded the bottom of the stairs and took them two at a time, turning at the top and racing forward through the upper deck to the cockpit where she yanked up the interphone and jammed her hand into the cipher lock.

"Captain! Let me in!"

She could hear voices and footfalls behind her coming up the stairs.

"What?" Phil's voice queried on the interphone. She knew the questions he was supposed to ask.

"No one is forcing me, no one is with me. Check your video screen. My hand scan is complete. LET ME IN!"

She heard the door locks coming open and pushed inside, slamming it behind her, taking time to make sure the heavy lock was in place.

"What on earth is going on with you?" Phil Knight asked as she turned around toward him, a wild look in her eyes.

"They're rioting down there!" she stammered, deciding that this wasn't the time for full disclosure of the little accident that had sparked the commotion.

"What do you mean, 'rioting'?" the captain asked, his face draining of color as Garth looked around from the copilot's seat, equally startled.

"There's an angry mob that chased me all through the airplane from coach."

"*Chased* you? I don't understand," Phil said.

She looked at him and shook her head, tears of anger and frustration forming in the corners of her eyes. "Neither do I, Captain . . . but you've got to stop them. They won't follow any of my commands. They're literally out of control."

"What . . . what are they angry about?"

"About the delays in London, the temperature, the . . . the thing about turning around in flight. Hell, I don't know."

Garth pushed his seat back and started to unsnap his seat belt then stopped, looking at Phil. "If it's not a takeover attempt, should I take a look?"

"Be careful of those bastards!" Judy snarled, her teeth clenched as she looked at the copilot. "They're what I have to fly with all the time these days. Animals, bitching about everything. I can't believe they attacked me."

"Judy, you didn't say anything about being attacked," Garth began.

She looked startled and tossed her head as if dismissing

the question. "It was just as good as an attack. Damned jerks chasing me down the aisles!"

Phil looked over at the copilot and said nothing until Garth pointed to the back. Phil nodded and waited until the copilot had cleared the door. He looked at the PA handset then and hesitated. "You . . . think I need to say something?"

"PLEASE!" Judy replied, anger coloring her voice. "Maybe they'll listen to a man."

Phil Knight pulled the handset from its cradle and punched in the digits connecting him to the PA.

This is the captain. If there are any of you who have any doubt that your crew is legally in control, you'd better think again. When one of our flight attendants tells you to do something, that's the law. Those of you who just chased our lead flight attendant through the airplane . . . if you don't sit down immediately I really will have you arrested when we arrive.

He replaced the handset, waiting for fists banging on the cockpit door and wondering what he'd do if it happened, but it was silent on the other side of the door, and the video screen showed no one waiting.

Garth punched up the various cameras, noting the number of people on their feet, talking in groups throughout coach.

"Maybe that did it," Phil said.

"I see no threatening activity back there," Garth

added. "But if they weren't already in revolt, your PA should do the trick."

Phil Knight shot his copilot a withering glance as Judy's voice broke through the silent exchange.

"That's it! That's just fricking it! This stupid airline doesn't pay me enough to deal with damned riots. I'm staying in here." Judy replied. "I'm so mad I could spit."

"Stay, then," Phil said, his voice flat, his eyes still boring into Garth.

TWENTY-THREE

Robert MacNaughton watched Brian Logan's reactions
carefully after the lead flight attendant retreated from the
first-class cabin. He saw the doctor look at his briefcase
as if seeing it for the first time, then open and close it
several times, finally opening it and moving something
around inside before securing it again. Logan placed the
briefcase in his lap again, tapping his fingers on its leather
surface.

As MacNaughton watched, one by one, three flight
attendants came into the cabin briefly, each of them
looking specifically at Logan before departing. An off-
duty flight attendant who'd introduced herself as Janie
Bretsen returned and settled into her first-class window
seat again. MacNaughton noticed her casting furtive
glances in the doctor's direction.

So why am I concerned? he asked himself. *They'll reach*

Cape Town ready to write three hundred furious letters, and at worst, they'll have to restrain the poor doctor.

Yet, the feeling persisted.

Obviously he'd made a poor decision to take a commercial flight to begin with—a mistake he would not make again, no matter how important the meeting was.

Except for the Concorde. As long as British Air could keep the Concorde flying, he had decided he would be a passenger.

Somewhere behind first class, MacNaughton could hear raised voices, and then running footsteps. He turned to his left in time to see Brian Logan leap to his feet and leave his briefcase behind as he rushed out of sight toward the commotion. MacNaughton hesitated, telling himself there was nothing he could contribute, but the pull of raw curiosity was strong enough to get him to his feet. He moved to the rear entrance to first class and watched as Logan moved toward the back.

MacNaughton glanced around casually, noting the physician's briefcase unattended on his seat. He moved quietly forward as he glanced around to make sure no one was watching, and leaned over, flipping up the two catches on the leather case. He lifted the lid carefully, noting several file folders and what appeared to be a pack of airline tickets in the upper pocket.

The lower section was empty except for a small pewter canister, which he lifted. It was fairly lightweight, and he tried the lid, which came open easily, revealing nothing inside but some sort of gray powder.

Robert MacNaughton reclosed the container and the briefcase and left it in place on the seat, his mind chewing over the question of what he'd just seen.

Judy Jackson had already been fleeing up the staircase to the 747's upper deck when Brian Logan emerged from the first-class section. There were three men chasing after her, and he now caught the third one by the arm.

"What happened?" Brian asked.

The man inclined his head toward the absent lead flight attendant. "That rancid woman dumped a baby on the floor back there and could have killed it," he said.

Brian hesitated as the man continued up the stairs, then moved aft to see for himself. He entered the rear of the coach cabin just as someone called for a doctor.

"I'm a doctor," he said, his eyes falling immediately on a man lying in the floor in obvious pain. Brian dropped to one knee to examine him.

"What happened?"

Voices from over his shoulder answered the question.

". . . hurt himself trying to save this woman's baby from hitting the floor."

". . . think he has a broken rib or two . . ."

". . . hit the bottom of that chair leg, I think."

"How're you doing?" Brian asked.

"It . . . hurts," the man said, his eyes coming open. "I'll survive, but . . . Are you a doctor?"

"Yes."

"Okay. I can breathe, man, but it hurts. Broken rib, maybe." The effort of the analysis caused the man to grimace again as Brian repositioned him and opened his shirt, carefully probing his chest and side as more voices filled in the story of Judy Jackson's wall-pounding officiousness.

"Is your child okay?" Brian asked Karen Davidson, who nodded before, answering, "Yes. He caught her in midair. She would have hit the floor headfirst."

Brian tried to focus on doing all the appropriate things for the injured man, relieved there was no evidence of internal bleeding or a compound fracture or anything that would require the immediate ministrations of his medical expertise. Having made sure the passenger was as comfortable as possible, Brian stood, his mind absorbing the outrage of the people around him, focusing like a crystalline lens on Judy Jackson.

"I'll check on you later," he said absently, pushing forward and striding up the aisle. He found the staircase and moved to the top landing three treads at a time, brushing past the three men he'd seen scrambling after Jackson, all of whom were standing empty-handed near the upper-deck galley wondering what to do.

The cockpit door was ahead, and as he approached it, the door to the rest room opened and a pilot with three stripes on each shoulder and an appropriately dour expression emerged.

"Hey! Captain!" Brian barked. The pilot froze in his tracks and turned, scanning the approaching angry customer as he held up his hand.

"I'm not the captain. I'm the copilot."

Brian pushed into the small alcove, trapping the pilot between him and the closed cockpit door.

"Do you have any idea what's going on here?"

The copilot snorted and rolled his eyes. "Yes, sir, I think I know what's going on here. But I'm not the captain, so I can't control it," Garth Abbott said. "May I ask who you are?" he added.

Something in the copilot's voice stopped Brian in his tracks. This was the enemy, but on a deeper level there'd been a sudden flash of kinship he could neither explain nor place, and he realized he was actually extending his hand to the copilot.

"I'm Dr. Brian Logan. Thanks to your lead flight attendant, there's an injured man downstairs. I've just been treating him. He's got several fractured ribs."

Brian heard his own words, metered and calm, as if they were coming from someone else. He wanted to scream and snarl and gesture, but if this was an ally . . .

The copilot sighed and shook his head. "She's a real piece of work, that one. What'd she do?"

Brian gave a quick synopsis before pointing to the closed cockpit door. "I think she's hiding in the cockpit."

"Could be. What can I do for you, Doctor?"

Brian hadn't expected that question. For a moment, he realized he hadn't a clue what the answer should be. He wanted what they couldn't provide. He wanted Daphne back. But in lieu of the impossible, he knew what he craved was mindless revenge. He wanted them bankrupt for what they'd done to him . . . to his wife, he corrected himself. He wanted their money, their corporate life, and complete and utter public condemnation of them. He wanted people to be ashamed that Meridian had ever been called an airline. He wanted the captain who'd killed Daphne to be fired, prosecuted, and ruined.

And here was one of the enemy's pilots *asking* him what he wanted.

Brian's jaw came open two or three times as he tried to spit out the venom sloshing in his mind, but it wouldn't come on cue.

"Doctor?" The pilot prompted him again.

"I want that woman to get back here and apologize to everyone."

Garth stood stock still for a few seconds, then began nodding. "Understood."

"There's not a passenger on this aircraft who hasn't had it with your crew, especially that idiot."

"You mean Jackson?"

"If that's her name."

"It is."

"So where is she? Hiding in the cockpit?"

He nodded. "Essentially, though she says she's too disgusted with everyone to come out."

"That bitch needs to be fired," Brian said, pointing again toward the closed cockpit door as the copilot scratched his chin. "Are you aware of what she did?"

"Yes, but the captain isn't, and . . . I think he needs to hear all this from you firsthand." Garth glanced at the cockpit cipher lock, then back at Brian. "Doctor, would you take that empty seat in the first row back there, please. I . . . can't talk to the captain with anyone standing here."

Brian complied as Garth raised the handset and asked for entry before sliding his hand in the appropriate position in the cipher lock.

"Who's with you? I can't see anyone on the monitor," Phil was saying.

"No, he's seated, as per the procedure, Phil. But I think you need to talk to him."

"You're sure?"

"Yes. You need to hear this."

The sound of the locks unlatching reached his ears and Garth turned and nodded to Brian Logan to come forward, motioning him into the cockpit before following and securing the door.

A startled Judy Jackson looked up from the copilot's seat with a trapped expression. "Phil, Judy has created a near revolt downstairs and didn't bother to tell us what really happened, but one of our passengers here will give you the straight story."

"You!" Judy said, rising from the seat, her eyes on Brian Logan.

"Sit!" Brian ordered, pointing at her as he turned to the startled captain in the left seat, who was alternately looking between Brian and Garth's surprised expression.

"Abbott, what's this about?"

"Tell him what happened, Doctor," Garth said.

Brian Logan described what had happened below as he watched Phil Knight turn and glare at Judy Jackson.

"Something you forgot to tell me, Judy?"

"It wasn't important," she replied.

"Captain," Brian continued, "I want you to arrest this woman for assaulting a passenger, after you have her apologize on the PA. And I want your public apology as well for never talking to us and for all the other ridiculous things that have happened on this flight."

Phil looked back over his shoulder at Brian, his face a scowl. "You don't make demands of me, I want you out of my cockpit."

"No, Captain," Brian replied, his voice hardening, "you're going to force this bitch to apologize."

Phil laughed nervously. "Who the hell do you think you are?"

"I have the authority of three hundred angry passengers who've had it with this lousy excuse of an airline, and are tired of being abused and lied to and fed garbage."

Phil tried to pull himself up in the seat as he glared at Brian Logan. "I said, get out of my cockpit!"

"No! Not until you apologize on that PA and force her to apologize publicly."

Garth placed a hand on Brian Logan's shoulder, but the physician shrugged it off and leveled a finger in the captain's face as Judy shook her head in disgust.

"In effect," Brian said, "you're no longer in command of this airplane, *Captain*. We are! Your passengers are in charge, and we're demanding immediate apologies, and the arrest of this woman."

There was a derisive snort from the copilot's seat and Judy rolled her eyes. "Yeah, like you're going to get anything but a decade in prison for making hijacking demands. You know what we do with hijackers these days?"

Phil Knight caught his copilot's eye. "Get this man out of here," he snapped, motioning to Brian. Once again Garth tried to put his hands gently on Brian's shoulders, but this time the doctor whirled around and raised a fist in the copilot's face.

"Don't touch me again!"

The copilot backed away, his hands in the air, his mind on the crash axe mounted on the inside wall of the cockpit just inside the door.

Brian sensed the change in Garth's attitude and began moving quickly past him toward the cockpit door. He put his hand on the door handle as he watched the three of them warily. "What's it going to be, Captain?" he asked. "Time's up."

Phil forced himself to swivel around in his command

chair and make eye contact with the man in the back of his cockpit. His heart was racing, and he struggled to stay calm.

"Look, she's going to stay up here, okay? I'm confining her."

"You're *WHAT?*" Judy snapped. "I'm not the problem here, buster!"

"Shut up, Judy," Phil replied.

"Go to hell, flyboy," she shot back, tossing her head and folding her arms.

"She's out of the way," Phil said. "But no one's apologizing on the PA. Now get the hell out of my cockpit!"

For several tense seconds they stared at each other. Brian nodded at last. "For now. But you will apologize." Garth opened the door for him.

"What was your name again?" Phil asked, trying to regain a modicum of control.

The effect on Brian Logan was immediate. He turned back to the front, partially closing the door behind him as he stared at each of them in turn, his expression only semirational.

"My name is Dr. Brian Logan. By the way, why don't you get on your phone and ask your corporate headquarters who Daphne Logan was?"

He turned and slammed the door behind him.

The cockpit was silent again except for the hum of the instruments and the myriad cooling fans. Judy exhaled first, inclining her head toward the door.

"You see what I've had to deal with? I can't believe you were mollycoddling him!"

"What did that mean?" Garth asked. "Ask about Daphne Logan?"

Judy was shaking her head. "I have no idea."

Garth was watching Phil Knight, waiting for the inevitable torrent of blame as the captain shook his head, his voice strained. "Nice move, Abbott, bringing a wild man to the cockpit. The company will probably fire you for that."

"I didn't know he was unbalanced."

"That's no excuse."

TWENTY-FOUR

WASHINGTON, D.C.
12:05 P.M. EDT

The loud chirping of his cell phone prompted an immediate apology as David Byrd reached for the offending instrument he had thought was in vibrate mode. The three other men around the table—all FAA management-level friends—waved it off as he punched the on button and said hello.

"How soon can you be at NRO headquarters?" an instantly recognizable male voice blared from the other end.

"Colonel . . .*Blaylock*?" David asked.

"Who else would be calling you from my phone? Please answer the question."

"In an hour or so, but . . ."

"Good. It's eleven-thirty now, and it'll take me ninety minutes. I'll meet you in the main rotunda at one."

"Wait! Why?"

"Why?" Blaylock sounded incredulous.

"That's right. Why?"

"You really want me to have to *shoot* you?"

"Of course not."

"Then don't ask. Trust me. This a very nonsecure line, and I'm a very nonsecure reservist."

"So I'm beginning to understand."

"Ah, good. Insults. The bedrock of a good friendship. See you in ninety minutes."

David punched off the phone and looked up to find two of his three colleagues also engaged in cell-phone conversations.

"Gotta go?" the other one asked.

"Not yet," David replied, shaking his head and smiling at John Blaylock's bull-in-the-china-closet style. "First, I'm going to finish my coffee."

John Blaylock was waiting when David Byrd entered the NRO's lobby, but the newly scrubbed and uniformed version of the man he'd met dockside in Annapolis looked wholly different.

A few hairs out of place, but within standards, David mused to himself as Blaylock stowed his flight cap and pointed to the security desk, deflecting the inevitable questions until they were inside and under the escort scrutiny of a senior analyst named George Zoffel.

"So, can you tell me now without risk of homicide?" David asked.

"I'm not sure," he said, turning to Zoffel. "Are these halls secure, George?"

Zoffel smiled and nodded without comment.

"Why are we here, John?" David pressed.

"Because you want to know about the state of alert we're in looking for a Trojan Horse, and because you need to know how commercial aviation fits into that twenty-four-seven search, and you need to see what the satellites are seeing."

"Something's up?"

"Something's always up, David."

Zoffel stopped in front of a door unlabeled except for a number, passed a card through a cipher lock reader, and motioned them in when it swung open.

"And this would be?" David asked.

"This would be very hard to explain to the civilian world," Blaylock quipped, "but despite its astronomical cost of several billion, Georgie here can sit us in front of an array of monitors and call up real-time satellite pictures of most of the fissile material on planet Earth."

George Zoffel was nodding.

David followed them into a room bisected by a curved table with a half dozen comfortable swivel chairs facing an equally curved wall of large liquid crystal screens. The table itself was really a control console housing a dizzying array of switches and push buttons and keyboards.

George Zoffel ran his hands over the panel with experienced ease, punching in authorization codes and responding to several prompts, including having to place his hand in an identification scanner. The screens came to life, thirteen of them showing a dizzying variety of views and maps.

"Our current European scan array," Zoffel said, giving him a quick briefing on the constant scan for fission-able nuclear fuels and the impossibility of detecting raw hardware such as nuclear triggers from space. "But what we also do is keep a gimlet eye on all commercial shipping. Airlines, ships, trains, even trucks, to the extent we can, as they move through high-risk choke points. Much of the evaluation is done by high-speed computers using very sophisticated algorithms we've developed, but they're anything but foolproof. For instance, we can't see a biological or chemical bomb generically from space, but we *can* see suspicious movement or shipments, and we're constantly cross-checking commercial shipping and known commercial flights against flight plans and known legitimate shipments."

"This is needle-in-a-haystack territory, then," David observed.

"Absolutely. And now it's getting worse. We've got a full staff working around the clock looking for that needle." He glanced at Blaylock. "Top-secret crypto clearance active for Colonel Byrd?"

"Confirmed." John Blaylock nodded.

"Okay. Twenty minutes before you gentlemen walked in, we were directed to divert as many of our resources as possible to watching sub-Saharan Africa for a possible terrorist incursion. That's a major shift. Before today, the big emphasis was our shores."

"Where'd the directive come from?" John Blaylock asked as he studied the world map on one of the screens.

"The White House. We've been told to expect a major terrorist attack on a major European city within forty-eight hours."

IN FLIGHT ABOARD MERIDIAN FLIGHT SIX
6:09 P.M. LOCAL

Phil Knight looked out over the southern expanse of the Sahara and tried to convince himself the remaining hours to Cape Town would pass quickly. He'd purposefully said nothing to his copilot for the past ten minutes, but Garth Abbott could see his eyes darting constantly to the large center instrument display as he watched the gauges for number four. He knew Phil Knight was waiting and probably hoping for any indication that he'd been right all along and number four was bad.

"It's steady as a rock, Phil," Garth said, deliberately throwing the fact in Knight's face. Predictably, there was no response.

Judy Jackson was silent as well and sitting like a dour sphinx in the jump seat behind the captain. She was still shaken by what had gone on in the cabin.

The interphone chime sounded, and Garth reached

for the handset when he realized no one else was going to answer.

"Is this the captain?" a stressed female voice asked.

"No. This is the copilot. Who's this?"

"Uh, Cathy, in coach." *She sounds agitated*, he thought. "Would you please make an announcement that the seat-belt sign is still on? They won't listen to us. Several passengers are wandering around refusing to stay seated. As a matter of fact, I know you're not supposed to, but if you or the captain could come down here and talk to them directly, it would help a lot."

Garth glanced at Phil Knight and repeated the request. Again there was no response.

"Phil, dammit, this silent treatment is childish," Garth said. "Answer the question if you're still in command. Should I go downstairs and take a look?"

At last the captain looked around, his face grim and tight, his eyes narrowed in anger. "You know what? I don't give a damn," he said. "But you know the rules. Someone threatens to cut your head off: I don't open the door, too bad. I don't open the door."

Garth suppressed the retorts that flashed through his mind, nodding instead as he unfastened his seat belt.

"I'm well aware of the rules," he said. "I'll be back in a few minutes."

He opened the cockpit door and moved into the upper-deck cabin, subconsciously expecting the usual friendly reception. But there was no friendliness in the eyes of those who looked up. It was as if he had stepped over the transom and fallen headfirst into ice water, the atmosphere of unrest and dislike almost as bad as the crucible of hatred he'd left behind. The idea of leaving the hostility of the cockpit had been inviting, but this wasn't much better, he thought. Uniformed pilots normally got smiles and nods in flight when they entered the cabin, but all he saw was a sea of distrustful eyes marking his passage as prisoners watch the movements of their captor.

Two of the flight attendants were waiting for him in the forward coach galley. "Who's giving you a hard time?" Garth asked.

"I'm Cathy. I called."

"Okay."

"There's a group of them. That doctor from first class came back just after takeoff asking who else was fed up, and he's been, kind of, recruiting others."

"To do what?" Garth asked.

"I don't know. I mean, I've never felt so much hostility. And they hate you guys in the cockpit. Every time you or Judy says anything, you'd think half these people were swallowing a lemon. They're jeering and booing."

"Did they really chase Judy to the cockpit?"

Cathy nodded. "There were a dozen furious men down here trying to catch her. I don't think they were going to hurt her, but they were madder than hell. She panicked and ran."

"She's in the cockpit."

"Which is where she'd better stay," Cathy continued. "Those guys were angry, and the truth is, she could have killed that little baby . . . and the man who caught the baby is back there in real pain. We've lost control, Garth. We don't have any real authority anymore. Y'know?"

"Believe me, I do," he said as he pulled one of the handsets out of its cradle and toggled on the PA.

Folks, could I have your attention?

"Hell, no!" a male voice bellowed halfway down the cabin as two men standing near the back of the first coach section turned and stared at him and several other voices responded with negative comments.

Ah, look, whether you want to listen or not, this is the copilot, and the first thing is, everyone needs to get back in your seats and fasten your seat belts. We're still climbing out and we've still got the seat-belt sign on.

"We're not taking orders from any of you for the rest of this trip!" another man yelled from a left-side window seat. "We'll obey the seat-belt sign when *we* decide to, since we can't trust anything this crew says."

"*Look . . . sir . . . ,*" Garth said, but the man was warming to his diatribe.

"Hey! You think I'm kidding? Let's do this democratically." He turned sideways, trying to catch the attention of the passengers in the middle section. "Come on, everyone. The copilot doesn't believe we're fed up. Let's show him how much we appreciate the way Meridian has treated us today. Everyone who's disgusted with this crew and this airline, please stand up."

Garth felt his jaw drop as the sound of opening seat belts clattered through the middle section of the cabin and first three, then five, then more than half the passengers got to their feet, the women standing more reluctantly than the men.

"There," the man said. "All we want from you, Mr. Copilot, is the time we're arriving in Cape Town. Other than that, you can go back to your cage."

There was a flurry of movement toward the back, and Garth looked past the angry men in the aisle to see the physician who'd accosted him a half hour before. The doctor stopped, as if assessing the situation, then pushed past two of the men in the aisle, patting one of them on the shoulder as he headed directly for the copilot.

Garth raised the handset to his mouth again, then thought better of it and clicked the PA off as Brian Logan came within speaking distance. He could sense Cathy and her partner backing into the galley.

"Doctor, what are you doing?" Garth asked.

"Reaching a consensus that we're all enraged at this ridiculous excuse of an airline. What do you think I'm doing?" the physician said, his jaw set in a defiant clench. "We're going to be calling the networks and the newspapers on arrival in Cape Town."

"Look, we're doing what you asked . . ." Garth said quietly.

"I haven't heard an apology from that bitch of a flight attendant."

"I'm working on that, but can't you please just relax?" He met Brian's gaze, seeing the same unfocused rage as before. It was different from looking at Phil Knight, he thought. Phil was simply upset. The doctor's eyes, however, were steady pools of pain and indignation and their unblinking intensity sent chills up his back.

Brian looked around behind him and turned back to Garth. "What are you doing down here, anyway?" His tone was almost conspiratorial, and the question caught Garth completely off guard. How could a copilot explain to an angry passenger the hostility he faced in the cockpit and the problems with the flight's captain? How could he explain how much he wanted to ameliorate all the passengers' concerns, but that the captain refused to let him? How could he explain anything and maintain any authority over him? Garth was the second in command, after all. He couldn't let himself enter an unholy alliance with an angry passenger, especially one whose conduct was bordering on air piracy.

"Look, Doctor, what else would you like me . . . like us . . . to do?"

Brian stared at him for an uncomfortable moment before answering.

"Tell me the truth. Are the both of you making the

263

idiotic decisions we've seen today, or is it just the captain?"

Garth swallowed hard, caution slowly sinking in the rising tide of indignation at Phil Knight's actions. "What decisions?"

"Oh, how about no communication from the cockpit, hours of delay in London, letting that woman lie to us on the PA, then hearing we've got a problem and are going back, no, we're going on, not to mention all the other affronts."

"Well, that's pretty much the captain," Garth said in disgust.

Brian nodded slowly, his eyes boring into the first officer's. "I thought so. You didn't seem like the . . . the same type. He isn't listening to you, huh?"

Garth snorted in disgust. "*Listening* to me? Hell, he's hardly talking to me. He's . . . he's got this idiot idea that if I make a suggestion it's for the purpose of undercutting his command. You know, if we're on short final with no gear and I point out it would be better if he landed with the rollers extended, he'd turn around in a purple rage and accuse me of just waiting for the chance to point out an insignificant error."

"In other words, he's a jerk?"

"To put it mildly. You think *I* wanted to go wheeling around in the sky changing destinations when it was obvious all we had was an indicator problem?"

"I didn't know. None of us down here know, because you two aren't telling us anything."

"He won't let me, Doc," Garth said, keeping his voice low but warming to the presence of a confidant, the memory of Brian's unstable acts melting rapidly in the welcome hope of camaraderie, however strained. Brian put a hand on Garth's shoulder and nudged him to turn away from the coach compartment and the glare of so many eyes. They moved into the galley.

"What's your name?" Brian asked.

"Garth Abbott, Doc."

Brian pointed up, toward the cockpit. "He's dangerous, isn't he?"

Garth nodded, then caught himself and shook his head no, a modicum of caution returning. "Not really dangerous . . . ," he hastened to add. The conversation with his wife replayed in his head. "And not incompetent, just . . ."

"Just acting arrogant enough to make catastrophic decisions if you're not there to counter him," Brian asked.

"Yeah. I'm afraid so. I hate to admit that," Garth said. "This airline has . . . gone downhill lately. All the emphasis on money, you know. They're too busy expanding to fine-tune the little things, like whether a guy's *really* ready for prime time."

"How'd this fool of a captain ever make captain?"

"He's . . . he's really not a fool. He was a very good domestic captain for many years. I know guys who flew with him. Steady, competent, knowledgeable about the technical details. But when your seniority number lets you have a shot at upgrading, too many airlines judge you just on flying ability. Meridian isn't doing anything to screen out the guys who can't handle the foreign languages, the diplomacy, the complexity of foreign airspace, and the fact that you've got to be a good commander and take care of all your people. Back home it was just a matter of hauling the winged cattle car to Tulsa and getting to the gate on time. Here it's much more demanding. Phil isn't prepared, he's scared to death, he won't admit it, and he won't take advice."

"Then, please," Brian said, "get back to the cockpit and try to keep us safely on course to Cape Town before he kills us with another stupid move."

Garth started to turn to go, but looked back at Brian. "Doctor, upstairs a while ago, you said something. You said to ask the company about a Daphne Logan. I didn't get the chance."

"And?" The hard edge returned.

"Well . . . is that your wife, or . . . or daughter?"

"Daphne Logan was my beautiful, loving wife, Garth. The love of my life. My soul mate. And she bled to death internally on one of your airplanes last year because the captain refused her pleas to land and get her medical help." Brian added the details as he watched the horror reflected in the copilot's eyes.

"I'm . . . so very sorry!"

"You know something? It's too late for anyone to be sorry. But you're the first Meridian employee . . . no."

He caught himself as he recalled Janie. "The first Meridian pilot to really mean that."

Logan turned and walked quickly back down the aisle toward the rear of the 747's main cabin.

As Brian passed, Brenda Roberts gripped her husband's arm and whispered in his ear.

"There he is again!"

Jimmy nodded.

"I'm worried, hon! You saw all those people stand up. Shouldn't we have joined them? I mean, aren't we just as ticked off?"

Jimmy shook his head and put his lips next to her ear. "We don't want to get involved in all the anger going on around this plane."

TWENTY-FIVE

NRO HEADQUARTERS
CHANTILLY, VIRGINIA
12:20 P.M. EDT

Before leaving the NRO's building, George Zoffel had given John Blaylock and David Byrd a quick tour of the new facilities, avoiding the most secret areas of the building where sophisticated satellite images of almost any spot on the planet could be called up at a moment's notice.

"I hear," David said as they walked toward the front entry, "that you also have control of several rockets, always in prelaunch readiness, that can insert a new satellite into any orbit you need within two hours."

Zoffel adopted a neutral expression. "You've heard this, have you?"

"Yes. How about you?"

"Interesting ideas," Zoffel said. "Sort of like the so-called Area Fifty-one in Nevada or the Aurora Project supposedly zipping around California at eight thousand miles per hour."

"Something like that." David smiled.

"You probably know more than we do," Zoffel replied.

"Understood," David said, well aware of how adroitly George Zoffel had sidestepped the question without the slightest validation or denial.

Zoffel waved to the two Air Force officers and disappeared back inside as John Blaylock gestured toward the parking lot.

"Time for an early-afternoon libation, Colonel? You like Guinness Stout on tap?"

"Of course."

"If you'd said no, I'd be very suspicious of your real identity."

"Where would you suggest we go?" David asked.

"A seedy little bar in Alexandria, and this evening, if you'd like, a sumptuous dinner over at the Willard so we can talk some more. I assume you didn't have other plans?"

"Not really."

"Good! Here's the bar's business card. Friend of mine owns it. He's an ex-spook. CIA, in other words."

"Understood."

"See you there in thirty minutes. I've got a stop to make." John Blaylock turned without waiting for a confirmation and walked briskly off toward his car. David looked down at the card, memorizing the address, turning it over by habit, and was startled to find a small note on the back.

269

*Col. Byrd: I get the impression that female senator really
turned you on when she called from London this morning.
Oh, and next time you visit an old intelligence operative,
don't ever leave him alone with your cell phone.
(I'll remove the bug at the bar.)*

John Blaylock was on his second draft of Ireland's
finest when David found him in a well-used mahogany
booth toward the back of the bar, which was a smoky,
diminutive place that easily lived up to the adjective
seedy. Blaylock waved him over and bellowed to an
underdressed barmaid for another round. She blew him a
kiss and curtsied before heading for the bar to comply.

"So tell me, Colonel Byrd, what did you learn
today?"

David plunked his cell phone on the table in front of
John Blaylock and pointed to it, smiling ruefully. "Blaylock, I think you broke about a half dozen federal
statutes, but . . . how the hell did you tap this phone?"

John was grinning. "Long experience, my boy. When
you were on my boat, if you'll recall, you went to the
can and left me alone with your phone for nearly a
minute."

"That's all it takes?" David said as he pulled out a
scarred-up captain's chair and sat down.

"Well, so happened, you have a type of phone I'm
prepared for." John picked up the cell phone with one
hand and popped off the battery, then reached in his

pocket and replaced it with another before handing the tiny instrument back.

"The bug is in the *battery*?" David said.

"You thought I'd whirled a few screwdrivers around and soldered a few wires in *sixty seconds*? Hey, I'm good, but I'm not a magician."

David sighed. "So, you asked what I learned. I learned I can't turn my back on you for a minute."

"No, you learned that we reservists are a lot more sneaky than you active-duty types would like to think."

"I guess."

"We have to be. We carry half the load and still get treated like second-class citizens."

"Not really true anymore, John," David said, trying to muster as much authority as he could manage in the face of what was obviously a very experienced senior veteran of the Pentagon. "We've activated half of you guys, and ever since the reserves became a separate command—"

John Blaylock cut him off with a big right hand raised in a stop gesture. "Granted, it's gotten better, but it's still the same old adage, Davy. Age and treachery will win out over youth and enthusiasm every time. That's the reserve credo."

"Okay, I'm warned."

"You shook my hand. Did you count your fingers?"

"Oh, cut it out, John." David laughed.

"Tell me about your divorce, David."

"My . . .*divorce?*"

"Let's see." Colonel Blaylock rolled his eyes to the ceiling as if the dossier on David Byrd were written across the tiles. "You were married in 1985 in Memphis to the former Katie Ann Lewis, a natural blond with an amazing figure, whose lawyer father was a two-term congressman from Tennessee, and whose mother was a pediatrician at Baptist Memorial, where Elvis died. Katie was an Ole Miss graduate, class of 1984, and you met her when the Air Force Academy played a strange exhibition game with Ole Miss in Oxford and those Mississippi boys slaughtered you zoomies."

"Where on earth . . ."

"You're an Air Force Academy grad, of course, who made it through with honors and no unwanted pregnancies in the surrounding community that we know about—though you *were* pretty worried for a few days of your freshman year about a little gal named Lucy in Colorado Springs. You were the top distinguished graduate from Undergraduate Pilot Training in the class of eighty-five-oh-one at Vance and chose an F-15 assignment to Soesterberg, Netherlands. But first, of course, you ran to Memphis and made an honest woman of Katie Ann, who'd been secretly living with you anyway during UPT, and whom you'd already married in a secret civil ceremony in eighty-four that even her mom doesn't know about yet. That means you're a traditionalist, which is good."

"There's no way you could know all that!"

"Now, you see . . . that's a really bad way to deny something, Dave. Hey. What can I tell you? I'm a damn good researcher and I found both marriage licenses and talked with people who were eager to help you win my favorite get-them-to-talk dodge, the 'Real Officer of the Year Roast,' which requires exposure of one's warts. Anyway, there's a lot more. Too bad you and Katie couldn't conceive. Maybe she wouldn't have developed a real hankering for that smooth-talking young captain from New Orleans while you were stationed at Hurlburt as a squadron commander flying Special Ops missions, and, I might add, doing a damn good job of surviving some tight situations and bringing all your guys home. You won the air medal twice. I'm impressed. She wasn't. The divorce was final in ninety-seven."

David was shaking his head, the previous smile gone from his face. "Why bother asking? You obviously know more about me than I do. I don't believe this."

"Uh oh. Now you're offended."

"No, I'm just . . ."

"Yeah, you're offended. Get over it. I have to know you to trust you."

"Hell, John, a profile is one thing, but it sounds like you've been hiding in my bedroom closet! I'll bet you've even got an accurate count of how many times Katie and I screwed."

"Actually, I'd estimate the final number at less than eight hundred times over a ten-year marriage, which comes out with weighted averaging between the hotter onset and the cooler end of the relationship to slightly more than one point five incidents of heterosexual coitus per week, which is terribly unhealthy."

"You're a real piece of work, Colonel. You know that?" David snapped.

"But, am I right?"

"None of your damn business!"

"Yeah it is, Dave. You're active duty. We own you, and life isn't healthy without a lot of sex, and you've apparently been behaving like a monk for the last few years, which makes you vulnerable. I saw your eyes pop out when Jill opened the bedroom door this morning."

David pushed back from the table, shaking his head in consternation. "Wait a damn minute here. My sex life and my private life are mine. You'd think I was interviewing for a job at CIA as a covert operative or something."

"Nope. More important than that."

David sat momentarily speechless for a few seconds trying to absorb the response. "What?"

"You want to get your star? You want to make general?"

"Of course, but what does that have to do with your invading my bedroom?"

John Blaylock leaned forward and drilled his eyes into David's. "George Overmeyer's a young buck for a three-star, David, but he's smart, and he thinks you're top material. You didn't know?"

"No. I mean, I suspected he was satisfied with me, but he's not long on compliments and positive reinforcement . . ."

"No, man, he's grooming you to make general and compete for chief of staff. They think you're general-officer material. I'm supposed to be the mentor. You should think of me as your personal trainer. Kind of like Yoda of the Jedi, but with smaller ears."

"What?"

"I'm not just a dumb old sybaritic, semiretired fool, David. I get some of the chosen guys like you ready for the big time. I show you the intelligence ropes, give you a good dose of reality in statecraft, and fade away like a strange nightmare to let you take all the glory and get promoted."

"You . . . make it sound like a program."

"It is, sort of. If you happen to get under the wing of a really good general, like Jim Overreactor."

"Is this current assignment not real, then?" David asked.

"You mean the current alert? Oh, it's very real. The intelligence community's been razor alert, ever since the war started in New York and here in D.C., but now they're on paranoid hair-trigger alert, and that's one of the things we've got to discuss, because we're in what I call the 'Mistake Zone,' when the gun's so cocked, a single mistaken response can start an unnecessary war. History's full of such moments, some of which exploded, some of which didn't. Sarajevo. The Cuban missile crisis. Berlin. The ninety-nine Kazakhstan nuclear missile launch."

"The *what*?"

"I'll tell you later. Not many people know. Meanwhile, don't be pissed off at my doing basic homework."

"Yeah, well . . . I guess my feelings are somewhat assaulted by all that personal revelation."

"I understand. And back a few years ago that would be my cue for snorting, pushing away from the table, and calling you a wimp for even realizing you *had* feelings. Times have changed, though. Now I'm supposed to ask questions like, 'How *do* you feel about my knowing all that stuff?' "

"Somewhere between violated and manipulated."

John Blaylock feigned a look of deep shock. "Wait a minute. You *did* voluntarily join the Air Force a few years back?"

"I *thought* so. They seem to have made me a colonel."

"Then I rest my case. The term *Air Force* is conceptually synonymous with being violated and manipulated. You should know this. That's what the folks at our personnel center at Randolph live to do."

David laughed, though he didn't want to. "So, where do we go from here, John?"

"Downtown D.C. to the Willard for dinner at seven. There's too much cigarette smoke in here again."

David was shaking his head. "No, I mean professionally."

"So do I. I've taken the liberty of inviting someone to join us for dinner whom I think you need to meet."

"Okay."

"She's . . . on the staff of the Senate Armed Services Committee."

"Okay. She?"

"And a real knockout, when she takes off those glasses."

"One of your . . . girls, so to speak?"

John Blaylock shook his head and grinned. "Nope. Mysteriously unimpressed by the Blaylock prowess, I'm sorry to say. She's fair game and unsullied."

David came forward in his chair, his index finger leveled at John Blaylock. "Wait a minute! You're not trying to play matchmaker, are you?"

John got to his feet, still grinning. "Mentors move in strange ways," he said.

"That's God, John. *God* moves in strange ways."

"Him, too? Interesting."

"You said we needed to talk shop," David said, still sitting.

"We do," John replied. "There's a lot more you don't know yet regarding our worries about the vulnerability of the airline system. But that can wait."

David stood and followed the older man toward the front of the bar, standing beside him as he paid the check.

"John, look . . . I'm impressed with what you've found out about my life, but some of it is pretty raw."

"I'm sure," Blaylock said.

"I mean, it's no picnic to find out your wife is giving it to another guy. It's taken me a few years to get on an even keel about that."

An exceptionally serious look crossed John Blaylock's face as he reached out a large hand to David's shoulder. "Dave, this may come as a shock, but the Air Force doesn't use Navy terms like *even keel*."

David chuckled. "Sorry."

"You more or less threw yourself into your work after the divorce, right?"

David nodded.

"I could see the earmarks. You've caught everyone's attention with superlative performance based on dedication that's seldom possible with a family at home. But that's not permanently sustainable, David. Life is more than the uniform."

"I know." He pushed open the door to the street and turned back. "So what's her name, John? This pretty woman you accidentally on purpose invited to dinner."

John moved through the open door and glanced back. "Her name is Annette. Like Annette Funicello."

"Who's Annette Funicello?" David asked with feigned innocence, coming up beside him as they headed for the parking lot.

John Blaylock turned with a scowl, not spotting the ruse. "*What?* Are you pulling my leg?"

"Me?" David replied, maintaining a blank expression.

"Yes, you. What kind of question is that? 'Who's Annette Funicello,' indeed!"

"I . . . guess I haven't heard of her, John," David fibbed. "Must be a generational thing. Is she an opera star or something?"

John Blaylock stopped cold and turned to put a hand on David's shoulder.

"*Opera* star? Where were *you* in the mid-fifties?"

"Ask my folks." David grinned. "I wasn't born until fifty-nine."

"Lord, " John Blaylock said, dropping his hand and shaking his head sadly. "Now I have to deal with children!" He rolled his eyes as he opened the door of his car and disappeared into the driver's seat, wondering how the Air Force could possibly trust anyone too young to have even heard of the cutest original Mouseketeer.

TWENTY-SIX

IN FLIGHT,
ABOARD MERIDIAN FLIGHT SIX
7:44 P.M. LOCAL

Garth Abbott closed the door of the small rest room aft of the cockpit, slid the "occupied" lock into place, and let himself luxuriate in the relative silence of the enclosure for a few minutes. The ubiquitous background hiss of the stratospheric slipstream on the other side of the 747's metallic skin was still audible, but much softer.

They'd been airborne for more than six hours, and Garth had decided to take a break in the rest room because there seemed to be no peace or place to relax anywhere else. The tension generated by sitting next to Phil Knight was exhausting, and the main cabin had become a war zone for crew members. Judy Jackson had fallen asleep in the jump seat, and the majority of the other flight attendants were hiding in their crew rest loft above the rear galley and keeping out of sight, counting the hours until the ordeal would be over with their landing in Cape Town.

Garth checked to make sure the top of the toilet lid was clean and sat down for a few moments, closing his eyes to imagine what it would be like to have a private bedroom in a private jet. Much like this, Garth concluded, at least in terms of noise. The background hiss was soft enough to permit sleep without the earplugs he always had to use in the cramped crew rest closet. Whatever Boeing had done to sound-insulate the little two-bed facility behind the cockpit, it wasn't enough.

He thought of Carol again, wincing at the pain. The satellite call he'd made ten minutes before had confirmed his fears that she wanted out. A separation, maybe a divorce, she'd said in anger, snapping at him for ignoring her request to wait until he got home to discuss it. If he was going to burn up satellite time on the company phone to force the issue, she said, then she'd just tell him. No, she wasn't seeing anyone or sleeping with anyone, and that, she said, was part of the problem. And yes, she wanted to know what life would be like without an always-absent airline pilot.

Phil Knight had pretended to ignore the call as he sat in thinly disguised disgust and looked out the window, and Garth had tried to make it less public than it felt.

"You asked, Garth. You insisted!" she'd snapped. "You couldn't just leave it alone. So there it is."

He looked around at the walls of the tiny enclosure now and wondered if there was still a fighting chance to keep the marriage intact, or if he even wanted to. How did he feel, other than numb? It was frightening to realize that he couldn't answer the question.

Garth sighed and got to his feet. He went ahead and took care of the routine physiological need that was supposed to have been the reason he'd left the cockpit in the first place. He had just finished washing his hands and was reaching for a paper towel when a muffled roar erupted some place to the right of the aircraft. The roar was followed by a distinct yaw and a pronounced shudder.

A second bang, and another shudder.

Compressor stalls! Garth thought. His mind raced through the fact that the captain had a propensity to snap off engines at the slightest provocation. He needed to get back to the cockpit. Less than three seconds had elapsed, but his mind was running at warp speed. Knight had tried to kill the engine without coordination before. Surely he wouldn't make the same mistake . . . they were over the middle of Africa with nightfall approaching.

Garth yanked open the rest-room door and grabbed the interphone as he worked the cipher lock.

"Phil! Let me in!"

The door locks began opening and he turned the knob and pushed open the door, his eyes scanning everything at once.

Phil Knight glanced around at the noise of the cockpit door opening, his face registering shock and concern. Garth could see that he'd disconnected the autopilot and was hand-flying the 747. All four groups of engine gauges were giving steady readings, except . . .

Garth's eyes tracked the throttle positions, realizing that number four was pulled back to idle. He'd felt the yaw to the right, and the readings on the forward panel for number-four engine were now dropping as number four—the outboard on the right wing that had already given them so much trouble—unwound.

Garth's eyes went to the T-handles that controlled emergency in-flight shutdown. An incongruous red light was burning, indicating a fire in number-four engine, even though the T-handle—the fire handle—had been pulled.

"What's going on?" Garth asked as he slid quickly back into the right seat and toggled it forward.

"I told you we shouldn't be flying with that engine," Knight growled out of the side of his mouth. Garth glanced at him quickly, spotting clenched teeth and a set jaw as the captain worked the control yoke back and forth, nervousness and panic apparently inducing more flight control instability than he was solving.

"You killed number four?" Garth said, his tone incredulous.

Phil Knight looked over at the copilot with a chilling combination of fright and uncontrolled glee. "Didn't you feel it trying to fall off the damn wing?"

"What?"

"Compressor-stalling."

"It started doing that just . . . all of a sudden?"

"No. First I got a fire warning, and then it started compressor-stalling."

Garth's eyes were ping-ponging back and forth among the various indicators and switches and panels. "So . . . then you pulled it back?"

"No. The fire warning corked off and then I pulled the throttle back and it started booming around out there like it was going to explode. So I pulled the fire handle."

"Jeez, Phil."

"Don't even think about telling me there's nothing wrong."

"You pulled the throttle back suddenly at high altitude, right?"

"Damn right! It shouldn't compressor-stall."

"Agreed, but pulling it back like that can *induce* a compressor stall if the bleed valve's sticky, and . . ."

The sound of a cabin call chime coursed through the cockpit, and Garth swept up the handset.

"Yes? Cockpit."

"This is the aft galley. We've . . . got passengers back here who want you to know that one of the engines looks like it's on fire."

"What do you mean? They see flames?"

"Yes. That's what they saw. On the right wing."

With the captain's interphone switch selected to the on position, Phil Knight was monitoring. He began nodding his head aggressively now as he reached out and punched a couple of deliberate keystrokes into the flight computer keyboard.

The screen instantly changed to a display of the nearest airports.

Garth Abbott was partially hunched over the control yoke, his mind racing as he tried to get a clear picture from the back. "I mean, are they seeing flames out there right now?" Garth looked up at the fire light for number four. Just as it had over the Mediterranean, it was glowing red. But now there was confirmation of a sort from the back.

"They . . . say it was on fire," the flight attendant reported, her voice tense. Garth could feel Phil banking the jumbo jet to the left and descending. He glanced at the captain's flight computer, his stomach contracting to see the list of emergency diversion airports displayed.

Oh God, he's going to try it again.

"Hold . . . hold on," Garth said to the flight attendant before turning to Phil. "Don't descend yet, Phil. We're over the middle of the damned continent, for crying out loud."

There was no response from the left seat, and Garth could see the same determined look on Phil Knight's face he'd seen before.

He turned his attention back to the interphone. The picture from the rear cabin was anything but clear. "Look, I need you to go look at number-four engine yourself," Garth said.

"Number . . . what? Which one is that?" she asked.

God, why don't we teach these flight attendants some of the basics? he thought. "It's the outboard engine on the right side. Not the right side as you stand and look back, but the right side of the airplane. Understand?"

"Yes. What am I looking for?"

"Look for fire, or flames, or anything wrong. Hurry."

There was silence as the woman let the handset clatter to the floor.

Garth turned to the left seat. "Phil? I've got her checking for . . ."

"I heard," he snapped. "But I've already fired the bottle."

Garth felt a numbness move through his body as he glanced back at the forward glare-screen panel, spotting the yellow lights he'd missed before. Knight had jumped the gun and fired off both fire suppression bottles on the right wing to number four engine. The yellow lights confirmed they were empty. The moment they landed anywhere, they were now legally grounded.

"It's still burning," Phil said suddenly, nodding toward the fire light.

"I'm checking, Phil. It may not be."

"We've got to get this thing on the ground."

"No, look . . ."

"We're landing, dammit. There's a commercial airport ahead about eighty miles, in Nigeria."

"Phil, not again. Let's please determine first whether there's really a fire out there."

Phil's head snapped to the right. "What about the compressor stalls? You trying to tell me *that's* normal?"

"No, but . . . but that doesn't mean it's burning. A

sticky bleed valve and a sudden yanking of the throttle back at altitude can induce a compressor stall, and people in the back will see flames momentarily. If that's all it is, we can fly to a better airport on three engines."

"It started with another fire warning," Phil replied. "It tried to boom off the wing, and you're *still* wanting to ignore the fact that it's dangerous? We're not having this debate again, Abbott."

"Yes, dammit, Phil, we *are*!" Garth reached for the satellite phone and pressed the auto-dialer for Denver Dispatch, unprepared to have the handset yanked out of his hands.

"I told you to keep your hands off that phone," Phil said.

The flight attendant's voice came back on the interphone line. "Okay, can you hear me?"

"Yes," Garth managed.

"Okay, I don't see any flames out there, but some of the passengers insist they do."

"What do your eyes tell you?"

"I . . . I don't know. It looks like it could be glowing."

Garth mumbled a thank-you and considered racing downstairs to see for himself, but it was the moment of decision. The captain was determined to set down at an unknown airport in the middle of Africa just before nightfall with God knew what hazards around the field. Even if he ran downstairs and came back ready to swear in a court of law that number four was *not* on fire, the chances of Phil Knight listening to him were zero. In fact, somewhere inside he knew that Knight would automatically oppose anything he suggested.

He had to stay, but should he seize command of the airplane? After all, the captain had a point. The engine-fire warning was on again, and the compressor stalls were real, and this was something entirely new.

What if he's right? Garth thought, the jolt of uncertainty crackling through his mind like an electric shock. *I know he's a flaming asshole, but what if he's right this time? I'll end up canned and lose everything. Meridian always has to find a head to lop off, and it'll be mine. No,* Garth concluded. *Better to stay up here and keep Knight from killing us with a botched emergency landing.*

He let out a ragged breath and leaned over to read the airport name from the captain's flight computer. "Katsina, Nigeria."

"That's it."

"Phil, let's go on to Abuja in Nigeria. That's the new capital. It's a big airport, and it's only a few hundred miles south."

"We've got an engine on fire. We're using Katsina. That's final."

Garth hesitated, his mind ranging furiously over the options again, but finding only the same answer. "All right," he said at last. "Let me declare an emergency while I try to find the approach plates." Garth keyed the radio and began a Mayday call. The Nigerian controller came back almost immediately asking the nature of the emergency.

"We have an engine shut down and an indication that it's still on fire. We'll need emergency equipment standing. We're doing an emergency descent and need clearance immediately to Katsina airport for landing."

"Ah . . . roger, Flight Six. Steer heading one-two-zero degrees now and descend to five thousand feet. And are you aware there is no emergency equipment at Katsina?"

Garth's stomach was already the size of a pea, but he felt it tighten anyway. "Negative. We didn't know. Is there a control tower?"

"Oh, yes. But they are having some problems now. We cannot talk to them. You will have to talk on the radio to them."

"Roger."

"Two-one-zero and five thousand feet," Phil was repeating as he dialed in the altitude and heading on the forward glare-shield panel.

Garth pulled the brown leather Jeppesen approach book containing the African plates from his flight bag and was trying to rifle through it for the Katsina plates, if they existed. His hands were shaking slightly, and he wondered why the captain seemed steady by contrast.

"You got the plates?" Phil snapped.

"I'm . . . looking. I don't know if they even have an approach there."

"I think I see the airport ahead."

"It's in the middle of a jungle, Phil, if I recall correctly."

"You've been there?" Knight asked, a hopeful note in his voice.

"No, I've flown over it. Here!" Garth liberated the instrument approach plate and handed it to Phil. "There's . . . only a nondirection beacon approach."

"You mean an NDB approach?"

"Yes."

"Then call it an NDB approach."

Garth ignored the verbal backhand. "There's that, and the field has only one runway, and it's six thousand feet long."

"We can make it."

Garth took a deep breath and turned to the captain. "Phil? Listen to me. What I'm going to say is going to be on the voice recorder, so the company and the whole world will know if anything goes wrong. This is a mistake. You hear me? This is a big, potentially disastrous mistake. We're a huge 747. If you're going to land, let's go to Abuja, the capital, where they can handle a 747 and there are facilities. I do NOT want to do this!"

"ENOUGH!" Phil yelled, his eyebrows raised, his expression maniacal. "YOU UNDERSTAND ME? I'M . . ." He lowered his volume, but his voice was still quavering with fury. "I'm the damn captain. Whatever I decide, you always want to do just the opposite to counter me. That stops now."

"Phil, that's not true, I . . ." Garth stopped in mid-sentence, his eyes fixated on Phil Knight's right index finger, which was pointed at him over the center console and shaking slightly as its owner spat out the words like a cobra spewing venom at its victim's eyes.

"READ . . . THE GODDAMNED CHECKLIST . . . OR GET OUT OF MY COCKPIT!"

Garth stared at the man in the left seat for an eternity of seconds, his outrage at the man's endless procession of stupid decisions muted by one, irrefutable truth: It was up to him now to keep the passengers safe, and having a physical fight in the cockpit didn't serve that goal.

"Okay, Phil," Garth said, quietly. "Okay. Calm down." He pulled out the checklist and settled on a plan. First he'd do the descent and approach checks. Then he'd make a PA announcement to the passengers, whether Knight liked it or not.

Then he'd do his best to keep them from crashing.

The massive, shuddering compressor stalls from number-four engine had shaken more than the airplane. The effect on the passengers had been somewhere beyond sobering. Suddenly all conversation had ceased, and even when the banging of the engine had ended, there were no voices to be heard in the cabin as the occupants gripped their respective armrests and wondered just how much trouble they were in. The background sounds began changing without explanation, the engine whine decreasing, the nose lowering, the aircraft banking first left, then right. The passengers could tell they were descending, and most knew they were somewhere over central Africa with nightfall approaching. Yet there was still no word from the pilots, and as the minutes passed in silence, wide-eyed looks of deep concern began to metastasize into mutters of anger and insurrection. Those who had been angry before when Garth Abbott appeared in the cabin now began attacking their flight attendant call buttons, and several men got to their feet to bellow for the crew to respond, their outrage reinforcing the dark feeling that there was a battle in progress aboard Meridian Six, and it came down to a simple equation: It was the crew versus the passengers.

In first class, Robert MacNaughton toggled on the moving map display on the small LCD screen at his seat. He knew this part of Africa all too well, having served during the sixties as a petroleum foot soldier in the escalating campaign to ferret out the obscure places nature had hidden the crude oil to which civilized humanity was hopelessly addicted. The southern area of Niger, Robert knew, was not as dangerous as the countries of Equatorial Africa, but this was no place to be landing an airliner if you could avoid it.

MacNaughton glanced to his left, unintentionally catching Brian Logan's eye for a second. The physician shook his head and pointed to the ceiling, toward the cockpit.

"If that clown doesn't come on the PA in thirty

seconds and tell us what he's doing," Logan said, "I'm going up there."

Almost immediately the strained voice of the first officer filled the cabin.

Ah . . . folks, this is the cockpit. We've . . . had to shut down our right outboard engine as a precaution because of those loud compressor stalls you heard earlier, and we're diverting to an airport in Nigeria to check it out. Please make sure your seat belts are fastened. Flight attendants, prepare the cabin for landing.

In coach, Jimmy Roberts motioned incredulously at the overhead speakers and looked at his wife, and then at the couple behind them.

"That's *it*? That's all that old boy's gonna tell us?"

"What's a compressor . . . whatever?" Brenda asked, her eyes inordinately wide.

"Technical words, I guess. Probably means backfire. That sure sounded like a big bunch of backfires," Jimmy said, fighting to hide a growing nervousness.

"But why don't he tell us . . . ?" Brenda began.

"Why *doesn't* he tell us," he corrected her before thinking. He knew better. She was acutely aware of her inadequate grammar and painfully ashamed of it. She could take correction from her husband, but it had to be done gently.

"There you go jumping on me again, Jimmy Ray," she replied, the hurt audible in her voice.

"I'm sorry, hon."

"I'm just a country girl. I don't talk fancy."

"Neither do I, honey. I'm sorry."

She looked up at him, the hint of a tear in her eye. "I am tryin' to get that kinda stuff right. I really am. *Doesn't*, not *don't*. *Dragged*, not *drug*. *He and I*, not *him and her*. I *am* tryin', Jimmy."

"I know you are, baby."

She leaned against him and tried to smile. "Dress me up but can't take me anywhere, huh?"

"You know I don't feel like that."

"*Doesn't* feel like that," she teased, and he laughed in response as he found her hands and squeezed them.

"So, Jimmy, why *doesn't* that pilot tell us what's really going on?" she asked.

"Because, darlin', he thinks we're all too stupid to understand."

TWENTY-SEVEN

There it was again. The high-pitched whine of turbine engines.

Jean Onitsa signaled his men to stop firing and waited for the crack and chatter of small-arms fire to slack off in response. The remaining government forces across the airport were panicked and reacting wildly to any incoming fire.

Jean cocked his head and tried to find the sound again. Slowly his ears registered the jet whine once more from off to the northeast.

"What is it?" one of his men asked in their native tongue.

Onitsa put his finger to his lips and shook his head for silence, but the rattle of automatic-weapons fire resumed suddenly from across the runway, bringing his full attention back to the tactical situation. It was just as well. No one in his right mind would try to land a civilian aircraft at Katsina in the midst of a rebel firefight. The lone occupant of the government control tower a mile to the east had to be hunkered down now on the floor with his microphone frantically warning away all traffic.

"Government plane?" Onitsa's lieutenant asked.

"No," he said, shaking his head as he gave a hand signal to deploy the right flank a hundred yards more to the west to reinforce the men he'd already positioned there. The lieutenant scrambled into motion, relaying the command and keeping low as he and fifteen other well-trained men moved with lightning speed into the under-brush, holding their guns precisely as Jean had taught them.

Jean nodded to himself and smiled, aware of how incongruous his life had become. It was a personal joke that all the years of classical education in Britain to become a physician had mixed with his noble determi-nation to return to Africa to contribute to his people, a desire that incongruously ended up making him a feared commander of rebel forces. He was known for his sense of humor and his steadiness—and his calm ruthlessness—and he enjoyed that reputation. A calm, jovial enemy displaying serene confidence always unnerved the opposition.

But a *Marxist*? He chuckled at the thought that the Nigerian government was attempting to rally the people against him based on that charge. The last thing on earth he could ever be was a Marxist.

More frantic, undisciplined firing broke out from the pinned-down government troops, who were essentially being led by a teenager. It was almost too easy moving the pieces on the chessboard of the battlefield against such poorly trained thinking. Mix the formal logic of warfare as taught by Karl von Clausewitz with the brilliant iconoclastic thinking of Sun-Tzu, then meld the tactical discipline of the British Army with the cleverness of American-style employment of technology, and the opposition hadn't a chance.

The jet sounds wafted over him again. It was becoming irritating, and he lifted his big head just far enough to scan for the source. There was always the remote possibility that the Nigerian Air Force, such as it was, would somehow lapse into momentary competence and arrive ahead of schedule, but with his well-paid spies in the south and at Air Force headquarters, being surprised by a warplane was even more unlikely than being out-flanked by an intelligent response from the government troops.

He looked at his gold Rolex President, an indulgence from his last trip to London. Twenty minutes more and his men should be able to finish the job, kill whoever surrendered, and purposefully mutilate the bodies in the creative and terrifying ways he knew would psycho-logically torture the army. Then he'd take the tower, proclaim the airport hostage, and open the negotiations with Abuja by satellite phone while safely withdrawing before the government reinforcements to the north arrived.

Jean knew the routine. It would take the army two days to realize they'd surrounded a nonexistent rebel force. In the meantime, he could wrest more concessions from Nigeria's government.

"Sir! Sir, look!" One of his men had scrambled to his side and was pointing to the east where a large aircraft had appeared, flying directly for the runway.

"What is it?" the man asked.

Jean peered carefully through his favorite set of field glasses, calmly analyzed the shape, then dropped the glasses.

"Calm down," he ordered. "It is a civilian airliner. American, I think."

"What do we do?"

Jean turned to the young man and smiled. "Why, we treat it as an amazing opportunity, of course."

Captain Phil Knight ordered the 747's flaps to the forty-degree position and throttled back, letting the giant airliner settle into the computed approach speed of one hundred forty knots as he aimed for the end of the runway.

"Forty feet," Garth called out, reading the radio altimeter. "Thirty, twenty, ten . . ."

Phil pulled the throttles to idle and flared the big ship,

breaking the descent rate until the sixteen wheels of the main landing gear thudded and screeched onto the poorly maintained concrete. Phil's right hand shot out to gather the speed brake lever and pull it to the deployed position a split second before the automatic system did the same thing. He applied reverse thrust as he began pushing hard on the brake pedals. The 747, still weighing over six hundred thousand pounds, shuddered and slowed, the antiskid system working hard to prevent any tire blow-outs as Phil stood on the brakes, finally bringing them to a halt at the western end of the runway with five hundred feet left to spare.

"Now what?" Garth asked, trying to keep the sarcasm out of his voice. "I never got a response from the tower."

There were small flashes of light from a line of trees to the right, and Garth let the fact register without examination as he waited for Phil's next move.

"There was a ramp back there," the captain said. "I guess we'll do a one-eighty on the runway here." He pulled the nosewheel steering tiller toward him, pivoting the nosewheel sharply to the left, and began turning the huge jet as Garth yelped. There were more flashes on the right along with what sounded like firecrackers. The sharp cracking sound reverberated through the interior of the 747, despite the heavy insulation.

"Oh, my God, that's gunfire!" Garth said.

The aircraft was just beginning to pivot to the left as several figures materialized from the tall grass and ran across the field in front of them. Garth leaned forward, his eyes large as he tracked the men and realized with a vascular cascade of adrenaline what he was seeing.

"Oh shit, Phil! We've got soldiers out there with guns telling us to stop."

"Where?"

"Just to the left!"

"Omigod!" Judy yelped. "They *are* shooting out there."

A group of six armed men had appeared to the left of the cockpit's viewpoint, one of them making a cut sign across his throat. On the right, eight men in army-style fatigues were dropping to the ground and pointing their weapons off to the north. Garth could see the muzzle flashes from their weapons. The 747 was less than fifteen degrees into its turn as Phil braked to a halt. The men were clearly visible now out Garth's window as one of the men on the right side stood to run, then stopped. Garth watched his body crumple, a diffused red mass where his head had been moments before.

"JESUS, PHIL! There's a war going on out here!"

"What?"

"I . . . I just saw one of those guys get killed! Forget their orders. Turn around. Take off. Let's get out of here."

Phil began moving the throttles on the right wing forward as the big Boeing began swiveling left once again.

"Go, go, go, GO, GO, GO!" Garth was saying, his eyes back over his right shoulder trying to track the small group that had left their fallen comrade and scampered away, still firing. Garth could hear the reports of the automatic weapons clearly now, his brain refining the muffled sounds into a clear and present danger.

"Please get us out of here!" Judy pleaded from the jump seat.

"What the hell is this?" Garth heard the captain say as he braked to a halt again. Garth looked left and realized with a flash of cold fear that they were trapped.

The aircraft was halfway through its turn and pointing south, perpendicular to the runway, but to the left, men in fatigues were scrambling out of vehicles that were blocking their path. The men were pointing their weapons at the cockpit as they fanned out and waited for a smaller jeeplike command vehicle to pull right in front of the 747 at the runway's edge. Garth watched a barrel-chested man in the passenger seat stand up, then step onto the hood of the machine, slowly, deliberately, making a "cut" sign across his throat with his right hand. The man smiled, a huge, toothy smile that seemed to bisect his face.

"He . . . he wants us to shut down, Phil," Garth managed.

"Okay," was the only response. "Engine shutdown checklist."

Garth fumbled with the laminated list and ran through the items, expecting the windshield to shatter in a hail of bullets at any moment. He could feel himself literally shaking inside, knowing a little of the brutal politics of central Africa and the high mortality rate for Westerners caught in the wrong place at the wrong time.

The engines began winding down as Phil brought the fuel and start ignition switches to the stop position one at a time. "I suppose," the captain began, "these people can help us get a mechanic out here."

"What?" Garth asked absently, his eyes riveted on the apparent commander standing in front of them.

"I said, maybe we can get these guys on the interphone and see if they can get us a mechanic to take a look at that engine."

Garth turned and looked at Phil Knight as if he'd spotted an extraterrestrial life form in the left seat, his mouth gaping open. "*WHAT?*"

Phil repeated the statement a third time, as if dealing with an idiot, as he reached for the satellite phone to call Denver.

"A *MECHANIC?*" Garth sputtered. "Jesus Christ, Phil! Don't you have any idea what you've done? You've just landed us in a rebel war zone in the middle of a friggin' firefight! We'll be lucky to escape with our lives!"

TWENTY-EIGHT

KATSINA AIRPORT,
NIGERIA, AFRICA
8:30 P.M. LOCAL

Jean Onitsa stood beneath the nose of the Meridian 747, marveling at the incredible size of the machine. He had flown on such aircraft, of course, numerous times. But passengers seldom confronted the gigantic size of the airplane from the surface of a ramp, and it was awe inspiring.

He glanced over his shoulder, impatient for the man he'd sent to the bullet-riddled terminal to return with the type of headset he needed to talk to the crew sitting some forty-five feet above. The man was back, now, screeching the jeep to a halt and running to his commander with the headset apparatus in hand.

Jean thanked him politely and reached up to find the small box on the side of the nose gear where he'd seen crewmen plug in headsets before. His experienced eyes meanwhile were simultaneously tracking his men as they

303

maintained a bead on the enemy from a dozen positions around the aircraft. There had been no more firing, and he intended to keep it that way until deciding how best to use this new, unexpected prize.

"Captain, this is the ground," Jean said, spacing his words carefully, both the depth of his education and the girth of his huge chest resonating in his broadly pronounced consonants. There was a pronounced African sound overlying his English, of course, but his mastery of the language was as complete as his formal education in Britain.

There was no response from above, and once more Jean reached up, this time pressing the call button several times until a startled male voice coursed through his headset.

"This is the cockpit."

"Very good. Is this the captain?"

"Yes. Who are you?"

"My name is General Jean Onitsa. I'm the commander of the forces that now control this airport, and you, ladies and gentlemen, are my hostages. So you'll forgive me if I ask how many people are aboard."

There was more silence on the headset, and Jean suppressed a grin. There would be wide-eyed confusion in the cockpit as the pilots tried to figure out what was happening.

"Ah," the voice came back, "we . . . we came in here, General, because we had a fire in one of our engines and had to shut it down. We were hoping to find a mechanic."

The officer Jean had commissioned, a major, arrived at his side, his face full of questions and his eyes huge as he approached the incomprehensible scene of his commander talking on a headset to the occupants of the 747 while the government troops undoubtedly had their rifles zeroed in on him. Jean Onitsa always wore bulletproof body armor, but his head and legs and arms were still vulnerable.

Jean smiled and motioned for the major to be quiet. "Captain, you say you had an emergency. Did you declare that emergency?"

There was another hesitation before the voice from the cockpit said yes.

"Very well, then, I cannot hold you, can I? Nigeria is a party to the international conventions regarding distressed airmen, and I shall respect that once I control this country."

"We're . . . not hostages, then?"

"Not at the moment."

The major gestured to the belly of the 747 looming above them. "You're going to let them *go*?" he asked in their native tongue.

"For the moment, they are to believe so," Jean replied.

The major smiled and nodded. He knew Jean Onitsa's clever ways. A promise was a promise until military advantage dictated something different.

Jean was pressing the transmit button again. "Captain, what can my men and I do for you?"

A new male voice broke in. "For starters, General, you can ask your men to stop aiming those high-powered automatic weapons at us."

"Is this still the captain?"

"No, sir, this is the first officer."

"Very well," Jean said, giving the command into a portable radio. In the distance, a dozen AK-47s were immediately lowered to parade rest.

"And we need maintenance personnel, whatever type they may have here," Garth added.

"Well, Mr. First Officer," Jean continued, "there are no maintenance men left here. I am so sorry to tell you we have apparently killed them all. Pity. We did not know, of course, that you would be needing them, or we would have let them live long enough to work on your engine."

In the cockpit of Meridian Six, Garth Abbott glanced at Phil Knight, wondering if he understood the gravity of the words the rebel commander had just spoken. Phil appeared unreasonably calm, as if the cavalry had arrived to save them, not destroy them, but Garth knew it was the short satellite call to Meridian Operations that had instilled the ridiculous air of normality. After the duty controller got over his shock, he'd promised to get a maintenance team on the way.

"They don't have a clue where Katsina is, Phil," Garth had warned, but to no avail.

"Damn!" Phil said. "We can't leave without fixing number-four engine."

"Phil," Garth said, "this is a very dangerous man we're talking to."

"What, now you know him personally?" the captain sneered.

"No, but I know *of* him, and General Onitsa is very clever and very brutal."

"Didn't you hear that pleasant voice, Abbott? The man's clearly educated and friendly and civil. He said we can't be taken hostages. So calm down."

"Phil, for Christ's sake, we can't trust Onitsa! He told you he'd killed the mechanics. We *were* hostages there for a moment, and the man could change his mind again. He's got a bloody reputation."

Phil Knight snorted contemptuously, but he was listening and Garth continued, talking rapidly, aware that the two huge, frightened eyes just behind the captain's seat belonged to Judy Jackson, who was shocked into silence.

"Okay, Phil," Garth said at last. "Look, let me go down there through the electronics bay and look at the engine."

"So now you're a qualified mechanic?" Phil said.

"No, but if I can get the cowling open, I can probably tell if the engine was on fire."

"I'm listening. Then what?"

The mellifluous voice of the rebel commander returned to their headsets.

"Captain? Mr. First Officer? I await your request, gentlemen. What would you like us to do?"

Garth punched the interphone button. "General, may we please ask you to wait one more minute? We're discussing our options."

"Very well. I am waiting, but there are opposing forces with guns out there whom I cannot possibly control, so please be quick."

Garth took a deep breath and closed his eyes. Going outside could get him killed, but there was obviously no way Knight was going to leave without an inspection of number four.

"Phil, I'll go down to the ramp through the electronics bay, stand on his jeep, look under the cowling, and if there's been no fire and no obvious damage to the bleed valve and I can guarantee that, and if Onitsa will let us go, will you agree to getting us the hell out of here?"

Phil had been surveying the surrounding terrain, wondering where those other gunmen might be. He nodded far more quickly than Garth had expected.

Garth punched the interphone button instantly. "Okay, General, the first officer here. May I come out of the airplane and get your men to help me look at one of the engines? I will need to stand on one of your vehicles."

"This is not a problem, Mr. First Officer. Do you need a ladder?"

308

A cockpit call chime was ringing, but Garth ignored it as he explained that there was a small entrance into the belly located behind the nosewheel and accessed through the main cabin floor. The rebel general readily agreed, a fact that did little to reassure him.

Garth pulled a small aviation band radio out of his flight bag and tuned one of the aircraft radios to the same frequency, piping it to an overhead speaker. "I'll keep you posted with the handheld," he told Phil. "We may want to start number-four engine while I can watch it from out there."

Garth left the cockpit and ignored the stares of the passengers in the upper-deck section as he hurried by. One man tried to hail him, and he raised a hand in response.

"Not now!" Garth descended the main stairs into the coach section. There were murmurings of urgent conversation everywhere, and clumps of passengers were peering through the windows trying to discern what was happening.

"Hey! One of the pilots," someone said, and heads began to turn as a half dozen people began asking questions.

"Not right now! I'll explain in a minute," Garth replied, walking as quickly as he could and dodging people in the aisle as he headed forward to the rear of the first-class section. He dropped to his knees at the appropriate spot and began examining the carpet as a crowd gathered around him. Somewhere beneath a hidden seam, there was a break in the carpet that hid the hatch to the electronics bay. He could see several of the flight attendants approaching as he found the spot and pulled the rug back, but the intrusion of a now-familiar male voice caught him off guard.

"Where are we and what the hell is going on?"

Garth glanced up to see Brian Logan standing over him.

"There's no time to explain, Doctor. I'm going down through a lower compartment to the ramp to see if the engine's okay so we can leave." Garth looked at the array of faces around the doctor. "We're in a place called Katsina in northern Nigeria, and unfortunately we've landed in a battle zone."

There was a gasp from one of the women, and Garth raised his hand. "No . . . they're not firing at us. We're talking to the rebel commander who's holding the airport, and he's helping us."

"We heard shooting out there," one man said.

"Are you aware, young man," a cultured British voice cut in, "that a soldier was killed just off to the right in full view of all of us as we stopped a while ago?"

"Yes, sir . . . I saw it, too," Garth said. "That's why I'm trying to verify that number-four engine is okay so I can convince this . . . this captain I'm flying with to get the hell out of here." Garth caught sight of two of the flight attendants as they stood in the galley, their faces registering fright as they reacted to his words.

"What's he trying to do this time, Garth?" Brian Logan asked. "Did he know this was a war zone?"

Garth had turned back to the task of working the seldom-used lock on the electronics bay hatch. He looked up again. "I don't think Captain Skygod up there can even spell Africa, let alone know anything about it. I told the bastard not to land here!"

The words hung in the air amid the silence they'd suddenly created, the reaction triggering more adrenaline in Garth's bloodstream.

Brian Logan knelt beside the copilot, a hand on his shoulder. "You know he's sending you out there to get rid of you, don't you? He'll probably start up and leave you out there."

"What? No! It was my idea. Why would he do that?" Garth said. "No, really. He's . . . probably right. I shouldn't have said all that. We did get another fire indication on the same engine, and I'm sure you felt it compressor-stalling."

Brian turned to the growing crowd around him and repeated the same incendiary explanation. "This pilot's the only ally we've got on this tub," Brian was saying, "and the captain's trying to get him killed."

Garth stood up and faced them, both hands out in a calming gesture that included Brian.

"Now . . . look, Brian . . . folks. This is really just a terrible maintenance day. Please don't get all riled up here. I misspoke, okay? This captain and I don't see eye to eye on everything, but he's still in charge."

"Maybe you should be in charge," one of the men said.

"Didn't you tell me that SOB up there isn't listening to you?" Brian asked.

"Well, yes, but . . ."

"And hasn't he landed us in some sort of war zone?"

"Maybe so, but those are just . . ."

"Can't you see what's happening here?" Brian asked. "You challenged his command, and he has to get rid of you."

It was a measure of his fatigue, Garth thought, that the doctor's completely mad explanation almost made sense. He tried to jerk himself back to reality.

"Doctor . . . guys . . . all of you . . . please calm down! The captain is not out of control; he's just headstrong. Now, please . . . I'm going outside and I'll be back shortly, and hopefully, if the engine checks out, we'll soon be out of here. I am having some trouble with this guy, I'll admit, but it's just pilot disagreement stuff. We're still a team, and I promise you, Captain Knight isn't interested in flying this ship alone."

"Garth?" one of the flight attendants asked, her tone urgent and scared. "What's happening?"

Garth gave her the same explanation before turning to the agitated group of men. "I'll be back in a few minutes. You folks just relax. Please!"

Janie Bretsen materialized at Garth's side and tapped him on the shoulder.

"You're the first officer."

"Yes," he said. "And I've got to get moving."

"Where's Jackson. Judy Jackson?"

Garth shot her an inquisitive look.

"I'm Janie Bretsen, the extra flight attendant who came along to make you legal."

"Oh. Okay."

"Where is she?"

"Hiding in the cockpit. She thinks these folks were chasing her."

"Damn right we were," another man said, "if that's the bitch you're talking about . . . the one who nearly killed that baby in the back."

Janie raised the palm of her hand to the man to ask for quiet.

"I don't have time for this. I'll be back," Garth said.

Nearly ten passengers had gravitated around Brian Logan, all watching the copilot now as he disappeared down the hatch in the floor into the electronics bay. Brian got to his knees to peer in, as did two of the men, the flight attendants merely watching cautiously from the forward galley.

Garth lowered his body through the hatch and toggled the electronics bay light on. The pressure hatch was in the floor of the compartment, and Garth worked the handle to open it and drop the small ladder. He swung his body over the hole and climbed onto the ladder, descending into the damp heat of an African summer evening.

The general Garth had been talking to was nowhere to be seen. Instead, three armed rebels approached him with their weapons pointed at his head, and instinctively

Garth raised his hands. There were vehicles, trucks and jeeps, ringing the back end of their 747, effectively blocking any gunfire or visibility from the forested area where the government forces had been.

Urgent, wild-eyed orders were given in the local language, and Garth shrugged to indicate he didn't understand. One of the three motioned for him to move to the right side of the aircraft out in front of the wing, and he complied, frantically scanning the surrounding tarmac for some sign of the general.

Another angry shout caused him to stop and look around. The three soldiers were all gesturing now for him to kneel, and Garth complied, his hands at his side, glancing up as he did and wondering what the passengers on the right forward side would think if they were watching. He could see faces in the windows with more appearing every second, and knew they must be as terrified as he.

In the first-class cabin Robert MacNaughton had been watching for the copilot through the windows. He leaned forward with a start and an exclamation. Brian Logan and several others moved immediately to his side, crowding around the adjacent windows to see what he was looking at.

"Good heavens, they're going to execute the poor bloke," MacNaughton said quietly. "Whenever they're without a plan, you see, they kill."

Several other passengers along with two of the flight attendants were plastered to the windows and watching every move outside as one of the soldiers down on the ramp broke from the group and walked over to the copilot, cocking his AK-47 and pointing the muzzle at the back of Garth Abbott's head. He held his weapon as far away from his body as possible, in the stance of someone preparing to shoot another human at close range.

In the cockpit, Judy Jackson gasped at the sight of the impending execution as she sat almost sideways in Garth's seat, unaware of Phil's sudden presence at her side, his eyes on the same grim spectacle, his voice almost too low to be heard.

"Oh, shit," he said.

On the ramp, with the barrel of the gun pressing against the back of his head, Garth realized he'd been tricked and closed his eyes, trying to concentrate on his wife's image, convinced he would be dead or dying in a few seconds. He wondered if he would hear the crack of the bullet before it took his consciousness. He remembered Jim Brady, the former White House press secretary, describing the explosion of a bullet ripping through his brain. He could feel the cold steel of the barrel against his head, and as seconds ticked past, he found himself almost clinically dissecting how it would feel, and what it would destroy.

The single explosion of an AK-47 round cracked through his consciousness and Garth wondered why he was still able to think, yet feeling no pain. A familiar voice reached him from somewhere behind him, beneath the 747, speaking a foreign tongue with a familiar lilt, and he realized with a start that the gunshot he'd heard had propelled a bullet somewhere off to the side.

Or perhaps, he thought, this was some celestial joke. Maybe the shot had blown through his head, after all. Maybe he was already dead and didn't know it.

But how could he be hearing measured footsteps now if that were true, footsteps that drowned out the very audible sound of his pounding heart? The footsteps were too real to be a delusion—that, plus the fact that his knees still hurt from the tarmac. The same mellow voice shifted to English, still coming from a distance, as if under the wing.

"Please, Mr. First Officer, be so kind as to stay very still. My men are not going to hurt you, but we must make the satellites believe so."

"The satellites?" Garth asked, feeling a slight prod from the rifle for being audacious enough to speak.

"Of course. That's what we're doing, you see, satisfying the United States's voracious desire for satellite pictures which will be relayed faithfully to the Nigerian military, whom I happen to be fighting. I do not remember the name of the spacecraft overhead at this moment, but it belongs to your Central Intelligence Agency and will be past in . . . thirty seconds more."

"How do you know this?" Garth asked in amazement.

"Quite incredible what the former Soviets have for sale these days, such as all the orbital charts of all the spy satellites including their own, which can be purchased on computer disk." Jean Onitsa looked at his digital watch. "Ah! Very well, the time has passed, now." He spoke another order. Garth felt the barrel withdrawn from his head as several large hands reached down to help him up. At the same moment, two men began pouring sticky red liquid on the ramp where he had been kneeling as several others pulled a rag through it, trailing the traces off to one side, as if a shattered body had been dragged away.

"There!" the general said with a huge smile. "Pure Hollywood, I'm afraid, but necessary. Another spy satellite will be overhead in eleven minutes with its camera clicking away, so we do not have much time. Now, Mr. First Officer, which engine did you say was the problem?"

TWENTY-NINE

The news that Flight Six was on the ground with the same recurring engine complaint at some unheard-of airport in the middle of Africa had caused the rapid assembly of a crisis team. There seemed to be no one to negotiate with, and several rapid, urgent calls to the State Department had triggered only a slow, confused response at first. After nearly a half hour, however, the government of the United States began to take very seriously the fact that over three hundred people, many of them Americans, were stranded in northern Nigeria.

The director of flight control had tasked his team to locate a maintenance shop at Katsina, but they were getting nowhere. The only airline serving the airport was a regional concern, but no one at the home office in Nigeria would answer the phones, and the news got worse when the State Department reported that rebel activity might have shut down the airport.

"Is their number-four engine inoperative?" The DFC asked the maintenance duty controller.

"I don't know," he replied. "They aren't answering my calls right now."

A tug on the DFC's sleeve brought him face-to-face with the senior vice president of operations, who had a funereal look and was motioning him into the conference room where he quickly closed the door behind them.

"What is it, sir?" The DFC asked.

"I just got a call from the CIA at Langley, Virginia. Flight Six has blundered into a small war at that airport. If you reach the crew, you are to order them to take off immediately, if possible. Langley is saying their chances of survival if the rebels get hold of them are nearly zero."

"Jesus! But we don't know whether number four is running."

"Can't he take off on three?"

"I doubt it. A DC-8 crashed in Kansas City trying to do that a few years ago. It's pretty dangerous."

He inclined his head toward the main control complex. "Go. Tell this to no one but the crew. But get them out of there if you can."

"Roger."

"I'm telling you, if someone in Africa doesn't kill that captain, I will."

NATIONAL RECONNAISSANCE OFFICE, CHANTILLY,
VIRGINIA
2:40 P.M. EDT

The somewhat routine notification by Nigeria's air traffic
control system to the originating European Air Traffic
Control authority in Brussels that a flight originating in
London had diverted to an African airport had been duly
relayed by Internet message to the FAA's System Control
Center in Herndon, Virginia, and sent over secure lines
in turn as a routine message to the CIA at Langley, where
it gained the immediate, undivided attention of a computer algorithm looking specifically for such anomalies.
Within minutes, a request was flashed from Langley to
NRO for immediate satellite imaging of the Katsina,
Nigeria, airport, which the State Department confirmed
was in a state of siege from rebel forces as earlier reported
by another obscure section of the CIA itself.

Deep within NRO's building in Chantilly, three
analysts—two women and a man—sat in comfortable
chairs in one of the compact viewing rooms as the first
images were downloaded from orbital relay.

"Okay, the 747 is at the west end and halfway turned
around, sideways to the runway," the man said.

"I've got two trucks, a couple of jeeps, and . . . some
sort of cart near the nose of the plane," one of the
women added, as they verbalized their way through the
shots. The next frame blinked into place, followed by a

dozen more as they boosted magnification and began peeling back the meaning of the images. Within eight minutes, one of the secure lines to Langley was engaged.

"This is very preliminary," one of the NRO team said when the CIA analyst had answered. "The aircraft appears to be surrounded by rebel troops, but apparently undamaged. We can't see the landing gear, of course, so we don't know if the tires are intact. However, it appears one crew member, one of the pilots, got out of the aircraft, perhaps from a hatch underneath. We see no emergency slides or portable stairs."

"Okay. Is that a real-time picture?"

"No. Last fifteen minutes."

"What do you show?" Langley asked.

The male analyst looked at his two female companions, who shook their heads and nodded. The story the pictures told seemed depressingly clear.

"We have two passes within ten minutes," he reported. "During the first images, they're forcing the pilot to kneel in front of the airplane. He's got three stripes on his shirt."

"That would be the Meridian first officer," the CIA analyst replied. "That ship carries only two pilots."

"Three stripes. We can't read a name tag."

"Go on. You said he was forced to kneel? Like at gunpoint?" their CIA counterpart asked.

"Definitely. That's probably an AK-47 to his head. Eleven minutes later, on the next pass, there's what appears to be a huge puddle of blood where they had him kneel. The computer's still refining the spectro-graphic image, but so far it's coming up consistent with human blood. Heavy on the iron and all the necessary traces."

"Aw, shit," was the response from Langley.

"There's a reasonably high probability they blew someone's head off in that eleven minutes on that exact spot. Since we see no more of the first officer, there's a moderate probability that he was the victim."

"High confidence?"

"Let's call it a notch lower. But it's not fuel or oil or water."

"How about the engaged troops?"

"These are rebel. It looks like they've taken the airport. There are bodies everywhere around the terminal and only a small platoon-sized element apparently huddling in a ditch to the northwest, and they're surrounded."

"Okay."

"But . . . there is a major force of several hundred with some armor to the north. The rebels haven't engaged them. We assume Nigerian Army."

"How close?"

"Within shelling range right now, but they're not deployed to fire. They're just oozing toward the field and a half mile out."

"Somehow they need to get that damned airplane off the ground."

"It could be too late," the analyst at NRO added. "There's one more thing you're not going to like."

"Go on."

"Eight buses, apparently rebel, on their way to the airport and one mile away with a dust plume on the last shot. Each bus of that type can hold fifty people. Do the math."

"Understood. Above the passenger count of a 747. When's your next bird overhead?" the CIA man asked.

"It'll be infrared. Daylight's fading."

"Yeah, but when?"

"Another half hour. I'll call you back."

THIRTY

As soon as one of the rebel jeeps had been positioned beneath number-four engine, a tool kit appeared, sophisticated enough to satisfy any Boeing mechanic. Garth's confidence was growing slightly as two of Onitsa's men helped him open the cowling and no immediate signs of fire greeted the beams of their flashlights in the waning light. Garth's legs were still shaky after what had seemed certain execution just minutes before, and his mind was a jumbled contradiction of deep, mortal thoughts and immediate impulses, accompanied by an unexplained, steady flow of tears that seemed to make no sense. He was glad for the increasing darkness of the tarmac, and hoped Onitsa's men hadn't noticed.

"Okay, Phil," he said into the handheld radio, "if there was fire in or around number four, there are virtually no traces out here."

The bleed valve was less certain. There were wrench marks around it, as if the wrong tool had been used to manipulate it, but there was no way for him to tell whether it was damaged or not.

"If it starts," Garth radioed, "then it should keep running just fine, unless we yank the power back at high altitude again."

There was a monosyllabic response, and Garth motioned to his impromptu team to close up the engine covers. As soon as the engine had been resecured, Garth got off the jeep and motioned for the soldiers to move it a safe distance away.

"Okay," Garth radioed, "Start number four."

Garth had never stood next to a 747 engine during start-up before. The whine of the turbines starting their spin-up was impressive and loud, and he could hear the repeated snap of the ignitors firing sparks through the misting jet fuel deep inside the so-called hot section of the engine just before the flame front took hold, the hot gasses spinning the turbine wheels ever faster and accelerating the huge jet engine to its minimum idle speed.

"How are the indicators?" Garth yelled into the sound-saturated radio. The reply from Phil Knight was inaudible, but Garth saw a thumbs-up gesture through the cockpit window.

"Okay, I'm coming back in now. Start the other three."

The first officer dashed toward the nose gear and the

hatch. Onitsa was waiting, flanked by several of his soldiers.

"We have one small additional duty, Mr. First Officer," the general said.

Garth felt a rush of appreciation and offered his hand to the big man, who took it with a smile and shook it solemnly. "I really appreciate all your help!" Garth said.

"No problem," the rebel general replied. "Except that I need to borrow your emergency slide." Onitsa laughed at the confused look on the copilot's face. "Only one will do."

Garth looked at the general. His huge smile was all but blinding.

"What do you mean, sir?"

"Please deploy and inflate one of the main door emergency slides. I will tell you when to release it. If you do this, we will let you take off."

This just keeps on getting more and more bizarre, Garth thought to himself.

"There is a river, you see," Onitsa said, "and these big slides make wonderful rafts. Our enemy does not expect this type of escape."

"Okay. I get it," Garth said, raising the handheld radio to his lips and punching the transmit button. "Okay, Phil. Here's the deal. If we do one more thing for the general, he'll let us out of here, but not until." Garth explained the request for the emergency slide, fully expecting resistance, but Knight agreed immediately. "I'm ordering it now," the captain confirmed.

"Ah, Phil. Better check the performance charts to see if we're okay to take off with this length of runway."

"Already have," Phil replied. "It's marginal, but legal. When you get up here, I'll want you to sign off the maintenance log, with your name. This was your idea, after all."

Garth ignored the dig and motioned the general to the left side of the plane. He saw movement above as door 1-Left was opened and the impressive mass of plastic and rubber ejected itself in a state of rapid inflation, stiffening almost immediately to provide a safe evacuation pathway down from the twenty-one-foot-high doorway.

"Very good," Onitsa said.

Just as quickly, one of the flight attendants pulled the release handle and the top of the slide detached from the door, which she closed.

Three of the soldiers dragged the inflated slide at double time to one side of the runway and out of reach of the idling engines.

"You may go now," Onitsa said. "But understand that there is a large government force trying to sneak up on us from the north, over there, behind the tail, and if you're caught in the crossfire, it may be too late."

"We're history!" Garth said as he waved and lifted the handheld to his mouth. "Phil, can you hear me?"

The reply was instantaneous. "Yes. What the hell's happening?"

"We're okay to go. I'm coming back aboard."

"Wait! I need you out there to make sure I stay on

the tarmac. I've got to move forward a few feet before I can cock the nose gear. I'm not sure it's going to stay on the runway."

Garth looked at the tires on the 747's nose gear, visible in the light of several old mercury vapor lamps still operating alongside one of the airport sheds to the south. "I see what you mean," he radioed. "Do you have all four engines running?"

"Yes."

Garth dashed to the left side of the nose far enough out to be seen from the cockpit. He could see Onitsa and his men racing back to their vehicles and moving off to the south side of the runway with more speed than he'd expected. "Okay, come forward Phil just to get her started. You've got about fifteen feet before you have to turn full left."

The powerful engines accelerated, and suddenly the big ship was moving, the nose gear rapidly swiveling full left as the 747 began turning to the east.

In the first-class section of the main cabin, Brian Logan heard the engines increase power and felt the 747 lurch as he waited by the hatch in the floor for the copilot's return. He looked around frantically for a crew member and spotted one of the flight attendants.

"Hey! What's he doing? The copilot's still outside."

She shook her head. "I don't know."

"Call the cockpit! Tell that SOB to stop!"

The flight attendant wasn't moving, and Brian turned to see Robert MacNaughton standing a few feet away.

"What is the trouble?" MacNaughton said, his voice calm and precise.

"That fool captain upstairs is trying to leave the copilot outside, just as I warned him."

"Has anyone informed the captain?" MacNaughton asked, but Brian was already maneuvering himself onto the small ladder leading from the main floor into the electronics bay.

There were racks of electronic black boxes on both sides as he reached the small floor and turned forward toward the open hatch to the ground. Brian could hear voices talking above him as he got to his knees and held on to one of the racks to poke his head out of the hatch. At first, the copilot was nowhere to be seen, but as he struggled to look in all directions while hanging almost upside down through the hatch, he caught sight of Garth Abbott running off to the left of the nose, apparently trying to keep up with the jet.

Brian reached down and waved frantically, trying to shout above the scream of the engines for the copilot to get aboard, but Garth couldn't hear him.

Brian had noticed a handset on the side of the electronics bay when he entered the compartment. It was identical to the one he'd used earlier to dial the cockpit. He pulled himself back up from the hatch and grabbed it, finding the two-digit code for the flight deck listed on the side and punching it in.

"What?" an angry male voice answered.

"Stop this damned airplane!" Brian ordered.

"Who the hell is this?"

"This is Dr. Logan, you bastard! You're trying to leave the copilot behind."

"No I'm not, I'm talking to him right now on the radio! Get off this line!" Phil Knight said.

"Give him time to get aboard. You hear me?"

There was no answer, but he could hear the engines winding down suddenly, along with popping sounds echoing through the open hatch.

A hundred and fifty feet to the left side of the Boeing, Garth was holding the transmit button down as he watched the nose gear tracking safely past the edge.

"Keep coming. Keep coming, you're fine on the nose gear," Garth radioed as he ran backward to keep pace while the Boeing completed its turn. He saw the nose gear swivel back to a forward position just as the sound of small-arms fire broke through his concentration. It was coming from behind him, from the north side of the runway. Garth glanced around to the north just as answering fire broke out from the opposite direction.

Jeez! We're already in a crossfire!

He could see muzzle flashes from both directions and hear the whirring buzz of bullets passing far too close, erasing any further hesitation. He broke into a run for the electronics hatch as he yelled into the transceiver.

"THEY'RE SHOOTING DOWN HERE! GET READY TO GO!"

"The wind's too stiff from the west for this runway," the captain said, his words barely audible between the crack and rattle of gunfire as Garth tried to keep the speaker to his ear while dashing head down for the ladder.

"We're too heavy for a downwind takeoff," the captain continued. "I've got to taxi to the opposite end."

Less than fifty feet remained to the ladder as the copilot raised the handheld radio to his mouth again, forcing his words between breaths.

"WE'VE . . . GOT TO GO . . . PHIL! FIRE-WALL IT WHEN . . . I'M ABOARD." He reached the foot of the ladder and tossed the radio up through the hatch without waiting for the answer.

Forty-seven feet above the tarmac, Phil Knight sat with his right hand on the throttles and keyed his transmitter. "Roger, understand you're aboard. Hang on." Phil jammed the four throttles full forward, his mind whirling as he tried to sort out how the military leader they'd dealt with so successfully could be letting his troops fire on their aircraft once more. It didn't make sense.

Garth had barely leaped onto the bottom rung and started to climb when his left leg suddenly collapsed in blinding pain beneath him, leaving him flailing for the ladder and hanging on with one hand, unaware that a bullet had just found its mark and torn through his upper left leg. His body rotated counterclockwise, leaving him hanging precariously as he tried to wrap his other hand around the ladder. He finally succeeded.

Phil felt the engines winding up just as he remembered he hadn't released the parking brake. He reached down to the center console and snapped it off, regretting the move instantly and hoping he hadn't knocked anyone down in the main cabin as the big jet jumped forward.

Just behind the nose gear, the sudden lurch dislodged all but Garth Abbott's right hand from the ladder as the Boeing began accelerating forward, dragging him along. His left side was in agony, his left leg useless, and he cried out for help. He hopped along on his right foot trying to reattach his left hand to the rungs of the ladder, but the acceleration of the jet was too great, and he was losing the battle.

In the electronics bay above, Brian had been thrown backward into a radio rack as the brakes were released. He grabbed for a handhold, his hands closing around a wiring bundle, which ripped away from one of the black boxes as he fell backward. Brian's head slammed into the bulkhead. He heard a shout down below above the scream of the engines but forced himself forward, peering over the edge in time to see the copilot hanging on by one hand. Brian fell on his stomach and hooked his left arm through part of the rack structure as he leaned down and reached for the copilot's other hand. Something hit the ladder at the same moment, and he realized it was a bullet.

"HOLD ON!" Brian shouted, encouraged that the copilot was looking up as he reached for his free hand and connected, pulling him far enough up the ladder for Garth to get his right foot on the lower rung. Brian could see his leg was covered with blood. The bullet could have severed an artery, he figured. He would have to act fast as soon as he could pull him in.

In the cockpit, Phil Knight glanced at the ground speed readout as it rose above sixty knots. *I'll hit eighty and then reverse and brake hard, turn us around at the end, and then go for it*, he told himself. There was still a light competing for his attention on the fault annunciator panel, and he glanced at it now long enough to realize it was the lower electronics bay hatch. *Abbott must not have had a chance to lock the hatch in place*, he concluded. He'd probably see it go out any second.

Seventy-five, and . . . eighty. Phil pulled the throttles back to idle and gauged his distance to the far end, braking hard.

Brian was in the process of reaching both arms down to pull Garth Abbott back up through the hatch when a series of frightening pings announced the impact of several high-energy slugs on the structure of the ladder. He felt the copilot jerk and drop and realized the gunmen had found his other leg. The man was hanging tight with both hands now, but both legs were dragging on the runway, and Brian realized there was no way he was going to be able to lift the man's dead weight all the way in.

"HANG ON!" he yelled to the copilot as he pushed himself back from the hatch and grabbed the interphone again, pulling it to his mouth and relieved for a micro-second to hear cockpit sounds on the other end.

"The copilot's been shot!" he barked. "Stop this damned airplane!"

Almost instantly the 747 heeled nose down as the captain tromped on the brakes, and Brian could feel the engines revving up in reverse and see the pavement slowing through the hatch.

He threw the handset down and dropped to his knees, getting in position to descend the ladder and drop to the ground as soon as they'd stopped. He could boost the copilot up and inside, he figured, but it had to be fast. There would be only seconds.

"HANG ON! HE'S STOPPING!" Brian yelled downward as the noise diminished.

"I'm hit!" The copilot said, his voice almost an octave above normal.

Brian Logan looked up toward the main floor to see several faces peering into the electronics bay. He started to yell at them for help, for someone else to come down, but a renewed flurry of gunfire broke out from beneath him and he felt the ladder sway.

Brian looked down and realized Abbott was no longer there. He scrambled back inside the hatch and turned around on his belly as fast as possible to stick his head out and look backward, searching for the copilot, spotting him at last lying on the runway a hundred feet or so behind the slowing 747. As Brian watched, a dozen soldiers in fatigues raced toward the prone figure from the north side of the runway and grabbed him, dragging Abbott away.

Oh, God! Brian thought, the outrageous helplessness of the situation all but overwhelming him.

The 747 had stopped and was swinging around to the left to prepare for takeoff, the nose passing from east through north as the captain turned toward the west.

Brian prepared to pull himself up and grab the handset again to yell for the captain to stop, but more soldiers appeared from the north side, several of them yelling and running directly for the ladder and the nose gear. Brian's head was upside down sticking out of the hatch, his eyes darting to the copilot's injured form as the soldiers dumped him on the side of the runway and took aim with their rifles. One of the onrushing soldiers raised his gun, trying to get a bead on Brian's head less than fifty feet away.

Brian yanked himself inside again and tried to retract

the ladder, but it wouldn't budge. There was a latch of some sort, he realized, and the hatch wouldn't close until the ladder was in.

Brian Logan heard the sound of shouting voices and running footsteps getting closer as the 747 steadied out on a westerly heading and the engines started rising in power again. He forced himself to slow down and quickly study the top of the ladder. The release mechanism was there and he found it just as the footsteps below clattered within yards. He pressed the release button and began hauling the ladder up as fast as he could, but one of the soldiers jumped on the bottom rung, pulling it back to full extension again. The man tossed his rifle to his companion and started climbing as Brian spotted a bright yellow metal oxygen bottle inside the compartment. The soldier was pulling himself into the compartment as Brian snapped off the latches holding the emergency oxygen bottle. He yanked it up and took as much of a backswing as he could before bringing the full force of it down on the man's uncovered head.

The soldier fell from the ladder with an audible thud. The 747 began moving forward again, the engines screaming.

Two more soldiers were on the ladder now and climbing, both holding guns, one aiming over his buddy's head and looking for whoever the attacker above might be.

Once more Brian took aim with the oxygen bottle and braced himself as the acceleration tried to push him backward. He could hear angry grunts and see a cocked pistol precede the first man into the compartment. Logan knew he would have only one chance to stop them.

Judy Jackson had been holding on to the captain's seat with white knuckles until he turned to her suddenly.

"Get down there and make sure that hatch is closed."

"Hatch?"

"The electronics bay. Move!"

She left the cockpit and descended to the main cabin, forcing herself to look at the passengers as she moved to the open hole in the floor, which was confusing. She'd never known such an entrance existed. She knelt down, trying to see below through the maze of equipment.

"Get back," one of the male passengers standing by the hatch demanded. "The doctor's down there. He went after the copilot."

She looked up in confusion, then turned back to the opening, sticking her head and shoulders far enough inside the hatch to see.

In the weak light filtering into the compartment from behind her, Judy could see a figure kneeling beside the open hatch as the 747 turned left for what seemed many seconds. The engines began revving up again and she saw what appeared to be the copilot's head pop into view above the lip of the hatch, and at the same moment, the man in the compartment swung a heavy yellow object down on the other man's head with incredible force, the impact producing a sharp "crack" she could hear from ten feet away.

Judy gasped as she recognized the assailant as Logan. He was fighting to keep the copilot out! She could hear the engines winding up to full power and felt the big bird rumbling forward, and suddenly Logan was at it again, swinging the bottle repeatedly below at the copilot, the impacts striking metal as well, creating a cascade of sparks as the bottle hit wiring bundles.

And within seconds he had succeeded. She saw Logan pull up the ladder and close the hatch.

Oh my God! Judy thought as she pulled her head back out of the hatch and wondered whether to slam it shut before he could emerge. Maybe if she had enough passengers stand on it, he couldn't get out.

She jumped to her feet and looked around with a feral expression, connecting with two of the men who'd angrily chased her to the cockpit hours before.

"That . . . that doctor just knocked the copilot out of the airplane. I think he killed him!"

"What?" one of the men said, incredulously.

"Down there," Judy said, hyperventilating and swallowing hard. "I saw . . . I saw him bash the copilot in the head as he tried to get back in! Quick! Please! Help me close this hatch and stand on it so he can't get in!"

"What, and lock the man in there? Hell, no," one of them said.

Judy dropped to her knees again and was starting to

close the hatch herself, when one of the men yanked her away.

"You leave him the hell alone, woman."

She turned to look at him, ready to protest, but the fight in her had been replaced by shock and panic and she got to her feet and retreated to the galley to find the interphone, her hands shaking violently as the acceleration of the departing airplane pushed her against the back edge of the galley counter.

"What's going on, Judy?" Cindy asked, breathing hard herself as she sat in the adjacent jump seat, too rattled to fasten her seat belt.

"We're . . . leaving the copilot behind," Judy said in a daze. "I saw the doctor kill him."

In the coach cabin behind them the passengers who were still standing following the rapid taxi down the runway were suddenly gripping anything handy and trying to maneuver their way back to their seats as Mary, one of the flight attendants in the rear galley, grabbed a handset and punched on the PA.

"SIT DOWN, EVERYONE! STAY SEATED! GET YOUR SEATBELTS ON! WE'RE TAKING OFF! STAY SEATED!"

Twenty knots, Phil thought to himself on the flight deck as he scanned the instruments and then looked at the runway ahead, ablaze in the 747's powerful landing lights.

He wondered if bullets were going to cascade through the cockpit at any moment.

There was movement to his left on the periphery of the lights and he glanced down, wondering why someone was lying in a white short-sleeved shirt on the left side of the runway in what looked like a pool of blood. There had already been too many shocks to digest, and this was just another outrageous sight he didn't comprehend, but his eyes involuntarily snapped back to the bloody figure, discerning more details of the image as the accelerating 747 rumbled past.

There were small, striped epaulets on the shoulders of the figure, and the sudden recognition of what he was seeing nearly stopped his heart.

Oh my God! That's Abbott!

Phil's mind reeled in denial. *But it can't be! He radioed aboard!*

He pressed his face against the glass, trying to find someone else there, but the figure on the runway raised a hand at that moment in a gesture for help just as the edge of the light beams passed over, leaving the image a nightmare now invisible in the wake of the passing jet.

The jumbo was accelerating through forty knots now, and there were trucks and soldiers on both sides of the runway, though no bullets seemed to be striking the aircraft.

He had a split-second decision to make: Yank the power off and stop, or continue the takeoff.

Phil fought the rudder pedals to keep the huge

airplane in the center of the runway, his hand poised on the throttles, the airspeed leaping upward every split second. He pulled the throttles back halfway, intending to pull them to idle, but the sudden loss of power shocked him enough to force his hand forward again to full throttle.

He was leaving his first officer behind. The first officer was injured, bleeding, lying on the concrete of the runway. How? He had reported himself back aboard, hadn't he? The thoughts were flying at light speed through his cranium as the airspeed came through eighty knots, but there was no copilot to make the "eighty knots" callout. Was that legal? He was back there bleeding on the runway. Why?

Once again Phil felt his mind order his hand to yank the power off, but this time the end of the runway was clearly approaching and he canceled the impulse, telling himself in the same microsecond that there was no longer room to stop.

Or was there? He couldn't tell, and he couldn't take the chance. Yet the indecision was tearing him apart. He didn't know what to do, so he pressed on.

Phil Knight held on and watched the airspeed climb above one hundred and twenty knots. It would be a close contest to see which value they hit first: flying speed or the end of the runway.

The speed was above a hundred thirty-five now. He needed one hundred and forty-five to fly and a few seconds to rotate the nose up so the wings could generate enough lift to pull them into the air. There were no red lights at the end as on most runways, and no runway-remaining distance markers. Only a dark void beyond. Even at a hundred and thirty the 747 seemed to be barely moving, the eye-to-runway height of forty-seven feet and the small circle of light from his own wings creating the illusion they were crawling.

One hundred forty!

The end was definitely in the landing lights now and less than a thousand feet ahead. There was no time left. Phil pulled the control yoke back sharply, feeling the nose leap off the runway and the deck angle rise to more than fifteen degrees as the tree line disappeared below the nose. He felt the shudder of the gear coming off the runway and kept pulling, the deck angle increasing second by second. The trees were right below their belly now, flashing past at over a hundred and seventy miles per hour as the Boeing clawed for altitude. He imagined he saw sparkles of light to the right and feared they marked the muzzle blasts of rifles aimed at his aircraft.

Gear! Phil leaned over the center console in a light-ning-fast gesture and pulled the gear lever to the up position. He could detect the big gear doors opening a hundred and fifty feet behind the cockpit and feel the corresponding shudder as the huge landing gear began retracting sideways.

An unexpected shudder rumbled through the cockpit, and a small icy feeling shot down his back as he imagined the gear plowing through the treetops and jamming in the up position.

But the green lights indicating the gear was safely up and locked came on simultaneously, giving him renewed hope that whatever they'd hit had done no damage.

His eyes dropped to the radar altimeter as it gave the absolute altitude above the surface.

Fifty. One hundred feet. One hundred and fifty feet.

A series of cockpit call chimes rang again, but he ignored them and concentrated instead on keeping the 747 climbing as he began to retract the flaps. He felt his heart pounding, and realized he had a blinding headache and a roaring in his mind.

We made it! Phil thought to himself, but the momentary feeling of deliverance sank at the same moment in the quicksand of self-recrimination for what he'd done, and not done. The emptiness of the copilot's seat mocked him, and the ghastly image wouldn't evaporate: Garth Abbott lying injured on the Katsina runway and looking up in agony, reaching out for help, as his captain left him behind to die.

On the tarmac below, Garth Abbott fought his fading consciousness and tried to deal with the image of his aircraft disappearing down the runway into the dark. Barely conscious, weak from loss of blood, and racked by immense pain, he suddenly heard running footsteps and managed to open his eyes enough to see several figures approaching in the weak lights of the airport.

But the effort was too great, and he closed them again, his last conscious thought a despairing and unanswerable *"Why?"* The sudden volley of shots ringing out at close range didn't register any more than the boot that probed his body.

THIRTY-ONE

Brian Logan sat in the gloom of the departing 747's electronics bay, breathing rapidly, his mind whirling. He was aware of the sounds and motions of the takeoff, and equally aware that the frightening rumble that shook the compartment moments before had been the heavy nose gear retracting into place a few feet forward of where he sat.

Anger was metastasizing like a mindless cancer, his outrage at the loss of the copilot propelled by preexisting hatred for Meridian Airlines and his deep and growing suspicion of the captain, who he alone knew had purposely left his first officer behind.

The copilot's face was vivid in his memory. *What was his name?* Brian thought, frustrated that he couldn't recall it instantly. At the very least he should be able to recall the guy's first name.

Garth. His name was Garth.

He remembered warning Garth that the captain was trying to get rid of him. *I was right all along.* Brian felt a twinge of illogic, but brushed it aside. He'd witnessed what the captain did himself, hadn't he?

The captain heard me. I told him on the interphone that the copilot was gravely injured and he had to stop the aircraft, and he hit the brakes instantly. He knew. But he took off anyway.

Brian shook his head against the fatigue and shock and confusion. He knew that somewhere deep within, the line between Daphne and this reality was blurring dangerously, but he was too tired mentally to resist the anger that was rapidly taking over. The image of the copilot's body lying somewhere behind them on the runway wouldn't leave his head, the accompanying stab of pain and guilt and helplessness bridging his last vestige of resistance as the copilot became the surrogate for his wife and son. In the slimy grip of Meridian, they were one and the same. That might as well be Daphne and their son back there on that runway, bleeding to death, abandoned by another murderous Meridian captain.

And once again he had been robbed of the chance to save them.

Brian sat forward with a start, forcing himself into the present. This was still a real and live and very dangerous situation, and he was in the belly of a jumbo jet full of passengers whose lives were being imperiled. It was too late for Garth, just as it was too late for Daphne, yet the same type of uncaring captain was at the controls of this aircraft, and there was still a chance to make a difference. Those people one deck above his head needed to know what had happened—what *was* happening.

Brian pulled himself up to a squatting position as he looked at the patch of light from the main cabin overhead and calculated what to do. Somehow they had to get the captain away from the controls, but who else could fly now that the captain had so effectively eliminated the copilot? There must be other pilots aboard. Somehow he'd have to find them quickly.

But why would a captain get rid of his copilot? Brian wondered. Somehow nothing made sense as long as he couldn't understand the captain's conduct. Meridian obviously bred hateful, uncaring pilots, but what was it that had driven this one to land in a war zone, and then get rid of his copilot? Why?

An answer came slithering in through the portal of his medical training. He wasn't a psychiatrist, but exposure to basic psychology was required for physicians, and some warning signs he'd missed before now began to emerge.

He thought back to two terrible crashes that had grabbed worldwide attention, one involving a suicidal Egyptian copilot on a Boeing 767 out of New York, the other an apparently distraught Singaporean captain in a 737 somewhere over Malaysia.

What if he's planning to kill himself? Oh God, that must be it! He's planning to kill himself and take us with him. How else to explain his conduct? Brian thought. Suicidal intent would explain everything bizarre the captain had done. *I guess I'm the only one aboard who understands what's really happening, and the only one who's witnessed hard evidence of lethal intent.*

The realization chilled him even more. *I'm the only one who understands the danger we're in.*

He had to change that. Somehow he had to find a way to wrest control from the captain before he succeeded in killing them all.

Brian stood up and glanced at the oxygen bottle and broken wires damaged by his attempt to repel the invading army. Brian moved quickly on rubber legs to the small ladder leading to the main deck and climbed up through the hatch, surprised to find himself surrounded by some of the familiar faces who'd rallied behind him before. They pressed around him in a whirlwind of concern and curiosity, asking what had happened and where the copilot was.

"The captain left him on the runway for dead," Brian said, unexpected tears cascading down his cheeks as he clenched his teeth in an effort to regain control of himself. Several hands reached down to pull him up and he shook them off, turning with his right hand up to quiet the questions.

"We're in terrible trouble here," he began. "The captain's suicidal."

Voices stopped for a moment as the men and women around him tried to come to grips with what he was saying.

"I'm sorry, what did you say?" one of them asked.

"I said, the captain is suicidal. I didn't understand that at first, but it's the only rational explanation I can come up with for this."

Quick, worried glances were exchanged among the group as Brian described the images he'd seen of the copilot slipping away, the call to the cockpit, and the captain's refusal to stop the takeoff. The color drained from the faces around him, and he felt a surge of hope that they would understand the truth of what he was saying. There would be many more to convince.

"We've got to find out quickly if there's anyone else on board who can fly," Brian said.

The chairman of English Petroleum was on the periphery listening carefully, and he nudged forward now. "You're quite certain, are you, Doctor, that the captain knew the copilot was injured?" Robert Mac-Naughton watched the recognition in Brian's eyes as the physician nodded energetically in response.

"He knew. That bastard definitely knew. I told him on the interphone that Garth was badly injured, that he'd been shot, that he had to stop the airplane, and he did stop. Did you all feel him hit the brakes before he turned around?"

MacNaughton nodded gravely, as did several others.

"Okay. He stepped on the brakes at the precise moment I told him what had happened. But then the unspeakable bastard turned around and took off, leaving the poor guy to bleed to death down there."

"Good heavens," MacNaughton said. "He was that badly injured?"

"When you've been shot several times with high-powered weapons and probably have an artery severed, you'll bleed out rapidly without immediate help. I could have saved him, but . . ." The words stung horribly the moment he spoke them, and Brian winced as he tried to control what was becoming dangerously close to hyper-ventilation.

The small, pretty woman who had identified herself sometime earlier as a deadheading flight attendant took his forearm, her eyes searching his.

"Why, exactly, do you think the captain's suicidal?" Janie Bretsen asked.

Brian looked at her. "The copilot told me a lot about what had been going on up there since we left London. There was a pitched battle between them. The captain kept trying to land in the most dangerous places, and now I realize it was to get rid of the copilot. When you add it all up, suicide . . . and killing all of us . . . is the most likely explanation."

Brian felt the panic rising again in his gut as he surveyed their eyes and realized they weren't grasping it.

"That's a rather substantial leap, don't you think?" MacNaughton replied, as Janie Bretsen stood silently surveying Brian's eyes.

Brian looked around quickly, as if the soldiers he had battled might climb out of the electronics bay and overwhelm him as effectively as their doubts were ensnaring his ability to save them.

They don't understand! They think I'm nuts, he thought to himself.

"Look, I'm not a psychiatrist," Brian said quickly. "Of course I could be wrong about his motive, but the reality of what he's done and what he's doing is still the same. I'm sure you understand that. We've got an out-of-control pilot in the cockpit who's already put us in great danger more than a few times today, and he's up there alone right now, in the air, and able to do anything he wants to. It's the middle of the night over the middle of Africa, we were peppered with bullets and may have lost God knows what systems, and no one's monitoring this wild man. We *know* he left his copilot behind to die on purpose, and I'm telling you we've got to find some way of controlling him until we get on the ground at Cape Town. Does anybody disagree with *that*?"

Thank God! Brian thought to himself. They were all nodding, except for the petite flight attendant, who was still skeptical.

"What do you propose we do?" Janie Bretsen asked, her voice soft and precise as her eyes bored into him like velvet lasers.

"I . . . guess we can't use the PA without his hearing us, so we'll have to fan out and try to find any pilots."

"Why?" Janie replied, her tone hardening. "You want to find someone who may be qualified on a Cessna 150 to replace a Boeing 747 captain? I'd call that a bit more than risky."

Brian looked into Janie Bretsen's eyes, realizing on a deeper level that she was penetrating his facade of control and that the others were watching the interchange carefully.

"No," he said evenly. "Not to take over. To monitor what he's doing. We only need a takeover if he tries to crash us."

Janie nodded at last, and Brian felt a small wave of relief course through him.

Judy Jackson had escaped from the forward galley as the aircraft lifted off the runway, and just minutes before Brian had emerged from the electronics bay. She'd made her way quickly past the grim and accusing faces of the passengers to the upper deck and the cockpit, going through the procedures to gain entry, which Phil Knight granted with the push of a button from inside. She reclosed the door and checked the locks.

"You left the copilot," she said in a matter-of-fact tone as she sat down in the jump seat behind Phil.

The captain looked around, trying to see her expression in the darkness. The glow of the instrument panel reflected in her eyes, which were staring into space.

He nodded. "I know. I thought he was aboard. On takeoff, I . . . I saw him off to the side. I couldn't stop."

"I know," Judy said. "I saw it happen."

He turned again. "Saw what happen?"

"That doctor. Logan. He clubbed Garth with an oxygen bottle when Garth tried to get back in."

"*WHAT?*"

From the jump seat behind him, she gripped the back of the captain's chair, her hands shaking on the top edge of it.

Phil Knight's head swiveled as he looked back and forth between the instrument panel and Judy Jackson. "Get . . . get in the seat over there and look at me," he ordered. "What the hell are you saying?"

Judy slid into the absent copilot's seat and repeated what she'd seen.

"Why on earth?" he asked.

"I . . . I don't know."

"Why would he kill a pilot?"

"He's insane, Captain. I tried to tell you both, but you wouldn't listen. All this has something to do with his dead wife. I think he's out to kill us."

She saw the pasty look on Phil Knight's face as he turned to her once again. "Judy, make sure the cockpit door is locked. I've got to talk to the company."

"I locked it."

Phil pulled the satellite phone from its cradle. The display was lighted but nothing he dialed would connect, and only static coursed through the earpiece.

"Damn!"

"What?" she asked, her voice shaking.

He glanced at her as if she were the source of his

irritation. "Our satellite phone is dead. Without it, I can't call the dispatcher."

"What are we going to do?" Judy asked, her voice shaky, the roar of the passing slipstream pressing in on her. "The passengers are with him."

Phil ran his eyes over the instruments, making sure the aircraft was still climbing. All the "door open" lights were out and even number-four engine was running steadily, but events were closing in on him, suffocating his thinking. If Judy were to be believed, they had a homicidal madman aboard who had clubbed his copilot out of the aircraft, and here he was, the only pilot left. At least the door was the new modified security version. No one could get through it, or so he'd been told. Yet, if that proved wrong, he had no gun to use to defend himself.

How am I going to explain leaving him behind? The question lunged at him like a snake, springing from the dark corners of his rationalizations. He closed his eyes for a second and forced the question away. He would deal with it later.

The idea that a passenger could have attacked Garth Abbott and dumped him overboard seemed too bizarre to be true. Could he trust Judy Jackson's account?

But, he'd seen the copilot himself on the side of the runway!

Yet, hadn't Abbott reported on the radio that he was back aboard? *I heard him say that,* Phil recalled. Abbott had come aboard, yet somehow he'd ended up back out on the runway, and that fact made Judy's tale all the more believable.

And wasn't it Judy who'd watched Logan dive into the electronics bay? Why *else* would he do that if not to attack the copilot?

This is surreal! Phil thought, glancing at the fuel panel and doing some quick mental calculations of distance, time, and fuel flow. Making Cape Town before running out of gas was becoming a marginal prospect, he realized. Getting them there safely would depend on the winds. If they continued southbound and ran short of fuel, where could he land? Certainly they were still closer to Europe than to Cape Town.

Maybe I should turn around, he thought.

Phil thought about the Nigerian air traffic controllers. Their frequency was still dialed into the number-one VHF radio, but he hadn't talked to them, and the realization was embarrassing. Here he was climbing into Nigerian airspace without a clearance or even the basics of a radio call. *Stupid move!* he chided himself. He jabbed at the transmit button and called repeatedly, but there was no response. He tuned the radios to another en-route frequency and tried again, but there was still nothing. The radios were clearly unpowered.

Now what? Phil thought.

"What's the matter?" Judy asked.

"The radios are dead! I can't talk to anyone." Phil felt his hand shaking slightly on the yoke. He was letting panic influence him, and he had to calm down.

"What . . . what are we going to do, Captain?" Judy pressed.

"You've already asked that question!" he snapped as the cockpit call chime rang. He could feel the situation pressing in on him again, controlling him, forcing him to flail at the process of deciding what to do.

Phil grabbed the handset and swept it to his ear expecting any voice but Brian Logan's.

"Is this the captain?" Logan asked, his voice low and threatening. The owner was breathing heavily.

"Yes. Who's this?"

"You know very well who this is, you murderer! And you know very well what you did."

There was tense silence for a few seconds before Phil could find a response. "What are you talking about? What do you want, Doctor?"

"You left your copilot to die out there! They shot him twice. I told you to stop so I could go out and get him, and you heard me, but you made sure to keep moving."

"I don't know what the hell you're babbling about, Logan, but there are enough witnesses to what *you* did down there to put you on death row. Nobody shot Abbott. You clubbed him with an oxygen bottle, and you're going to the gas chamber for it."

There was silence for a few seconds on the other end. "You *are* mad," Logan said at last. "I was trying to keep soldiers out. I was clubbing soldiers, you bastard."

"Then where's my copilot?"

"You left him! Listen, I don't know what's wrong with you, but there are three hundred passengers down here who're taking over as of this moment, you son of a bitch, and you're going to do precisely what we tell you from now on with no more unscheduled stops and no more lies and no more tricks."

"Or what? You'll club all my flight attendants to death with more oxygen bottles and come fly the airplane yourself?"

"Head this aircraft to Cape Town as fast as it'll go. You understand that?"

"We're already headed to Cape Town. You . . . you just sit down and leave my people alone. "

"Are you trying to kill us all, Captain? Are you suicidal?"

"WHAT?"

Brian Logan repeated the question, misinterpreting the silence from the cockpit.

"Of *course* I'm not suicidal, for God's sake!" Phil managed at last. "I'm trying to keep everyone safe. We had an engine problem, we had to land back there . . ."

"We're in control of this airplane now," Logan interrupted. "And we're going to send several off-duty pilots up there to watch you, and if you try anything else, we'll pull your miserable carcass out of that seat and let someone else fly, you arrogant little bastard!"

"No one's entering this cockpit, Logan." Phil could hear the doctor's voice increasing in volume as he almost sputtered into the microphone, the venality of his words deeply chilling. "You're just an arrogant little Caesar, aren't you, Captain? You can just sit up there and let people die because you don't care. A copilot, some poor schmuck in coach with broken ribs, a baby . . . You don't give a damn. You want to finish yourself off and you don't care one whit about the other lives on board. That poor copilot had both legs shattered and needed your help, and all you could do was leave him to die. Someone's got to stop bastards like you, and this time, there's someone on board to do it."

Phil Knight's voice rose in timbre and volume under the stress. "What . . . you're trying to do is commit air piracy . . . ah . . . in addition to attacking the copilot, and . . . and it's punishable by death!"

"Who cares," Logan replied. "I'm already dead inside, thanks to you."

"I'VE GOT A GUN UP HERE!" Knight bellowed out of fear, well aware his voice was too loud and too high but unable to control it. "If you try to come through that cockpit door, I'll shoot you on sight!" Phil slammed the handset back in its cradle before he could hear a response. His hands were shaking visibly as he turned to Judy Jackson who was watching him closely, her face a mask of fear.

"You have a gun?" she asked.

He shook his head. "No, but I don't want him to know that." Phil breathed rapidly, half expecting to hear a crowd trying to batter down the door at any second.

He reached for the interphone handset again, stabbing in the PA code.

This is the captain. I want all of you to listen closely. We're headed for Cape Town, and we're lucky to be alive. Stay in your seats or I'll have to land again at the first available airport with security. Stay in your seats! I'm not going to tolerate a riot! And one more thing. There's a wild man down there in the cabin you'd better get under control. His name is Logan. Don't let him talk you into doing something stupid.

Phil replaced the handset and turned to Judy. "You're sure Logan clubbed Abbott?"

"I saw him. I know what I saw. I'm sure."

"Okay. There's a crash axe on the back wall behind me, Judy. Get it."

"What are you going to do with an axe?"

"I've got to fly. It's up to you," he said.

"What's up to me?"

"To keep them out of this cockpit. If they get to me, we all die." Phil looked down at the center console, trying to think. He had to communicate with the outside world, let them know he was being hijacked.

Hijacked. That was the right word, wasn't it?

The hijacking code! He glanced at the radar transponder, the small radio that responded to any air traffic control radar beam by sending back a burst of identifying information. The little green light on the front of the unit was blinking now that he'd climbed above ten thousand feet. Someone's radar was "watching" and the unit was working, so he could dial in the international code for hijacking. No matter how crude the African radars, the hijacking code should be seen by the controllers below.

Phil leaned over and worked the small thumbwheels, intending to enter the hijack code, but changing it to the radio failure code instead.

Okay! He thought. *Squawking hijack. The whole world will know.*

His eyes swept past the ACARS control head, the telemetry system that communicated constantly with the company by satellite. There was a small printer in the console that could spit out weather and gate information and messages, and a small keypad he could use to send messages. Maybe it was still working. Phil snapped on the autopilot and leaned over, slowly typing the words he needed Denver to see.

Passenger riot on board. Have been hijacked by angry passengers. First Officer Abbott apparently badly injured and dumped out on takeoff from Nigeria by passenger named Logan who is leading revolt. Have been threatened and ordered to continue to Cape Town but must secretly turn around and return to London due to insufficient fuel. Request armed intervention on arrival. Head flight attendant barricaded in cockpit with me, and she's holding an axe. Do not know whether they have weapons, but assume they may use force. Other pilots on board threatening to take over. All radios out.

The typing completed, he hit the transmit button and watched the display until the small symbol appeared confirming the message had been transmitted to the satellites overhead.

Phil scanned the forward panel again and looked outside. There was no moon to reveal anything on the ground, just occasional lights from widely scattered African villages.

He reached up to the glare shield and grasped the heading knob, turning it a degree at a time and watching the slight left bank of the 747 as it gently and imperceptibly began turning away from the computed course to Cape Town.

THIRTY-TWO

The rapidly growing CIA team spilled into a secure conference room and reestablished the connection with the National Reconnaissance Office a dozen miles away at Chantilly. Chris Marriott, a senior analyst with twenty years of African experience, toggled the call to the speakerphone and identified himself.

"Sandra Collings here at Chantilly, Chris," a feminine voice responded. "We've got the latest transmissions, and this is getting very strange, even if we weren't watching all the air traffic in Africa. The 747 is airborne again and apparently resuming its course southbound to Cape Town, but they're not talking to anyone on the aviation radios, and their company can't raise them on their satellite phone. They left without an air traffic control clearance and then began transmitting the international radio failure code of seventy-six hundred on their transponder. At Katsina, the last pass showed those buses near the airport. Forty-three minutes later the buses are heading south *from* the airport, and it appears there are people aboard. We have several arms protruding from windows that appear to be Caucasian. Further, back at the airport, we have a discarded emergency exit slide off to one side of the runway."

"You're suggesting," Chris began, watching the faces of the others in the room, "that the rebels may have offloaded the passengers via the emergency exit slide into the buses?"

"Yes," Sandra Collings responded. "It's an early interpretation, of course, but all the basic pieces to the puzzle are there. The question we can't answer is, Why did the aircraft leave if everyone aboard was taken hostage? If we're right about the copilot having been shot, then, since this flight carried only two pilots, the captain would have had to depart on his own. The airline confirms there were no relief pilots or deadheading pilots aboard that they know about. Meridian also confirms that this captain is not a risk taker, although I guess he could have panicked and just wanted to get the hell out of there. The point I'm trying to make here is, Why the radio silence? Whether the passengers are aboard or not, why wouldn't the crew be screaming on every available radio to tell their company what had happened back there?"

"You have the airplane live on camera, so to speak?" Chris Marriott asked.

"We do," Sandra replied. "We're using a number of

different birds and methods for a digital composite, but we're watching him, and now, suddenly, all four engines are apparently running just fine. Plus, we're not sure the aircraft could have left Katsina's relatively short runway with passengers aboard. Three hundred–plus passengers weigh nearly fifty thousand pounds. So our confidence is growing that the aircraft departed without its passengers, and maybe without its crew."

"Without its *crew*?" Chris asked. "You mean, without the pilots?"

"Possibly. Remember we have enemies out there who can find someone to fly a 747 if they need to. After the World Trade Center attacks, you can be sure *we* didn't train them in the U.S., but, for enough cash, it wouldn't be impossible to find a crew."

"Sandra, flying an aircraft for a terrorist organization has been made a universal life sentence or death penalty offense by every civilized nation on earth," Chris said. "Just last year."

"Yeah, but the pilots may have no idea who they're working for, and someone's flying that aircraft. Look, I don't know what all this means, but we're watching the buses, and the next bird will acquire the area with sufficient resolution to help us in about eight minutes. So I'd say that if we see a stream of people getting off those buses somewhere, we've most likely got a hostage situation under the control of a very clever rebel leader. Onitsa has a long history of taking no prisoners and killing hostages after receiving ransoms."

"Right," Chris replied. "State needs to know this immediately. They're going to need to alert the Nigerians that they're about to be hit with a hostage crisis and outrageous ransom demands."

"I agree," Sandra Collings said. "We'll make the call and check back with you in ten minutes. And, Chris, one other thing you might need to know under the current alert from the White House and the Pentagon."

"Go ahead."

"We've called George Zoffel back in. You know George?"

"No, I don't think I do."

"She's our ranking expert on the Trojan Horse scenario. Just in case this begins to look like a European threat."

Chris hung up as one of the women in the room spoke up.

"He's got a point, Chris. No passengers, no radio response, and a dead copilot, meaning all we need is one coconspirator pilot and we've got a flying terrorist bomb."

"But, could a passengerless takeoff be the *result* of a hostage taking? That sounds pretty far-fetched."

"Not a result. Part of the plan. I know Onitsa's methods," one of the men said. "He loves to do interlocking deals. Say some group approached him with a plan. They've got a well-paid cockpit turncoat who's going to create an artificial need for an emergency landing in the middle of Africa. If Onitsa's men are ready to take the passengers as hostages and help load the plane with whatever weapon of mass destruction they're using, they both win. He gets bargaining chips in the form of hostages, they get an airplane with a valid flight number to use as a flying bomb, and we've got a Trojan Horse."

"Yeah, but good Lord, he'd be putting his head in a noose and declaring war on the U.S. and the world for aiding a terrorist act! The man wants to rule Nigeria and be accepted in the world community, not become another Saddam Hussein."

"Now wait a minute, everyone," Chris said. "Don't forget this aircraft is now headed for Cape Town. The alert that has us all jumpy is for Europe."

"For the *moment* he's headed south," was the reply. "For the moment we've just got a mystery. But if he turns north, we've got a Horse."

ABOARD MERIDIAN FLIGHT SIX
9:25 P.M. LOCAL

The wildly varying rumors that the copilot had been killed and his body either dumped or left on the runway burned through the shell-shocked passengers of Flight Six like a prairie fire.

The flight attendants had given Brian Logan and the passengers around him a wide berth. With Judy Jackson leaving her crew in the dark about what she had seen, the flight attendants had no idea what to believe. Cindy and Cathy had overheard as much of Brian Logan's words as possible after he emerged from the electronics bay, and had huddled in the first-class galley with Elle to call Judy Jackson in the cockpit.

"What do you want?" Judy had replied flatly.

"What do we *want*? Judy, how about a little guidance. What in the world is happening?"

"That doctor clubbed the copilot to death and pushed his body out before takeoff," Judy said. "We've got to keep him from attacking the captain."

"The *doctor*?"

"Yes."

"But . . . he's up front right now telling everyone the captain did it. Left Garth back there, I mean."

"I saw him do it!" Judy snapped, repeating the basics of what she'd witnessed.

"Judy, he said he was fighting soldiers trying to get aboard. He thinks the captain may be suicidal."

"Bull. He's fine."

Silence filled the gap until Cindy spoke. "So what do we do down here, Judy?"

"Keep him from trying to get through this cockpit door. It's supposed to be unbreakable, but the captain has me guarding it with an axe. Get some of the men, I suppose, and subdue him. We've got handcuffs down there in the supplies. Call me when you've cuffed him."

The sound of the connection being broken ended the call and all three women pulled back, looking at one another for some clue as to what to do next.

"Okay, so whom do we believe?" Cindy said after a few moments of silence.

Elle was shaking her head. "I have no idea."

Outside the galley curtains Brian searched through the overhead compartments until he found a battery-powered bullhorn. He pulled it from its bracket and stepped to the forward section of coach as eight other men and two women stood alongside and behind him. Brian triggered the megaphone, the electronic pop getting everyone's instant attention.

Folks, this is Dr. Brian Logan. I know you've been hearing different versions of what happened back there, and I just want to . . . well . . . let you know what really happened and what's really going on here. Most of you already know our copilot went outside through a hatch in the forward compartment. What you don't know is that he was shot trying to come back aboard, and the captain just . . . left him out there to die. I was down in that compartment trying to help him get back aboard. I grabbed the interphone at one point and begged the captain to stop the airplane, but he wouldn't. This captain is out of control. He's a murdering maniac, and we don't know why. What you also don't know is that the copilot had been trying all day to get the captain under control. He told me so before he climbed down to the ground to check the captain's fictitious claim that the same engine that caused our first emergency landing had gone bad again. His name was

Garth, and we left him back there with both legs shattered by bullets, bleeding to death.

Brian's voice choked off for a few seconds and he stood with his eyes closed, trying to regain control.

Garth was really on our side. Now there's no one in the cockpit to keep this captain under control. We don't know what he's doing, and we don't know what his motivation has been for purposefully trying to imperil all of us in Nigeria. You know, don't you, that he landed us in the middle of a civil war? I tried to talk with this captain a few minutes ago by interphone. I told him we all were demanding he fly on to Cape Town as planned and that he could consider that we were taking over, but I have no idea if he'll pull another stunt or not. One thing I do know: We desperately need to find any of you who are qualified pilots who could watch him up there and make sure he doesn't try to do anything else dangerous, such as land short of Cape Town, or . . . or do something else crazy. Let me know if you're a pilot. Especially any military pilots. Our lives depend on it. As long as he's the only pilot at the controls, he could kill us all in a heartbeat.

A silver-haired man in a casual sweater two rows away raised his hand, catching Brian's eye.

"You a pilot, sir?" Brian asked.

The man shook his head. "No, but why would you think an airline captain would try to imperil us?"

Brian met the man's gaze. "Remember EgyptAir?"

369

The questioner froze, his eyes flaring slightly as he nodded quickly and lowered his hand.

In the cockpit, the call chime rang, and Phil reached to answer it.

"Yes?"

"Captain? This is Mary in the rear galley. That doctor is down here using a bullhorn to speak to the passengers."

"What's he saying?"

"He's trying to find pilots to go up there and take over. He says you killed the copilot. Lori Cunningham and Barb Weston and I are hiding in the crew rest cubicle above the rear galley and we're really scared, and we need to know what to do and where the heck Judy is."

Phil handed the phone to Judy without comment, and she took it reluctantly.

"Yes?" she said, her voice distant and distracted as she listened. "Is anyone trying to hurt you?" Judy asked.

"No, but . . . what do we *do*? I mean we may be trained in how to handle suicidal hijackers now, but no one ever trained us how to handle a passenger riot, and these people are rioting, Judy! They *hate* us. I mean, I'm not sure what a riot is, but they're all agreeing with anything that doctor says, and there are several others down here stirring everyone else up, too."

"I can't come down there," Judy said. "You'll have to take care of it."

"Yeah, well . . . are you our leader or what, Judy?" Mary asked, sarcasm infusing her voice.

"I'll tell you what I am, little girl!" Judy snapped. "I'm disgusted with all of them and I'm not about to try reasoning with them. Let the bastards riot if they want to! You two just follow the manual."

She heard a rude sound from the other end. "*WHAT* manual? There's nothing in the manual about this."

But Judy had already handed the handset back to Phil, who quickly replaced it in its cradle.

THIRTY-THREE

David Byrd hardly noticed the drive from John Blaylock's favorite Alexandria watering hole to Capitol Hill.
He was too busy trying to digest Blaylock's words.

I'm being groomed for general?

The thought was a thrill, and a worry. And even
more bizarre than the concept of Blaylock as a personal
trainer was the idea that James Overmeyer thought that
highly of him. The news had triggered a sudden burst of
pride immediately leavened by caution and followed by
the ridiculous image of Blaylock as Yoda of *Star Wars*.

David suddenly realized a female driver in an adjacent
car was smiling at him, reacting to the fact that he'd been
shaking his head and gesturing in resonance with his
thoughts as he sat in his car. He smiled back at her and
laughed, rolling his eyes in shared recognition of the
humor, and gave the woman a small wave as he peeled

away left at the L'Enfant Plaza exit and accelerated toward the Capitol building and his town house five blocks beyond.

Purchasing the hundred-and-fifty-year-old house had been hailed as an act of insanity by other officers at the Pentagon, but he'd banked much of his money since the divorce and could easily afford it. Besides, he could always rent it out later on. Even with the hefty and unexpected renovation costs, he'd never regretted the decision.

"We know what you're up to, Byrd," one of his FAA acquaintances had needled him. "Whenever a decent-looking divorced guy buys up there, it's for one reason. Trolling for cute female congressional aides."

"No, I'm trolling for the female congresswomen they work for," he'd responded, a line that now rang rather strangely in light of Senator Douglass' call and his response.

Amazingly, there was an open parking place in front of his door and David took it, bounding up the front steps with key in hand as the cell phone rang again. He opened the door on the rich, walnut-trimmed interior of his living room as he flipped the instrument open.

"Hello?"

"Well, forget dinner at the Willard, my friend. What we talked about a few hours ago is happening as we speak. They're going off half-cocked."

This time the voice was instantly recognizable as Blaylock's.

"You mean the Trojan Horse thing, John?"

"You talk around secure subjects well, although you know we aren't supposed to do that. But what the hell. Yes. Something's happened, and they're coming unglued at Langley and the Pentapalace. Can you get back to NRO? I think this is going to be very instructive."

"It's afternoon drive time, John. It'll take me an hour even if I drive like a maniac—longer if I decide to obey any of the laws."

"I knew you'd say that," John replied, "So that was Plan B."

"Do I want to know Plan A?"

"You afraid of helicopters?"

"Of course not. I'm a pilot, right?"

"Yeah, but you're fixed wing, not a fling-wing pilot. Fixed-wing pilots are generally suspicious of helicopters and bumblebees, for damn good reason. Plan A calls for you to go immediately to Hangar Five at Reagan National where a civilian helicopter, a Bell JetRanger, equipped with a real helicopter pilot, will snatch your commissioned body up and bring it here."

"Understood. I'm on my way."

"*Ex*-cellent, as children say these days after their minds have corroded to dust under the influence of such alien forces as *Wayne's World* and MTV."

David found himself closing his eyes and shaking his head. "John, what the hell are you talking about?"

"The collapse of American culture and language into guttural triviality, among other things, but that can wait.

Hurry. We'll try not to start World War Three without you."

IN FLIGHT,
MERIDIAN FLIGHT SIX
9:45 P.M. LOCAL

Janie Bretsen wasn't certain when she reached her personal breaking point, but in the minutes following Brian Logan's emotional speech on the PA she found it virtually impossible to sit by any longer and tolerate the void Judy Jackson had created by running away. Previously, the state of the cabin crew and their utter impotence when it came to dealing with the passengers had just left her disgusted.

Now she was alarmed.

Janie moved into the empty forward galley and used one of the interphone handsets to reach Judy Jackson in the cockpit.

"What on earth do you think you're doing up there, Judy?" she asked. "Where does it say in the manual that the lead flight attendant hides in the cockpit?"

"I have no choice," Judy said, relating her duties with the crash axe that had become her relieving central focus.

"Then neither do I," Janie replied. "I'm next in seniority, and I'm taking control of this cabin crew. Stay up there and rot, for all I care."

"Go to hell, Bretsen."

Janie slapped the handset down and turned to find a wide-eyed Cindy Simons staring at her.

"Where are the other girls?" Janie asked.

Cindy pointed forward and aft simultaneously. "Hiding, mostly."

"That stops here. I'm taking over. Any objections?"

Cindy rolled her eyes. "Are you, like, *kidding*? It'll be a relief to have some direction and help."

"Get Elle and the others up here for a quick huddle. Tell them to take inventory of the food and drink stocks in the back before they come. Okay?"

"Okay! Cindy shot off toward the rear of the cabin as Janie rifled through the carts and the compartments, trying to discern what they had left. It was a lot easier to riot when you were hungry, thirsty, scared, and mistreated, which was the general condition of most Meridian passengers these days, she thought to herself. Certainly, the awful leg from Chicago had been no exception, but this . . . this was becoming uncontrollable. A life had been lost and a passenger had been injured. She was beyond thinking about legal liability. There were passengers actively trying to stampede other passengers into doing something stupid with a captain who had, indeed, imperiled them.

Janie peeked around the curtain in coach and tried to assess the state of the revolt. She didn't hear Robert MacNaughton approaching until he touched her shoulder, causing her to jump.

"Oh! Sorry."

"We met earlier, Ms. Bretsen, but I'm still unclear whether you're part of this crew," he said.

"Yes, I am." She related the circumstances of her clash with the lead flight attendant and her retreat to the cockpit. "I'm taking over the cabin crew."

"Good. We've got quite an emergency here, I'd say."

"Mr. MacNaughton, I need to ask you a very direct question, since you were ... talking with Dr. Logan much earlier, too."

"By all means."

"What's *your* assessment of him?"

Robert MacNaughton studied Janie's face for a few seconds as he formulated an answer. "Very well. Two points. Dr. Logan is predisposed to hate this airline, with substantial justification as I understand it, and he came aboard very upset."

Janie was nodding. "I heard about his wife and child."

"Therefore," Robert continued, "he may be expected to exaggerate any problems."

"I thought that as well," she said.

"But ... it's also quite clear that our strange captain has indeed left his copilot behind, apparently on purpose, and it's quite clear that we have a very odd and dangerous situation here, and the doctor is probably correct that we're dealing with either a seriously incompetent flyer, or a suicidal one. In either event, we can't afford to sit and wait for the next act."

Janie shook her head. "Suicidal I can't buy."

"Logan has a point, you know," Robert added.

"Merely finding a qualified pilot to watch him is a rather smart suggestion, don't you think?"

Janie hesitated, then nodded. "Within limits."

"Of course."

"But . . . we can't corner the captain and run the risk of his doing something dangerous in response," Janie said.

"Such as landing in the middle of a firefight in a civil war?" Robert let the words hang there as he watched Janie swallow and look away momentarily before meeting his eyes again.

"Point well taken."

"I must tell you that except for yourself and some of the other ladies, this is the worst crew I have ever had the misfortune to encounter. Especially Miss Jackson. I hope that doesn't offend you."

"It doesn't," she replied. "And you're right about the service and the decisions made by the captain."

"One more thing. If the good doctor returns empty-handed from searching for another flyer, it so happens I, myself, am a pilot, though I'm not qualified on something this large."

"What's the largest plane you can fly?"

She thought she noticed a small grin as he replied.

"The Boeing 737."

The soft dual tone of a cabin call chime rang, and Janie turned to look at the overhead light as someone shouted from the first coach cabin. She pushed through the divider curtains as Brian Logan rushed back into the forward coach area from the rear section of the huge aircraft, following a small, bald man she hadn't seen before as he pointed to one of the windows and leaned across two passengers.

"See? We are turning!" the man said.

Janie moved toward them as several others rushed to other windows, straining for a view of whatever had attracted their attention.

"Where?" Brian Logan was asking.

"There. See that W-shaped constellation? Watch it move to the left. We're turning very slowly, but he's already changed course over ninety degrees. Cassiopeia was squarely off the left wing when he started."

Brian nodded and pulled away, his face ashen as he strode forward to find Janie in his path.

"Please move," he said.

"What's the problem, Doctor?" Janie asked, holding her position.

Brian looked at her quizzically for a few seconds before responding. "He's drastically changing course. We're supposed to be going south."

She took a deep breath and glanced over her shoulder at Robert MacNaughton, who was watching without comment, then turned back to Brian.

"What are you planning to do?"

"I'm going to call the bastard and see what he's up to now," Brian said, as he gently pushed past her and headed for the same interphone he'd used before. Janie made no attempt to stop him as he consulted the numbers printed on the back of the handset and punched in the flight deck code.

On the flight deck, Phil Knight picked up the receiver and growled a response. "What?"

"What the hell are you doing up there?" Brian snapped.

"I . . . have to go around some thunderstorms."

"There's nothing out there but stars."

"You don't have radar. I do, and I'm looking at thunderstorms and I'm not going through them."

"A ninety-degree course change to avoid weather? That sounds pretty drastic. You're headed due east."

"That's the way it goes over Africa. Now get off this interphone."

"Understand this, Captain," Brian said, well aware of Janie Bretsen standing beside him and listening carefully to every word. "There are several people back here who can read the stars, and they'll know which way we're heading at any moment. If we're not back on course for Cape Town very quickly, we're coming up there."

"And I'll blow your head off, Logan, if you even try to open this door. Understand?" Phil replied, but the other end had already been disconnected. He sat in silence for a moment, trying to recall some of the tricks other crews had used with hijackers. One method in particular had impressed him as clever. Maybe, he thought, he could make it work, too. After all, he was hijacked, wasn't he? Logan had clearly told him that on the interphone, which meant the man's words would be on the cockpit voice recorder, and they had the new version that recorded all the radio calls and interphone and cockpit chatter throughout the flight, not just the last thirty minutes.

There's enough there to put him in the gas chamber, Phil told himself as he glanced at the overhead panel, thinking through the steps he'd have to take if he used the method he was considering. There would be some serious physical risks to the passengers, but weren't they responsible anyway? No, he concluded. He had every right to take such a chance.

"Judy?" Phil said sharply.

"Yes?" The answer was cautious, but maybe he could force her into action.

"We're going to end this revolt right now."

THIRTY-FOUR

David Byrd greeted the NRO aide in the lobby of the headquarters building and clipped on a security badge as the young man motioned for him to follow. The high-speed dash to Reagan International Airport and the equally fast helicopter flight to Chantilly had been a whirlwind of sights and sounds competing with his growing curiosity.

After a quick walk down several corridors, the aide ushered him into a slightly larger version of the high-security room he'd seen earlier in the day. Three NRO analysts, including George Zoffel, were sitting at the circular console and hunched over their computer keyboards in the midst of an intense exchange as he moved into the room. David spotted John Blaylock seated behind them at a second-tier continuous desk and waved. Blaylock motioned David to the chair beside him and offered him the same type of lightweight headset the others were wearing, along with the whispered information that an intensive discussion with a CIA team at Langley was under way.

John adjusted several switches in front of him, his deep voice suddenly booming in David's ears.

"Can you hear me?"

"Yes," David replied, inclining his head toward the others.

"They can't hear us talking when we're in a private chat mode," John said. "That's Sandra Collings next to George Zoffel, by the way. I don't know the other guy."

"What's happening, John? Why are we here?"

"Very strange situation, it's evolving rapidly, and it involves a civilian 747," he replied, filling in the basic facts about the departure from the Nigerian airport after the apparent murder of the flight's copilot and removal of all passengers. Something in the intense background discussion snagged John's attention and he raised his hand, silencing David's impending reply.

"Wait!"

"Pull that in closer," George Zoffel ordered as one of the many electronic images on the screens began changing. "This is the other end of the runway," Zoffel continued. "The east end . . . six thousand feet away from where the copilot was apparently killed, or at least, where he was last seen."

"Okay," a voice from CIA headquarters said.

"This is a frame taken as the aircraft was climbing to

the west, before it turned south. There's a body on the runway, as you can see, and shooters on both the north and south sides."

"An active crossfire?" Sandra Collings asked.

"I think so, but look at the blowup here using just available light . . . not infrared. The body appears to be in pants, probably male, bleeding badly, and wearing a white shirt. Closer, Ray, on the shoulders," George Zoffel ordered, watching as the frame pushed in even closer. "It's too blurry."

"Hold on," the analyst named Ray replied. "I'll computer-enhance it in a second." He worked through a series of keyboard orders to the computer, and they watched in silence as the pixels of the image began to migrate toward one another to form a sharper picture, step-by-step. There were black patches on the shoulders of the figure, and as the computer improved the frame for the sixth or seventh time, one of the patches began to show alternating stripes.

"Oh, shit! There we are," George Zoffel said, sitting back.

"What?" Langley asked.

"You getting this shot at Langley?" Zoffel asked.

"Yes, but where's the 'Oh, shit' material?"

"See the black patches on the shoulders? Those are epaulets. Civilian pilots wear those. That's how we ID'd the copilot. There were only two pilots aboard. As I told you, we believe the copilot was killed at the west end just after they landed. Here's the other pilot. I'm unable to tell whether I'm looking at a four-stripe captain's epaulet or not, but if it's four, then we're looking at a deceased or badly injured captain whose aircraft is airborne without him."

"Hard to tell from this angle," Ray added, still cajoling the computer to improve some more. "But, that's as far as I can take it. Not bad from two hundred miles at night."

"So . . . ," a male voice from Langley asked, "you think both the captain and copilot have been killed and dumped out?"

"I'd class that as high confidence," George Zoffel replied, "which then raises a little technical question about who the hell's flying Meridian's airplane."

John Blaylock checked the switches to make sure they were still in private chat mode and turned to David, who had been following the exchange carefully.

"David, this could well be the attack everyone's been on alert for. The jet took off, we think without passengers, and about a half hour ago the live shot showed they were changing course and flying almost due east on a heading of about zero-seven-five degrees, which is how you get to Yemen, among other not-so-friendly places. That was the last satellite shot. They're just now working to reacquire the aircraft with another satellite."

"How do we know the passengers got off?" David asked.

There was a small yelp in the background, and they both turned.

"Okay, we've got another course change, folks," Ray was saying. "He's going north!" They watched the ghostly white infrared image of the 747, its hot exhaust plumes streaming white behind each engine.

"What's the course you're reading, George?" the CIA man asked.

There was a rueful laugh as George Zoffel shook his head. "Oh, how about roughly in a direct line to London, just as the message said, or for that matter to Rome, or Paris, not to mention Geneva, Brussels, Amsterdam, and possibly Copenhagen."

"He can't aim at all of them simultaneously," the man at Langley said.

"No, but with small alterations in course, he could head for any one of them."

"Your fissile scan still negative?" the voice from Langley asked.

George Zoffel nodded before replying. "We have no indication of any fissile nuclear material on that jet . . . *yet*. But you know the problem if they've got incredibly well-shielded nuclear material aboard. We may not see it for a few hours until the satellites can ping it and collect enough particles."

"The next shots are coming up in sixty seconds," Ray said.

John Blaylock turned back to David and ran through the evidence and pointed to a freeze-frame on an upper-left screen. "This one just came in as well. The buses that we think carried the passengers away from the plane are still in motion, but they were heading down a road leading to what appears to be a warehouse as the last live satellite moved over the horizon and out of range. On top of everything else, the aircraft has started squawking seventy-six hundred."

"Radio failure code," David said.

"Right."

"Did he have a clearance?" David asked, his eyes boring into the various images on the screens.

"Never called," John Blaylock replied. "No satellite communications with his company, either, after an initial call on the ground. But, he . . . or someone . . . sent a cryptic message over the satellite ACARS system. We got it in here about twenty minutes ago." John pushed over a copy of the message from Phil Knight as he read the first few sentences. "He says, 'Passenger riot on board . . . Hijacked by angry passengers. First Officer Abbott apparently badly injured and dumped out on takeoff from Nigeria by passenger named Logan who is leading revolt. Have been threatened and ordered to continue Cape Town but must secretly turn around and return London due to insufficient fuel.'"

"Good grief!"

"He goes on: 'Request armed intervention on arrival.' And he says all his radios are out."

"But, that's consistent, John, with his squawk."

"Right. He may well be needing to squawk *both* codes, but the fact that he's using only the radio failure code is interesting. Hijacking's a greater priority, to say the least, but the radio failure thing is a perfect ploy if you're going to pretend to be running for home but don't want anyone analyzing the voice of whoever's at the controls. Remember, they probably aren't aware we can read the stripes on the shoulders of bodies on a runway. Point is, that message makes no mention of the passengers having been removed. It does mention the loss of the copilot, but the captain that we're supposed to believe is in that cockpit is more than likely the dead or dying airman we're looking at who's been abandoned back at the Katsina airport."

"But, maybe not. We shouldn't stampede to a conclusion that this is a terrorist."

"I agree, it's too early to conclude one way or another. But it's also not too early to look at the alternative theory and take protective steps."

David Byrd shook his head slowly as he tore his eyes away from the screens and met John Blaylock's gaze. "John, keep in mind what you said to me this morning about the improbability of someone actually using a commercial airliner as a Trojan Horse. What was it, the conservation-of-paranoia principle?"

"You listen well, Colonel Byrd."

"I try."

"But neither of us considered someone creating the *illusion* of an air rage incident to *mask* a Trojan Horse attack. We were discussing how someone might use a genuine, spontaneous air rage incident as a diversion."

"The guys I told you about in General Overmeyer's

office weren't thinking about diversions, John. They were all worked up over the possibility that some remaining terrorist cell could whip a mild air rage scenario into something lethal just by manipulation."

"I really think this is something else," John said, rubbing his chin, his eyes on the monitors. "We've got no evidence of any air rage except that message, which is quite likely bogus and carefully planned. And, this involves Dr. Onitsa, which means it's got to be a package deal, which means it's very well thought out and extremely well funded and they're very well informed to know how to press our air rage buttons."

"Wait . . . *Doctor* Onitsa?"

John searched through a folder in front of him and pulled out a two-sheet classified briefing paper, which he handed over. "He's called general now, but he's a physician and a very clever rebel driving the Nigerians crazy."

David skimmed the paper before looking up. "Never heard of him. John, we're not losing sight of the possibility of that message from the cockpit being authentic, are we?"

John Blaylock shook his head. "No. They know that. It's always possible. But if so, then where did the extra dead pilot on the runway come from?" He glanced over at David.

"Have we checked the passenger list?" David asked. "Where did this flight originate, by the way? For some reason, the call sign seems familiar."

John filled him in. "We don't have the passenger list yet."

"You know what worries me?" David added, his eyes back on the activity at the front of the room. "The phraseology in that message. 'Passenger riot on board' sounds very American. All of it does. If it's American, there has to be an American pilot on board."

"Or they've got an American turncoat on their staff who knows our idioms. Do you know you may have had a passport-carrying double in training in Moscow in the eighties?"

"Sorry?"

"Our old buddy adversaries, the ex-Soviets, had a lot of tricks up their sleeves. One was to select and train select Soviet personnel who physically looked like American officers or senior enlisted counterparts and put them through an Americanization course at KGB university that approached the flawless. If they ever needed to insert them into reality, just eliminate the real Major Byrd, for instance, and insert the well-trained imposter. Their linguists are still around, as are their students. Discount no possibility before its time."

"We've got pictures," Ray said as new images flashed on the main screen. They looked closely at the picture as a small cursor appeared on the screen.

"Okay, I'm controlling the cursor," George Zoffel was saying. "This appears to be some sort of large shed, right here . . . probably corrugated metal roofing, looks like, perhaps, a hundred feet by eighty feet."

"Enough to put three hundred twenty people under," Sandra added.

"Yeah . . . and . . . we've got the buses all parked outside, and . . . wait a minute! We've got people sitting in rows spilling out of the structure."

"How many?"

"Ray, can you get a live shot?" George asked.

"Yeah, with unfiltered infrared." Ray punched his keyboard and a more fuzzy version came up, white human images burning their way across the scope of the picture as they moved around the seated objects.

"Those are living humans, all right, sitting in rows. I count about twenty-five visible. Any way they could be troops?"

Ray toggled the picture back to the composite freeze-frame and enlarged it, eliminating the infrared images and leaving regular light. "They have electricity there and lights inside," he said, as he once again enhanced and zoomed until wristwatches and small carry-on bags and Western-style clothing were clearly visible. "I see what's probably an electric power plant to the right."

"What are we seeing in terms of racial makeup? If those are passengers from Meridian, you'll see a cross-section of dark and light skin."

"And we do," Ray replied. "I've clearly got light-skinned people as well as some blacks. Too many to be explained by a few stray white mercenaries in the employ of General Onitsa."

The door to the room opened and an aide moved

quickly to George Zoffel's side with a folded message. He read it before turning around and nodding to John Blaylock and David Byrd as he spoke to his counterparts at Langley on his headset.

"Well, guys and gals, we've just received another little missile that fits the nightmare. The folks at the State Department report that General Onitsa has just contacted the Nigerian government in Abuja by satellite phone to demand three hundred million American dollars wired to an offshore account within two hours, or he starts executing his three hundred twenty hostages. He claims he let the pilots go."

"But we know better," Sandra said.

"In other words," the voice from Langley said quietly, "whatever Flight Six is trying to carry back to Europe, it isn't the passengers they started with."

"I see no reasonable alternative explanation at the moment," Zoffel agreed with a tired sigh. "Provided all these facts hold up. Better sound the Klaxon at the White House and the Pentagon. This appears to be the real thing."

THIRTY-FIVE

Janie Bretsen raised one of the interphone handsets to her mouth and toggled in the code for the PA as she looked up at Cindy, who was watching the process with a frightened expression. It was bad enough that the majority of over three hundred crowded, tired, angry passengers were already in passive revolt against the captain and crew. But the collective attitude was spiraling toward something worse, and Brian Logan was the catalyst as he walked back and forth answering questions about the copilot and the captain and the loss of his wife at the hands of this same evil airline.

Janie took a deep breath and forced herself to punch in the PA access code. It was time to act, but the gamble she'd decided to take was unprecedented and dangerous.

The sound of the speakers coming to life caused the usual flurry as conversations stopped and heads turned.

Folks, I need your attention, and please hear me out.

She could feel her heart pounding and imagine the outraged response at Meridian headquarters in the coming weeks when the cockpit voice recorder yielded the record of what she was about to say. *So much for my airline career,* she thought.

A new lead flight attendant has taken over this cabin crew, and that's me, and things are going to get much better. My name is Janie Bretsen. I was a deadheading crewmember going along to Cape Town, but because of what's happened and the way Miss Jackson, the previous lead flight attendant, has grossly insulted, manipulated, and lied to you ever since push-back in London, I've finally come to the conclusion that I can't tolerate this any more. I'll probably be fired, but I've relieved Jackson. She's the acid-tongued flight attendant some of you chased out a while back.

There was a ripple of exchanged glances in the cabin, and more eyes meeting hers directly, but no one was grumbling or moving in her direction.

Okay. Look, I'm . . . just as disgusted as you, and I'm just as scared. I don't understand any of what's happened today any more than you do. Please believe me, though, when I tell you that your flight attendants are not the problem. We are NOT your enemy. With the exception of Judy Jackson, that is. In fact, your flight attendants were being ordered by Jackson not to get you water and coffee and food except when she decreed it, and they were threatened with being fired if they bucked her. Now I'm in charge of the cabin, and we're going to do our dead level best for you by serving every drink we've got, every snack we can find, and by trying to get this captain under control.

It's true that none of us can understand the loss of Garth Abbott, the copilot, or how the captain could leave him behind. We can't understand much of anything this captain has done. But I have a big, big request of you. I know that some of you are openly talking about going to the cockpit. Please . . . no matter how furious you are . . . don't even think about trying to get through that cockpit door. All of us want to live, and starting a fight with a lone pilot while airborne could be fatal for all of us, not to mention the fact that the captain is still legally in command, thus any attempt to break in could be a crime.

And I have a second big request. Please try to stay seated with your seat belts fastened. In return, I promise that your flight attendants, under my command, will NOT lie to you about anything, and we'll do our best to make you as comfortable as possible until we can all get off this airplane.

"We understand that we have your sympathy, Janie," a male voice bellowed from the rear of the cabin. "But are you *with* us?"

Janie raised the handset again and hesitated before answering. Calculating the consequences of the various things she could say. It was still better, she decided, to be an ally trying to soothe them from within. It was the best chance she had to keep them under some sort of control.

This captain's conduct is not what my airline is all about. So, yes, I'm with you. Now, we've got to be very careful what we do, because the situation is so dangerous. But, yes, my crew and I are with you.

The man who'd shouted the question stood and started clapping slowly, loudly, and others gradually joined him until most of the passengers were also standing and applauding.

Janie nodded to them as she lowered the handset, gratified to see almost everyone sit down and reach for their seat belts. She wondered if the captain had been listening on the flight deck. The fact that she'd already discussed this sympathize-and-control ploy with the rest of her crew might insulate her career from Meridian's inevitable outrage, but it was still a gamble—not that there was any real choice. No one but Brian Logan had been leading the passengers up to now.

She saw a short man with a completely bald head leaning over another row of passengers and staring out the window. He was motioning to Logan, and she saw the doctor move rapidly from several rows away to the man's side.

"He's turned north," she heard the man say. "He's steering about ten degrees left of due north."

"Back to London, in other words," Brian answered.

The man nodded, then shook his head as he glanced around at several others. "Could be anywhere along the way. He could be taking us to the middle of the Sahara. In fact, it could be Libya."

Logan turned and caught Janie's eye as he pointed to the window and shook his head. She could see his lips compressed in anger, but she hurriedly motioned for Brian to come to her.

He hesitated and looked around before complying.

"Come in here," Janie said when he'd reached her. She pointed to the privacy curtains which screened the galley from view.

"Why?" Brian responded, suspicion evident in his tone.

"Because we're both trying to get some control over this situation," she said, as if cooperation between them was an agreed goal. She held her breath and turned without waiting for a response, pushing through the curtains to move to the far side of the galley's interior before turning to see if he'd followed.

He had.

"The son of a bitch has changed course again, Janie," Brian Logan said, coming up to her. "Now he's heading north."

"Do you think," she replied, "he could be trying to go back to London?"

Brian Logan was breathing hard, his right hand flailing the air in frustration as he glanced in both directions, then met her eyes once more.

"I don't know where he's going, but I do know we can't trust him for a second."

"But, there are no other pilots aboard, and without him, we're dead. That's the reality, isn't it?" she replied, quietly, watching his eyes and keeping them locked on hers.

He hesitated, then nodded. "That's what's driving me crazy. We're hostages here!"

Janie reached for his left arm, touching it gently, then closed her small hand as far as it would go around his upper arm, momentarily stunned by the rush of attraction she felt toward him. He was looking at her intently, and she wondered if he felt the same thing, but she hurriedly pushed the thought aside.

"Doctor . . .*Brian* . . . as long as we're still airborne and moving toward some safe airport, shouldn't we just wait it out? I'm afraid of panicking the man."

He made no effort to pull away, and she felt a tiny bit of tension evaporate. He *could* be talked to. She was going to have to build his trust, but he wasn't unreachable. *Thank God*, she thought as he broke lock on her eyes and looked away.

"We can't let the arrogant little bastard kill us all," Brian was saying.

"But . . .*But* . . . ," she said, squeezing his arm slightly, "if we try to take over, and we have no one else qualified to fly a 747 . . ." She let the rest of the sentence trail away and suppressed a small flutter of guilt at using the technicality to mask a lie. Technically, Robert Mac-

Naughton was not qualified to fly a 747, but he *was* qualified in a 737, so he understood big airplanes and systems. However, putting MacNaughton in the pilot's seat would be nothing more than an emergency backup if all else failed. "I agree the captain's a bastard and worse, Brian, but be practical! If . . . if there were another 747 pilot aboard it might be different, but not just any pilot can land this large a ship. *Besides, that's a reinforced door up there, and I don't have a key. There's no way you could get in unless the captain opens it, and he's trained to never open it just because someone's threatening his crew.*"

"I know *all that!*" he said, grinding his teeth and closing his eyes as her alarm grew. She could feel his anger rising again, his frustration about to boil over. She tugged on his arm in an attempt to turn him back to look at her, but he wouldn't turn. She saw him pinch his nose as he cleared his ears and shook his head slightly.

And suddenly he was looking at her with the same distrust as before.

"My ears!"

"I'm sorry?" Janie said, thoroughly off balance.

"You feel that? The pressure's changing."

"No, I don't."

"Why is the cabin pressure changing?"

Three other men pushed through the curtain from coach.

"Hey, Doc?" the first one said. "Hickson back there says he's trying to go to Libya now."

Brian whirled around, breaking away from Janie's

grasp and ignoring the statement. "Are your ears clicking?"

The men exchanged glances as they paused to take stock of their ears, one of them shrugging. "I don't know . . ."

The first man began nodding energetically, his eyes wide. "Hey, yeah! Mine *have* been clicking. What's that mean, Doc?"

"Did you have to do a Valsalva maneuver to clear them?" Brian asked, his voice intense.

"Val . . .*what*?" he asked.

"Valsalva. Close your mouth, pinch your nose, and blow until your ears clear."

The two exchanged another glance. "Ah, no. They've just been popping."

Brian moved across the galley and ripped the curtain back, surveying the passengers.

"So what does that mean?" another man asked behind him.

Brian turned to Janie, who was feeling stunned at the sudden loss of connection with him. "Okay, Janie, what *does* it mean?"

"I . . . I don't know," she answered, her mind racing over the question. "Probably he's climbing to a higher altitude. Why?"

Brian inclined his head toward the cabin. "Because they're all working to clear their ears back there, and mine are still popping, and I didn't hear the engines change pitch."

"Then, I don't know," she said. "But don't worry about it. Changing altitude during a flight is routine. The pilots are . . . I'm sure he's trying to find smoother air."

Brian let go of the curtain and turned to her, shaking his head.

"It wasn't bumpy."

"Well . . . I don't know, then."

"You're lying, aren't you?" he snapped.

"*No!*" Janie said, feeling light-headed as she heard her own ears pop again.

Brian Logan pointed to the ceiling as he moved slowly back toward Janie. "He's pulling something up there with the pressurization, and you're pretending you don't know." The other two men stepped aside to let him pass until he was standing in front of her, towering over her petite figure and looking down, hands on hips, his eyes hard and angry.

"What's he doing to us, Janie? TELL ME NOW!"

She shook her head, her hands out in a gesture of immense frustration. "I don't KNOW! Honestly! My ears are popping, too. Either we're climbing, or . . . or . . ."

"Or what?" Brian shot back, his breathing becoming more rapid.

Janie felt her own breathing accelerating, but not from fright. Something *was* wrong, but it was gradual, so it couldn't be a rapid depressurization.

"Wait," she said, pointing to the entrance. She moved past him and pulled the curtain to look at the passengers herself, just as he had done. As many as two dozen were sleeping, she saw, but as she watched, an older woman in a forward row suddenly let her head loll to one side as she, too, dropped off.

Janie let the curtain go as a small kernel of fear begin to grow in her stomach. She turned and moved to the opposite side, to the curtain separating the galley from first class, searching the seat backs for any signs of deployed emergency oxygen masks.

When do they drop? she asked herself, the answer almost instantaneous and echoing through a decade of recurrent training. *Twelve thousand feet, of course. When the cabin reaches twelve thousand, the masks deploy automatically. But we can breathe just fine below twelve thousand feet, so if they haven't deployed . . .*

Janie turned to face Brian and the other two men. "Are any of you feeling light-headed?"

"Yeah," one of the men responded. "I am."

"Me, too, I think," another answered.

Brian glanced at them, then looked back to Janie. "He's depressurizing us, isn't he?"

She nodded, slowly and reluctantly, yet unable to hide it. There was no point in lying about it, she decided. With her ears popping, the masks would probably drop at any second. "Could be," Janie said, "although the masks haven't dropped, so we should be below twelve thousand cabin altitude." She quickly explained the mechanism. "No masks, no problem. We might be a bit light-headed, but he can't really knock us out from lack of oxygen unless the cabin is much higher. A cabin altitude of twenty-five thousand feet, for instance, would be a big problem, but even then we're okay for about thirty minutes without the masks, and maybe good for as much as an hour with everyone using oxygen. Of course, if he climbs the cabin above twenty-eight thousand, that's another story."

"Why twenty-eight?" Brian asked.

Janie bit her lip and looked at him, aware she was blurting out everything. But it was boilerplate aviation physiology, and she thought back to the Air Force altitude chamber class she'd taken once at the insistence of a fighter pilot boyfriend. He knew she needed such knowledge if she was going to spend much of her life at high altitudes, and he'd been appalled that most flight attendants never received such training.

"Above twenty-eight thousand," Janie continued, "we'd need oxygen under pressure and special masks and regulators, like the pilots have. The passenger masks don't deliver oxygen under pressure. So above twenty-eight thousand, we'd all pass out in about a minute. It's called pressure breathing, and time of useful consciousness."

Three more passengers, two men and a woman, came through the curtain from coach and Brian turned to them. "Any other pilots back there?"

All three shook their heads. "We asked everyone," the woman replied. "There are two private pilots in coach who used to fly single-engine airplanes, but they said they'd be clueless in a 747 cockpit."

Janie recognized one of the passengers from the

Chicago-to-London leg. The man had been in coach and slow to anger, but he'd sought her out in flight to complain about the attitude of her Chicago crew, and she'd helped him write a complaint. Brown was his name, she remembered. Dan Brown.

"You told that fool to go to Cape Town, didn't you?" Brown asked. "And now he's defied us again and turned north, hasn't he?"

"Yes," Brian said, "but we've got another problem." He briefed them on the decreasing cabin pressure.

"Then we've got to get up there and confront him," Dan Brown added.

"He claims he's got a gun, and an unbreakable door." Brian replied, unconsciously looking at the ceiling as his breathing quickened. He looked at Janie with an accusatory expression. "This feels a lot higher than twelve thousand," he said.

Janie glanced through the curtain at the first section again, verifying the absence of oxygen masks before turning back to Brian. "The masks haven't dropped, so we can't be above twelve thousand feet cabin altitude. He may be trying to make everyone sleepy, but I can't believe he'd try to knock us out."

"I can," Brian said. "You forgetting this is the guy who just left his first officer for dead?"

Janie looked at the others standing around them, reading a combination of panic and anger in their eyes.

"I'm feeling hypoxic right here, right now," Brian said. "Janie, are you sure that mask system is automatic?"

"Yes," Janie replied, her mind racing through the possibilities.

"How does it run? What powers it?"

"I don't know. Maybe electricity."

Brian looked at her for several long seconds.

"If it's electrical," Dan Brown said, "it's got to be protected by a circuit breaker."

"Probably," Janie said.

"Located in the cockpit?" Brian asked.

"I . . . I don't know. Maybe. Most things aboard are, except for galley equipment."

"That must be it," Brian said, breathing hard and feeling weak. "The bastard's pulled the circuit breaker so the masks won't come down," Brian said, turning to the others. "He's going to raise the cabin altitude until we all pass out from hypoxia."

"What's hypoxia?" Brown asked.

"Lack of oxygen in the bloodstream. Leads to confusion and unconsciousness. Long exposure means brain damage . . . eventually brain death."

Janie watched the stunned expression on Brown's face. Brian raised his voice so the other passengers gathering around could hear him.

"Okay, people, that has to be his plan. He's going to depressurize this cabin until we all pass out, and he probably doesn't know he could kill us."

"Brian—" Janie began, but he interrupted her.

"You've got portable oxygen bottles back here, right?"

"Yes, but just a few."

"Where are they?" Brian asked.

Janie shook her head. "Brian, look. Let's call him . . ."

"No! There's no time. He won't listen, and we've got to act now."

"He's armed up there," Janie said. "I told you, having a battle with a single pilot is insane, and you'll never get through that door anyway. You heard these people. There are no other—" She stopped cold, remembering Robert MacNaughton's qualifications, and realizing the time had come.

"We're dead down here if he succeeds," Brian was saying, reasoning his way through the case for taking over as the others listened and nodded and gained in numbers. The small space of the galley was already glutted with passengers, all of them breathing more rapidly than normal and all of them increasingly alarmed.

Brian's right hand closed firmly around Janie's arm. "This is deadly serious! The cabin altitude's probably already above eighteen thousand feet. He may not know what he's doing, but if we spend too long up here, he'll be flying a load of dead bodies."

"What do you mean, Doc?" one of the latest to arrive in the galley asked, his face flushed.

"Remember the golfer in the runaway plane? Payne Stewart?"

They nodded.

"Same thing."

An interphone call chime sounded, indicating a call

from the rear galley, and Janie automatically scooped up the handset to hear a familiar and plaintive voice. "Janie? Elle's passed out back here, and we're all feeling very faint. What's happening? The masks haven't dropped, but it feels like a rapid decompression."

"Get out the portable bottles and sit down. Share the masks," Janie ordered, toggling the connection off and punching in the cockpit code.

The electronic ringing tone sounded repeatedly, but no one answered.

"You're calling him and he's not answering, right?" Brian asked.

She nodded and started to replace the handset as Brian took it from her, punching in the memorized PA code and raising it to his mouth.

Captain? If you can hear me, this is Doctor Logan. We know what you're trying to do with the pressurization. You either stop it right now and repressurize this airplane, or we'll batter down that damned door and come in after you. You understand me, you bastard? Repressurize this cabin immediately!

Brian turned and reached past two of the men standing nearby, yanking the curtain back as he held the handset to his mouth with the PA still engaged.

Folks, the captain is trying to make us all unconscious by depressurizing. That's what's happening. He's trying to kill us, in other words.

The words seemed to echo through the cavernous 747 cabin as he replaced the handset, aware that the exchange had probably frightened the passengers of Meridian Six to the depth of their beings.

"Let's go get the son of a bitch," one of the men growled.

Janie turned on him, her voice hardening, her breathing rapid. "And then do what?"

Brian answered instead, his hand gently placed on her shoulder. "If we can find the circuit breaker he's pulled, we can push it in and drop the masks," Brian said.

"Wait a minute!" Janie said, "Wait! There may be another answer. I'll be right back."

Brian glanced after her, but turned immediately to the others. "Okay, all of you, go back there and open all the overhead compartments and find the oxygen bottles and bring them here."

Dan Brown and four other passengers turned instantly and disappeared back into the coach cabin as Brian turned to watch the feminine form of Janie Bretsen disappearing into the first-class cabin. He caught himself wondering in a tiny flash of puzzlement how such a pleasing image could register so suddenly on an oxygen-starved brain, and he wondered at the same moment why she seemed to be having trouble keeping her balance.

Janie stopped at the rear of the first-class section and popped open an overhead compartment, scooping the oxygen bottle and packaged mask out of its bracket with one hand before moving quickly to Robert Mac-

Naughton's seat, where she knelt down by the sleeping man. She shook his shoulder and he stirred, but only slightly, and she felt a flash of alarm as she shook him again and again, more violently each time.

MacNaughton came awake with a start.

"Yes?"

"Mr. MacNaughton, Janie Bretsen."

"Yes?" He sat up and rubbed his eyes. "I'm feeling rather odd."

"You said you could fly a Boeing 737, right?"

He looked at her and nodded slowly. "What's happened?"

"Nothing yet, but we're out of time. He's truly gone nuts up there." She quickly summarized the situation. "If they get that cockpit door open and disable him, you're all we've got."

"Take over the flight, you mean?"

"Yes, sir."

"That could be considered an act of piracy, you understand."

"Yes, sir, I do. But I'm trying to control this, and . . ."

"Strange method of control for a member of the crew," he said, still rubbing one eye.

Janie stood suddenly, feeling herself wobble on her feet as the truth of his words sank in. *Good God, what am I thinking?*

"Stay here. I'll be back," Janie told him as she forced herself to walk back toward the galley, leaving the oxygen bottle beside his seat. She pushed into the galley to find Brian Logan holding another portable oxygen bottle and passing the mask around as he spotted her.

"Okay, Janie. We're heading upstairs. What was the urgent errand?" he asked her, gesturing toward first class.

She ignored the question and willed herself to grab the interphone handset and pull it to her face. It took three tries before she could get the cockpit number punched in correctly. Her fingers were not working right, and her frustration was filtered by a growing fuzziness.

This time Phil Knight answered on the second ring.

"Yes?" the captain said, his voice muffled by what was obviously an oxygen mask.

"Ah . . . captain?" she began, gasping for breath as Brian slipped the oxygen mask between her mouth and the handset. She breathed deeply a few times, wondering why the colors around her suddenly seemed brighter. She pushed the mask aside. "Captain, this is Janie Bretsen, one of your crew."

"Oh, one of *my* crew? I heard your announcement, Bretsen. You are so fired. Ever heard the term *mutiny*?"

"Captain, you've got to lower the cabin altitude now. They know what you're doing, and if you don't reverse it, this crowd's coming upstairs after you and there's nothing I'll be able to do to stop them."

"Anyone who starts banging against this cockpit door gets a bullet in the chest. Tell them that."

She ignored the threat.

"You're going to kill some of the passengers, Captain. They're already passing out down here. You can't do this."

"The hell I can't!" he snapped.

She felt short of breath again. The cabin was getting very cold as Janie tried to think of the right thing to say to counter him, convince him. She felt her anger building from somewhere within, and her voice took on an unearthly quality as she all but screamed into the phone: "LISTEN, DAMN YOU! I'M TRYING TO CONTAIN THE ANGER DOWN HERE."

The passengers crowding around her moved back slightly, startled by the ferocity of her words. She felt another wave of light-headedness as she forced her voice back to normal. "Captain, please! I'm trying my best, but I'm losing control of these people, and they're going to come after you if you don't listen, and there's something else you should know."

"And what's that?" Phil snorted in reply.

"There's another Boeing pilot aboard, and he's ready to take over if you won't listen."

She heard a summary click on the other end at the same time she felt the sudden silence around her.

"You've found another pilot?" Brian asked incredulously. "Who?"

She looked up, trying to decide what to say as Robert MacNaughton stepped into the galley carrying the portable oxygen bottle and mask.

"I'm terribly afraid it's me," he said. "And judging from the people passing out all around us, I'd say we haven't got long."

Brian looked at MacNaughton as he took another long draw on the oxygen mask and then handed it to Janie. "The cabin's probably above twenty thousand by now. She tells me above twenty-eight we're screwed."

"That is essentially correct. Let's go," Robert said.

Brian looked quickly at Janie. "Do you have a key to the cockpit?"

She shook her head no. "Not any more. After the World Trade Center, the keys were history. He has to let you in, *and* your handprint has to be registered by a . . . a thing up there."

"Then we'll batter it open, however long it takes. As soon as we're sure he doesn't have a gun," Brian nodded to MacNaughton, "you come in, take the right seat, and stabilize things while we drag his sorry ass out of the left."

"I'm inclined to agree," Robert replied.

"This is crazy!" Janie said, looking between the two of them. "Suppose he clicks off the autopilot when and if you burst in? What then?"

"Then," Robert MacNaughton added, "I'll have only a few seconds."

"We've only got seconds now," Brian said. "Everyone else stay here." He turned and moved rapidly toward the foot of the stairway to the upper deck, taking the steps two at a time as Robert MacNaughton followed and Janie tried to keep up. Two of the other men started after them, but slowed, one of them sitting on the bottom of the stairway to catch his breath as the other simply pitched forward, falling to the floor, unconscious.

Brian reached the top step and turned, dismayed to find Robert MacNaughton stalled halfway up.

"The oxygen!" Brian yelled, gesturing for the older man to don the mask and turn the bottle on. "Put the mask on!"

MacNaughton looked increasingly puzzled as his right hand moved the mask back and forth toward his face in confusion while Janie came up behind him, fading as rapidly.

"I'll . . . do it," she said, panting for breath as she pulled the mask from his hand. She turned on the regulator and took several long breaths herself before putting it on his face.

Brian watched MacNaughton slowly revive and reach for Janie, pulling her along as they continued to the top and turned toward the cockpit.

They moved rapidly through the upper cabin, Brian's pulse pounding as he realized they were almost out of time. There were unconscious passengers all around him as he reached the cockpit door and raised the steel oxygen bottle in a wide backswing, bringing it down hard on the cockpit doorknob.

It didn't budge, but he heard startled voices within and leaned to one side, half expecting bullets to come tearing through the surface of the door.

Nothing.

Again he slammed the bottle into the doorknob, but to no avail. The effort hadn't made a dent.

The big jet suddenly lurched and rolled to the left, the motion throwing Brian in the opposite direction. He fell heavily against the rest-room door and let himself roll to the floor as the bank angle increased and things began sliding to the left. He glanced back in time to see Janie grab successfully for a railing, her feet swinging almost out from under her as the roll continued and the 747 yawed left.

Robert had lost his footing before reaching the small hallway leading to the cockpit. Brian watched him grabbing air now in slow motion as his oxygen bottle slipped away and he leaned uncontrollably to the left before falling headfirst into the sidewall, the oxygen bottle skittering uselessly to the floor, the mask detached from his face.

Janie let go of the railing and slid toward Mac-Naughton, scrambling for the oxygen mask and putting it on herself.

There was nothing but darkness outside the 747's windows, but it felt to Brian as if they were turning upside down. Yet, Janie and Robert MacNaughton were still on the floor as the gyrations continued. She tried to shake him awake, but it wasn't working, and she turned to Brian and shook her head. She pulled the mask from her face long enough to shout the words.

"He's out," she said. "There's no one to fly!"

The PA activated as the captain's voice echoed through the cabin.

Okay . . . goddammit . . . whoever's banging on the cockpit door, you'd better understand I'm going to maneuver this airplane as wildly as necessary to prevent you from getting in . . . and if I have to turn us upside down again, the airplane could break up in flight and . . . and kill us all. No one's getting in this cockpit, so BACK OFF! Understand? Enough is enough! Logan, this means you and whoever else is out there.

Brian felt numb, which didn't make sense. He was wearing the mask and breathing pure oxygen, but his mind felt full of cotton and Janie was faring no better fifteen feet away. He started to swing the oxygen bottle at the door once more despite the warning, but the bottle was growing inordinately heavy, and he happened to glance at the small quantity gauge on the bottle, wondering in almost detached fashion how the needle could have landed in the red zone already.

He tried sucking harder on the mask. The oxygen was coming, but not enough, and he shivered as a sudden chill shuddered down his back. His concentration was drifting somewhere else, and it didn't seem to matter. What was it he was trying to do?

Cockpit! Yeah, I have to . . . get in! he thought. That was the mission, but he was having trouble forming the words in his mind. There was something about a bottle, but he'd forgotten what it was. Brian let himself sink

415

down to the floor as he leaned against the bulkhead. He felt rather good. Relaxed.

No worries, mate! Who says that? he thought.

The door. A door somewhere. He would have to swing that heavy bottle again by a door or something.

But first, he decided, it wouldn't hurt to take a little nap.

THIRTY-SIX

William Sanderson, the White House Chief of Staff and former four-star Navy admiral, followed his normal pattern by materializing before the Situation Room staff expected him.

This time, however, they were ready, having learned the lesson months before that wherever the Chief of Staff was supposed to be, he would appear ahead of schedule and arrive with the stealth of a B-2.

Sanderson slid into a chair at the end of the small briefing table in the relatively compact basement room and motioned to the electronic display on the wall, now blinking with several scrambled, highly classified live shots being relayed from Chantilly.

"I have the basics," he said. "Why do Langley and NRO think this is a possible Trojan Horse attack?"

The director of the Situation Room slid several papers bearing red classified markings across the table.

"Sir, these are the bullet points backing the initial conclusion. Langley believes General Onitsa worked some sort of package deal, with whom we don't know. He's never been in bed with terrorists before, and never put himself in our crosshairs. But if he's made a trade, he gets three hundred and twenty hostages, then whichever organization put this together gets a place to prepare a commercial airliner carrying a legitimate flight number with some sort of mass destructive weapon. We've got space-based verification that the passengers are on the ground and being held hostage, we have photographic evidence of two dead pilots from an airliner that only carries two pilots, we have an airborne 747 with apparent radio failure squawking a radio failure code, and we have an exceedingly clever digital message supposedly from the captain claiming the aircraft has been hijacked by the very passengers Langley is sure are still back in Nigeria. And just five minutes ago NRO believes one of their satellites picked up initial indications that there may be fissile material aboard."

"What happened? They get a positive neutron hit on the aircraft?"

"Not exactly, sir. A few bursts that could be from something shielded on the plane, or it might be nothing at all. In other words, it's low confidence at this point, but it's not impossible that there could be a nuclear weapon on that aircraft. NRO also reports that there was no indication of anything nuclear at the Nigerian airport before they landed. Then again, it could have been well shielded."

"Doesn't impress me one way or another unless confirmed," the Chief of Staff replied. "They could be carrying anthrax or something chemical."

"Bottom line?" the director continued. "Langley is recommending we brief the President immediately."

The admiral snapped his eyes from the papers to the director. "And ask him for what?"

"Authority to sound the alarm at NATO and SHAPE, as well as alert the Israelis in case the aircraft makes a sudden right turn, and authority to unleash State to contact everyone in the possible European path of the 747."

Sanderson looked back at one of the papers. "This says that Doctor Onitsa's already made a demand. What's Nigeria going to do?"

"Wait to see if we'll give them the money. Otherwise, they'll wait to see what Onitsa is demanding of the Nigerian military. The first deadline—the money demand—expires in a few minutes."

"Where's the Pentagon on this?"

"Watching and waiting, Admiral, and alerting the Seventh Fleet in the Mediterranean in case we need them."

Sanderson looked up again and smiled. "Good. We just may need them. The *Enterprise* is out there, along with *Eisenhower* and . . . I forget who else."

"Once the Chief of Naval Operations, always . . ."

"You betcha," Sanderson replied, sliding the papers back across the table. "Very well. Where's *Air Force One* right now?"

"Signals has him near Des Moines. The President's on the phone with the first lady."

"Interrupt them, hook us up, and have the Pentagon stand by to brief at a moment's notice. You know how he always asks me right out of the box for the Pentagon's point of view? Well, if we're going to be shooting down an American 747 over the Med, I want everything on the table from the first."

The director hesitated, obviously unprepared for such a prospect. "You . . . think that may be the result?"

William Sanderson stood and moved to a small table at the edge of the room to pour a cup of coffee, as he looked back over his shoulder.

"If we can't be virtually certain they're not a threat, we may have no choice. He's already given a standing order authorizing a civilian shootdown over the U.S. if necessary. But at least, unlike that Quantum Airlines flight a few years ago with the suspected virus aboard, this time there are no passengers to worry about."

NRO HEADQUARTERS,
CHANTILLY, VIRGINIA
4:45 P.M. EDT

George Zoffel swiveled around in his chair to catch John Blaylock's eyes. He pointed to the main screen where another ghostly infrared image of Meridian Six streamed white heat plumes from its four engines.

"What do you think, John? Was that some sort of aileron roll we just saw?"

John Blaylock nodded energetically. "It was, and I'll tell you, no sane commercial captain's going to do such a thing in a 747, then gyrate around with steep bank angles like that. Whoever's flying that ship isn't one of Meridian's boys. That tells me more than any of the pictures of pilot bodies on the runway or demands from Onitsa."

"You flew the 747 as captain, didn't you?"

"More years than I'll admit," John replied. "You *can* roll it. That's not a problem. It's just that none of us would ever do so voluntarily."

David Byrd leaned forward, watching both Zoffel and Blaylock carefully as he raised a finger.

"Colonel, you have a comment?" Sandra Collings asked.

"Well . . . I'm just an observer, but something's really troubling me here."

"Go on."

"Well, first . . . what if there really is a passenger riot aboard that aircraft? Is an aileron roll such an outlandish maneuver if there's a fight going on? I mean, remember on the day of the New York and Pentagon attacks, we had a group of heroic passengers who fought the hijackers in the cockpit and brought the plane down."

"Hard to have a passenger riot without passengers, Colonel," Sandra replied, gesturing to a freeze-frame shot of General Onitsa's camp with the telltale line of buses outside.

David sighed as he scanned the shot once again, then met Sandra's eyes.

"True, but . . . I guess I'm not completely convinced all the passengers are off. Look, if Onitsa arranged this thing as some sort of deal with Group X, it's obvious they weren't just looking to steal a 747 . . . which is a bit hard to hide anyway. So what's their purpose?"

"The most obvious purpose is what we're suspecting here," Sandra replied, "taking advantage of the routine international acceptance of what appears to be a regular commercial flight using the cover of an emergency diversion to deliver a weapon. It's a great idea, and they've made it even better because there's this perceived emergency aboard and a poor, lone captain battling it out and looking for a place to land."

"Yeah, but hold on," David said, pointing at the screen. "On that monitor we've got visual confirmation that the passengers are off the aircraft. Right?"

"Right," Zoffel echoed.

"Now, if General Onitsa's plan was to take the passengers and crew off and hold them for ransom, surely his partners, Group X, knew he was going to do that. After all, that's the benefit Onitsa gets for the deal: the use of hostages to extract concessions and money from Nigeria. That means that Group X knew Onitsa was going to tell the world at some point that the 747 they just stole has no one left aboard except the pilots. So, Group X sends a carefully planned written communiqué claiming an air rage incident and says they're being hijacked by their own passengers, which I agree is both clever and unprecedented. But at the same moment, that claim is completely discredited by Onitsa's statements to the Nigerian government that there *are* no passengers aboard! So . . . why would Group X set themselves up to fail?"

"Who says they're failing?" George Zoffel asked. "They've got our undivided attention."

"Yes, but, what do they want us to believe? See, something's wrong here in our reasoning."

John Blaylock had been smiling and keeping quiet, but now he was chuckling and David turned to him in slight irritation.

"*What*, John?"

John shook his head. "I'm sorry . . . it's not you, Davey . . . it's General Onitsa. Actually, it's *Doctor* Onitsa."

"I don't understand," David replied, fighting a flash of irritation at the older colonel's smugness. "I mean, I

423

know I'm as green as they come with respect to international intelligence matters, but logic is logic."

John Blaylock looked at the table and cleared his throat, the smile fading and the chuckling gone. "I know this guy's history and profile. The doctor is a master at the art of double-cross, and he's far too intelligent to become an instant enemy of the United States in a time of war. So what's he doing? In this case, I'll betcha a B-1 that he's outfoxed and double-crossed Group X, and I'll guarantee you they don't know it yet."

"Okay, I'm getting confused here," David said.

"So am I," George Zoffel echoed with a wry smile. "You don't own any B-1's, do you, John?"

"I certainly do," Blaylock shot back. "And it's a beautifully built scale model in my den." He got to his feet and stretched to his full height before nodding to the screen where the 747's image was still streaking northbound. "It's a clever plan, boys and girls," John continued. "Group X, as you call them, plans to either use that 747 to release a biological agent, or detonate a nuclear weapon, over the heart of some European city. More than likely it's biological. The pilots are probably *not* suicidal. They're probably not aware of what they're really carrying, or what's going to happen. But to carry out the mission, they need to hide behind the illusion they've tried to create that the passengers are rioting and there's a beleaguered captain barricaded in the cockpit conveniently accompanied by a lone flight attendant. Onitsa undoubtedly swore to Group X when he was making the deal that he'd wait for them to release their anthrax or detonate their bomb before making his demands to Nigeria and destroying the illusion that the passengers remained aboard. Now, afterward, Group X won't care where the passengers are, or were. Their mission will be complete. The U.S., however . . . either mourning the loss of a few million souls or the impending epidemic of just as many . . . will be inordinately relieved to find that at least the three hundred Meridian passengers are still alive in Nigeria. Knowing us, we'll pay anything to get them back. So Onitsa gets his money, the passengers get to live, and Group X gets to wipe out a few million people in Rome or Geneva or London and then race underground after fingering Baghdad or Tehran, hoping we'll pound the shit out of some civilian population center and damage our worldwide coalition against terrorism. That would explain the basis of the deal Onitsa struck." John began pacing along the perimeter of the room, gesturing grandly. "But!"

"I knew there was a 'but' in there," Sandra replied, winking at David, "there always is with John Blaylock."

"Kindly refrain from interrupting your elders, young woman," John said, winking at her as he held up an index finger to resecure the floor. "But," he continued, "our crafty Doctor Onitsa has a flaw that so far hasn't been fatal to him. He's a *healer*! A physician. A Hippocratic oath-taker on a mission to save his people. He doesn't really relish killing, although he's good at it. Mainly, he's as good at theater as he is at military tactics, and he's been amazing at building a terrible, bloodthirsty reputation while sparing as many as possible during the civil insurrection he started eight years ago. But when it comes to wiping out London or Geneva or Paris, he doesn't care much for the idea because the man happens to love those cities and Europe in general."

"You're saying . . ." David began.

"I'm saying he knows *exactly* what murderous thing Group X is planning and has purposefully jumped the gun on making his demands to Nigeria's government, knowing we'd find out and be on the case in a New York minute. He knew we'd figure out that the 747 is now a flying threat long before it even reached the southern shores of the Mediterranean."

"There's another loose end, John," George Zoffel interjected. "How'd they harvest that airplane to begin with? How did they get two airline pilots to land at a remote airport like Katsina, for God's sake?"

"That one's obvious, George. They rigged some sort of maintenance problem to trigger over Nigeria at exactly the right moment, or they had one of their captured Nigerian fighters shoot one of his engines out. And they probably had a powerful radio transmitter on the ground overriding Nigerian air traffic control and directing them to Katsina. In either event, Meridian's pilots had to be terminated on the ground, although Onitsa and Group X screwed up by not considering our satellites."

George Zoffel was nodding. "*Most* of that makes sense. No, I think all that makes sense."

"So, thanks to Doctor General Jean Onitsa's kind assistance, we can now proceed to shoot down the empty 747 as soon as it soars over water, meaning that in a twisted way, Onitsa has become an ally," John Blaylock said. "And I," he added, holding both arms out and taking a small bow, "thereby rest my case. Thank you so much."

George Zoffel and Sandra Collings both laughed and began applauding in perfunctory fashion as David Byrd joined in, stunned by the brilliance of the plan even if disturbed that something inchoate and incomplete was still scratching at the back of his mind.

"That's why they pay me the big bucks, folks," John said, enjoying the moment, "although I'd much rather be paid in blondes."

Sandra cleared her throat and rolled her eyes as she swiveled back toward the screens while George Zoffel picked up the tie-line to the Situation Room.

"You phoning that in to Sixteen Hundred Pennsylvania?" John asked.

George nodded.

"Good. Tell them if we're wrong, it's the fault of a rookie colonel named Byrd."

THIRTY-SEVEN

Several minutes had elapsed since the last loud crash against the cockpit door. Phil Knight turned to look over his shoulder. Judy Jackson's eyes were wide with fright over the oxygen mask obscuring her mouth and nose. Her hands were still clutching the crash axe in her lap.

He reached back in the other direction and ganged the switches on her oxygen regulator to the 100 percent and emergency position to match his, making sure she was receiving enough pressure to stay conscious.

Phil glanced up at the cabin pressurization panel again. The cabin altitude was just above thirty thousand now, and his breathing felt strange, as if the oxygen system were forcefully inflating his lungs and making him work to exhale each time. Somewhere in training he had heard about that, positive pressure and something called reverse breathing at higher cabin altitudes, but he couldn't recall the details.

The cabin pressurization controller was in manual, and he toggled the switch slightly now until the large outflow valve two hundred feet to the rear closed slightly, causing the rate-of-climb indicator for the cabin to stop climbing and settle back to zero. Thirty thousand was good enough, he figured. Ten minutes more or so without supplemental oxygen and even the portable bottles would be exhausted, leaving only Jackson and himself awake. He would send her back, then, to use the plastic handcuffs and immobilize Logan, who he'd seen on the TV monitor ineffectually battering at the door. He could see the doctor now slumped on the floor in the small hallway.

Phil looked at the forward panel, his eyes focusing on the altitude indicator. They were in a twenty-degree left bank again. He returned the 747 to a magnetic heading of 350 degrees and reengaged the autopilot, his heart still racing as he waited for the next assault on the door.

Something on the radar screen caught his attention, and he realized he'd been too distracted to pay attention. They were cruising at thirty-nine thousand feet, and the powerful radar beams the Boeing was sending into the night were returning substantial electronic evidence of huge thunderstorms over a hundred and eighty miles away. As he watched, a huge north-south line of yellow radar returns heavily splotched with red crawled onto the screen, indicating severe convective activity over the western Sahara. That much red on the screen that far out meant the storms were massive. He'd have to fly around them.

Phil reached up to the auto-flight panel and slowly rotated the heading knob clockwise, bringing the selected course to the right, ten, then twenty degrees, as he studied the radar scope to make sure his intended flight path would remain far to the east of the storms. The tops of such monsters routinely soared to altitudes above sixty thousand feet, he knew. He'd seen and avoided countless such thunderheads over the midwestern U.S., but over the vastness of the Sahara, they were sure to be worse.

Where is that on the map? Phil wondered, looking for the high aeronautical chart and deciding just as quickly that it didn't matter. He was over the trackless Sahara anyway. Who cared which country claimed it? Besides, he was in emergency status and squawking a hijack code, and the world was legally required to let him do anything he needed to do to get back safely.

Fifteen feet to the rear on the other side of the cockpit door, Brian Logan watched the world swim back into focus as a fresh gust of oxygen forced its way into his lungs. Colors flashed around him as he regained his bearings and realized someone's hand was holding the mask hard to his face.

Brian looked up, finding Janie Bretsen's eyes. They

were green and wide and expressive, he noted, and very prominent above the facial anonymity of her oxygen mask.

She swept the mask aside for a few seconds to speak.

"Can you hear me, Brian?"

He nodded.

"Keep the mask on. We're pressure-breathing and your other bottle ran out." She replaced her mask and breathed deeply a few times before pulling it aside once again. "We've only got a few minutes if he doesn't lower the cabin. I think we're the last ones still conscious. These bottles don't have much left."

It was Brian's turn to speak, and the renewed rush of oxygen in his brain was spurring him to the reality that breaking through the door would only bring more dangerous gyrations at the hand of the frightened captain. And there was also the annoying fact that he hadn't been able to break the lock. If they had just a few minutes of consciousness, then negotiation was the only remaining solution.

He pulled his mask aside. "Where's the interphone?"

Janie looked up and around, spotting one within a few feet. She left him with the fresh oxygen bottle and stood to grab the handset.

"Keep that mask on. Your time of useful consciousness may only be thirty seconds with it off."

He nodded and put the mask back in place.

"You want to call him?" she asked, pointing to the closed cockpit door.

He nodded more energetically and she punched in the numbers and handed it to him.

Phil Knight hesitated before answering the call chime. He estimated that at most one or two of the flight attendants might still be conscious as they sucked the last of the oxygen out of their bottles, but now he felt a flash of worry that once more he'd somehow miscalculated. Raw curiosity won out. He swept the handset to his face, startled to hear Logan on the other end. He glanced down at the console video screen. Logan was no longer in view.

"I've got enough bottles," the physician began, "to give me enough time to break through and kill you where you sit, and there's another pilot aboard who can take over, but . . . I'll make you a deal."

"What?" Phil asked after several seconds of tense silence. "What deal?"

"Lower this cabin back to ten thousand or better immediately, and we'll . . . leave you alone. But . . . but you also have to promise you're really going to London, or somewhere we can accept."

"I'm going to London, dammit! I told you that."

"And no more acrobatics?"

"All right."

"And turn on those screen things . . . that moving map that tells us where we are, so we can make sure you're complying."

"I guess I can do that."

"So . . . we have a deal?" Brian asked.

More silence as Phil Knight tried to break through the roaring in his mind to consider the offer. No more break-in attempts in exchange for oxygen. He could get in deep trouble anyway if any of the passengers sued Meridian for making them pass out, so maybe this was a better solution.

"Understand, Logan," Phil replied, "if you go back on your word, I'll just turn off the pressurization and open the valve and we'll go straight to thirty-nine thousand feet and you'll be unconscious almost instantly."

"Yeah. I understand. Of course I'd be in there and have your neck broken before I passed out, but I hear you. Do we have a deal?"

"As long as you comply," Phil said, caution still ricocheting around his head. In the background he could hear a female voice murmuring something about the passenger oxygen masks as Logan's voice returned.

"Okay. Hey, you pulled some sort of circuit breaker for the passenger masks, didn't you?"

"Yes," Phil answered hesitantly.

"Push it back in."

Seconds ticked by before a sudden flutter of noise coursed through the upper-deck cabin as a rubber jungle of yellow oxygen masks cascaded from the overhead panels.

"All right. The breaker is in. Have the masks dropped?"

"Yes. I just hope you haven't killed anyone. No one's awake to put the masks on."

"I have the authority to do anything necessary to put down a mutiny in my airplane," Phil snapped.

"Lower the cabin altitude. Quickly. I want to feel my ears popping, *now*!" Brian added.

Phil Knight reached to the overhead panel and flipped the appropriate switches, his eyes shifting to the cabin altimeter to verify that the cabin pressure was starting to increase, and the cabin altitude descend.

"All right. I'm repressurizing."

"You've probably given a dozen people the bends back here, you stupid fool. You know that?"

"Screw you, Logan! You're going to the gas chamber for air piracy and murder anyway. Do you know *that*?"

Silence filled the void for several seconds as each man dealt with the standoff and the futility of his respective rage.

"Look," Brian said, "you said a while ago that you weren't suicidal."

"Of *course* I'm not suicidal!"

"Then you've got to have a plan, and I want to know what it is. Why did you turn around when we told you to go to Cape Town?"

Phil Knight snorted into the receiver.

"You were too busy issuing threats to hear me, Logan. We didn't have enough fuel to make Cape Town. It's that simple. We're going back to London, as I said, and even then, if I have to deviate around too much weather, we might have to land in Paris instead."

Brian looked past Janie into the upper-deck cabin. None of the passengers seemed to be stirring yet, but he was already having to clear his ears, so the pressure was increasing.

"You need to make a PA announcement for everyone to clear their ears," Brian said.

"You're so good with your rabble-rousing, riot-inciting PAs," Phil replied. "Make it yourself."

A few profane retorts popped into Brian's mind, but the reality that the captain's beginning compliance might be fragile dictated caution, and he decided to hold back the avalanche of insults and invectives he wanted to scream at the man.

"All right," Brian said, toggling the handset off, then on, and entering the PA code.

Folks, this is Doctor Logan. Listen to me! Wake up! WAKE UP, everyone! We're repressurizing the cabin, but you need to stay ahead of your ears. When they begin to feel full, hold your nose firmly, then close your mouth, and then blow into your nose. Your ears will click and clear. That's a Valsalva maneuver. Do it every minute or so.

Brian toggled the phone again, and for a reason he couldn't quite fathom, reentered the cockpit code.

Phil answered just as quickly.

"Yeah?"

"I want to know something."

"What, Logan?"

"Why did you leave the copilot back there? He was

bleeding to death. How could you do that, for God's sake?"

"I didn't leave him! I mean, I didn't see him until we were on takeoff roll, and if you hadn't noticed, I had about three hundred others to think about, too. I thought he was aboard when I started the takeoff. That's the honest truth."

"I *told* you he wasn't aboard. I *told* you he'd been shot."

"I never heard you say anything like that until we were airborne and you were screaming at me."

"Godammit!" Brian snapped, "I know you're lying. You know why? Because I told you to stop the plane and you hit the brakes instantly in response."

"I never heard you say anything about stopping, Logan."

"The connection was good. I could hear cockpit noises," Brian said.

"Maybe you did, but the handset was on the floor. I was trying to control the damned airplane, not talk on the phone. It so happens the end of the runway was coming up and I was taxiing at high speed. I *had* to stop or run off the end. It had nothing to do with you."

"You're saying you didn't hear me?"

"Hell no, I didn't hear you! But I sure as hell heard my chief flight attendant and what she saw you do to Garth . . . my copilot."

"I tried to save him."

"Yeah, right."

"Wait a minute! Exactly what did Jackson say to you?"

"She's an eyewitness to the fact that you clubbed him to death and dumped him out of the electronics bay, or at least kept him outside long enough to fall off."

"WHAT? Jeez, man, that's a complete lie!"

"Don't . . . don't deny it, Logan," Phil Knight replied. "She's sitting right here and nodding. She saw you clubbing the copilot with an oxygen bottle."

"That wasn't the copilot, you idiot! I told you before. That was . . . there were . . . two soldiers trying to get in *after* the copilot had been shot and had fallen off!"

There was more silence from the cockpit.

"Why should I believe *you*, Logan?"

"Why in hell would I hurt the copilot? He'd already told me what an asshole you are. If I'd wanted to club a pilot to death, it would have been you, not him, considering what you've put us through."

"Just stay out of here," Phil snapped in response, the tension returning to his voice. "I can still blow the cabin altitude with the flick of one finger."

Brian started to reply, but there was a summary click as Phil Knight broke the connection.

THIRTY-EIGHT

The fact that the thrice-weekly airline flight called Meridian Six had made an emergency landing in Nigeria in the previous six hours had already attracted the attention of Libya's extensive security apparatus. Flight Six was routinely monitored by Libya since its flight path passed close to Libyan airspace. But the sudden reemergence of the normally southbound flight on a northbound heading became a matter of heightened interest even before Nigerian air traffic control informed most of the world that Flight Six had been hijacked.

Libyan Air Force radar began searching to the south and waiting to acquire Flight Six as curiosity turned to concern, but when the American 747 finally appeared on Libyan radar, the controllers suddenly realized the pilots had altered course. Flight Six was tracking straight for the southwest corner of Libya without clearance.

Despite the fact that the southwest corner of Libya encompassed some of the most inhospitable desert on the face of the planet, an approaching hijacked American aircraft was more than an automatic affront to the hair-trigger sensitivities of Libyan dictator Mu'ammar Qadhafi. It was a license to shoot, given the American war on terrorism. Never again, Qadhafi had decreed a decade before, would the Americans be able to sneak up on him the way a flight of U.S. Air Force F-111s had done in the early eighties when Tripoli had been pounded and the Libyan dictator had barely escaped death. The mere possibility that the Meridian 747 could be a flying bomb was enough to spur immediate action, especially when word of what had happened in northern Nigeria reached Libyan intelligence.

Within fifteen minutes, doors to an alert shack on an impossibly remote Libyan Air Defense base in the southern Sahara clanged open and four fighter pilots raced through the doors, pulling on their gear as they ran across the gritty nighttime tarmac to their aging, well-armed MiG-21 fighters with orders to get airborne and prepare to intercept.

The rules of engagement were simple and came straight from Qadhafi himself: If the 747 violated Libyan airspace, it was to be destroyed.

SITUATION ROOM,
THE WHITE HOUSE,
WASHINGTON, D.C.
5:15 P.M. EDT

The image of the President of the United States digitally assembled itself in full color on the liquid crystal display covering the entire wall at the far end of the small conference table, the multiple digital cameras aboard *Air Force One* sampling enough angles of the President at his airborne desk so that a high-speed computer was able to assemble and transmit a live stream of three-dimensional information to be reassembled as simulated reality on the Situation Room wall. It looked, staffers were always remarking, as if the President were merely on the other side of a crystal-clear window, not hanging in the sky aboard *Air Force One*. The state-of-the-art system had been installed in the year following the WTC attacks when *Air Force One* had been forced to dash to the old Strategic Air Command headquarters near Omaha just to give the President visual teleconferencing capability with the White House Situation Room.

Chief of Staff William Sanderson nodded to his old friend as he looked at the display, still amazed that the twenty-eight camera lenses looking back at him were an invisible part of the LQD display. It worked even better than they'd planned.

"Okay, Bill," the President said. "What's the latest?"

Admiral Sanderson chuckled and shook his head. "Sorry, sir. I can't quite get used to you just materializing like that. You look like you're right here. This technology is incredible, as you know."

"Yeah, same here. I was about to conclude you were a stowaway. You look that real on this end." The President shuffled some papers and looked up again. "Okay, where are we?"

"Meridian Six has changed course. It's headed squarely for the southeastern border of Qadhafiland, and the looney colonel himself has scrambled four MiG-21's to wait for the crossing." Admiral Sanderson saw the President shift position and cock his head.

"Really?"

"Yes, sir."

"The picture I'm getting here, Bill, shows severe weather radar returns along the Libyan-Algerian border"—he leaned forward, studying a corner of the screen—"or, more precisely, along a north-south line perhaps a hundred miles west of that border."

"That's right."

"So, the question is whether the pilot of that craft intends to violate Libyan airspace, or whether he's trying to get around the weather and doesn't realize where he's headed."

"Hard to believe," Sanderson began, "that someone who can handle a 747 can't figure out where the Libyan border is, especially if he or she's a trained terrorist."

"Maybe he or she *isn't* a trained terrorist."

"Sir?"

"Maybe whoever's in that cockpit is just some fool pilot with the right qualifications hired for a ridiculous sum of money to do what he's doing on the naive assumption it's a benign smuggling mission or something and that his employer is going to let him live to collect."

"That's possible. Hard to believe anyone would knowingly fly a terrorist mission these days."

"What does Langley think?" the President asked, pointing to another man at the table in the Situation Room. "Jeff, is it?"

"Yes, sir. Our best guess, Mr. President, is that this aircraft has a European target, as I mentioned in our first contact last hour. If this was a Libyan operation, this aircraft wouldn't be flying toward Libya, since Qadhafi knows only too well the immense and immediate penalties you'll trigger if he's even involved with such an attack. It *is* remotely possible the plane is headed to attack Tripoli, but we think not."

"And if it's an inadvertent mistake on the part of the pilot?"

"Qadhafi will shoot it down the moment his border's crossed. Remember, the plane is of American registry, which makes it de facto hostile, and this southwest corner of Libya and southeast corner of Algeria are disputed territory claimed by Libya. And with our new worldwide rules of terrorist engagement, an unresponsive, hijacked civilian airliner is to be shot down long before reaching population centers."

"Okay. Where's the Pentagon on this?" the President asked.

"Off line for the moment, sir, but I can brief you," Sanderson replied, consulting some papers. "All our naval assets in the Mediterranean are on alert, as per your orders, and as previously briefed. Other than sending some sort of radio warning to the pilot of that 747, which we can't do since he's not communicating, we have no assets capable of interdicting southern Libyan airspace even if you wanted to risk it."

"Mr. President, there's one other consideration," Jeff said.

"Go ahead."

"Since we believe the passengers and crew are *not* aboard that aircraft, and since we believe that whatever it's carrying is more than likely a nuclear, chemical, or biological weapon of mass destruction, and since we're preparing to intercept and destroy it over the Mediterranean . . ."

"Wouldn't it be nice if Daffy Qadhafi could do it for us?" the President interrupted, chuckling. "Is that where you're headed?"

"Yes, sir."

"Well, it looks like we're just helpless observers at this point until and unless he makes it to the Med, but I'll sure feel more secure when our F-14s get a close-up look at that 747. Before I have to decide to bring it down, I mean."

"They will have thought of that, Mr. President," Jeff

replied. "Whatever our pilots see in the windows of that jumbo jet will reinforce the idea that it's a civilian airliner full of passengers, and thus no harm to anyone."

"Maybe so, but . . ."

"Sir, may I suggest something more?"

"Go ahead."

"If . . . Qadhafi were to think that this aircraft was headed for Tripoli, his fighters would be ordered to down it even if it wasn't over Libyan territory."

"Which," the President began, "would constitute a reprehensible act in violation of dozens of protocols, not to mention a violation of the territorial rights of Algeria, which is where the wreckage would come down."

"Exactly."

"And, you're looking for me to sign a finding, are you?"

"No, sir. I didn't say that. I suppose I was just wondering if we should be really, really careful to make sure Mu'ammar doesn't get that idea, or should we just let him interpret our background communications any way he wants?"

The President looked at Bill Sanderson through the almost transparent medium of the advanced teleconference wall, and Sanderson looked back, his right eyebrow raised slightly, a lifelong gesture of conditional disapproval the President knew well.

"Very well, Jeff," the President replied, shifting his gaze to the man from Langley. "I will not sign any finding that authorizes the CIA to purposely instill a false belief in the Libyan government that this Meridian airplane is on its way to Tripoli with lethal intent, and I do not approve any specific attempt to lure the Libyans out of their own airspace. Short of that, if they stupidly misunderstand some . . .*private* message we're sending to third parties that they happen to illicitly intercept, such misunderstanding will be at their own peril."

"Yes, sir."

"Bill, you say the Seventh Fleet is ready?"

"Yes, sir, it is."

"How long before the flight reaches the Med?"

"A little under ninety minutes, Mr. President."

"Okay. We'll reestablish this conference in ninety minutes with some serious decisions to make. As soon as our pilots can safely intercept the flight to the north of Qadhafi's airspace, I want to know what they're seeing. But make sure they're ready to shoot. Once we've solved that, we'll turn our attention toward ransoming our people in Nigeria."

THIRTY-NINE

Janie Bretsen sat beside Brian Logan in the small alcove behind the cockpit door for what seemed an eternity, breathing what remained of the oxygen in her portable bottle as Brian did the same, both of them clearing their ears as the cabin repressurized. When it was obvious the bottles were no longer necessary, Janie motioned Brian to where Robert MacNaughton had fallen, putting the portable mask on MacNaughton's face and blasting him with pressurized oxygen until he began to stir.

"What ... I mean, where ... ," he said, looking around at both of them.

"We're stabilized for the moment," Brian told him, quickly describing what had happened.

"Good heavens!" Robert said, rubbing his forehead. "Is everyone awake again?"

"I'm going to find out," Janie replied, getting to her

feet and moving down the aisles, putting the yellow supplemental oxygen masks on the unconscious passengers one by one as Brian stood and helped Robert to his feet.

"That, most decidedly, was the last straw," Robert MacNaughton said.

They descended the stairway and Janie motioned to Brian to help with the masks in first class while she looked for her crew and helped revive the rest of the cabin. Brian moved into the cabin, relieved to see all the occupants standing or sitting and rubbing their eyes.

"Everyone up here okay?" he asked.

There were nodding heads and questions, and he quickly filled them in.

"He did it on *purpose*?" one of them asked, an incredulous look on his face.

Brian nodded, chilled by their rapidly growing outrage.

There was an empty rest room between coach and business class, and a suddenly protesting bladder forced him inside.

In the main cabin, the passengers whose masks had been snapped in place slowly began opening their eyes and refocusing while those still without masks remained unconscious. Many of them were in extraordinarily awkward positions, some draped over armrests into the aisle, but some draped over each other as well, whether they were acquainted or not. Slowly they, too, began to wake, many in pain with ear blocks from the pressure change, all of them upset to learn that the captain had tried to hurt them.

Dan Brown had collapsed by door 2-Left while his wife passed out in her seat, oblivious to anything until Janie passed her row and pulled her mask in place. The small trickle of oxygen accelerated her return to consciousness, and the sight of her husband's empty seat propelled her into the aisle in search of him. There had been nightmares, or dreams, or something in her head about shooting and shouting and something terrible happening to him. There was a taste of panic in her mouth as she moved forward and spotted him at last asleep on the floor.

There was an open oxygen mask compartment next to the flight attendants' seat and she grabbed one of the masks and put it to his face, and was greatly relieved to feel his pulse. She massaged his hands and watched him slowly come back.

"Honey? Are you okay?"

His eyes were open and glazed, but his mind was engaging slowly, and within a minute he was sitting on his own.

"What happened?"

"I don't know."

"We're still flying?"

"Yes. I passed out, too. I think everyone did."

"The masks are down," he noted, looking around and wincing at the headache which shot across his forehead.

"I'm a little nauseous, but okay otherwise. How are you?" Linda Brown asked.

"Confused," Dan replied. "There was something . . . the PA I think . . . the doctor said the captain was raising the cabin altitude, right?"

"I think so," Linda replied.

"Then . . . the son of a bitch." Dan shifted his body and started to clamber to his feet, but hesitated as the aircraft seem to undulate around him. He rubbed his head and sat back down.

"Honey, let's get you seated," Linda said.

"Wait." He opened his eyes again and took a deep breath. "No. This has gone far enough. Where's that doctor?"

"I don't know. Why?"

"Does everyone know what happened?"

"I'm not sure," she said.

There were footsteps behind her, and a male hand reached out to Dan Brown to pull him to his feet.

"You all right?" he said.

Dan nodded.

"How about you, little lady?"

Linda felt a flash of anger at the sexist phrase as she looked up, recognizing a loudmouth she'd noticed before. The hardened look on the man's face told the tale.

She stood and looked around the cabin, shocked at how many people were on their feet and talking, angry expressions on their faces as the words of the captain, the oxygen deprivation, and the wild gyrations of the plane all coalesced into a growing firestorm of indignation.

"On *purpose!* That's what I heard."

"What was he yelling on the PA? I was about out of it when . . ."

"I tell you what. I wasn't in favor of interfering before, but that jerk in the cockpit's gonna finish us off if we don't do something."

The flight attendants assigned to the rear cabin were coming forward, but they were being met by an aisleful of upset people asking questions and pointing out the few passengers who had yet to awaken. For the first time, the roar of human voices began to rival the background roar of the slipstream.

Dan Brown was fully awake now and out of control. He'd seen where the bullhorns were kept in the overhead compartments and moved to grab one, clicking it on and facing the sea of outraged faces as he pulled the trigger to activate the amplifier.

Hey! Anybody doubt Doctor Logan now?

A noisy chorus of "no's" broke out and died down.

You all realized that son of a bitch in the cockpit just tried to kill us?

A ragged "yes" rippled through the crowd, less satisfying in its volume, but just as determined.

Robert MacNaughton had entered the front of the

coach cabin as Dan Brown began using the bullhorn, standing quietly a few paces behind him until Brown looked around and saw him. Robert nodded toward the bullhorn and Brown handed it over, not expecting the controlled vitriol that rolled off the corporate chairman's tongue as he began to outline a renewed plan to remove Phil Knight from the controls.

Brian Logan emerged from the rest room into a cauldron of milling anger, his reappearance in the cabin greeted by a spontaneous cheer from those closest to the front. Robert MacNaughton was leading the way and began outlining for Brian the new plan for storming the cockpit, as both men and women pressed in from behind. Brian spotted Janie Bretsen standing to the left, an ashen expression on her face, and two other flight attendants farther back who were caught up in the crowd and the emotion. One of them even raised her fist in defiance along with the rest of the passengers when Robert turned and asked for another unified response.

"We can't . . . do that," Brian said to Robert, trying to keep his voice too low to be heard by the others.

"We can and we must," Robert MacNaughton replied. "This captain is incredibly dangerous."

"But . . . ," Brian began, stopping himself as he surveyed the angry eyes in every direction around him.

"We should have listened to you, Doc," one of the men said, whose face he didn't recognize.

There was noisy agreement as Robert resumed briefing him on what was a serious plan of attack: five men using a metal galley container as a battering ram to blow through the cockpit door without warning.

"Any comments?" Robert was asking, his eyes boring into Brian's. "Are you quite all right, Doctor?" he added.

"What?"

"I asked if you were all right. We must act right now."

Brian felt the cabin undulate violently. He was aware of the thirty or forty or more passengers standing in furious anticipation and waiting for his answer, waiting for his continued leadership. Robert MacNaughton's initiative in formulating a new assault was tactical leadership, but they obviously considered Brian the leader of the revolt. This was *his* work, *his* revolt, *his* mob, all of them out of control and enraged. These were the people he'd cajoled for hours directly and indirectly to do something about the arrogant and uncaring Judy Jackson, her crew, and the captain, inciting them to rise up and refuse to be victimized by the agents and employees of the entity he hated most in the world: Meridian Airlines.

And he'd succeeded. . . . But at what?

The magnitude of what was happening pressed in on Brian, colliding with shifting realities and changing perceptions. Even the angry exchange with the captain had rattled his previous conclusions about Meridian.

The copilot, for instance, had turned out to be a decent man, and Janie . . . Janie over there had turned out to be a caring ally. Only Judy Jackson and the captain had remained in his crosshairs, and the dark possibility was looming in his mind, however remote, that the captain might not have understood that the copilot was bleeding to death outside.

He looked at the angry mob again, delivered ready for action by perhaps the most restrained, erudite, and judicious man on the flight, Robert MacNaughton. Had his rage blinded MacNaughton as well?

My God, what have I done? Brian felt the words form in his mind, already understanding their import.

He took a quick breath and held up his hand as he glanced at Robert MacNaughton, then back at the crowd.

"Hold it! Wait a minute! I . . . didn't have time to tell you that we've forced the captain into an agreement."

"An *agreement!*" someone said in a sarcastic tone. "With *that bastard?*"

"WAIT! LISTEN TO ME!" Brian moved forward a few inches, forcing Robert to step to one side.

"What are you doing, old man?" MacNaughton said in a low, irritated voice. "We're wasting time."

Brian ignored the question, his hand still in the air in a stop gesture as he reached for the bullhorn with the other and activated the trigger.

Okay, everyone! Hang on! I know the SOB upstairs tried to knock us all out and almost succeeded, but he didn't because we were up there trying to batter down the door. So I worked out a deal with him. Remember, all he has to do is flip one switch and we're all unconscious within seconds, so in return for our not trying to break in, the captain has promised to continue on to London and to keep the cabin pressure normal, and not try any more moves like that. I wasn't able to budge the door anyway.

Brian released the trigger, aware of the ripple of negative responses before him.

"Have you forgotten we were going to bleeding Cape Town?" One of them shouted.

"And what about the copilot you said he murdered?" yelled another.

He said we don't have enough fuel to make Cape Town. That's why we're returning to London. He . . . also swears he didn't hear me telling him on the interphone back in Nigeria to stop the plane. He swears he didn't know the copilot wasn't aboard until he was on the takeoff roll.

Robert had Brian's left forearm in a vise grip, forcing his attention.

"Doctor, the element of surprise is paramount. We must act now."

"And what if we don't need to? He could still kill us if we tried to get him out of there. Don't forget they've got a crash axe in there, and although I don't believe it for a moment, he claims to have a gun."

"If we move rapidly enough," Robert retorted, "there won't be any time for him or that ridiculous lead flight attendant to mount a defense. I don't care how reinforced that door is, with all of us hitting it with everything we can find, we'll get in and get him out."

"Robert, I . . . I've gotten everyone too riled up

without thinking this through. We can't lose control of this."

"We never had control, Doctor. We're trying to get it, in fact."

"What are you guys talking about up there?" one of the men said from several feet behind Robert. "Are we going to do this or not?"

Robert turned to him and raised a hand. "Stand by. We're dealing with tactics."

"I'm sorry, Robert," Brian continued. "We've got to stop this. I think now it's best to wait him out. I mean, I talked to him, and I was wrong. The man is a terrible captain at the very least, but he's not suicidal, or we'd already be dead."

Robert MacNaughton looked him carefully in the eye. "You think we've become a bit hysterical, then?"

Brian nodded. "I do. I have. *I* have. I've been too hysterical."

"Perhaps, but may I remind you that, unless I'm somehow mistaken, it wasn't you who decided to make a strange, apparently useless emergency landing in Nigeria. It wasn't you who abused these people for hours on end, lying to us, as you pointed out, in London about the Queen and almost everything else."

"I know."

"And it obviously wasn't you who shot the copilot. So, are we overreacting when the captain attempts to kill us all with oxygen deprivation?"

"I'm not sure . . ."

"Not sure that he was attempting to render us unconscious in a manner that could kill?"

"He may not know the lethal effects of sustained hypoxia, Robert. Most civilians don't, and the copilot told me this guy is a very weak pilot."

Robert kept his jaw clamped shut as he shifted position and turned to survey the faces around him, looking back finally at Brian after what seemed minutes.

"Very well. I suppose you did have me violating one of my personal maxims, you know. Acting without thinking." Robert turned to the glut of passengers behind them, raising his voice. "We're going to wait! Doctor Logan is right. Armed intervention may not be necessary, but I'd like those of you who were going to break down the door, to stay ready in case we need you again."

Perhaps it was the ramrod-straight bearing of the man or the polished, authoritative accent, Brian thought, but the corporate chairman's words instantly deflated the explosive tension.

Most of them don't even know who he is, Brian thought.

Robert moved into the crowd, explaining the decision and calming tempers as Janie caught Brian's eye and gave him a fleeting smile. He smiled back, almost overwhelmed with the need to reexamine all he'd said and done since London, and feeling wholly off balance and embarrassed.

He looked up again to where she'd been standing, but she'd already moved down one of the aisles and out of sight.

There was a glow from a panel on the bulkhead wall to one side and Brian looked up, relieved to see that the captain had kept another promise and turned the Airshow display back on. He moved around to get a better look and studied it for a minute, his eyes tracking the blue of the oceanic sections bordering North Africa and the west African coastline and recording the position of the small icon representing their 747 as it flew north. He was too preoccupied to catch the meaning of the lines and symbols at first, but something there was vying for his attention, and in frustration he focused on the electronic map and what it was showing: a projected flight path about to cross the southwestern border of Libya in less than a hundred miles . . . on a course roughly aimed at Tripoli.

FORTY

The e-mail message flashed onto Robert Hensley's computer screen just as the prospect of an early dinner promised respite from a boring shift.

Aw, what the hell, he thought as he dropped his jacket back on the back of his chair and reached over to trigger the incoming text. There was always the possibility that such a message contained the elusive elixir that gave real newsmen their greatest highs: the wholly unexpected, late-breaking story no one else yet knew about. The chance of being first on the electronic rooftops with such revelatory information was as powerful a magnet as the promise of a jackpot to a gambler, or the hope of sex to the dating male of the species.

The message, he saw, was from an e-mail address he vaguely recognized. He toggled up his database program and ran a quick search, finding a seldom-used contact at

Meridian Airlines in Denver as the explanation. He made note of the name and returned to the message.

"We've got a strange emergency in progress over Africa," the man had written, filling in the details of Meridian Flight Six and its odd emergency landing and the message from the flight deck, which had been sent verbatim.

Robert sat back and reread the words again. *A 747 hijacked by its own passengers? Is that what the captain's saying?* He tried to imagine three or four hundred passengers in revolt.

There was a note from the sender at the end warning that disclosure of his name to Meridian would get him fired.

Then why screw your own employer? Robert thought to himself, but the man had already anticipated the question.

If this company were the Meridian Airlines we all used to respect, I'd never leak this to you. But today I wouldn't be at all surprised at a passenger riot. We still treat our passengers so badly, I'm surprised it doesn't occur every day. And then we lie, lie, and lie some more. I'm sick to death of it. We took the public's money back there after WTC to keep us afloat and then we proceeded to keep screwing the public. I'm trusting you, Robert, not to reveal me as the source, and whatever you do, for God's sake don't call me here. I'm sending this on my Palm Pilot PDA.

Robert got to his feet and paced slowly around his desk, trying to figure out whom to call first, if not the sender. Surely Meridian Airlines would instantly deny everything, though he would have to talk to them, too.

Come on, man, think! Who in D.C. would be privy to such information. Okay, CIA, maybe FBI, maybe not . . . the Pentagon . . . NRO . . ."

An old memory flashed into his head. The writer had used the term *ACARS* to describe the cockpit machine supposedly used by the captain of Meridian Six to send his plea for help. ACARS signals traveled by satellite, and he'd toured one of the main facilities of the organization that provided airlines with that service.

Robert returned to his desk and keyed in the appropriate company name, his excitement already building. With any luck, he could get the corroboration he needed and put the story out on the wires in twenty minutes or so.

Suddenly, all thoughts of dinner evaporated.

NRO HEADQUARTERS,
CHANTILLY, VIRGINIA
5:28 P.M. EDT

Colonel David Byrd had left the secure monitoring chamber as much to think as use the rest room. There was a break room around the corner and he drifted in, relieved it was empty. He fed a dollar to a Coke machine and sat down for a second, lost in thought, trying to pinpoint what was eating at him about the conclusions being sanctified down the hall.

You're not a spook, and you're not an analyst, he kept telling himself. *Don't get in the way of this.*

But relief wouldn't come.

David popped the can open and sipped at the soft drink as he drummed his fingers on the table and went over the pieces. Angry passengers hijacking the airplane, yet wanting to go to its original destination. The message was full of contradictions even before considering the bigger picture of hostages on the ground and the sudden course reversal to the north. Did "angry passengers" mean air rage? And was the captain talking about some, or all? More important, how could foreign terrorists construct phraseology like that?

I'm forgetting, David reminded himself, *that we've got pictures of two seriously injured pilots on that runway.*

He thought about his first impression when he'd walked in and been briefed on what they knew so far. He'd fully expected John Blaylock to be more skeptical, yet John was essentially convinced beyond a doubt, and he, the rookie, was the one feeling strangely uncertain.

That's why I stayed out of intelligence! David thought with a chuckle. *Too many shades of gray.* Certainty was more satisfying, like a switch that could be either on or off.

John Blaylock's voice boomed into his consciousness from behind, causing him to look around suddenly.

"So this has something to do with the Coca-Cola Corporation?"

"What?"

John pulled out an adjacent chair and spun it around, sitting down backward and resting on the back as he pointed to the soft drink. "You were contemplating that Coke can as if it held the secret of life."

David laughed. "Coke thinks it does. Pepsi disagrees."

"Something's really bugging you about all this, Colonel Byrd. I can tell. So what is it?"

"I don't know." David sighed. "That's the problem. There's an incredible drama going on half a world away and we don't have any idea what it really is. Are there people on that plane or not? I've been sitting here running it back and forth and I can't find any logical holes in your conclusions, John, but something's really nagging at me."

"When that happens to me, I go for the basics one by one. We've made a lot of assumptions today. So, go back and see if you can find a flaw in any of the big ones."

David chuckled. "You mean, like, are we *sure* he landed at Katsina, or was that a cardboard cutout?"

"It's a start."

"Anything new, John?"

"Yes. When I stepped out two or three minutes ago, our wayward 747 was precisely forty miles away from bulling their way into Libyan airspace, but suddenly they altered course twenty degrees to the left. Now they're tracking a projected course that will bring them within two to three miles of the Libyan border in about fifteen minutes, and then they'll have a second encounter with the border in forty-five minutes where it kind of juts out to the west into Algeria."

"How's Qadhafi taking it?"

"His boys are orbiting at the point of projected closest passage, and you can be sure they're armed and eager. Will they come over the border into Algerian airspace and shoot the Boeing? Who knows? Who knows what crazy communications Tripoli has been listening to? We'll see. Oh, by the way, the news services just broke the story of a 747 hijacked by its own passengers. CNN and everyone else will be launching camera planes within minutes. Someday they'll have their own satellite surveillance network."

"I don't doubt it." David fell silent for a few seconds. "So what's your opinion, John, about the course change?"

"Convinces me more than ever there's no commercial throttle jockey in that cockpit," he said, getting up from the chair. "You coming back in? Might be fun to watch this all the way to conclusion."

"I wouldn't miss it . . . but I need to find a phone."

John Blaylock nodded and fished in his pocket for a card. "George anticipated that. Says to tell you to use his office down the hall." He slid the card across the table with the room number. "A really cute little brunette named Ginger will be sitting there emitting copious pheromones and playing the part of the dutiful but distractingly pretty secretary."

David smiled and shook his head. "You ever think of anything but women and sex, Colonel Blaylock?"

"Hell no, Colonel Byrd! What else would I think about? Women and sex, preferably together, make the world go around. In fact, that's the treasured objective of virtually everything else we do as males. Don't kid yourself."

"Ginger, huh?"

"She knows to expect you. Be gentle."

"Oh, cut it out, John."

"Not a chance. See you back inside."

He turned and disappeared into the corridor as David took the card and got to his feet, chewing over the contradiction of the satellite shots of the hostages with the plaintive message from the flight deck of Meridian Six. To have angry passengers, you had to first have passengers. And they had to be angry about something. What was it that Senator Douglas had told him just that morning about the system falling apart?

David was moving down the corridor looking for George Zoffel's door when the memories finally merged and he came to a dead stop.

Wait a minute! Senator Douglas had just flown to London on a Meridian flight, and it was a terrible experience. She said she was almost ready to attack the crew herself. What was that flight number?

David quickened his step, propelled by a growing feeling of urgency. He seemed to be the only one harboring any doubts, but they needed to be resolved fast. Two aircraft carriers of warplanes were waiting to destroy the aircraft called Meridian Six.

CNN HEADQUARTERS,
ATLANTA, GEORGIA
5:38 P.M. EDT

The interval between the first appearance of the Associated Press wire report and the first break-in announcement of the story on CNN was six minutes. News that an American 747 had been hijacked by its own passengers was a major story, and within fifteen minutes the appropriate bureaus, stringers, and correspondent television news outlets in a dozen countries were struggling to respond to the uniquely American demand to accomplish the impossible sometime yesterday. As ABC, NBC, CBS, and Fox News joined the fray, jets were being chartered, camera crews were being rousted out of bed, and diplomatic clearances for news crews were being negotiated on the assumption that whatever was going to happen to Meridian Flight Six wouldn't happen until a live worldwide television audience was watching. Surely, the common wisdom among the various newsrooms held, this type of hijacking would require more than one night to resolve. Besides, the flight was returning to London, and

London was an easy stage for live coverage. But it was equally apparent that the flight path from Nigeria to London would be close to Italy, Spain, France, Switzerland, Malta, and Belgium, and all possible landing sites had to be covered.

The usual editorial debates were also in full swing about how much to report of what was allegedly known. Should they release the report that a copilot named Abbott—the only copilot aboard—had been badly injured and dumped somewhere in Africa? Had the man's family been informed? And even if they didn't use his name, wouldn't the wife and kids and parents and whoever else cared about him recognize the flight number the moment they heard it?

The London news bureaus in particular began ordering their people into action with the urgency of a fire department responding to a general alarm. Within an hour correspondents were manning phones and waking a wide variety of sleeping people, the so-called "usual suspects" when commercial aviation went sour. For Meridian Airlines, the list began with the home number of Meridian's station manager for Heathrow, James Haverston, who reluctantly sat on the edge of his bed rubbing his eyes and dealing with a steady stream of incoming requests for information he didn't have and interviews he had no authority to grant.

"Go ahead and talk to them, James, but just stick to the basic facts," the staff vice president for media relations told him when Haverston succeeded in calling head-quarters for advice.

"You realize Flight Six had quite a delay leaving Heathrow?"

"Yes, but as I say, just give them the facts."

James replaced the receiver in disgust. Years of experience had taught him to distrust such glib and overly broad instructions. If he stuck to the facts and got Meridian in trouble with the media, the vice president's report to upper management was a given: "I *told* him not to say that!" the man would complain, and James would end up sacked. Veteran managers for Meridian knew from bitter experience it was always better to develop a case of selective amnesia in such moments, though ducking the media was always counterproductive in the long run.

He padded to the kitchen and poured a hastily brewed cup of coffee, absently stirring in too much cream as he thought through what had happened and what he could say. The London delay had been due to an engine difficulty that cost them nearly three hours on the ground, but there had been no radioed indication from the flight crew of any difficulty with the passengers. After the flight left, it would have been up to Denver to answer any questions. He knew there would have been a threatened return to London, of course. The entire airline seemed to be chatting wildly on e-mail about that. And before leaving his office in the terminal, there had been word of the worrisome diversion into an African airport. But officially he could know nothing of that.

The prospect of news cameras held little terror for him, having dealt with the aftermath of several accidents over the years. What *was* disturbing, he admitted to himself, was the singular memory of Janie Bretsen's beautiful face evincing fatigue and disgust as she prepared to work yet another long leg to Cape Town. That and the fact that Judy Jackson was aboard, the same "lead flight attendant" now reported by the captain to be hiding in the cockpit of Flight Six.

James sighed and checked his watch. He had thirty minutes before the camera crews would expect him to appear. He wondered if Janie was all right. She had always been a good leader, caring and friendly and at the same time tough and capable. But a passenger *riot*? Perhaps it was his old periodic longing for her that was contracting his stomach so. Or perhaps, he thought, the balloon had finally gone up, as his American friends would say. Perhaps Meridian's arrogant attitudes had finally pushed a load of passengers too far.

He felt a sick sensation rising in his gut, a dark and depressing premonition that this was not going to end well.

The captain's message included the name of a passenger, Logan, who had reportedly attacked the copilot. The name had triggered no recognition at first, but then, James remembered a note he'd left on a small pad on his desk.

Please, let the name be different! James thought to himself.

He finished his coffee and hurried to his car, wheeling onto the deserted nighttime streets and following the familiar route to Heathrow. The name was that of an angry man whose face still burned in his memory. It was all too easy to recall the source of the man's anger, and the cold note on Meridian's computer listing under that name had mentioned the death of his wife and unborn child. That was the passenger who had worried them at the gate, the worries prompting him to call for security.

But James had decided to let him go aboard. His decision. His call.

Had he been wrong?

For the second time a small wave of nausea rolled through his midsection.

Could I be the cause of all this? he wondered. The thought deeply disturbed him. Had the copilot really been injured and left behind on a remote African airfield? James recalled the copilot's face from the brief encounter at the gate. He'd been a friendly sort. Certainly nowhere near as dour as Captain Knight.

James parked his car and hesitated before opening the door. *What if the name on the notepad is Logan? What can I say to the press?*

But the answer was all too obvious. He could say nothing.

469

FORTY-ONE

A live picture, appropriately scrambled, encrypted, transmitted over secure fiber-optic lines, then decrypted and reassembled on the liquid crystal display wall of the Situation Room, had been holding the attention of all present for the previous half hour. The White House Chief of Staff, Admiral Bill Sanderson, had tired of raising and lowering various telephone handsets and had opted for a lightweight headset instead, ignoring the prevailing snobbish attitude that only functionaries and secretaries wore such things, not senior leaders.

"B.S.!" Sanderson had snapped when his communications director had made the point weeks earlier during another Sit Room–level crisis involving the ongoing war with the remaining terrorist cells in the Middle East.

"Sir?" the Situation Room's director said quietly. "The President, line one."

Sanderson toggled the appropriate switch. "Go ahead, Mr. President." He nodded while listening, his eyes locked on the infrared image of Meridian Six and the white images of four MiG-21s flying in a loose formation five miles to the east. "We know . . . or at least NSA assures us . . . that Tripoli was listening when the appropriate message went out. It was moderately clever, but so is Mu'ammar. In any event, his four horsemen are still flying formation and waiting. Nearest approach to the border is coming up in about two minutes, and with the course he's flying, we estimate passage within two miles, but still physically clear of Libyan airspace. If they're going to jump out of their border and shoot him down, this is their last chance to argue that Meridian had strayed over their border."

Admiral Sanderson eased his six-foot-two, rail-thin frame into a chair and nodded silently some more as the President spoke. "I'm watching the same shot right now. I'll keep the line open." He pressed a hold button and glanced around the room before hovering a finger over the live line to the fully staffed Pentagon war room. If the stolen 747 survived its close encounter with Libya, the Sixth Fleet would be on stage. Regrettable, he thought. Much better to let the Libyans destroy the plane and suffer a firestorm of condemnation than have the Navy do it.

Sanderson glanced at a young Air Force major assigned to the Situation Room team and tried to recall when he'd held the Navy equivalent rank of Lieutenant

Commander. It was confusing sometimes, he thought, when military matters arose, to be both a former Chief of Naval Operations and yet have to respond like a civilian as Chief of Staff at the White House.

"Sir, they're moving in," the major said, pointing to the images.

"How far from the border now?" Sanderson asked.

"The MiGs are crossing into Algerian airspace now. The Meridian 747 is still six miles away, but in six miles he'll be almost exactly two miles to the west of their border."

"But he'll still be clear of Libyan airspace, right?"

"Yes, sir. No question. NRO says they've checked and rechecked these projections to exhaustion, and they've got a host of videotapes rolling."

The computer projection of the Libyan border showed it jutting out more sharply to the west as the jet flew north and the boundary edged to its westernmost point. The four MiGs were moving rapidly behind the 747, now clearly in Algerian airspace, though the Algerians had inadequate radar coverage in that section of the Sahara to monitor anyone accurately.

"NRO says at least two of the missile warheads are in active tracking mode," the Air Force major said, his background some eight years in F-15 Eagles. "They have tone. In other words, one missile now has locked him up. There's a second . . . and now a third."

Bill Sanderson took a deep breath as he watched the high-speed geometry unfold.

"How much longer do we have with this satellite?" Sanderson asked, aware of the echo of his question being passed to Chantilly and the almost immediate answer.

"Four minutes, but there's no gap. The next one is in position over the horizon now."

"We have lockup for missiles five, six, and seven . . . and eight. Eight missiles locked."

The fighters were now in four-abreast formation trailing the 747 by eight miles.

"He's three miles from the border as it curves in toward him," the major was saying. "Closest passage in forty seconds."

"They're going to try engineering the wreckage into Libya," Sanderson said. "Bet you anything they've locked up the right engines to force a right turn after impact. They'll fire four now at the right side, then finish him off when he's clearly across the border."

There had been flashing red aircraft beacons in the night sky to the east for the previous ten minutes, but no one aboard Meridian Flight Six had noticed in the initial confusion following the depressurization attempt. Suddenly a startled passenger on the right side spotted the other aircraft and told her seatmate, and the realization spread through the cabin that they were not alone.

Cindy was the first crew member to hear the report, and the first to lean down and spot the same lights blinking away steadily in the distance to the right side of the 747. She passed the information to Janie, who asked Robert MacNaughton to take a look.

"Hard to say," he concluded. "There are several beacons, so those are probably some nation's fighters tracking us." Robert turned back to his seat and flipped out the Airshow screen, toggling on the picture. He watched the display until it shifted to the tighter view of North Africa with political boundaries displayed, and let out a low whistle.

"Good heavens," he said, mostly to himself, unaware that Brian Logan had also plastered his nose against a right-side window to see the same thing.

"What?" Janie asked.

Robert tapped the display. "Libya. We're extraordinarily close, and that's very dangerous. I'm not willing to guess that our crazy captain has bothered to get clearance across Libya."

"What happens without it?" Janie asked.

"You remember Korean Airlines double-oh-seven in the eighties when they strayed over the Kuril Islands and the Soviets shot them down?" Robert asked, maneuvering out of the seat.

Janie nodded.

"Well, that was a 747, too, and Qadhafi's crazier." Robert pointed to the galley. "Where's that interphone?"

In Phil Knight's mind, word from the cabin below that they were being paced by fighters became immediately secondary to the fact that the caller was apparently the pilot Logan had said was standing by to seize control.

So it hadn't been a bluff, Phil thought. The man had made too many references to aeronautical terms and procedures to be faking. He'd spoken of things only a heavy-jet pilot would know, and that realization slowed for a few seconds the additional shock that the other pilot was none other than the chairman of English Petroleum.

Wait, Phil told himself. *He claimed to be MacNaughton, but that's got to be a lie. He's obviously a pilot, but MacNaughton's a damned corporate chairman carried around on a lettuce leaf. He'd be lucky to know how to drive, let alone fly.*

Yet, the caller was worried about being too close to Libya. Why? Even Libya had to respect a civilian aircraft in emergency status. The whole world had to know by now that Meridian Six was hijacked and not responsible for wherever its captain was forced to fly.

Phil strained his neck to look to the right for the flashing red beacons the man had mentioned, but it took unsnapping his seat belt and leaning over the empty copilot's seat to do so.

There they are! Behind the right wing, and off a considerable distance to the east. Obviously whoever was out there presented no immediate threat.

Probably just the standard escort of a hijacked airliner.

Phil brushed by the ACARS control head as he settled back in his seat. It was the same system he'd used to transmit the hijack message to the company, and he realized with a start that the message light was on and yet he'd been canceling the chime without checking to see what was waiting. He triggered the printer and waited for it to finish before tearing off the paper and snapping on a light.

> *Captain, Flight Six, from Ops—London ready to receive you with security as requested on arrival. Please note, no air traffic facility has had contact with you, nor do you have ATC clearances. Can you coordinate through us? Do you have time to describe nature of radio failure or permit troubleshooting from here? Please respond.*

Phil looked behind him at Judy Jackson, who was asleep and snoring softly, her head against the left window frame. Just as well, he thought. The axe lay in her lap, one hand still gripping it, but his threats had apparently calmed things down in the cabin. He could let her sleep for now.

The lights to the right were worrying him. Ops was correct. He had no air traffic control clearance because he was squawking the international hijack code. He'd reply to them on the ACARS in a minute, he decided.

Where is that damned map? Phil thought, scrambling around on the floor in search of the high-altitude chart. He remembered vaguely that it had fallen as he was yanking the jet around to keep Logan out.

There! He pulled the map from the floor and opened it to the general area they were traversing, turned up the overhead light, and checked the latitude and longitude on the flight-management computers before looking for that exact spot on the map.

There. We're right . . . here.

Phil sat back, thinking quickly. The border between Libya and Algeria was a curvy line moving roughly southeast to north-northwest He'd been tracking well to the Algerian side, but just ahead a part of Libya jutted into Algeria, and it looked like they would pass almost squarely over the tip.

He checked again. Just a few miles to go. He looked out to the right but the flashing lights were gone now, and he wondered whether they'd broken off or just fallen back some more.

He'd read something about Libya in the past week, but the names seemed to fold into one another. Libya, Chad, Egypt, and whatever else. He was hanging in the sky over a trackless desert. Why would anyone give a damn about borders out here? After all, he'd been flying them over Algeria for more than an hour with no consequences.

But the name "Libya" was sounding sinister, and there was Libyan territory just ahead.

Phil reached up to the auto-flight panel and took the aircraft out of the navigation mode that hooked it into the computer navigation system. Instead, he punched "heading select" and slowly rotated the course knob around to the left some fifteen degrees, then let the big Boeing steady out. Undoubtedly, he thought, it was a useless gesture, but maybe it was wiser to give Libya a wider berth.

For ten minutes the President had been watching the computer-enhanced images uplinked by secure military satellite from Chantilly as the distinctive and ghostly infrared image of the 747 became the clear prey of the four MiG-21s now trailing it, their missiles armed and locked. The thought of effectively presiding over the destruction of an American airliner had triggered several anxious moments of reexamination, but he'd returned each time to the reality that there were no passengers or crew members, as far as they knew, aboard the flight. In fact, there was every reason to believe that Meridian Six was a flying weapon of mass destruction, so why not applaud the Libyans' efforts if they blew it out of the sky?

Yet, he'd been holding an unconscious vigil and waiting for the first bright streak of light indicating the first missile launch from one of the MiG-21s.

Now, at the last second, the 747 began turning left and away from the Libyan border with the fighters in hot pursuit.

The President came forward in his chair and pulled

the telephone handset back to his ear. "Bill? What's he doing?"

"I don't know, Mr. President . . . turning, of course, but . . ."

"He's right on that border protrusion!"

"He was going to miss it by about two miles, now . . . more like three or four. More important, even if they go for the right engines, he may not go down in Libya."

"Dammit! Are they still trailing?"

"Stand by . . . we're talking to Chantilly. They say they're picking up excited radio communications between the pilots and their command post."

The President put his hand over the receiver and turned to his national security advisor. "I thought for sure they were going to go for it. Now I'm wondering if this doesn't look like a Libyan operation. You know, are they putting on a charade?" He repeated the question to the Situation Room.

"Chantilly's still in shock that he turned at the last moment," Bill Sanderson replied. "Okay, wait . . . the MiGs are standing down. The radar locks are coming off."

"I see it, Bill. The MiGs are breaking off to the east. Dammit!"

"Well, sir, the best laid plans . . ."

"*Their* plans, not ours, Bill."

"Are you ready for Plan B?"

"Plan A, actually."

"Understood, Mr. President."

"Get the Seventh Fleet ready and tell me who's first up?"

"The *Enterprise* has the first intercept group. I'm sure we won't need the *Ike*, but she's ready, too. Engagement in about forty minutes. You ... still want a visual inspection first?"

"Unless someone has a good reason why that might imperil our pilots, the answer is yes. Now that they've slipped past the Libyans. Keep me posted, Bill."

IN FLIGHT,
ABOARD MERIDIAN FLIGHT SIX
12:15 A.M. LOCAL

Jimmy Roberts had emerged confused from the fog of hypoxic unconsciousness with a splitting headache. He found his wife collapsed in the seat beside him. Someone had put oxygen masks on both of them, but she remained unconscious for several frightening minutes while he massaged her face and hands and called her name, fighting down the profound fright that he might lose her.

Brenda Roberts came around at last, somehow aware that both of them had been in great peril. Her tears didn't stop for many minutes as he held her and let her sob away as much of her fear as possible.

"Okay," she said, after drying her eyes and blowing

her nose. "I don't want to know another blooming thing about this airplane or its captain or anything else. Where are those earplugs?"

"You mean those headphones, darlin'?" Jimmy asked.

"Yeah. That entertainment system."

Jimmy located her headset on the floor and his in the seat back and hooked them up to the in-seat entertainment system.

"You flick that little thing, and it changes the channels to whatever you want, I guess."

"That screen there?" she asked pointing to an embedded liquid crystal display on the seat back in front of them that suddenly bloomed with color as Jimmy hit the right switch. He stepped through the various channels while Brenda studied an information card and looked up.

"It says here they've got CNN, Jimmy. How 'bout that? CNN in the middle of nowhere."

"Really?"

"Live broadcasts . . . by . . . satellite, it says. Try channel thirty-nine."

He entered the numbers, but a scrambled picture of static appeared over the occasional background noise on the headsets, then suddenly stabilized. One of the CNN anchors in Atlanta was in the middle of a story with a background graphic of an airplane.

. . . no more details from the remaining pilot, and, in fact, there has been no further communication from the aircraft for the past hour, according to sources close to this emerging

story. To recap, a passenger riot aboard a Meridian Airlines Boeing 747 over northern Africa earlier this evening has apparently resulted in the passengers hijacking their own flight. The captain and one flight attendant have barricaded themselves in the cockpit in an attempt to retain control. Meridian officials refuse to comment on preparations to storm the aircraft and arrest all aboard when it lands in London. Whatever is really happening aboard, the possibility of air piracy charges being filed against a large number of passengers would be unprecedented in U.S. airline history. Air piracy is a capital federal crime that carries a maximum penalty of death.

Jimmy Roberts felt his insides contract at the same moment he saw Brenda's eyes flutter open in shock.

"Jimmy? That's ... that's *us* he's talking about, right?"

"Damn," he said, feeling wholly inadequate at being unable to find something more profound to say. "The *death penalty*? Good God, Brenda, he's saying they consider all of us hijackers!"

FORTY-TWO

David Byrd replaced the receiver once again in George Zoffel's office and sat in growing frustration, wondering what was happening to Meridian Flight Six and whether there was any point in trying to follow his hunch. Locating Senator Sharon Douglas in the middle of the night had proven far more difficult than he'd expected. She was still in London and would undoubtedly be asleep, but there were far too many fine hotels and little time to permit his simply calling down the list.

A phone rang, and David saw one of the lines light up. Ginger, George Zoffel's secretary, answered it, and just as quickly caught his attention through the open door as she held up two fingers and mouthed the word *line*.

David punched up line two.

"Colonel Byrd? Ron Olson, Senator Douglas' administrative assistant. I just got a call from the White House switchboard saying you desperately needed to talk to her."

David phrased his words carefully. They were on a nonsecure line. "I . . . have a matter of utmost urgency to discuss with her, and it can't wait."

"You can't tell me what this is *about*?"

"No, Mr. Olson, I can't."

"And yet, you want me to wake her up at, what, three A.M. in London?"

"If you *don't*, sir, she'll probably have you flogged. Look, it really is that vital. Just give me her hotel number, and I'll call."

"How the heck do I know you're who you say you are?"

"Think about it. Who called you on my behalf?" David asked.

There was a moment of silence before Olson responded. "Oh, yeah. The White House operator. Okay, hold on while I get you that London number."

He returned with an endless series of digits for the London hotel.

The phone in the London hotel room was answered by someone having a hard time controlling the receiver. It banged around on the nightstand and apparently fell to the floor, eliciting an audible grunt before it found its way back to what was presumably Sharon Douglas' ear.

"Um . . . Hello?"

David identified himself and apologized for the call before racing through the case for her help. There was a confused sigh on the other end and the sound of the receiver being shifted to another hand.

"Who's this again? David . . . Byrd?"

"Yes, ma'am."

"The Air Force guy I talked to earlier today . . . yesterday?"

"Yes, Senator."

"What time is it?"

"Very early, and I'm sorry about that."

"More to the point, where am I? It's dark in here."

"London."

"Oh. That's right. What can I do for you, David?"

"That terrible flight from Chicago you were telling me about? Do you recall the flight number?"

"Uh huh. Meridian Six," she said. "Couldn't this wait till morning?"

David caught his breath. "I thought I remembered that flight number."

"But . . ." She cleared her throat in the background, then composed herself. "Why? Why do you need to know?"

"There are . . . some aspects of this I can't talk about on a nonsecure line, but let me give you a quick rundown." He briefed her on the continuing odyssey of Flight Six since she'd left it at Heathrow. While he talked, he heard the covers rustling as she sat up and cleared her throat again.

"Good Lord! Hijacked? But you said, by the *passengers*?"

"That's what I need help finding out, and quickly. The captain reported a riot on board, which sounds like an air rage situation, and I'm trying to find out if that makes any sense." David paraphrased the ACARS message from Flight Six. "The thing is, officially we don't believe that came from the captain."

"David, who is 'we'?"

"Ah ... Senator, I can't tell you. I've just been pulled into an official analysis of a situation involving this flight, and all I can really say is this: I need to try to find out if there really is a serious chance the passengers could have revolted on that flight. Have you heard of any passenger anger, for instance, on their departure out of London?"

"Are you joking? If there's one single Chicago passenger still on that plane, there's a whale of a chance of passenger fury. All of us were primed to be furious. As a matter of fact, I witnessed a man verbally assault the captain out on the jet way as he got off, and I believe he and his wife were going on."

"Okay."

"I have no idea, of course, what kind of crew they had out of London. They could have been completely different from the rotten group we flew in with. Well, one flight attendant wasn't rotten, but she was the exception. Look ... I've got the number here of the London station manager. I think it's his cell phone."

David could hear her shuffling things around in search of the number. "He called last evening," she continued, "and profusely apologized, then sent over wine and flowers and did a great job of trying to make amends for his airline. But, frankly, I think they're hopeless. Here it is."

David wrote down the number as she read it.

"Thanks a lot, Senator."

"One more thing," she said. "Would you call me back after you talk to him? I'm both awake and very concerned now."

He promised to do so and hung up, dialing James Haverston's number immediately. The station manager answered in a crisp, wide-awake voice, startling David.

"Yes, we had a long delay out of London, but that's all I can tell you. I know of no specific anger incident on the outbound flight. Who are you, again?"

"Colonel David Byrd, U.S. Air Force."

"Look, Colonel, I'm sure you are who you say you are, but I have a company to protect from clever reporters. Do you have a phone number I could call back that might settle my worries?"

"Stand by."

He got up and moved into George Zoffel's outer office and to Ginger's desk to get a main NRO switchboard number and their extension, then returned to pass it on to Haverston.

Ginger appeared in the doorway as he waited for the incoming call.

"Mr. Zoffel says to tell you they've passed the Libyan threat and are headed for the Mediterranean."

"Thanks," he said, giving her a fleeting smile and indulging himself in the act of noticing that John Blaylock was right. She was a lovely woman.

The phone rang and Ginger moved to answer it, turning to David once more and indicating the line number by the number of fingers she held high.

"Colonel? James Haverston here. I'm now appropriately satisfied that you're not a reporter, but I'm not sure I can help you."

"Can you tell me anything more?" David asked.

James Haverston related the presence of the English Petroleum Corporation's chairman. "I'm sure that will all be a matter of public record very soon, but I have no idea whether it means anything. You did ask, however, whether the captain's message could be valid."

"Have you seen a copy of that message?"

"I'm heading to the airport to meet a covey of camera crews, Colonel, and I've had the message read to me at least twice."

"So, could it be valid? Could there be a major incident of enraged passengers on that flight?"

"I don't know. Other than what I told you about Mr. MacNaughton." There was a long hesitation on the other end. "Of course, my personal opinion is that anytime a big airliner stuffed full of passengers has two delays in one day . . ."

"Two?"

He related the diversion on the ground in London. "I know nothing of what the crew said to the passengers or what the attitude was in the passenger cabin, but the maintenance problem was solved in little more than two hours."

"Look, Mr. Haverston, this is very, very important, and you're going to need to take a leap of faith here if you know anything else. I simply can't reveal why I'm asking, but if I could, I know you'd immediately bend heaven and earth to get me what I need. If we can't show that the message from Flight Six is logical and reasonable and that a passenger uprising is more likely on that particular flight than not, every life on board may be lost."

"I'm sorry, what?"

"I can't tell you more, but you can imagine these days, the government of Great Britain and those of most of the E.U. nations as well as the U.S. get very excited when a big airplane starts heading to a major capital without communicating."

"I'm not understanding this, Colonel. What are you asking?"

"I think there's something you're not telling me, Mr. Haverston, and it could be fatal to your passengers and crew. Please. What else?"

David could hear the phone being transferred to the other hand. Haverston cleared his throat.

"I'm parking at my office now, and there's a note inside I need to see."

"Tell me why."

The sound of a car door being slammed echoed in the background followed by footsteps and the jangling of keys.

"In that message there was the name of a passenger whom the captain points to as having hurt the copilot."

"Yes. The name is Logan."

"Quite."

David could hear the sounds of a door being unlocked. "There was an angry American physician yesterday going on this flight, you see. I need to check the name as I wrote it down to make sure it isn't the same man."

"Logan, you mean?"

"Yes."

"You had a problem with him?"

James Haverston summarized the report in Meridian's computer about the death of the man's wife and child. "It was a most unpleasant encounter, but we . . . I . . . judged him to be no threat and allowed him to board. I'm at my desk now. Wait a flash."

David could hear papers shuffling, then silence.

"Mr. Haverston?"

More silence.

"Sir?"

"Well, dammit all."

"Say again?"

"I can't find the bloody thing. I thought I'd left it here."

"And, you don't recall the name for certain?"

"No. I'm sure the name is different, but, look, Colonel. I'll call you back if I can find it."

"Please! The second you locate it, if the name is the same, call me on my cell phone." He passed on the number and replaced the receiver, sitting in rapid thought. *I can't do this alone!*

He swept past Ginger and headed for the hallway, barely aware that she had bolted from her desk to chase after him.

"Colonel? I'll have to let you back in."

"Oh." David fell in step behind her, trying to keep his eyes off her figure as she flowed down the corridor, worked the cipher lock, and threw her lithe body into the job of moving the heavy door inward.

"Thanks, Ginger," he said, feeling a flash of warmth in her smile as he moved inside and took the same seat and slipped the headset on again.

"What's going on?" he asked.

"He's coming up on the coastline," Blaylock reported, summarizing on the private channel the encounter with the fighters and the sudden turn. "He knows exactly what he's doing, David. That pilot may well be Libyan, and those MiGs may have been a protective escort. If so, they locked him up with their missiles just to make it look good."

David was chewing his lower lip as he looked at the various screens.

"How long?"

"The *Enterprise* is launching her Tomcats now. The plan is to intercept, try to establish radio contact, and failing that, try to turn him back to North Africa. There's a remote airfield well south of Algiers that the Algerians are saying we can use. But if whoever's in that cockpit won't talk *or* turn, he's going to die rather quickly. The rules of engagement have already been passed to the F-14s."

FORTY-THREE

Jimmy Roberts stood in the aisle after telling Brenda to stay put. He moved rapidly past the forward galley and into first class, not caring whether he should be there or not. He hated putting himself in places where someone might make him feel inadequate or unwelcome, like a skunk at a garden party. Usually he avoided such places like the plague, but this was different. He and Brenda and everyone aboard were being accused of a crime, and it scared him.

The huge seats in first class were intimidating, but he forced himself to move into the cabin, searching the faces of the passengers until he spotted the doctor who'd been the ringleader of the revolt they were talking about on the news. He was leaning over a pair of seats on the right side and looking out the window into the blackness as another man he recognized from coach was doing the same thing in the row behind, talking with the woman who'd identified herself as the new lead flight attendant, Janie.

"Doc? Excuse me," Jimmy said, stuffing both hands in his slacks.

The doctor didn't look like such a giant up close, Jimmy thought. He'd loomed large earlier when he was tearing around the cabin with the bullhorn.

The doctor pulled back from the window and looked around, his eyes weary and his face almost pasty. He straightened up, looking Jimmy in the eye.

"Yes?"

"Ah, look, my name's Jimmy Roberts and I'm from coach back there, and my wife and I just picked up a news broadcast from CNN, and the announcer was talking about this flight and saying that all the passengers were hijackers, and I'm . . . well, we're not, and I need to know, what . . . in hell is going on here."

" 'Hijackers'?" Brian Logan repeated.

"Yeah." Jimmy repeated the words the announcer had spoken as well as he could recall. The other man who'd been looking out the window and the lead flight attendant had heard him, too, and were moving closer.

"What's scaring my wife and me," Jimmy continued, "is that they're saying we're all going to be arrested and charged with piracy. I don't know about you folks, but we haven't done anything back there. We're just on a trip we won and trying to mind our own business."

Robert MacNaughton pulled himself out of his

seat and offered his hand to Jimmy as he introduced himself.

"Glad to meet you, Mr. MacNaughton," Jimmy said, shaking MacNaughton's hand.

"Don't you worry about such nonsense, Mr. Roberts," Robert said. "The only activities here that border on criminality are those of the pilot, not Doctor Logan or myself. There . . . may well be some sorting out to do with the police when we arrive, but I can assure you no one's going to be filing charges against you or your wife."

"But why would they *say* that?" Jimmy replied, looking Robert MacNaughton in the eye. "I mean, I heard what you fellows said on the PA. You especially, Doc. I think you said we were taking over."

"Just . . . ," Robert interrupted, his hand raised, "just taking over in terms of telling this captain that he was required to continue on to his destination. That's certainly not like . . . like . . ." Robert hesitated as he went back over the events of the previous hour from a legal point of view, the reexamination bringing him to an embarrassing halt.

"Look," Brian Logan added, "you can't hijack an airplane to its original destination. That's ridiculous. The captain has obviously been broadcasting these allegations on the radio with none of us around to counter him, but it's all B.S."

"I hope so," Jimmy added. "We're not, you know, experienced fliers or anything. My wife and I."

495

Brian nodded, but he wasn't really paying attention to Jimmy's last remark. His attention was focused instead on Robert MacNaughton, who had fallen silent and was scratching his chin.

"Mr. Roberts, is it?" Janie asked.

"Yes, ma'am."

"Let me go back with you and reassure your wife, too," she said.

"I'd appreciate that," Jimmy replied, letting Janie guide him back through the curtains toward coach as Brian turned to the E.P. chairman.

"What's wrong?"

"From the mouths of babes, or shall we say, the innocent, come painful truths."

Brian held on to the seat back and studied the older man. "What do you mean?"

Robert MacNaughton sighed and eased himself down in the seat, folding his hands neatly over his stomach as he looked up at Brian and shook his head. "I hate to admit it, but I'm afraid our friend there may be right, Doctor. You and I have attempted to seize control of this airliner, and without regard to the reason, that quite literally meets the threshold definition of air piracy, regardless of what we demanded the captain do."

"No! Bullshit!"

"I'm not a solicitor, of course, but I deal with legal matters all the time, and I'm afraid it does. Now, that doesn't mean anyone's going to file charges, but . . ."

"But what?"

"Well, considering the fact that you counseled restraint a while ago and it was I at the time who wanted to bash down the cockpit door, I'd say we both should just stand down and hope the fool up top gets us back to London in one piece. We can deal with the police there."

"Police?"

Robert cocked his head as he studied Brian's face. "How . . . did you think this would end, Doctor? I'll admit, I *didn't* think, other than to react like a bellicose commander. I rather imagined we'd be turning the *pilot* over to the authorities at the gate, but now I'm more than a bit concerned that he may well reverse the sequence."

"You're . . . not seriously suggesting that I've . . . or we . . . or anyone's committed a crime?"

"Doctor, forgive me, but that is precisely what I'm suggesting."

In the cockpit, Judy Jackson awoke with a small start, remembering where she was . . . and why. She looked around carefully, but no one else had entered the flight deck while she'd been asleep. It was just she and the captain, now, against the rest of the passengers, and the crew as well. Janie Bretsen had seen to that.

Judy could almost feel the empty copilot's seat mocking her, reminding her that the nightmare was still under way. Angry passengers, a strange landing in the middle of a gun battle, and the most embarrassing moments of her career all merged together in a frightening mélange.

Apparently, whatever mob had been outside the door had given up. Despite what she'd told the captain about fearing for her life, the mob that chased her to the cockpit scared her less than the embarrassment of her own cowardly disappearance.

She felt her face flush again at the memory, and especially the utter void in her head where she'd always had the appropriate, immediate, and self-justifying excuse for any mistake she made. There *were* no excuses this time, and she couldn't even explain it to herself. It was as if Judy the flight attendant had been a fragile construct of brittle glass, and now, in the face of such rage and hate, the fragile creature she'd been was shattered.

She sat up in the jump seat and reached out to tap the captain on the right shoulder. He turned to look at her through his peripheral vision.

"Yes?"

"Sorry," she said, wondering why she led with an apology, yet knowing why. "Where are we? I don't know how long I was out."

"Just coming up on the coast of North Africa. We've got less than three hours to London now."

"What are we going to do, Captain?" she asked. "When we get to London, I mean?"

"They'll arrest everyone in the cabin, I expect, and we'll have to go file our statements."

Judy exhaled sharply, trying to imagine the magnitude of such an arrest.

"We've got over three hundred passengers. They can arrest *all* of them?"

Phil Knight shrugged. "All I know is what Logan kept saying, that he represents everyone, and they chased you upstairs, and we know some of them were trying to get through the door. So I'd say, yes, three hundred or more arrests."

"Not everyone was involved, you know."

"They'll have to sort that out. Logan, at least, will be facing the death penalty for hijacking."

"I don't know the law . . . ," she began, letting her thoughts trail off.

"They'll be depending on you to testify about what you saw between Logan and Garth Abbott."

"Testify?"

"You said you were sure of what you saw, that he was clubbing Abbott in the electronics bay."

"Yes."

"You're absolutely sure it was Abbott, and not someone else trying to get in?"

"Yes."

Phil turned further around to try to see her eyes, dissatisfied with the monosyllabic responses.

"Judy?"

"Yes!" she repeated, a defensive tone in her voice.

"Did you know that Logan told me on the interphone

a while ago that he was clubbing soldiers, and that Abbott had already fallen off at that point? You know you're the only witness to what happened?"

"I know what I saw."

He hesitated, his eyes on hers and aware she had looked away to the left, out the window.

"You know I've trusted that. I told the company, and God knows who else knows about it now. I didn't say, 'Judy told me,' I just stated it as a fact."

He heard the sound of a seat belt being snapped open as Judy catapulted herself out of the jump seat to stand just in front of the door. Phil could see that her whole body was trembling, but her jaw was set and her eyes aflame as she stared at him.

"Dammit! DAMMIT! I TOLD you what I saw. You stupid fool, why are you browbeating me?"

"I'm not, Judy, I . . ."

"That son of a bitch is not going to get away with this!"

"You mean, challenging you?"

"Yes! No. No, I mean . . . with changing his story, or . . . or what I saw. I know what I saw! He killed the copilot."

"All right, all right. Calm down, now. Sit back down."

"I have to use the bathroom," she said, turning to look through the cockpit door peephole, then back at him. "Will you let me back in?"

"Yes. The usual procedure." She looked back

through the peephole for many seconds before swallowing hard and glancing over her shoulder.

"I . . . I think it's okay."

"Go ahead," he said. "I've checked the screen. It's clear. I'm going to have to do the same when you're through."

Humor was the last thing on his mind, but the way Judy Jackson responded to the thought of being alone in the cockpit while the captain went to the can almost made him laugh. She nodded in staccato fashion and opened the door slowly, then carefully opened the bathroom door before pulling the cockpit door closed.

The same flashing red light on the panel caught Phil's attention. It had been going off periodically for the past two hours and he'd been routinely canceling the warning, checking the engine temperature, and trying not to think about it.

Damned number four!

It had been the progenitor of all his problems, and Abbott had apparently been right. The continuous fire warning he was still getting was obviously false. Number four was running as steadily as the other three, mocking all the decisions he'd made before, and making the loss of Garth Abbott even more of a travesty.

The presence of the sophisticated digital flight data recorder in the tail of the 747 was something all pilots took for granted, but Phil thought of it now with disgust. Every time that engine fire warning light had illuminated, it had also recorded itself on the flight data recorder. Phil realized his right hand still wanted to grab and pull the fire handle for number four. He'd been overriding the urge, and he did so again. There was no point.

Janie Bretsen and the rest of the flight attendants had worked quickly to pass out the last of the bottled water and snack packs along with every aspirin or Tylenol she could find to those still suffering from altitude-related headaches. Three passengers were showing some signs of decompression illness with tingling sensations in their elbows, and one woman couldn't stop scratching her arm—a symptom, Janie knew, of a mild form of the bends. Amazingly, however—despite the physical stress of the decompression on all three hundred passengers spanning an age range from infants to octogenarians—everyone seemed to be calming down under the constant attention of what was now *her* crew.

Janie toggled on the PA at the forward part of coach. She began in a gentle tone of voice:

Folks, I know a lot of you are as weary as I am. Could I see a show of hands on how many of you would like me to turn off the cabin lights? It would be easier for you to try to sleep, and you'd still have the reading lights . . .

More than half the hands went in the air.

Thank you. Those who didn't raise your hands, do you have any really strong objections if I go with the majority and turn them out?

No hands. *Good*, she thought. *If we can hold on a few more hours, this will be over.*

Okay. I'm turning them out now. Thanks.

She turned back to the galley and worked the appropriate switches, then leaned against the sidewall for a moment to close her eyes and regain a little strength. She needed a second wind, and it wasn't coming.

Eighty feet toward the rear of the Boeing Jimmy Roberts had raised and stowed the armrest separating himself and Brenda, pulling her close after turning off the small TV screen. She'd accepted the explanation that they weren't in legal trouble. Janie, the flight attendant who'd returned with her husband, had seemed so nice and so concerned, and Brenda had believed her. Now she was sleeping softly and Jimmy held her, his mind slowly becoming aware of a small sound it couldn't place: a tiny, periodic sound somewhat like static and somewhere behind him. It sounded like the business radios he used at the shop back in Midland. Static and voices, and more static. Faint and barely audible, but pricking his curiosity too profoundly to permit sleep. He was in grave need of getting rid of pent-up nervous energy from sitting for so many hours. The inactivity was causing his muscles to tickle.

He looked down at his wife and began slowly, carefully moving her to the left as he adjusted a pillow for her head against the window frame. She was an incredibly sound sleeper when they were together. He'd joked

503

that a freight train in their bedroom couldn't wake her. But those few times he'd had to work all night on someone's truck, she'd been bleary-eyed and exhausted in the morning because the slightest noise during the night had jolted her awake.

Jimmy covered her with an extra airline blanket and leaned over to kiss her gently, then quietly undid his seat belt and slipped into the aisle, moving back row by row until he was standing beside the shadowy form of a young boy in a window seat three rows back. The aisle seat next to him was vacant, and Jimmy could see enough in the dim light to tell the boy was in his mid-teens. He was hunched over the digital controls of a small radio with an earplug in his ear—the source of the small sounds Jimmy had picked up. The boy noticed him and looked up.

Jimmy smiled and pointed to the radio. "Whatcha got there?"

"Just a police scanner," he said.

"Mind if I sit?"

"No," the boy said as Jimmy maneuvered into the aisle seat.

"You're picking up police calls way out here?"

"Not really . . . airplane stuff mostly, and some of it I can't understand."

"May I listen?"

"Sure," the boy replied, pulling the earpiece connector out of the radio and turning the volume down. A male voice crackled over the speaker, ordering someone to turn right, and receiving a quick response.

"What was that?" Jimmy asked.

"I don't know. I've got it on the aviation band right now, and it's scanning through a bunch of frequencies. I think that one's a control tower or something, and it sounds like Spanish they're speaking."

Another voice, a different one carrying distinctly American tones, broke the squelch:

Meridian Six, Meridian Six, Navy on guard, respond one-twenty-one-point-five. Repeat, Meridian Six, U.S. Navy on guard. Come up immediately one-twenty-one-point-five.

"Wait a minute . . ." Jimmy began, but the boy was already nodding.

"Yeah. That's our flight, but the captain's not answering. That's been going on for the last few minutes."

FORTY-FOUR

As always when air operations were in progress, the quiet efficiency of the electronic nerve center of the USS *Enterprise* had been shaken every few minutes by the *whoosh* of the steam catapults on the flight deck as several flights of F-14 Tomcats were launched fully armed into the night. Twenty minutes had elapsed, and the Tomcats were now on station at thirty-seven thousand feet and waiting for their target as the ship continued to broadcast on a variety of frequencies in an attempt to raise the pilot of the renegade 747. Meridian Flight Six was approaching the midpoint of its track across the Mediterranean, and the plan was to bring it down as far from land as possible.

In the cockpit of the lead Tomcat, Lieutenant Commander Chris Burton, radio call sign "Critter," checked his position once more and began a turn back to the south. The 747's radar target was already crawling onto the radar screen of his backseater, Lieutenant Luke Berris, his weapons officer. The plan was to fly the flight of four southbound for thirty miles and do a one-hundred-and-eighty-degree turn to come up behind the Boeing, with the other flight of four coming down from thirty-nine thousand only if needed. It would be up to Lieutenant Commander Burton to report what, if anything, he saw in the windows of the craft, as well as try to turn the 747 back to the south, but the final, private word at the door of the ready room had put a special spin on the mission. "The skipper wants you to know," his OPS officer said, "that we may be piping any description you give directly to *Air Force One*. The President wants a live hookup."

"What's the range, Blackberry?" Burton asked, using Berris' formal call sign, which he normally shortened to Blackie.

"Coming up on ninety. Five-point-five minutes to the turn."

NRO HEADQUARTERS,
CHANTILLY, VIRGINIA
6:23 P.M. EDT

David Byrd got to his feet and leaned over to speak in John Blaylock's ear. "I need to talk to you outside. Urgently."

John looked at him, hesitated, then nodded as he stood and addressed George Zoffel.

"We need to step outside, George. How do we get back in?"

Zoffel kept his eyes on the screens as he answered, "Use the phone out there on the wall, and I'll come out and get you."

They exited into the corridor and made sure the security door was closed behind them.

"John, I know you're the expert and I know very little about the intelligence community," David Byrd began, "but they're making a huge mistake in there, and somehow we've got to stop this."

"Why? Because you have a hunch?"

"Yes, I have a hunch. Just like you, I've been around the Air Force and aviation a long time and I'm not beyond having solid hunches."

"Didn't say you were, Davey. But convince me. Tell me why, with solid photographic evidence that the passengers are off that airplane, and both pilots are dead, and with all the warnings the community has received that something like this might be tried, why *shouldn't* we blow that tub out of the sky before it incinerates or infects part of Europe?"

"Because it isn't what it seems."

"Meaning?"

"I think the captain is still alive and on board."

"So, perhaps he's the turncoat, and he thinks he's going to survive whatever they want him to do."

"Now where's *your* evidence?" David asked.

"My evidence is in those shots of the rebel camp in

Nigeria, David. You saw them, too. We had the circum-stantial evidence with the evacuation slide and the buses, but we have real, live pictures of human beings, the majority were light skinned, and we've now counted close to two hundred of them in and around that shed. What did they say a while ago? The other section someplace here in the building that was analyzing those shots?"

"They said they thought they were over eighty per-cent Caucasian," David repeated, chewing his lip and raising an index finger. "But! We have not seen them all, and there may be a bunch more of the passengers on the airplane. Hell, John, that captain may not even know people were forced off."

"Describe the main burr under your saddle. What's the number-one incongruity in their reasoning in there?"

David nodded, thinking it through and glancing in both directions to make sure they were still alone in the corridor.

"What the alleged captain said in that message has not been disproven. Because of the hostage pictures we're concluding . . .*they're* concluding . . . that a passenger riot, an air rage incident, is not possible simply because there are no passengers. But we don't know as an indisputable fact that there are no passengers aboard."

"I disagree," John Blaylock said.

"Go at it in reverse, John. If there is *any* reasonable possibility that a bunch of furious passengers could have seized control, even if few in number, then we cannot discount the captain's message as a cynical component of an overall master plan. Any possibility! And there *is* a reasonable possibility and perhaps even probability. I'm here to tell you that, as bizarre as it may sound, I've studied passenger groups that were on the ragged edge of just such a revolt. Why is it so hard to believe they could frighten a captain into thinking he was in danger? Especially in an aircraft that's already made an emergency landing in the middle of an African civil war. A passenger revolt wouldn't seem much more bizarre."

"The point, Colonel?"

"I'm giving you the damned point, John."

"Intelligence proceeds on assessments of reliability, confidence levels, and guesses, all based on available evidence. You're trying to trump the proverbial thousand-word picture with a philosophical argument."

"The hell I am!" David replied, turning and pacing a few feet away in thought before turning suddenly and snapping his fingers.

"Okay, John, you want hard facts? Here's a hard fact. I talked to Senator Douglas a while ago in London. Woke her up. She was on that flight, Meridian Flight Six, on its first leg from Chicago to London." David related the litany of delays and abuses Sharon Douglas had outlined. "I also talked to the station manager at Heathrow. Over *one hundred* of those upset people continued on to Cape Town."

"I see," John replied, unconvinced but listening.

"In addition, the Meridian London manager had a

nasty encounter with an angry American physician yesterday boarding this flight to Cape Town. He's trying to find his note about the man's name because he's not sure, but the physician's wife died on a Meridian flight last year because the crew wouldn't listen to her when she asked for emergency help. He's suing the airline for millions. So why is such a guy flying that airline himself? Maybe because he's planning to start a riot."

"Or maybe because he's arranged a hijacking and been paid by a terrorist group," John added, holding his hand out, palm up. "Okay, David, look. Let's agree that the passengers had a preloaded amount of anger. There are dozens of ways this could have been a planned terrorist action. Fact is, whoever staged the commandeering of that 747 probably had either a confederate or a hireling on the flight from Chicago, and that's how they knew about the angry passengers, and how they would have decided at the last minute to utilize that information to make what they were about to stage sound even more real. Remember, we're up against a very sophisticated group here. They would have had numerous contingency plans."

"If we're up against a group at all. See, we've been stampeded, John. We've been stampeded by a totally legitimate determination never to be caught with our pants down again, but it's still a rush to judgment, and if we're wrong, our Tomcats are going to blow a bunch of innocent Americans out of the sky in a few minutes and the fallout and conspiracy theories and political damage will be immense, not to mention the lost and shattered lives."

"Wait, David. You're saying the process has been prejudiced in the direction of attacking?"

"They're assuming that no radio contact and no clearance and no evidence of passengers mean you *automatically* get a Trojan Horse. That's just not supportable. That's why it's a prejudiced decision. There could be other explanations, for Christ's sake! I mean, John, do we have *any* hard evidence, even anecdotal or circumstantial evidence, of a weapon?"

"No."

"No! We don't. We're just *assuming* that the suspicious nature of the 747's flight path and the no-passenger conclusion mean that there has to be a bomb or a biological weapon aboard."

John Blaylock was shaking his head.

"If they were approaching New York or Washington, would you hesitate?"

"No, I suppose not."

"You haven't been privy to what I've seen, David. The warnings that the remains of the terrorist networks we've been slowly rooting out all over the world have been planning something exactly like this has been increasing in intensity for months, and . . . there are two recent incidents that make this a higher probability than you know."

David fell silent for a second, thinking through his words. "John, you've got to listen to me now. We're about to make a historic error in there. I asked if there was any evidence of a bomb or anthrax or anything, and you said no. The warnings on which we're basing the conclusion that this is a flying weapon are even more circumstantial and suspect than the evidence I've just given you. How, John, could a terrorist pilot or a terrorist group know that there was enough anger aboard to justify spinning up the story of a passenger riot?"

"I told you, maybe they had a confederate in London, or aboard the plane."

"But, John, even if they did, they wouldn't have been *planning* on using an air rage story. Think about it. All the other elements of the plan were already in place. These thieves and terrorists, if they exist, wouldn't have left that message from the cockpit to chance, to be written at the last minute. It was too important. It was designed to keep everyone off their back and divert any suspicion. Who in hell would have thought up a passenger riot, let alone written it in an American voice? No, John, that's a real Meridian pilot up there, and he's got passengers in the back, and we're about to murder them."

"Onitsa's been pretty convincing, Dave. Nigeria just blew our minds and wired him ten million dollars to keep him from starting the threatened executions. Eventually they'll want to recover that from us."

David sighed and shook his head. "They may have some of the passengers, but not all. And, again, where's the weapon that was supposedly loaded on board? The satellites saw no big packages or bombs coming aboard."

"Could be a small package, or maybe Onitsa had the satellite schedules memorized and worked around them." John was nodding to himself. "Yeah. That would be like him." He looked back at David. "Look, what you're arguing has solid logic, David, and it's well thought out, except for one fatal flaw."

"What?"

"I'm going to raise this in there anyway, but . . . the pictures of the passengers as hostages are so close to conclusive, and the actions of the aircraft are so innately threatening, that in the minds of this community, they simply override your logic and constitute all the proof they need. Remember, we're fighting a war, and there's no spot on the planet not included in our alert zone."

"What will it take to convince *you*, John?"

John Blaylock shook his head and sighed as he studied his uniform shoes for a second, then looked back up. "I've gotta see something in that message that no one but the real captain could know. And we're just about out of time."

---

123 MILES WEST OF THE USS *ENTERPRISE*
12:24 A.M. LOCAL

Chris Burton watched the beacon and position lights of the Meridian 747 slide by five miles to the left with a closing rate of over a thousand miles per hour. With his three wingmen in an extended trail position, he rolled into a left ninety-degree bank to turn and pull up behind Meridian Flight Six as they followed in close interval. Burton steadied the Tomcat out on the same heading and accelerated toward the 747 as his wingmen followed.

"Okay, Critter, confirming ID on the Meridian Airlines logo and tail number. I'm pulling alongside on the left."

Chris nudged the throttles back and extended the speed brakes to slow the closing rate as he slid into position almost abeam of the 747's left side.

"What do you think?" he asked Berris on the hotmike interphone.

"Mostly dark, Critter. I see a few reading lights. Looks like . . . I don't know, *could* be a few people in there reading. Hard to say. I wouldn't want to swear to it."

"Could be dummies, too, Blackie," Burton added, letting the Tomcat move to the left quarter of the 747 as he searched the rest of the windows, finding almost all of them dark.

"Could be. I don't see any of them moving."

"I'm going in closer and get abeam the cockpit." Chris moved the controls almost imperceptibly to rise thirty feet or so above the wing level as he edged the Tomcat in front of the Boeing, taking care to keep the slipstream of his fighter from flowing directly onto the wing or tail of the airliner and disturbing the flight path.

"You see anyone in there?" he asked his backseater.

"Yeah . . . maybe. I've got one head in the window against the background of the instrument lights. Looks like."

The lead reported what they were seeing back to the ship.

"Roger, Critter. Try him on victor guard," the ship replied. "We've received no answer from down here."

"I'm doin' it, Critter," Berris said from the backseat as he selected the appropriate radio with VHF frequency capability and dialed in 121.5 before pressing the transmit button.

"Meridian Six, Meridian Six, U.S. Navy fighter at your ten o'clock calling on guard. Respond on one-twenty-one-point-five."

"Any answer?" Burton asked.

"Negative." Berris tried again, and then a third time, as the lead checked their position.

"No joy, home base," he radioed back to the ship. "Negative answer. We're going to try to turn him."

Burton let go of the transmit button. "Blackie, keep trying, okay?"

"You got it. I'd recommend we not get too close there, sport."

"Another ten feet or so, and that's it." Burton nudged the throttle again and inched forward as he reached down by feel and snapped on all the Tomcat's lights. He pulled a flashlight out of his flight-suit pocket and aimed it at the cockpit, flashing it back and forth for attention. Whoever was in the left seat was looking to the right.

Chris could see the flashlight beam illuminate the back of the figure's head, but whoever it was apparently didn't notice the reflections of the flashlight in the cockpit.

"Okay, Blackie, I'm going to thump him," Burton said, purposefully descending to let the wake turbulence from the Tomcat wash over the jumbo's wing and cause the jumbo to lurch. He craned his head around to watch the predictable response as the position lights of the 747 indicated a sudden left roll, then right, then a return to steady flight.

Burton maneuvered back to where he could see in the cockpit again, but the figure in the window faced the other way.

"Still no answer," Burton reported.

"I thumped him, but the autopilot's on."

"Chris . . ."

"I know, I know . . . we're running out of time, aren't we?" He could feel himself tightening under the increasing tension. He started rocking his wings and flashing his position and running lights in accordance with the international rules governing in-flight intercepts, but no one on the 747's flight deck seemed to be reacting.

"I hate to tell you, Critter, but we're almost out of the ID box. We've got less then fifteen miles to turn him or burn him."

"I'm going to try the other side." He hit the transmit button. "Two, three, and four, hold your positions. I'm trying to get his attention." Burton popped the F-14 up above the top level of the fuselage and banked slightly to the right, bringing himself smoothly to the right side, slightly ahead of the cockpit, then let himself settle back down to the same eye level. He tried the wing rocking and the flashlight again, and this time there was movement as the lone figure in the cockpit suddenly disappeared.

"Home base, Critter. I thumped him and lit him up with a flashlight on the left and made all the standard moves and got no response. Now, on the right side, the one pilot inside ducked out of sight as soon as he saw me."

"One person, copy?"

"Roger."

"Male or female?"

"Couldn't tell."

"Stand by, Critter. You're almost at the end of the box."

Burton shook his head and whistled into the interphone.

"What do you think, Blackie?"

"I think they're going make us splash him, Chris, and God have mercy on us if they're wrong."

FORTY-FIVE

'I think we ought to tell someone, don't you?"

Jimmy Roberts watched the fifteen-year-old nod and hand over the portable scanner.

"I guess."

"I'll be back in a few minutes, okay?"

"Sure."

Jimmy unfolded himself from the seat and moved rapidly up the aisle, stopping at his own row briefly to check on Brenda. She was asleep, the blanket he'd lovingly tucked around her still in place. He fought the urge to lean over and kiss her, forcing himself to keep moving as fast as he could through the darkened cabin to find a flight attendant.

There was another voice coursing through the hand-held scanner, and he stopped and raised it to his ear. The volume had been turned down and he tried to find the right control, but the voice didn't return, so he resumed walking.

The lights were out in first class as well, but he spotted Janie Bretsen sitting sideways on an arm rest.

"Excuse me. I'm sorry to interrupt . . ."

She stood immediately, and he could see a tired smile in the subdued illumination of an overhead reading light.

"No problem. What can I do for you?" she said.

He held up the scanner, explaining what he'd heard minutes before and trying to demonstrate, but the radio wasn't cooperating.

"It was there a minute ago. It was something about a Navy guard calling Meridian. That is us, right?"

"Yes," Janie said, guiding him through the curtains into the galley and turning up the lights as she focused on the radio. "They were calling for Meridian Six?"

"Yes, ma'am. Several times. I figured I needed to let you know."

"This is your radio?"

He shook his head. "No. A young fellow back there. He's two rows behind us. I heard some noise and went back."

Janie motioned toward a small, circular window embedded in the entry door. "Maybe if we put the antenna by the glass we can pick it up again."

She looked at the radio and worked the knobs. "It was off."

"Off? Oh. Sorry. I must have done that a minute ago when I was coming to get you."

Janie moved the knobs on top until loud static caused them both to jump, and she quickly turned the volume down. She could see the liquid crystal display showing a single frequency of 135.0.

"Is this the frequency?"

Jimmy looked closely at it. "I . . . don't know. Those numbers were jumping around, you know, scanning a lot of them. The voice mentioned a particular one, but I didn't memorize it."

"You know how to work this?" Janie asked.

"Not really. I've seen police scanners before. Friend of mine has a towing business, and he listens to all those calls."

"I'm not hearing anything, and I think it's stuck on just one frequency."

"Well, I really am sure I heard them calling us," Jimmy said.

Janie reached out and put her hand on his shoulder. "I have no doubt about that. I just have to figure out what to do. The person who owns this knows how to work it, right?"

Jimmy nodded. "You want me to get him?"

"Please."

Jimmy turned and disappeared toward the back as Janie grabbed one of the interphone handsets and punched in the cockpit code.

Thirty seconds went by before the call was answered. The sound of Judy Jackson's tentative voice saying "hello" startled her for a second.

"Judy? Where's the captain? This is Janie."

"Why?"

"Look, dammit, I asked you an important question. I have something to tell him that may be very important."

"He's . . . doing something right now."

The aircraft lurched to the left in a burst of turbulence, almost knocking her off her feet. There was a small, simultaneous yelp through the interphone.

"Judy, what was that?"

"I don't know. Nothing," she said.

More turbulence shuddered through the 747's interior, and once more the big aircraft steadied out. Janie grabbed the edge of the folded jumpseat to stabilize herself. She molded her back to the doorway and looked inward, away from the small, convex viewing port, completely missing the flashing red beacon of the lead Tomcat, which was now pulsing away at the upper edge of the glass.

"Put the captain on, Judy. And I mean now."

"I can't for a few minutes. He's busy."

Janie closed her eyes and sighed. "Judy, listen to me. He needs to know that the Navy has been calling us on the radio. I don't have any idea what channel or frequency, and we're not hearing it now, but a passenger with a police scanner picked it up."

"Okay. I'll tell him."

"Judy, is he okay? What's going on up there? We all have a right to know."

"He's okay. He's just busy right now."

"Are you going to tell him?"

"Yes."

"I'm at door One Left. Have him call me for the details. We'll wait right here."

"Okay."

She heard the connection broken and stood in confusion for a second trying to imagine what might be happening ten feet above her head in the cockpit.

In the cockpit, Judy replaced the handset in its cradle as she tried to fight down the panic in her gut. She knew the captain had felt the burst of turbulence. She could hear him scrambling around in the bathroom just aft of the cockpit door. Phil Knight emerged holding his pants up and peeked into the cockpit.

"What the hell was that?" he snapped.

"I don't know. Just turbulence, I guess."

She saw his eyes running over the instruments. "You didn't touch anything on the yoke or the panel, did you?"

"No."

"Okay." He withdrew back into the bathroom and closed the door as Judy sat sideways on the captain's seat and listened to her heart pound, not even wanting to think what she'd do if the airplane suddenly entered a dive.

There were reflections of light in the cockpit, but she kept her eyes glued on the cockpit door, almost holding her breath until he returned.

A burst of light caught her eye from somewhere on the right side, and she felt her heart falter for a few beats.

What was THAT?

There was something else out there, she could see. Another airplane, maybe, and whoever was in it was shining a light in the cockpit.

Judy catapulted herself from the seat and lunged for the cockpit door, holding on to it as she pounded on the rest-room door.

"Captain! Captain! There's another airplane out there!"

"What?" Phil Knight's slightly muffled voice responded, and she repeated the message. She could hear him scrambling around behind the rest-room door before it came flying open and he shoved past her, almost diving into his seat, his head swiveling as he looked all around. Judy was right behind him, pointing to the right and relating the sudden light in the cockpit.

"I don't see anyone," he said.

"There was a call from Bretsen downstairs," she said, filling in as many of the details as her panicked mind could recall.

"What frequency were those calls on?"

"What?"

"Goddammit, woman! WHAT FREQUENCY?"

"I . . . I don't know. She said call her at door One Left. I don't know."

Phil jammed an index finger grabbing for the handset and punched in the number. Janie Bretsen answered immediately and repeated the information.

"The radio's owner is coming forward right now," Janie said. "We couldn't get the message to repeat, so I don't know the frequency."

"I can't transmit to them anyway," Phil said. "All our radios are dead. If you get that radio working, bring it upstairs to the cockpit immediately, okay? If there's someone out there calling us, I need to know what they want."

NRO
CHANTILLY, VIRGINIA
6:31 P.M. EDT

David Byrd had watched John Blaylock quietly argue his case with the two chief NRO analysts and their CIA counterparts for several minutes before a small realization grew to large enough proportions to get his attention: The room he was sitting in was far too deep in the NRO complex to admit cellular phone signals.

David glanced down at his cell phone. The light was blinking red.

"Excuse me. I've got to check on something," he

said, interrupting Zoffel and Blaylock as he moved to the door of the monitoring room and pushed it open. Ginger was waiting on the other side.

"Ah, Colonel Byrd. Just the gentleman I was coming to get. A Mr. Haverston from London has been trying to reach you on your cell phone."

"Oh, Lord," David said, pulling the antenna to the fully deployed position and checking for signal strength.

"When he couldn't reach you, he called the number you gave him here and gave me a message for you."

"Yes?" David shifted his eyes to hers.

"The name is the same. He said to tell you that he found his note, and the man he was worried about yesterday was a Dr. Logan, L-O-G-A-N."

David pointed to the room he'd just left. "Let me back in, please, and come in with me."

She was already working the cipher lock, and when the small light turned green, they both pulled the heavy door open and slipped in.

David motioned for Ginger to follow as he moved to the forward tier of seats where John Blaylock was leaning over, talking to George Zoffel and watching the screens.

"John, I need your attention, right now," he said. Zoffel and Collings turned, as John Blaylock straightened up.

"David, they're about to get attack authorization. There's no one on that airplane but a pilot who's—"

"We've got to talk," David interrupted, physically pulling John to one side and speaking rapidly.

"I just heard back from London, from the Meridian manager who was worried about a very upset passenger yesterday."

"Yeah, you briefed me about that."

"You said that to convince you, John, you needed a piece of information known only to the pilot of that 747, something only the real Meridian captain could have known. We have it. The transmission from this 747 hours ago said that a passenger named Logan was leading the revolt. Remember?"

"Yes."

"And do you remember I told you about the American physician suing Meridian for millions because his wife died on one of their flights, and he was angry as he boarded this flight yesterday?"

"Get to the point."

"The point, John, is that the name of that angry passenger is the same as the name transmitted by the pilot of that 747. The same! There's no damn way a terrorist would have known that name and pinpointed it in such a message."

John Blaylock was pulling at his chin as he looked at David in silence for a few seconds, then nodded. "That's not conclusive, but . . ."

"It tips the balance, John. We've got to stop this."

John gave a questioning glance at Ginger, who was standing a few feet away.

"I wanted her here in case anyone asked her to repeat the message from London," David explained.

John Blaylock turned and moved to George Zoffel's side, explaining the new information in a low voice as Sandra Collings leaned in to listen, then briefed their counterparts at Langley. There was a buzz of back-and-forth conversation on the headsets. John suddenly left Zoffel's side and literally jumped over the desk behind to pick up a handset and start punching buttons on the phone. David followed and slipped on his headset as the voice of the President came through from *Air Force One*.

IN FLIGHT,
AIR FORCE ONE

"What's the report, Bill?" the President asked as he slid back into his desk chair and surveyed the Situation Room on the other end.

The White House Chief of Staff motioned to one of the aides, and a grid map of the middle Mediterranean popped up on the left side of the President's screen.

"We're almost out of time, sir," Sanderson said, "and the Tomcats can't get anyone's attention on board." He ran through the list of everything they'd tried.

"He's sure there are no people on board?"

"We can't say that for certain, sir. The pilots report what could be a few people with overhead reading lights on, or they could be effigies . . . dummies . . . placed in the seats."

The President sighed. "How far are they from the coast?"

"They're on a beeline to Marseille, France, Mr. President, and the French Air Force is already scrambling several flights of Mirages. He's coming up on the end of the zone the Navy established for the shootdown."

"So, how long, Bill?"

"Two minutes maximum. We need a decision, sir."

The President sat back in the chair. "Run through the logic again of why we're assuming this plane is lethal."

"Sir, CIA, DIA, NRO, and our European counterparts are all in agreement that we've almost certainly got a Trojan Horse here and a major attack in motion. The main points? We know most, if not all, the passengers are still in Nigeria. We think both of Meridian's pilots were killed or injured back there, so whoever's flying this aircraft stole it. We have a report from the airplane that they've had a passenger riot on board, but we know there are no passengers, or very few, if any are being held hostage. In other words, we've caught somebody in a ruse, and the magnitude of the ruse and the preparation indicate great sophistication, which supports the overall theory. This stolen aircraft is headed to Europe for unknown reasons, and we've had six months of continuous warnings from the intelligence community and from our clandestine sources on the ground in various locales that a major terrorist strike with a weapon of mass destruction will be attempted, and . . . according to the briefing I know you received at Camp David . . . Langley and DIA have concluded that the recent activities in Nova Scotia and Atlanta, Georgia, were most likely a diversionary tactic to divert us from paying attention to an impending strike at the European community. We have an immediate alert out of the Mideast to expect just this attack coming from precisely the area this aircraft left, sub-Saharan Africa. And, we've had at least one satellite indication, although many hours ago, that might have shown the presence of fissionable material on this aircraft."

"Okay."

"In addition, NATO has formally requested our military intervention in preventing this craft from entering European airspace, and the French have expressed their extreme concern. In other words, we have the right, and considering the American flag nature of this airline, probably the responsibility, to handle this ourselves."

"I agree that it's our ball game as long as it's over the Mediterranean."

"So, Mr. President, we're out of time," Sanderson said. "We have very good reason to fear this aircraft getting too close to the coast, and no solid evidence that it's *not* a terrorist strike, and we can't get a response from whoever's flying it. In fact, as I told you, the one person seen in the cockpit has ducked out of sight."

"What if we're wrong, Bill? What if they're what they say they are?"

"Sir, what if we're right and don't act? What if that was New York up there and not Marseille? This is your decision, but we're balancing the possibility of a nuclear strike or a biological strike against France or the U.K. against the slim possibility that we have innocent Americans held hostage aboard that craft."

"Hook me up to the lead fighter, Bill."

"Mr. President, as we've been talking here, the aircraft has flown out of the so-called kill box. We're literally out of time."

"Hook me up, Bill. Now."

"Yes, sir," the Chief of Staff said, trying to restrain his own feelings as he turned to one of the technicians in the room and motioned for the connection to be established immediately.

"He's listening, Mr. President. You'll be talking to Lieutenant Commander Chris Burton. Call sign Critter. And you're talking in the clear on a nonscrambled channel."

"Commander? This is the President. How do you copy?"

"Loud and clear, Mr. President," Chris Burton's voice came back almost instantly.

"I've had a briefing on all you've done to check this out, but now I need your personal opinion. Have we done everything possible to make sure that aircraft is not a friendly?"

Static filled the channel momentarily.

"Ah, sir . . . if I can have another five minutes, I can answer that with more certainty."

There was no hesitation from *Air Force One*. "You've got three minutes, Commander. No more than that. I'll be waiting."

FORTY-SIX

Phil Knight saw a red beacon in his peripheral vision as an unknown aircraft moved alongside his cockpit on the left. In the intermittent flashes of the 747's strobe lights he could make out the shape of a twin-tailed fighter of some sort, with what looked like American markings. A small beam of light flashed across his face from the fighter's cockpit, startling Phil, who raised his hand to ward off the beam. Whoever was in the fighter's cockpit swung the light away from the 747 cockpit and shone it on himself.

A flashlight, Phil concluded. *But what's he trying to say?*

Alarm accelerated his heartbeat. The possibility that he'd handled it wrong again and ended up with fighters sent to intercept him sent another jolt of adrenaline through his system. But he was squawking the hijack code, wasn't he? And he'd told the company what he was doing. Maybe the fighter was just trying to escort him to safety.

That must be it. This is an escort.

Another large chill shuddered through him as he remembered the ACARS system. He hadn't answered the company's last query hours ago about clearances, and what was it Abbott had said about things not being the same out here?

He reached around to feel for an additional message, but there was nothing sticking out of the printer, and he had other, more immediate things to consider than the possibility the small machine was simply out of paper.

Phil stared hard at the cockpit of the fighter, realizing the pilot was motioning with his hand as if saying "Follow me," and blinking his position lights.

What in the world does he want me to do?

Meridian had never provided training on what to do if you were intercepted on commercial air routes. At least, if they had, he'd missed it. He'd heard military pilot veterans talk over the years about certain hand signals used by fighter pilots during the cold war, specific gestures to tell an intercepted pilot what to do. But wasn't that when someone had violated a communist nation's airspace and they wanted him to land? Phil searched his memory, but there was nothing there about hand signals. Maybe in some of the manuals, but there was no time to search.

The fighter pilot was rocking his wings, flashing his

lights, and pointing down repeatedly, but none of it made sense to the captain of Flight Six.

I guess he wants me to follow him. He probably wants me to land somewhere closer than London.

Once more the fighter pilot's flashlight was trained on the 747 cockpit, and Phil gave him a thumbs-up response.

That was it, Phil thought. *He's returning the gesture.*

His eyes shifted to the flight computer. The coast of France was a hundred or so miles ahead, and the flight path was aligned with Marseille.

Is that where he wants me to go? Phil wondered. How could he ask him without a radio? Phil reached to the overhead panel and switched on the cockpit dome light, flooding the cockpit area. He waved again at the fighter and pointed ahead, making a downward gesture, unsure if it was acknowledged. He started digging in his brain bag for the legal pad he always carried and the black marker zipped in a side pocket. He hurriedly wrote "Land Marseille?" on the pad and turned the face of it to the window, holding it back far enough for the cockpit lights to flood the message.

But the fighter was moving forward now, too far ahead to read the sign.

"He's finally acknowledged my gestures, and I think he understands to follow me," Lieutenant Commander Burton reported to the President.

The flare of a new video window inserted on the liquid crystal teleconferencing wall snagged the President's attention. Once more he was looking at a live nighttime infrared satellite shot of the Meridian 747 and the Tomcats. The lead F-14 was practically touching the nose of the 747 while the other three maintained formation behind and to the side. He watched the lead Tomcat pull out ahead and begin a gentle bank to the left and heard him instruct his wingmen to follow in loose trail. The F-14 continued the left turn, but the 747 bored straight ahead, as confirmed by one of the wingmen who punched the transmit button at the same moment.

"Lead, two. Target is not following. Repeat, not following. Course remains three-four-zero."

IN FLIGHT,
ABOARD MERIDIAN FLIGHT SIX

"Okay, we're starting down," Phil said, mostly to himself, as he took the auto-flight system off altitude hold and dialed in a descent rate and an altitude of five thousand feet. He pulled a laminated checklist into his lap and went over the items before looking back up. Normally the copilot would read the checklist and he'd respond, and the empty right seat suddenly loomed large in his thinking, triggering guilt along with the chilling image of Garth Abbott lying on the Katsina runway in a pool of blood.

Phil shook the nightmarish image out of his mind and strained to see the fighter. But the other aircraft was gone, which must mean that he'd interpreted things correctly.

Marseille . . . I need approach plates for Marseille. He pulled out the leather-bound Jeppesen charts for Europe and flipped through the listings for France until he found the right ones and removed them from the binder, glancing up as he did so to check the altitude.

Descending through flight level three-six-zero. No way to call anyone on the radio. I'll just have to fly to the runway and land.

Phil turned the approach plate over and studied the airport diagram, memorizing the heading of the longest runway. Hopefully it would be lighted.

Of course it'll be lighted, he corrected himself. *They'll know I'm coming.*

NRO
CHANTILLY, VIRGINIA

George Zoffel turned around in his seat to look for John Blaylock, who still had a receiver pressed to his ear.

"John?"

"Yeah?" the older colonel said, looking up.

"He's disregarded the fighter's instructions and started descending, and it looks like he's headed for Marseille."

"What are they going to do?" David asked.

John glanced at David briefly as he held his hand over the receiver of the phone, a "Let me handle this" expression on his face. John looked back at Zoffel. "Status?"

"Langley is concluding this is a planned feint. They're pressing the President for immediate shootdown approval."

"No," David barked.

"Colonel Byrd, please!" John snapped.

"Screw the protocol, folks. And screw the pictures from Nigeria. That plane is *not* a flying terrorist attack. We can't shoot them down."

John Blaylock was on his feet, the palm of his right hand held out to David to quiet him down as he addressed Zoffel and Collings.

"I have solid reason to believe David's right," he said.

George Zoffel shook his head. "We've considered all

that, John. Group X could have had a confederate aboard who already knew about Logan's discontent and was ready to use Logan's name. I'm sorry. We're not interfering here."

"Did you tell Langley?" John asked.

"Yes, but they don't believe it's significant, and neither do we."

"Well, tell them again, dammit. They're trying to get a shootdown authorization."

"No, John," Zoffel repeated quietly. "Now, stand down."

"Goddammit, George, listen to us. This is a mistake. I didn't think so before, but now I'm convinced David's right, and I'm trying to get one more piece to the puzzle here, but I need a few more minutes."

"We don't have a few more minutes," Sandra Collings said.

John Blaylock started to say something more, but Sandra had already come out of her seat and turned to face him. "SIT DOWN, Colonel! You're out of line. You're a guest only here. One more interference, and we'll have to have you two removed."

For a few tense seconds, David Byrd watched John Blaylock stand in silence, trying to decide what to do. Slowly he pulled the telephone receiver back to his ear as Collings disengaged and resumed her watch. In his headset, David could hear the relayed sounds of the pilots still trying to find a way to force the 747 pilot to comply. The lead F-14 had flown back in front of him and turned to the left again, but the 747 was still descending in a straight line for Marseille, undeterred, as the request for immediate shootdown authority was once again flashed to the President.

IN FLIGHT,
ABOARD MERIDIAN SIX

Jimmy Roberts had herded the young owner of the scanner radio to the forward section, where Janie was waiting. She quickly greeted the boy and thrust his radio at him with an urgent plea to get it working again. The boy fiddled with the knobs on top, and once more the numbers on the display began frequency-hopping, confirming the unit was working.

But there was no one talking.

"You're sure it's covering the same frequencies as before?" Janie asked.

The boy nodded.

Something caught her eye through the small circular window mounted in the 747's door 2-Left on the right side, and she excused herself for a second and walked twenty feet to the other side to peer through.

"What are you seeing?" Brian Logan asked from just behind her as he came out of first class.

"Another aircraft," Janie said, turning briefly to verify it was he. "Two, in fact, I think, flying alongside out there."

Brian looked and just as quickly pulled away. "Fighters. I can't tell whose, but I'm not surprised."

The 747 jumped ever so slightly, and Janie felt the throttles coming back and the beginning of descent as she looked wide-eyed at Brian, who checked his watch.

"Could we be starting down for London so soon?" Janie asked, already suspecting the answer.

"No way. We just passed by Libya and we're over the Mediterranean, but I don't know how far out," Brian replied. "I saw the map a few minutes ago. Something's going on with us and those fighters."

Janie returned to the other side of the galley where Jimmy Roberts and the teenager were working with the scanner, trying in vain to find the frequencies that they'd heard before.

"Any luck?"

Jimmy shook his head. "No, ma'am. We're hearing nothing."

"Please keep trying," Janie said, turning then to Brian. "What are you thinking?"

"That we're being forced down somewhere."

"Forced *down*?"

"Forced to land, and if so, there will be an armed group waiting for us on the ramp. Who knows what the captain's told them."

ABOARD *AIR FORCE ONE*

The President shook his head and sighed, the gesture watched closely in both the Situation Room and the Pentagon as he made his decision. There was simply too much at stake to take a chance, he thought. A true terrorist operation would have worked hard to make the decision just this difficult, fuzzing up the line between a clear threat and a possible horrific mistake.

If it was anthrax, or a nuclear weapon, millions could die if he took a chance. If he was wrong, some three hundred people would pay the price. The numbers alone made it inescapable. The risk was too great.

"Very well," the President said in a defeated tone. "Destroy the aircraft."

"Yes, sir," Bill Sanderson said, nodding to someone else in the Situation Room who relayed the command, unaware that the Pentagon had already heard it.

The order was flashed from the Combat Decision Center of the USS *Enterprise* to Lieutenant Commander Chris Burton within seconds.

"Green light, Critter. Repeat, home base relays green light."

"Roger," Burton acknowledged, his voice betraying defeat. "Moving in position now."

The background sounds of an air-to-air missile warhead growling its silicone acknowledgment that a target was in its sights and being tracked was audible on the channel, a noise that rapidly escalated to a radar lock-on.

"In position for Fox one," Burton transmitted.

The controller aboard the *Enterprise* came on the channel again, his voice urgent. "Critter, your target is eighty miles from the coast. Bring him down now. A flight of eight Mirage fighters, French, approaching as backup, range four-six miles."

"We have them on the scope," Burton acknowledged. "Two, three, four, lock up Fox one and two. Tiger flight, stay high."

The wingmen acknowledged as they, too, locked their Sidewinders on the engines of the Boeing.

In the cockpit of the lead Tomcat, Chris Burton felt his finger brush the launch trigger and hesitate as he spoke to his backseater.

"Help me here, Blackie. Anything we haven't tried?"

"Go for it, Critter. For God's sake, that could be a flying nuke."

Chris felt his mind issue the tiny electrochemical order to move his finger back against the trigger, but he consciously overrode it, his internal conflict rising exponentially as he looked for something, anything, to calm the fear that he was about to murder innocent civilians.

"What are you waiting for, Critter?" Blackie asked.

"One more thing!" Chris responded, hitting the transmitter to tell his wingmen to hold their position. "Blackie, hit that VHF radio again on one-twenty-one-point-five and tell him if he doesn't follow me, we'll shoot him down."

"Roger," Blackie replied.

"Home base," Burton transmitted, "I'm trying one more maneuver to get him to follow."

He safed his missiles and nudged the throttles up, accelerating once again to catch up to and slide just forward of the Boeing.

"Negative, Critter," home base replied. "Execute your orders now."

"Not yet, sir. Something's not right about this."

"Critter, you are to fire immediately."

"Stand by, home base."

"Negative, dammit. Fire those missiles now!"

"Stand by, flight. Home base, I'm going to fire a burst of cannon to get his attention."

"There's no time, Critter. Carry out your orders."

In the backseat of the lead Tomcat, Blackie was holding the transmit button down.

"Meridian Six, this is your last warning. Repeat, this is your last warning. We see no one aboard except in the cockpit, and if you do not turn your aircraft and follow on a reverse course for a landing in Algeria, we will shoot you down. Repeat, in the absence of any evidence of passengers or any evidence of compliance, we will shoot you down. This is your last chance." He released the transmit button, hoping against hope to hear a reply, but there was nothing.

Burton had already slid into position alongside the

747 and toggled the necessary switches to arm the guns. He pressed the trigger and fired a volley of cannon fire into the night, the tracers streaking off ahead of the 747, the noise instantly impressive. Once more he shone his flashlight at the cockpit and then on his right hand, motioning the pilot to follow and turn left. The 747 pilot appeared to nod, and once more Burton banked left as gently as possible, praying the pilot would follow.

"I'm watching, Critter . . . hang on . . . ," Blackie said as he swiveled around in his seat, straining against the belts and straps. "Dammit, he's still holding course. He's not following."

There was a low oath from the forward cockpit.

"Critter, what's your status," home base asked, the voice clearly that of his squadron commander.

Burton sighed and pulled his throttles back as he toggled the speed brake to slide behind the 747 again, bringing his missiles up once more and letting them lock on as he prepared to fire.

"I'm getting back in position. I've tried everything."

FORTY-SEVEN

The American voice that suddenly blared from the speaker of the small scanner radio caused Jimmy Roberts to almost drop the scanner. The words sank in rapidly, sending a sharp chill of fear through all of them.

> . . . *shoot you down. Repeat, in the absence of any evidence of passengers or any evidence of compliance, we will shoot you down. This is your last chance.*

Janie had heard it too, and she turned now, her face betraying utter shock.

Jimmy pressed his face to the window on the left side at the moment a staccato sound erupted from the same direction.

"They're firing on us," Jimmy said over his shoulder. "Those planes, they're firing. I saw the bullets."

Janie was beside him in a second as Brian Logan and

Robert MacNaughton fled back into the galley area from first class.

"He was just in front of us," Roberts was saying.

"What did he say again, exactly?" Janie asked, her heart pounding as Jimmy strained to see anything outside. All he saw was a flashing red beacon that dropped back and disappeared.

"He said there was no evidence of passengers," Jimmy repeated. "And he said he'd shoot us down unless we complied."

"Complied with what?" Brian asked as several other men pressed into the galley.

"What on earth?" Janie said, her confusion growing by the second. "Why does he need to see passengers?"

In the cockpit, the shock of seeing the burst of tracers and hearing the muffled report of the Tomcat's guns had left Phil Knight in momentary confusion. He was descending for Marseille, wasn't he? Hadn't the fighter pilot given him a thumbs up to the sign? Then why was he firing?

Phil saw the fighter break off again and slide off to the left, leaving him with a growing feeling of dread. Live bullets meant he was doing something very wrong again, and he didn't know what. He didn't have a clue what.

Phil scanned the radio heads in desperation, trying to think of something to use to communicate with them.

He needed someone to ask someone else's opinion, but there *was* no one else, no experienced copilot, however arrogant, no guru on the radio.

The presence of the PA system flashed in his mind, an incongruous thought. What was he to do, ask the passengers for help?

Yes, Phil thought, the idea gaining ground by the nanosecond. *What else do I have as an option? Nothing.*

He grabbed the handset and activated the PA function.

> *This is the captain. Look, please just listen. We may be in real trouble here, and . . . I'm going to need any help I can get figuring this out. There's a fighter out there, maybe more than one, and as some of you may have seen, he just fired warning shots. I thought he wanted me to land in Marseille, France, just ahead, but now I don't know, and without radio contact, I can't talk to him. I need . . . Okay, people, I don't know what I need, I'll just admit that. I know you've been madder than hell, and . . . that works both ways but . . . we're in this together now, so if there's anyone with a . . . a two-way aviation radio aboard, or a cell phone that works in France, or something . . . now's the time to let me know. I have no idea whether they would shoot at us for real or not.*

He started to disconnect, then raised the handset again.

> *Ah . . . for the record . . . I apologize for all you've been through.*

The cockpit call chime rang almost instantly.

"Yes?"

"This is Janie. I turned the cabin lights out an hour ago to let everyone sleep. But we just picked up a broadcast on a handheld scanner saying that those fighters don't think there are passengers aboard and they need proof, so should we turn on the lights?"

"My God, YES! Get 'em all on, Janie, and . . . and get people in the windows so they can be seen, please."

Janie snapped the cabin light switches on and punched the PA code into the handset.

Attention, everyone! Wake up! Everyone! WAKE UP NOW! All of you anywhere near a window seat, turn on your overhead lights and put your faces in . . . Well, wait a minute. Make sure the overhead lights are shining on your faces and someone outside could see as many of us as possible. We have a fighter out there who's demanding to see us for some reason. Make sure he sees you. Make sure we've got lighted faces in every window. Wave at him, move around, and make sure he sees you. Hurry! Please! Hurry!

She lowered the handset as she watched Brian Logan drop to his knees and claw away at the hatch to the electronics bay.

"What are you doing?" she asked.

"The radio," he said, explaining nothing as he yanked the hatch open and dropped down into the compartment. She moved to the edge of it, searching the dimly lighted gloom below, seeing nothing until his head shot back through the hatch and almost collided with hers as he clambered out holding something.

"What is that?" Janie asked, following as he motioned to the stairway and broke into a run.

"The copilot's two-way radio," he shouted over his shoulder, weaving past several passengers as Janie followed, turning at the top of the stairs and realizing he was headed to the cockpit. She stopped and grabbed a handset, punching the cockpit code into the keypad.

"Yes?" Phil Knight answered.

"Captain, this is Janie. Open the cockpit door. Brian Logan is coming in to help you. He found the copilot's two-way radio."

"Logan?"

"Do it, Captain, if you're serious."

"Opening now," Phil replied.

Janie cupped her hands and yelled at the physician's receding back.

"He's opening the door for you, Brian!" She saw him wave as he approached the cockpit entrance.

Phil Knight reached for the cockpit door release.

"What are you doing?" Judy asked in instant alarm when she heard the door release click.

"Logan's coming with the copilot's radio."

"Logan?"

"Yes."

"NO!" she screeched, grabbing the back of his chair, "Don't let him in—it's a trick!"

He heard the cockpit door being pulled open as Judy swiveled out of the jump seat and turned to face the door. Too late he saw the crash axe in her hands.

"Judy, don't!" Phil shouted as he clawed for his seat belt and thrust himself out of the captain's chair and backward, catching his leg on the center console and kicking the control yoke as he lunged for the axe and missed.

"STAY OUT!" she yelled, lashing out at the intruding figure.

Phil was falling face first to the cockpit floor as Brian threw himself hard right to avoid Judy's attack, his left arm rising protectively. But the space was too narrow and the surprise too great, and the axe struck his left upper arm, slicing all the way to the bone and spinning the physician uncontrollably to the left as he fell forward on top of the captain.

The axe skittered free of Judy's hands as she thudded into the aft bulkhead of the cockpit and instantly picked herself up, looking for another weapon. There was a red light blinking on the instrument panel and a warning noise, but it didn't reach her consciousness that the 747 was steepening its descent and rolling to the right, its autopilot disconnected by the captain's accidental kick to the control yoke.

The thunderbolt of pain in Brian's left arm had left him writhing around in agony as he tried to get to his feet by using an arm he could no longer control. He twisted his body to the left, triggering a level of pain he'd never before experienced. He looked up into the maniacal eyes of Judy Jackson just as she prepared to bring a fire extinguisher down on his head.

Phil was puzzled by the growing pool of blood around him as he saw Judy raising the extinguisher, but his reaction was instantaneous. "JUDY! DROP IT! DROP IT NOW!" He struggled to pull himself out from beneath the injured doctor and watched her as she hesitated.

Stunned, unsure of what to do, and shaking uncontrollably, Judy stood wide-eyed with the heavy bottle still suspended over her head until Janie Bretsen thrust herself through the cockpit door and grabbed her.

There was still a persistent warning horn blaring in the cockpit. Phil scrambled to his knees, fighting for footing on the blood-slick floor, and with a hand on the jump seat, managed to look around at the flight instruments.

The autopilot. We're diving.

He slipped repeatedly but managed to claw his way back into the left seat.

"What the hell are you doing?" Janie Bretsen was saying to Judy as she pulled the metal bottle from Judy's hands and tossed it aside. "What have you done?" She yanked Judy backward, out of the cockpit, shocked by the sickening sight of a badly injured Brian Logan on the cockpit floor. She manhandled Judy outside the cockpit and turned to several men who had come forward. "Hold her, please. Restrain her." Janie ordered, as one man pinned the hysterical woman's arms.

Janie raced back to the cockpit, unprepared for the extent of the wound to Brian Logan's left arm.

"Oh my God."

"She got him with the damned axe," Phil said, working to right the Boeing as he pulled the throttles back and rolled to wings level, nursing the nose up gingerly. Phil glanced frantically at Janie as she worked with the latches on the cockpit first-aid kit.

"I've got to get a tourniquet on him."

"And I've got to get that radio," Phil countered.

"Under . . . the right side . . . ," Brian managed through gritted teeth. "Climb . . . over me . . . ," he added.

"Where?"

"Right side . . . on the floor . . . ," Brian answered.

"Hurry!" Phil added. "Please hurry!"

NRO
CHANTILLY, VIRGINIA

"He's either started evasive tactics," David Byrd heard the Navy Tomcat pilot say as he began his return to the firing position, "or he's beginning to turn around. I'm not sure which. Wait a minute . . . he may be putting it into a dive."

David held John Blaylock's arm, gaining his attention
for a second as the older man·hunched over the phone
and tried to squeeze a determination from another section
of the NRO's complex.

"What?" he whispered.

"John, this is it. Now or never. They've got the green
light. They're going to shoot."

Blaylock sighed and nodded. "Hang on. Please keep
working," he said into the phone as he stood. "We need
the bare basic analysis . . . don't wait for certainty, just
give me the raw data as soon as the computer spits it
out."

He lowered the phone and turned to the two analysts
at the front of the room.

"George? Sandra? Tell them to stand down. I now
have proof that the pictures from Nigeria were faked."

George Zoffel swiveled around, his tone pained and
sharp. *"What?"*

John repeated himself, but stopped short of a complete sentence. There was no time left. Even if George
Zoffel and Sandra Collings agreed completely, they
would have to first convince the CIA at Langley and
reach some sort of consensus.

John Blaylock yanked up the receiver and toggled an
outside line, consulting his Palm Pilot as he punched in a
number as fast as he could, raising his hand in a "wait"
signal to Zoffel and Collings.

"What are you talking about now, John?" Zoffel

asked, as he turned in frustration to David Byrd. "Do you have any idea what he's on about?"

David shook his head.

In the background the Tomcat pilot reported in position once again and ready to fire. *"Roger, home base,"* Critter was saying. *"I'm locked up again. He's shallowing his dive and turning again. I'll wait until he steadies out. Confirm we're still cleared for launch."*

David's heart sank.

"Put Sandy on," John was saying. "This is Big Bird. NOW!" He could hear the *Enterprise* repeating the attack authorization.

There was a pause of no more than five seconds before the connection was made.

"Bill, stop the attack and give me two minutes to justify."

On the other end of the line in the Situation Room, Admiral Bill Sanderson came out of his chair. "John?"

"Trust me, Bill. I'm at NRO. Stop them. I'll hold."

Sanderson yanked up the hot line to the *Enterprise*'s CDC without hesitating. "Tell Critter to hold his fire."

Lieutenant Commander Chris Burton had locked up the left side outboard engine of the 747 after its gyrations and diving descent, his finger holding on the button as his backseater's voice rang in his helmet.

"Critter, pickle it. We're inside seventy-five miles.

Even if we blow all his engines off at this range, he can still crash on the coastline."

Images of a long-ago Russian shootdown of a loaded Korean 747 had been playing in Chris Burton's head since he'd first pulled up behind the commercial jetliner. There had been neither forgiveness nor respite for the Soviet pilots who killed over four hundred passengers that night, even though they were only following their orders. The pilot who launched the fatal missiles was forever branded a murderer, and here he, Chris Burton, sat on the brink of the same fate.

Maybe.

The thoughts and images were passing in microseconds now as he willed his finger to fire the missiles. After all, the thought ricocheted through his head at lightning speed, *I am a military officer. I have no choice.*

"HOLD YOUR FIRE, Critter! Repeat, hold your fire. Acknowledge."

The voice from home base was so incongruous at first as to seem self-generated, and for a moment he didn't believe he'd heard correctly.

"Say again?" Chris asked.

"He's . . . telling you to hold off, Critter. Home base said to stand down. Don't fire."

"Roger, home base," Chris transmitted. "Holding fire." He relayed the order to the wingmen and waited, wondering why he was seeing lights reflected off the 747's wing where none had been before.

What is that? he asked himself.

He pulled the Tomcat to the left a few hundred yards to get a better look.

In the cockpit, Janie snaked her body over the center console and reached beneath the copilot's rudder pedals for the two-way aviation radio.

"It's not here."

"I dropped it . . . there . . . I felt it fall," Brian said.

"Captain, do you have a light of some sort?"

Phil nodded and scrambled through his briefcase for a few seconds before tossing over a small flashlight. She snapped it on and dove beneath the right-side panel again.

"I've found it . . . It's wedged behind the rudder pedals."

"The rudder?"

"Can you . . . can you move the left pedal backward?"

Phil complied, skidding the 747 to the right.

"Got it," Janie said, working hard to pull herself back to her feet without kicking or hurting Brian Logan further.

She held the radio out to Phil Knight, who still had both hands on the yoke.

"Hang on," he said, completing the pullout. He reached up to the glare-shield panel and snapped on the autopilot again, adjusting the descent rate and heading before grabbing the radio and scrambling to select the emergency frequency.

SITUATION ROOM,
THE WHITE HOUSE,
WASHINGTON, D.C.

"Okay, John," Bill Sanderson told John Blaylock by phone. "He's holding fire, but we're awfully close to the French coast. Talk fast."

"Two things," John Blaylock said. "One, the message from the plane hours ago included a name no one but the original captain would have known, that of a physician named Logan who boarded in London madder than hell at that airline for letting his wife and son die on an earlier flight. The possibility of a terrorist knowing to use that name in this case is very remote. Point two, I just received the basic results of an analysis I had one of the specialty sections do here at NRO, and it reverses our conclusions."

"How?"

"Our determination that this was a true Trojan Horse incident rested on the assumption that the passengers were removed from the plane in Nigeria, and that, in turn, rested on the believability of the satellite shot that we thought showed some of the passengers in hostage status, and we believed those shots because they showed a lot of light-skinned arms in a region of dark-skinned people. I ordered a spectrographic analysis of the Caucasian skin of those hostages on the next pass. The results are sixty-eight percent calcium phosphate and assorted clay-based compounds, twenty-one percent dihydrogen oxide, and trace minerals."

"In English, John," the Chief of Staff replied. Twenty seconds left.

"Mud, Admiral. White, west-African, full-of-clay mud, which, when rubbed on your arms, makes them look white to a satellite. We've been bamboozled all evening, my friend. Those are all Dr. Onitsa's men down there masquerading as palefaces, and we bought it. Call off the dogs."

"Stand by, John," Sanderson said. The White House Chief of Staff turned and quickly relayed the new information to the President with a warning.

"It is still possible that the aircraft is on an attack mission with passengers held hostage aboard."

The President shook his head. "That's a risk we *will* take, Bill. Get him on the ground safely."

The radio channel between the *Enterprise* and the lead Tomcat pilot was still being piped to the combined command posts, and it came alive with Chris Burton's excited voice.

"Home base, this is Critter. I, uh . . . Thank God you had us hold fire. The aircraft has just turned on all internal cabin lights, and there are faces in every window. Sir, this aircraft is full of men, women, and children."

ABOARD *AIR FORCE ONE*

The President took a deep breath for the first time in what seemed like an hour as he sat forward. Bill Sanderson relayed the rest of the details of John Blaylock's call and the corresponding confirmation from the lead pilot that the aircraft was loaded with passengers.

"I think our pilot said it all, folks," the President said softly. "Thank God. We almost destroyed over three hundred lives."

Bill Sanderson sighed. "Well, sir, sometimes the process gets it wrong."

"We're going to want to review the process, yet again Bill. Hindsight can be good sometimes." The President's remaining words were covered by another transmission from the lead Tomcat.

"Home base, we've just made radio contact with the 747's captain for the first time. He's talking on a handheld emergency radio. He says he's got a badly injured passenger losing blood who needs immediate medical help, and says he needs to make an emergency landing in Marseille."

Bill Sanderson gave a "wait" gesture to the President as several voices at once filled the air in the Situation Room and Critter's transmission continued.

"We've got two flights of French Air Force fighters here, too, sir, but we can't talk to them directly."

Sanderson turned away for a moment as he issued a

series of commands, then turned back to the President with a relieved sigh.

"The French Air Force command is accepting our assurance about the aircraft."

"What did we tell them?"

"That . . . the alert was our mistake."

The President laughed briefly. "They'll love that, Bill. I'll hear about that at the next summit."

"Undoubtedly."

"How is he doing?" Phil Knight asked Janie as she worked with the tourniquet on Brian Logan's upper left arm.

"Okay . . ." Logan answered for her as Janie looked up from the cockpit floor and said, "We're controlling it, but I'm going to need a hospital. Fast."

"We're just thirty miles out," Phil responded, banking the 747 slightly to keep the nose pointed directly at the Marseille airport.

"Meridian Six . . ." The voice of one of the Navy crewmen crackled through the handheld.

Phil picked it up to respond. "Go ahead."

"Ah, we relayed your emergency medical status, and Marseille tower has cleared you to land on runway three-four, straight in, sir. Do you have the lights yet?"

Phil glanced at the flight-management computer, which showed twenty-nine miles to go on a course straight to the end of the runway. He looked out of the windscreen into the real world, letting his eyes focus on the flashing strobe lights and sequential approach lights pulsing away in the distance.

"Roger," Phil said into the walkie-talkie. "I have the runway."

"We're told you should turn off the runway to the right at the end, sir, and shut down. Portable stairs and medical equipment will meet you there."

"Thank you, Navy," Phil replied.

There was a pause before the voice came back. "We're really glad you got those cabin lights on when you did, sir."

"Roger" was all Phil could manage, the reality that they had almost been on the receiving end of a guaranteed fatal missile attack still sinking in.

"Can you do . . . something for me?" Brian Logan asked Janie, his voice thready and weak.

"Sure. What?"

"My . . . briefcase. In first class. Please don't let them take me out of here without it."

"We'll get it to you."

"No! I mean, I can't leave it."

Janie studied him for a second, remembering the way he'd clutched the briefcase. "Why?" she asked. "What's in there?"

He shut his eyes against the pain for a few moments, then opened them slightly to look at her. "It's personal."

"Hang on. Just hang on," she said, her voice distracting the captain as he tried to focus on the airport ahead.

The second-nature familiarity of slowing and configuring the aircraft as the runway lights swam ever closer diverted Phil's attention from the smoldering fear that this could be his last landing as a captain. He lowered the landing gear, ran the "Before Landing Checklist" himself, and brought the flaps to full extension before pulling the throttles back and flaring carefully, feeling the tug of the main landing gear kissing the concrete in one of the smoothest landings of his career.

EPILOGUE

"What happened in there, John?" David Byrd asked, as he leaned against John Blaylock's oversized fire-engine red double-wheeler pickup and watched him fish a couple of cans of Guinness out of a rear locker.

"Well . . . I'd say you saved the lives of about three hundred people, Colonel Byrd, sir."

"*I* saved them? Hardly."

John turned and grinned at him. "All in a day's work."

"Is it *always* that intense in this place?"

"No," Blaylock replied as he tossed one of the cans over. "Most of the time, guys like George Zoffel are fighting terminal boredom. The job of analyzing pixels can be very tedious. But these days, with all the real-time satellite capabilities and other high-tech goodies in this new building, when some major problem unfolds, such as airplanes flying over or tanks rumbling over a border or whatever, it can seem like a high-speed video game . . . only with real lives at stake." He pointed back toward the NRO building a few dozen yards distant. "But I'll admit, this was different. *This* was nerve-racking."

David laughed. "I didn't see you looking ruffled."

"Of course not," Blaylock replied, pulling the tab on the can of stout for emphasis. "Those of us intelligent enough to turn down fighter assignments to fly large transport-type airplanes properly equipped with flush toilets are used to being virtually imperturbable. Oh, I'm sorry," he said in mock alarm. "I forgot you were a fighter jock."

"That's fighter *pilot*, not fighter jock."

"Once a fighter jock, always a fighter jock."

John retrieved two glass beer mugs, offering one to David, who shook his head in response. "I can't believe you carry a bar in the back of your truck."

"I believe in being prepared."

"Ah, the Scout motto." David smiled. "And I'll bet you made Eagle Scout, too."

"No, I was a girl scout. Found quite a few of them, in fact."

"'Scuse me?"

"Well, I was technically in the Boy Scouts, and yeah, I did make Eagle, but I was far more interested in looking for girls during those summer camps than I was in tracking squirrels, or whatever the rest of the troop was doing." John lowered the pickup's tailgate and climbed up to unfold a couple of lawn chairs, before turning to David. "Come on up here and sit."

David climbed into the cargo bed and pulled up one of the chairs, and they both settled into silence for a few minutes, nursing the Guinness and watching the unusually bright canopy of stars overhead, sprinkled with the sparkling lights of airliners arriving and departing from nearby Dulles.

It was David who broke the silence.

"John, when on earth did you get to know White House Chief of Staff William Sanderson well enough to have his direct numbers, and have him trust you instantly like that?"

The distant roar of a departing jet rumbled over them, and John Blaylock waited it out before replying.

"Before Desert Storm, Bill Sanderson was a Navy captain assigned to Defense Intelligence, David. I reported to him for three years, and we got to be close friends." John looked over and took a deep breath before continuing. "I love the night air, don't you?"

"Yeah. So you and Sanderson are friends."

John nodded, tapping the beer mug lightly on the arm of the chair to the rhythm of some unheard tune. "He's a brilliant fellow. The President's very lucky to have him as chief of staff, and I've been very fortunate to have his confidence as well as his friendship."

The sound of crunching gravel caught their attention as George Zoffel appeared around the back of the truck.

"Señor Zoffel," John said with a broad smile. "I thought we'd bade you good night."

"You did," George said, his eyes boring into John Blaylock's for a second before holding the palm of his right hand up and looking around. "What . . . are you guys *doing*? I was going to have security stop you at the gate on the way out to tell you something, but they said you were still out here in the parking lot having a tailgate party in the back of a truck."

David shook his head. "This is serious decompression, George, not a party."

Zoffel nodded, his face serious. "Yeah, I can tell."

"You still sore at me?" John asked.

George Zoffel regarded the big colonel in silence for a few seconds as he cocked his head, his expression slowly softening.

"Blaylock, that's the most consternating thing about you. It's damn tough to stay mad at you, regardless of what havoc you wreak."

John turned to David and raised his glass. "I'll drink to that. I'm a wreaker of havoc."

Zoffel grimaced in mock disgust. "I mean, we just went through one hell of a crisis in there, during which you managed to upset the entire intelligence community, and now you're out here sucking up beer as if nothing had happened, and you're corrupting the morals of an active-duty officer to boot."

"Guinness Stout, I'll have you know."

"Whatever."

"So what brings you out here to talk to the bad boys?" John prompted.

"I thought I'd let you know that the French have confirmed that there were no bombs, viruses, or nasty chemicals aboard the Meridian flight. The rest rooms were semitoxic, but that's about it."

"Well, thank God I got the word on that spectrographic analysis in time," John said breezily, noticing George Zoffel's wry expression.

"Yeah . . . well," Zoffel continued, "it's apparently been a circus for the French authorities, not to mention the media, who don't know the half of it. They're focused on the passengers rioting, not the fact that the Meridian crew nearly got themselves blown out of the sky."

"They're still rioting?" John asked.

"We're told about half the passengers came off the 747 demanding the captain and the lead flight attendant be arrested, while the lead flight attendant came off demanding they arrest the doctor she'd tried to cut in half with an axe, and meanwhile the captain is apparently refusing to say anything to anyone until he has a lawyer with him."

David Byrd leaned forward. "You said a doctor?"

"You recall the name Logan?" George Zoffel asked, relaying what he knew of the accused hijacker's disastrous entry to the cockpit. "In any event, whatever'd happened before, when she tried to hack him apart he was bringing the captain an emergency radio, not breaking in. They got him to the hospital in time, by the way. He'll make it."

"So, why did that captain land in Nigeria in the first place?" John asked. "And what happened to his copilot?"

George Zoffel leaned against the side of the truck. "The copilot is missing, and the airline's trying to sort it all out, but meanwhile, I thought you'd be amused to know that our old friend General Onitsa is now ten million dollars richer. Almost as soon as the ten million first installment of the money from Nigeria hit the bank, Onitsa had it wired somewhere else and withdrawn. We figure it was just about a half hour later that the Nigerian leaders saw the 'hostages' live on CNN as they were emerging from an airplane in Marseille. The same hostages . . ."

". . . who were supposed to be with Jean Onitsa in the middle of the jungle." John chuckled. "I would imagine the Nigerians are a bit irritated."

"You might say that." George grinned. "But the best part is the e-mail we intercepted from Onitsa to the Nigerian government a few minutes ago. With great seriousness he announced that the hostages were in Marseille only because he knew the Nigerians would pay the ransom, and he *personally* ordered their release in anticipation of their doing the right thing. Then he had the temerity to give them a bank routing number so they could send the rest of the two hundred ninety million."

"You're joking," David said.

"No, he's not," John replied. "That's our Dr. Onitsa, all right. The man is perhaps the world's greatest living opportunist, with a wry sense of humor to boot."

"Yeah, spoken as if you knew him personally, huh?" David kidded, his laughter dying off when he realized George Zoffel wasn't reacting and John Blaylock was nodding.

"No. NO! Really?"

"Long story, David," John replied. "But Doc Onitsa's quite a guy."

Zoffel pursed his lips and looked at John Blaylock.

"One other item, Jonathan," he said.

"Sure."

"Remember how you spoke to Randy Brady, one of our spectrographic technicians from the control room, and asked him to do that emergency analysis of the light bouncing off the arms of the alleged hostages?"

"Of course," John answered. "That's what turned the tide. You know, when he gave me the preliminary results."

George Zoffel had a smile on his face. "Uh huh."

"What about it?"

"Well, Randy was very apologetic that it took him so long to call you with his analysis, and was quite concerned when he was told you'd already left."

"Oh, he called with the *final* analysis? Good. But he shouldn't be apologetic," John said. "That *early* evaluation of his did the trick. So . . . what's his final analysis of what made those arms in the pictures look lily-white?"

"Essentially what you told Admiral Sanderson: white mud, composed of clay, chalk, shale, and water, rubbed onto their skin to make them look Caucasian. Fast, cheap, and effective for the satellites."

"Good. Damn clever of Dr. Onitsa," John said. "Say, George, one other thing . . ."

"And," George Zoffel continued, ignoring Blaylock's attempt to change the subject, "Randy said to explain to you, John, that during those intense moments when we were getting ready to blow the 747 out of the sky and you called him, he had to first send a string of commands to the satellite's camera array before it could perform the evaluation for you. He had just received the preliminary results when I talked with him . . .*after* you'd left."

"'Preliminary results'?" David repeated, looking puzzled and wondering why John had fallen silent.

Zoffel nodded. "Yeah. Preliminary. As in, his first report. Randy called just now, before I came out here." George Zoffel turned and waved. "Good night, gentlemen. Well done." He walked back toward the building leaving John Blaylock in silence as David Byrd slowly turned to look at him.

"Preliminary?"

John shrugged.

"You *guessed*?" David said.

"Well . . ."

"You . . . you told the White House Chief of Staff, for God's sake, that you had evidence you didn't have?"

John Blaylock sipped his beer with exaggerated relish

and sat back in the lawn chair, looking off in the distance. "We didn't have time to haggle," he said. "They were going to shoot those poor buggers out of the sky."

"But, good Lord, John, what if the airplane had been empty and the hostages still in Nigeria and the 747 really was a Trojan Horse?"

"*You* were convinced," Blaylock said, without expression. "And that was unbelievably impressive to me. We reservists always defer to our active-duty counterparts, you know."

David was all but sputtering. "But . . . that was my *analysis*, not . . . not based on anything solid. What if you'd been wrong?"

"That's not the right question, Davey," John replied, his left hand behind his head. "The right question is, 'What if I'd been hesitant to act?' What if I'd waited for the confirmation which I already knew would not come in time and which, indeed, only came just now? We'd have killed over three hundred men, women, and children on the basis of a flawed assumption." He reached out with his beer mug and tapped David's shoulder for emphasis.

"You convinced me, David. I wanted more proof, all right, but we'd run out of time. I had to trust my instincts, as well as yours."

MARSEILLE INTERNATIONAL AIRPORT
5:15 A.M. LOCAL

"Now I have a question for *you*, Inspector," Janie Bretsen said, as she looked at the English-speaking French police official. The two other men and a woman who had been taking notes during the questioning of passengers and crew all looked up.

"Certainly," Monsieur Christian LeBourgat replied.

"Is there a plan yet for getting these people on their way? It's been four hours since we landed."

He laughed pleasantly and nodded. "Your airline has a replacement aircraft and crew on their way right now from London. They will take your passengers on to Cape Town, and a new set of pilots will fly your aircraft back to London. You didn't know?"

She shook her head.

"I know you're exhausted, Miss Bretsen, and we're finished here."

"Are you arresting anyone?" she asked.

The inspector shook his head. "No," he said, closing the notebook in front of him. "Everyone is free to go. Including you, of course. You had requested an international telephone, *oui*?"

"Yes."

He showed her to an adjacent office and spoke with an operator before handing the receiver over. "The operator is ready to put you through."

Janie thanked him and pulled a note from her purse. She found the number in Switzerland she was looking for and relayed it to the operator, emerging several minutes later to find the inspector waiting.

"You are smiling, Miss Bretsen. There was good news?"

Janie nodded, relating the story of Janna Levy's near-fatal car crash and her parents' desperate race across the Atlantic the day before and the obstacles that Meridian and the air traffic system had thrown in their way.

"Their daughter regained consciousness shortly after they arrived at her bedside, and the doctors think she has a chance to make it now," Janie said. "I can't begin to tell you how very relieved I am."

"Unusual, that an airline employee would be so moved by concern for her passengers," the inspector said. "Especially these days."

In a row of seats less than fifty feet from where Janie had spent nearly two hours answering questions, Martin Ngume's right elbow was slipping off the edge of an armrest. Once again the sudden motion jolted him awake.

He rubbed his eyes and sat up with cotton in his head, looking at a nearby clock.

Four hours, he thought. *Four hours since we've landed, and I should be arriving in Cape Town right now instead.*

The memory returned of following the other passengers from the Meridian 747 into an overcrowded waiting area where everyone had been questioned one by one.

He could see the phone booth across the waiting area. Someone in the phalanx of police and airline representatives had promised in heavily accented English to help make a call to South Africa in the morning. There would be no point in the middle of the night. No one would be hanging around the little store in Soweto to answer a dusty public phone, let alone be able to tell him anything else about the fate of his mother.

Martin turned to an equally sleepy man next to him.

"Do you know when we'll be able to fly on to South Africa?"

The man shook his head and sighed just as the PA system came alive.

Mr. Martin Ngume, would you please identify yourself to the agent standing at the door? Mr. Martin Ngume.

For a moment, Martin thought he was still dreaming. He was reliving his summons to the podium back in London so many hours ago.

But, no, this was a different voice.

Martin pulled himself up from the chair and waved, and an agent moved rapidly toward him.

"You are Martin Ngume?"

"Yes, ma'am."

"Would you follow me, Mr. Ngume? There's a telephone call for you."

"For me? But who . . . ?" a jolt of dread shuddered

through his mind as he followed her, the distance traveled blurring the time it took to be ushered into a small office and handed a receiver.

"Hello?"

"Martin? Is that you?" a familiar male voice asked in an excited tone.

"Yes. *Phillip?*" The image of one of his roommates flashed through his head. "Is this Phillip?"

"Who else, man? I'm here at the apartment. We saw you on CNN after hearing your flight was in trouble, or everyone had hijacked it, or something, and, well, anyway, I'm sure glad you're okay. It's taken an act of Congress to get this call through."

"I am fine, Phillip, but . . . I still know nothing about my mother, and it's going to take that much longer now to get to Soweto."

"She's fine, Martin. Believe me." There was a chuckle in Phillip's voice.

"I *would* like to believe you," Martin replied, "but it is very frightening when an old woman disappears and no one knows where she's gone or what's happened to her."

"Well, guess what, roomie? We know where she's gone and we also know she's just fine, though worried about you."

Martin let the words sink in. "You . . . you know? How? You have *talked* to her? You got through on the telephone?"

"No. I mean, yes, we talked with her. I'm pretty sure it was she."

Martin closed his eyes and shook his head. His ears were playing tricks on him, making him hear what he'd like to hear.

"You're not positive, then, Phillip? What did her voice sound like?"

"Martin, is your momma a small black lady, very distinguished-looking, with a big, broad smile?"

"Well . . .*yes*, but why . . . I'm not understanding you."

"You remember that article about you in the paper?"

"Yes."

"Well, some softhearted rich guy here in Chicago was apparently touched by what you said about attending college for your mom, and he decided she ought to be able to come to Chicago now, rather than later. He paid some Cape Town lawyer to arrange things, and when the lawyer wrote your mom, she kind of dropped everything . . . right, Mrs. N?" he said off to the side. "Yeah . . . she's nodding. When she got the lawyer's letter, she left without telling anyone and took the train to Cape Town and just arrived here in a limo a few hours ago looking for you. It was all supposed to be a surprise. Here. Let me put her on."

"Martin?" At the first sound of her voice, Martin felt his eyes welling up and tried to fight the reaction, but it was no use. The cold feeling that he would never see her again had been in his gut for so many hours and the relief he felt now was so strong, he felt himself sobbing quietly as his mother continued talking excitedly about her great adventure.

"You have made wonderful friends, Martin," she was saying. "They have bought me one of those hamburgers and made an old woman feel very welcome."

"Stay there, Mama," he said, finally laughing through his tears. "I'm coming. I'm coming home to you in America, and we have much to talk about."

CHICAGO
FIVE WEEKS LATER

Deputy Assistant United States Attorney Debbie Randall sat in the comfortable backseat of the hired Town Car, pointedly ignoring the disapproving look from her colleague as she concentrated on the papers in her lap.

"Can't you just enjoy the ride and talk to me?" Alex Brownlee complained.

"I could," Debbie replied, her eyes still on the charging papers for the murder prosecution of one Brian Logan, "but before we meet this informant, whoever he is, I want to review the case."

"It's simple, Debs," Alex said, letting his eyes wander along the pleasing lines of her body. "Fired physician gets so angry at an airline, he decides to club the copilot to death in cold blood."

Debbie looked over at him and shook her head. "It's anything but simple. It's a tragic case of blind rage and sudden opportunity, and while they'll claim insanity, in the end we'll convict him."

"It's going to be a tough case without the copilot's body," Alex said.

"That problem may be going away."

"You mean . . . the guy we're meeting may know something?"

She nodded and looked up, recognizing the area. They were still about ten miles from Palwaukee Airport, a private field north of O'Hare.

"All I know," Debbie continued, "is that our boss took a call a few hours ago from someone who was in flight to Palwaukee. Our fearless leader said that since you and I are the firebrands who pushed him to approve this prosecution in order to make a statement about air rage, we're the ones who need to go interview this guy."

"It's not just a statement about air rage, Deb. We're prosecuting a doctor who murdered an airline crew member."

"Well, you know the boss's reluctance to let us file these charges in the first place was due to the lack of a body. The Nigerians have been searching for three weeks and have turned up no trace of it," she said.

"I still wish we were nailing Logan for air piracy, Debbie. That would be more fun to prosecute."

"Oh yeah, great fun to have a case that's dead on arrival. Let's see, not enough evidence, most of the passengers are contradicting the charges, the captain is unsure of what happened, and all we really have against Logan are the cockpit voice recordings of what he said on the PA system and on the interphone demanding that the Cape Town flight go to Cape Town."

"He tried to take over the jet by force, Debs," Alex said. "We've had this argument before."

"Yeah, we have. And he'll say he had no intention of taking over anything; he was just verbally lashing out. After all, he ordered the captain to fly to where the captain was supposed to fly anyway. That's a pretty lame hijacking. You ever have a jury start snickering at you and keep on until they all break out in a belly laugh and fall out of their chairs?"

"No," Alex said, having trouble suppressing a smile at the ludicrous image.

"Trust me. It's not fun."

A sleek corporate Gulfstream V was slowing on the runway just as they pulled up to the private jet terminal.

"Is that him?" Alex asked. Debbie consulted a small notebook and nodded. "I think so . . . if I'm reading the tail number correctly. It's all letters instead of the usual numbers, whatever that means. It may be British registry. And he's early."

She looked around, making note of the other cars and people apparently waiting for the same arrival. There were two customs agents standing next to a limousine.

Debbie craned her neck in the other direction, trying

to discern the identity of several individuals waiting near the door of the lounge.

"We're evidently not the only ones meeting him," she remarked.

The Gulfstream braked to a halt, and the engines began winding down as the forward stairs were lowered. The two customs inspectors climbed aboard and disappeared, but one of them returned within thirty seconds and walked directly toward the driver's side of their car.

"You have some people from the U.S. Attorney's Office in here?"

"That's us," Debbie called out.

"Good. They need to see you aboard." He turned and walked back to the Gulfstream without explanation, as Debbie and Alex left the car and followed.

The smell of rich leather was redolent as Debbie entered the alcove of the private jet. The customs man pointed to the right, and a strikingly beautiful black woman in a flight attendant's uniform escorted them into the luxurious interior where a casually dressed man was waiting.

Debbie extended her hand and introduced herself.

"Good," the man said. "I appreciate your coming." He shook hands with Alex as well and motioned them to sit down.

"May I ask your name?" Debbie said.

"First," the man began, "I want to know if you're the lawyers handling the prosecution of a Dr. Brian Logan?"

They both nodded and he continued. "I also want to know what you could have charged him with, what you *have* charged him with, and why."

Debbie hesitated and glanced at Alex as the man spoke again.

"Look, you're only out here because the head of your division wanted you to come cooperate with me, and I guarantee I've got the most important information you've had yet in this case. So please answer my questions."

Debbie sighed and nodded as she went through the various potential charges they could have filed, and the decision to prosecute Logan for first-degree murder.

"He's been charged and arraigned, and released on bail, but with the exception of not having Abbott's body to complete the evidence, we have a solid case with a prime eyewitness."

"That would be the senior flight attendant, right?"

"Right."

"Judy Jackson?"

Alex and Debbie exchanged glances as Debbie nodded. "Yes."

"I would have expected Meridian to have fired Jackson by now for a whole bunch of reasons."

"That's correct and they have," Debbie said. "But the reasons don't diminish her credibility as a witness to Abbott's murder."

"Really? Well, folks," the man continued, "truth is, even though Judy Jackson certainly believes she's got it right, she's dead wrong. Brian Logan did not kill or harm Garth Abbott in any way."

Alex leaned forward, his hands clasped, his face displaying a carefully practiced look of disapproving skepticism.

"By what authority do you make that assertion, sir? What evidence do you have?"

"Me," the man said. "I'm the authority."

Alex sat back in the chair, shaking his head and scowling. "You arranged to bring two very busy assistant U.S. attorneys all the way across town to hear nothing more than a personal opinion?" He turned to Debbie and began rising from the chair. "This is absurd. Let's get out of here."

"Wait," she said, her hand out in a stop gesture, her eyes studying the man across from her. "What, exactly, do you mean that you're the authority?" she asked.

"Don't you need Garth Abbott's body before you can prosecute Logan?"

"No. Well, I mean, certainly it would help to have the body, but . . ."

"Good. Because I know exactly where it is."

Both lawyers exchanged wide-eyed glances as Alex sat on the edge of the plush swivel chair. "Where?"

"Here."

"Here?" Debbie asked. "Aboard this airplane?"

He nodded. "Yep. Right in front of you." He reached down and pulled up his left pant leg, revealing a combination brace and cast as he watched their expression. "I'm Garth Abbott, and as the old saw goes, reports of my demise have been greatly exaggerated."

Carol Abbott had been ready for hours, sitting in their living room with several friends arrayed around, none of them understanding the depth of the turmoil inside her, none of them aware of the sharp words that had passed between husband and wife the last time they'd talked.

Garth's satellite call had come unannounced from somewhere over the Atlantic, a bolt from the blue that sliced through the acrid guilt of the way they had parted. But he hadn't died, and now he was here, and yet, the confusion in her heart was mixed with utter relief whirling around through the weeks of anguish and the mourning of a husband she'd all but decided to leave anyway.

He came to her now from the front door on a crutch, his left leg in a brace, his right leg marginally working, throwing the crutch to the rug as he grabbed her and held her tightly. He tousled her hair as he nuzzled her neck and kissed her before pulling back to look into her troubled eyes.

"I thought . . . ," she started, unable to finish.

The others began crowding around, and he accepted their hands and their hugs and let Carol guide him to the couch as the questions began and he raised his hand to try to slow the barrage.

"The report we got said your leg had been shattered,

Garth. They thought . . . that doctor they charged with murdering you thought you'd bled to death."

He shook his head. "I was bleeding pretty badly when I slipped off the ladder, but the bullet didn't get an artery. Turns out it was the damned government forces who shot me, not the rebels. I got caught in a counterattack."

"So they left you dying on the runway," one of the men said.

"Not 'they,' Keith," Garth said, looking at one of his fellow Meridian pilots. " 'He.' Our old buddy, Phil Knight."

"You do know they fired him?"

Garth shook his head. "No. I guess I'm not surprised. I was ready to kill the bastard myself, especially when I lay there watching that aluminum overcast we'd been flying in rumble past me and take off *without* me. I can't tell you what that felt like. I couldn't believe it! Utter betrayal, utter abandonment."

"The whole airline was in shock, Garth," Keith said.

"So was I. But you know something? It took me all these weeks to figure this out, but it's true. The fault was more Meridian's than Phil Knight's. What the hell were they doing dumping an unprepared domestic captain into the international division? Where were the training and the checking? They led him to the slaughter, and I don't intend to be quiet about it."

"What happened when Knight left you there?" Carol managed.

"There was a counterattack to the counterattack," Garth said. "After I watched the aircraft leave, I heard one of soldiers who'd shot me walk over to see if I was dead. He kicked me in the ribs and turned me over, and I tried to look dead and not react to the pain. My eyes were open just a little bit, and I could see him take aim at me again, but a shot came from nowhere, and *he* keeled over dead. Suddenly, this same huge, barrel-chested rebel commander I'd dealt with right after we landed came over and scooped me up while his men were laying down covering fire in all directions. I think it was the pain from moving my legs that finally knocked me out. Anyway, I woke up three days later in a little field hospital to find this same man, General Onitsa, sitting there smiling. Turns out he's a physician and surgeon, and he more or less put me back together."

"But . . . how did you get out of there?" Carol asked.

He told them about the ransom demand and the ten million paid, and the fact that Onitsa had become a wealthy man in the past few years effectively looting the government and toying with their forces as he pressed his rebellion.

"I don't know if he's morally bankrupt in what he's trying to do or not, but he's a gentle guy when he wants to be, and very intelligent. The government forces went berserk for weeks afterward looking for us . . . for him, I mean. That's why he said he couldn't let me call home. He has satellite phones, connections, equipment . . . I mean the man's an electronics junkie. He plans his attacks

Fortunately, neither the media nor any angry Meridian employees had shown up to harass him, and for that he was grateful. After having been hounded for months and vilified in the newspapers and in the weekly news magazines, he could hardly believe they were leaving him alone.

"You okay, Phil?" the lawyer for the Air Line Pilots Association asked.

"Yeah," Phil said flatly, unsure anymore what the phrase even meant. How could he ever be "okay" again? All he knew was how to be an airline pilot, and now that was gone. The union had made brave noises about reinstatement and scheduled the statutory hearing he was about to attend, which was the only method a fired union pilot could use under the Railway Labor Act to petition for reinstatement.

But he knew it was useless. They were acting out of their contractual duty to defend him, but their hearts weren't in it. Every decision he'd made had been adjudged wrong or stupid or worse, and most of the pilots agreed. Landing in Nigeria, leaving a copilot he thought was dead in order to save over three hundred people, all of it was colored by the collective decision that Phil Knight did not have the right stuff to be an airline captain, and thus the facts had been conveniently assembled to fit the conclusion.

There was no participation in the field of blame for Meridian. They would battle the various lawsuits and public vilification by merely pointing to the professionally mummified head of Phil Knight and proclaim they had been hoodwinked themselves. If the system had failed in any way, they would say, it was only in failing to detect the fact that Phil Knight was a fraud who should have never been allowed in a commercial cockpit.

The toll on his wife and kids had been fearsome, their faith in him shaken, their faith in the system lost. If they had a chance as a family now, it would be elsewhere, moving away to a more modest home while he tried to find aeronautical work flying for some midnight check carrier or, perhaps, an overseas airline. The two-hundred-thousand-dollar-per-year paychecks and the unlimited passes for his family and the pride of being a major airline captain were gone forever.

"Phil, before they get started, maybe we should go over this again," the ALPA lawyer prompted.

He shook his head. "Nothing to go over. This is a waste of your time."

The trek into the hearing room was an agony. There was a cloth-covered table facing him, behind which sat the vice president of operations, the chief pilot, the chief of training, and several other senior captains. He might as well have been a Navy captain who'd lost his ship and was being brought before a panel of furious admirals. The principles were similar, the conclusion equally foregone.

The give-and-take was predictable, the anger from those who would judge the appeal of his firing barely hidden behind a facade of pretended equanimity.

"No, sir," Phil answered at one point. "I do not believe my decisions were in error as a matter of regulations, but if they were . . . and I know no one wants to listen to this . . . I was a product of my training, or the lack of it. No one told me the things I was expected to just somehow know."

ALPA had brought in a clever slate of expert witnesses to back up the technical correctness of his emergency landings, given the incomplete state of the Meridian regulations on what to do and when to do it. Meridian had countered by fielding its own witnesses to contradict, indict, belittle, and neutralize every point in his favor, yet halfway through, Phil found himself indulging in a glimmer of hope that minds could be changed. His spotless record as a domestic captain was laid out in detail, including the testimony of a longtime friend and former copilot who had braved the disgust of the other pilots to speak for him.

But the end of the favorable witnesses and the ameliorating statements came too soon, and he could see the faces of his judges beginning to harden again, a realization that obscured the sound of the door opening behind him.

"Excuse me, am I too late?" a male voice asked from behind. The tones were vaguely familiar, but Phil didn't turn.

"Who are you?" the hearing examiner asked, obviously taken aback.

The man moved to the forward table and began

handing out papers to the various members of the panel, then turned to hand copies to the company's lawyers before stopping to nod to Phil Knight, who finally looked up. Phil felt his heart sink even farther as the man smiled and turned to the hearing examiner, his left arm still in a sling.

"I'm Dr. Brian Logan," he said as the door behind them opened once again. "And I'm here with one of your people, Meridian First Officer Garth Abbott, who just came in."

The examiner sighed and nodded and gestured to the witness chair. "We did have you on the witness list, Dr. Logan, along with Mr. Abbott, but we were about to give up on you both."

"I apologize on behalf of both of us," Logan said. "Mr. Abbott was waiting for me, and my flight from Boston was late."

Brian held an index finger in the air to keep the floor.

"Before we get started, I want this hearing board to know precisely why I'm here. You all know that I'm suing your airline for millions because one of your crews denied my wife and son medical help on one of your flights. You also know that I've been personally vindicated of the charges that your airline worked hard to bring that I'd murdered Garth Abbott, who's now standing behind me here very much alive. So you know there's been a lot of bad blood between us, and you also know . . . because I said it publicly in the press . . . that I wanted Phil Knight fired, and that was the one thing you did rather promptly. Well, Garth Abbott and I are here to make damn sure the blame for all the stupidity that happened aboard Flight Six falls where it's due. But I'm going to shock you, because that doesn't mean I'm here to place blame. I'm here to *share* the blame with the captain, with all the furious passengers, and with you, as the leaders of a very flawed, very culpable system that failed utterly to prepare this man for his job as an international pilot."

He paused, letting the words sink in.

"In other words, gentlemen, we're here to support Captain Knight's appeal for reinstatement."

"When do they announce their decision?" Brian Logan asked as he reached in to shake Garth Abbott's hand through the open passenger window of his wife's van.

"Two weeks to a month. I'll call you when I know."

The van moved off with a parting wave from Garth, and a late-model sedan pulled up in its place, the driver reaching over to open the passenger door for him. He climbed in and turned to the elegantly dressed woman behind the wheel.

"I appreciate your coordinating all this, Janie," he said. "Picking me up at the airport and waiting and everything. That's above and beyond."

"Nonsense."

"I also want to thank you for calling me in the first place and suggesting this."

JOHN J. NANCE

"So how'd it go in there?" she asked as she steered the car toward the nearby freeway entrance to head for O'Hare.

Brian had almost finished his narration of what had transpired as they pulled up to the American Airlines terminal and she put the car in park.

"If your flight's on time, you've got forty minutes."

He was hesitating, his hand on the door release, his eyes on the driver.

"You ever come to Boston?"

She smiled, a radiant, lovely smile that warmed him in ways he hadn't felt since losing Daphne.

"I love Boston, but I seldom get an invitation."

He could feel his smile spreading involuntarily.

"Would you like one?"

"Depends on who issues it," she said, cocking her head and sending a cascade of dark, wavy hair into motion.

He took his right hand off the door and reached across to gently take her right hand from the wheel and squeeze it.

"Would you consider coming to Boston sometime soon and let me show you the town?"

"I would consider it, yes," she said, squeezing back before removing her hand from his and replacing it on the steering wheel. "Just give me a call, if you're so inclined."

Brian Logan nodded. "Okay, I will."

"Did you put them to rest?"

"Sorry?"

"The ashes of your wife and child. You had them with you in that briefcase on the flight."

Brian's jaw dropped slightly as he looked at her. "How did you know?" he asked at last.

She smiled back. "I figured it out."

He nodded then. "Yes. Daphne loved the ocean. I rented a boat."

"That's best."

"Thank you again," he said, opening the door somewhat awkwardly as an irritating recorded voice from a set of speakers along the drive intoned dire consequences for anyone lingering in the unloading zone.

"You did the right thing today, Brian," Janie said through the open door.

He nodded and lifted himself out, closing the door before leaning back in the open window.

"I don't know if what I said in there today will help Phil Knight, but I can tell you it's already helped me. And I have you to thank, Janie."

She smiled at him as he pushed away from the window with his good arm and waved before moving rapidly into the crowd.

Janie Bretsen watched him go, letting her eyes linger on the automatic doors of the terminal that had swallowed him. Taking a deep breath, she shifted her gaze to the traffic ahead, her smile broadening as she put the car in gear.